MW00659306

The Dark Frontier

A.B. Decker

Clink Street

Published by Clink Street Publishing 2021

Copyright © 2021

First edition.

The author asserts the moral right under the Copyright, Designs and Patents Act 1988 to be identified as the author of this work.

All rights reserved. No part of this publication may be reproduced, stored in a retrieval system or transmitted, in any form or by any means without the prior consent of the author, nor be otherwise circulated in any form of binding or cover other than that with which it is published and without a similar condition being imposed on the subsequent purchaser.

ISBN:
978-1-913962-18-0 - paperback
978-1-913962-19-7 - ebook

To my wife Penelope
for her patience

Chapter 1

It was a sunny afternoon in early spring. 1972. On any normal day at this hour in late March, Ellen would have been hurrying home across Putney Bridge. Still wrapped in her winter coat against the North Sea chill blowing off the Thames. But this was not London. And Ellen had not known normal for a good twelve months or more.

The sun that was doing its best to embrace Ellen on this particular afternoon shone over Locarno, Switzerland. And it was only now, sitting here on the Piazza Grande, that it finally sank in. She was never going to see Frank again. And the knowledge was driven home with an exquisite sting by the words of Vicky Leandros: 'Aprés toi je ne serai que l'ombre'. The words wafted out from the café behind her. They sang of a cold dark solitude. A vast pitch-black shadow, made all the murkier by the light and convivial warmth on the piazza around her.

Those lyrics were all she had heard since Marthe first played her the song. Every radio in every café seemed to be playing it now. They kept intruding on Ellen's mind wherever she went – from the moment she saw the last hint of his existence vanish for all eternity. That was last Friday. Ever since then, the song had been a constant companion on her journey.

It was already a good three weeks since she had last seen Frank himself. Neatly draped on the slab. In truth, the shock of seeing what had become of him after the long intervening months following his sudden disappearance was tempered by his prolonged absence beforehand. An absence that had gnawed deep gaping wounds in her knowledge and understanding of him. And she wondered now whether she had ever known him at all in any real sense of the word. For it had been a whirlwind romance. Barely three months into bliss before they married and then a few more months before he vanished.

Had he really been living a double life all the time, as events seemed to suggest?

The eyes that fixed their gaze on Ellen as she mulled over this history went unnoticed. It was a slightly furtive gaze. And carried a hint of trepidation. Sitting at the table next to Ellen, the elegantly dressed lady opened a large Louis Vuitton bag on her lap. And as if to calm her nerves with a little distraction, she spent the next few minutes busily burrowing inside it. Like a nesting bird.

It was this activity that eventually broke Ellen's concentration. When she turned her head, the burrowing stopped for a moment. She caught sight of a brief glance in her direction before the elegant lady quickly resumed the search of her bag. Relieved to have some distraction from her own dark thoughts, Ellen watched, wondering what precious object lay hidden inside. And whether it would ever be revealed. She judged the woman to be late fifties to early sixties. Her thick grey hair still showed strong hints of a jet-black mane from years gone by that perfectly matched her black twinset with cream trim. Ellen had seen something very like it in a fashion magazine at Marthe's place. She fancied it was probably from Chanel. Over the woman's shoulders there draped a large scarf that hindered her search. And eventually she gave up.

She closed the Louis Vuitton bag, revealing the letters P.R. embossed in gold on the tongue, looked over at Ellen and smiled.

"I saw you in Basel recently. On the bridge in the centre of town," she said. There was a conspiratorial edge to her words.

Ellen smiled back, unsure she was ready for any kind of conversation.

"You were with a friend and looked a little agitated," the woman continued. "But it was the boots that really caught my eye."

She cast a glance down at Ellen's feet under the table next to hers. Ellen was still wearing the same high-heeled boots with thick platform soles that she had been wearing ever since she arrived in Switzerland. She had bought them at Biba in Kensington High Street just over a year ago. It was the weekend before Frank had flown out to Switzerland. He had been busy working on an assignment all weekend, so she had taken herself off shopping.

"I do admire girls these days. I'm sure I could never have worn boots like that in my day."

By now, the mournful words of Vicky Leandros had been swapped for the catchy T. Rex melody 'Ride a White Swan'. It seemed oddly out of place for a quiet Ticinese piazza. And the strikingly beautiful warble of Marc Bolan's voice did nothing to lighten her mood, but reminded her of Frank with even greater poignancy.

"Is this your first time in Switzerland?" the P.R. lady persevered. Ellen was jolted from her thoughts, and for an instant she gave in.

"Yes. Well no, not really."

"You don't seem too sure."

"I was here last year." Ellen was conscious of sounding abrupt, but she was in no mood for further explanation and changed tack. "You speak very good English."

"I had a very good teacher." The words came with a wistful look that plainly held an entire chronicle of special memories.

Raising her left hand as she smiled across to the woman, Ellen attracted the waiter's attention. She really had no wish to be drawn any further into conversation and, placing three francs on the table to cover any tip, she got up to leave.

"I have to get back to my hotel," she said, and continued smiling politely across the table. "It was very nice talking to you."

With a look of strangely knowing curiosity, the mysterious lady watched Ellen stride across the piazza towards the lake in her platform boots. They lent an air of confidence to Ellen's walk that belied her underlying anxiety. When she reached the lakeside, she stood for a moment by the water next to a *gelateria* that was playing the ubiquitous background melody of Vicky Leandros.

A lonely bedraggled swan floated adrift beneath the jetty to her left. Ellen smiled and almost unconsciously began to hum the T. Rex melody to herself as she was reminded of the times Frank would take her mudlarking along the Thames when the tide was low. Of the shabby swans that swam past and would inspire him to poetry as he tugged an old camera from the mud. Or a broken vase. Repeated reminders of Frank that left Ellen trapped in the arms of one vast shadow.

She watched the activity around her: young families gathering for their ice cream; an elderly man and a woman admiring each other's dogs; and out on the water a scattering of white yacht sails bobbing like lost punctuation marks against the backdrop of the mountainside.

Like a boat beneath a sunny sky. Those words from Frank came to Ellen as she watched the yachts out on the lake. They reminded her of the sunlit day they stood on Putney Bridge together. Watching the water. A solitary boat floated silently downstream. And under his breath, Frank whispered: "Still she haunts me, phantomwise / Alice moving under skies / Never seen by waking eyes."

Ellen recalled gaping at him in bewilderment and saying something like: "Where did that come from?"

It was the first time she had noticed the trace of a soft Lancashire accent in his voice. The lilt brought memories of the Liverpool poets to mind and of the poetry readings Frank would often take her to. They were a far cry from the Coleridge and Wordsworth that she had read for A-levels. And they fascinated her. But the words he spoke now were a source of complete bemusement.

"Lewis Carroll," Frank said. He seemed to her to be a million miles away as he spoke. "Like a boat beneath a sunny sky. It's an acrostic. So beautiful. Such a lovely device."

"Acrostic?"

"A poem where the first letter of each line spells out a name," he explained.

Ellen had never ceased to marvel at Frank's knowledge and his way with words. And he in turn had always been in awe of her memory for the lyrics of every song that she had ever heard in her entire life. He found it hard to believe she had such a total recall for words as she claimed to have. But she never failed any test to which he put her. And for all the mystery of the words that Frank had spoken then, they were no less mystifying to Ellen now, as she slowly repeated them to herself – *Still she haunts me, phantomwise / Never seen by waking eyes* – and gazed out at the boats beneath a sunny sky on Lago Maggiore.

What did he really mean, who was he talking about when he spoke those words? Ellen wondered.

The white punctuation marks that were yachts on the water had already turned a light shade of grey. The sun was starting to fade. Even the bedraggled swan beneath the jetty had left the water and settled down in the dry. And for Ellen, the dark mountain that draped its twilight cloak right down to the shore on the other side of the lake held shades of menace – like a black glove remorselessly squeezing out every last drop of the day that remained.

Marthe had recommended it as the perfect place to recuperate from all the heartache of the last months. And when she insisted that she would follow in a few days' time, Ellen was persuaded. But since receiving Marthe's phone call in the hotel to say that there had been a change of plan and she would be unable to join her after all, Ellen could see no purpose at all in being here. She felt uncomfortable in Locarno. And as she stood at the lakeside now, contemplating that sense of menace, she questioned the wisdom of ever following Marthe's advice.

For all its beauty and conviviality, Locarno was proving a sombre place that left Ellen feeling deeply disturbed. Far from spreading out in width like Heaven, as Wordsworth might have led her to believe when she was studying for her A-levels, it seemed more like a dark underworld. Recovery seemed the last thing she was likely to find here.

Her sister Beth had suggested she go and stay with her for a few weeks to recover. But after the disaster of the last time Ellen stayed with her sister, this was plainly not an option. So she decided then and there that she must return north to Marthe's place in Basel the next day. Then straight back home to London, where she could start picking up what pieces of normality remained in her life.

Ellen's hotel lay about a ten-minute walk away in a narrow side street on the other side of the Piazza Grande and not too far from the railway station. But with time on her hands, she took a circuitous route that skirted around the piazza for fear of running into her cappuccino companion again. With slow deliberation, she meandered through the backstreets. The few little shops here had either closed already or were about to close. And the streets themselves were remarkably empty. The shoppers had either left for home or congregated now on the piazza just a street or two away for their après-shopping gossip. At street level, these narrow lanes that Ellen was negotiating might be considered by most people to be charming and full of atmosphere. For Ellen they spawned a sense of claustrophobic angst. And the echo of her footsteps did nothing to dispel this feeling.

When Ellen was suddenly jolted from her apprehension by another sound – like a ping-pong ball bouncing erratically across a table – she stopped and span round. The street was empty. The echo of her footsteps had been silenced. She was alone. But this only added to her sense of disquiet. Then, just as abruptly, two little boys about fifty metres back down the street dashed out from a door, shouting and laughing as they chased after a ball, then disappeared around a corner as swiftly as they had appeared. Ellen turned and continued on her way at a more hurried pace, keen to reach the comfort of her accommodation.

Her hotel was a small family-run place. An unpretentious building that bore no comparison with the grandiose Lombard-style architecture and inviting porticos around the piazza. And while it offered the seclusion she was seeking, it also reflected the same sense of dark menace she felt emanating from the mountains around the lake. It had been a bad choice to stay here. And this probably helped nurture her decision to return. The owner of the hotel was Signor Sciarone.

A portly, avuncular sixty-something with a bushy grey moustache, thick flowing hair to match and a perpetual twinkle in his eye, he seemed affable enough. He was at the desk when Ellen arrived back at the hotel. And he reached down the key to her room as he saw her coming through the door.

"*Buona sera, signora.*" He handed Ellen the key.

"It is so nice to have an English lady as our guest."

Ellen smiled politely.

"I love your country," he continued. "A lovely country. But such a tragic place. Like a – how you say *tentatrice* – she draw so many people to an early death."

Ellen stopped in her tracks. She shot a startled look across the desk at Signor Sciarone. The twinkle in his eyes had gone.

He pointed to the wall behind him. It was covered in faded photos, ragged newspaper cuttings browning at the edges and one that appeared much cleaner and fresher. Ellen recognised the picture in this one instantly. She recalled the iconic image plastered across the front pages of every newspaper just a few years previously. The arms of the Bluebird rearing up out of the lake at Coniston like a crab out of water.

"That's Donald Campbell's awful crash," she said.

"I meet his father when he make record here on Lago Maggiore," Signor Sciarone nodded, and pointed to the most faded of the cuttings. "Thirty years before. Such a beautiful sunny day. Now they go to England to make records. And die there."

Stepping back towards the wall, he planted a deliberate stubby forefinger on a face that meant nothing to Ellen.

"Jo Siffert. Another great driver. He win Grand Prix in England. And three years later he also die there."

Signor Sciarone banged a huge fist down on the reception desk as he spoke these words. Ellen jumped. The brutal violence of this fist on the desk was totally at odds with his affable manner. She found this other side of him disconcerting.

"I don't follow the sport," she whispered timidly. "But I do recall reading something about the accident a few months ago."

She was about to turn and climb the stairs to her room, then added "It's very sad" in an effort to comfort her host. But he had already turned his back and was shuffling off down the corridor to the back of the house.

The dimly lit stairwell was steep and narrow, and by the time she reached her room on the third floor she was quite out of breath. The room itself had also seen better days. There was a slight mustiness about the air in the room as she entered. But it was not unpleasant. It lent a sense of history to the place. And Ellen could imagine the many travellers who must have passed through here over the decades. Single ladies in lace with matching parasols. Salesmen with suitcases packed full of their sample products. And lovelorn writers escaping the heartbreak of being dumped. The age and history that seeped out from the furniture and the heavy curtains over the window gave Ellen a feeling of comfort, a sense of not being quite so totally alone.

She drew back the curtains and opened the doors onto the narrow balcony to let in what remaining light there was. Sadly, although she was on the third floor, it did not offer the view over the lake that she had hoped for when she checked in. Instead she had to make do with a view of the balcony on the other side of the street – almost close enough for her to leap over with little trouble. This intimacy with the neighbourhood increased Ellen's sense of vulnerability. She went back inside, closed the curtains, removed her platform boots and lay down on the bed.

Holed up in this history-laden room with not even a view to speak of, Ellen let her thoughts turn to the events and non-events of the last months. To Frank's protracted absence. To what he had been doing here in the first place. And who he even was.

She recalled him in her arms that morning, just before he left, as they lay bathing in the spent tension of their bodies. Their languid limbs still tangled together. His drenched body wedged between hers. With the memory of that moment she felt a tingling sensation course through her body. During all the time that Frank was away, she had been too pent up with worry even to recall the many wonderful times they had enjoyed together – let alone try to get to know herself. But for the first time in a long while she conjured images of Frank's slightly tanned, perfectly proportioned body – and she began to remember who she was. A frisson of electricity, like the static of a nylon blouse, began tingling again with the memories. The feel of his velvet skin on hers. That perfect smell. The tenderness of his lips on her neck. She let the tips of her fingers dance lightly over her skin.

The suddenness of the knock on her door dragged Ellen brutally back to earth. She got up, adjusted her clothes and went to the door. She was greeted by the figure of Signor Sciarone, wheezing slightly from the climb up the stairs and holding two neatly folded towels.

"I forget towels for bathroom."

Ellen raised a hand to take them and thank him for his trouble. But before she could get the words out, he had brushed past Ellen and into the room. Placing the towels on the end of the bed, he ambled over to the other side of the room, drew back the curtains and opened the doors onto the balcony. Then pushed wide the door just next to it to inspect the bathroom. Slowly he turned to face Ellen again and continued his inspection. He scanned the dressing table, the room, the bed – then smiled at Ellen in a way she found more unsettling than friendly.

"The room need light and air," he said, moving back towards the door and brushing past Ellen as he went. Ellen backed up nervously against the wall to let him pass.

"I forgot to mention," she said, made slightly breathless by her nerves. "I will be leaving tomorrow".

With his hand on the door to leave, Signor Sciarone cast a slightly injured yet accusing look at Ellen.

"You leave us? You no like it here?"

"It's not that. I need to get back."

Signor Sciarone shrugged, turned and closed the door behind him, mumbling to himself as he went.

As she listened to his steps disappear down the stairs, Ellen began to relax. Locking the door, she went straight over to the balcony and drew the heavy curtains back together. True, the room needed light. But for Ellen the dark seclusion offered greater comfort. And since the light of the day was already fast fading anyway, she decided to have an early night in bed with a book. She took a collection of Daphne du Maurier stories out of her case and laid it on the bedside table. *Not After Midnight.* It seemed the perfect read.

She slipped out of her clothes, laid them neatly on the chair beside the table and slunk into bed. Although it was more than a year now since Frank walked out of her life, she still slept naked. The only sound as she lay there was the occasional bounce of a ball in the street below. But this soon faded as the dusk deepened and Ellen became immersed in her book. It was not until she reached the third story in the collection – 'Don't Look Now' – that her concentration began to wander. Set in Venice, it not only seemed so close by culturally. But more importantly it put her in mind of their honeymoon.

She let the book fall onto her chest as she recalled that blissful sunny afternoon just a week before Christmas. They stepped out of Venice railway station to be greeted by a magical scene that gave her the feeling she had just walked into a modern-day Canaletto painting. A waterway teeming with activity, elegant old buildings rising out of the water either side of the canal washed in pastel shades of pink and yellow, and people everywhere getting on and off the boats that drew up outside the station. Ellen was mesmerised. It was the perfect honeymoon. She stood in wonderment, lost in the magic of that moment.

"What do you think of it?" Frank asked, turning his mop of thick brown hair in her direction with a broad captivating smile. There was a slight mournfulness about his dark, gently drooping eyes that sat oddly with the smile. They always put her in mind of a loyal Basset hound. It was the eyes – and that mop of hair – that had attracted her the very first time they met: the sparkle that coalesced with a hint of sadness accentuated in turn by a certain unevenness. It was partly this asymmetry about his eyes that intrigued her – the way they were slightly skewed by a strangely buckled bridge of the nose that lay between them.

As if he'd been shot between the eyes at birth, his father used to tell him.

It was a cruel description that Ellen had found hard to cope with from the very first moment she heard it. But set against this Canaletto backdrop, the intriguing charm of his eyes blotted out every trace of that fragmentary vignette. Made them all the more bewitching with his smile. Ellen could find no words to express her joy.

Frank put an arm around her waist and gave her a squeeze. He knew Venice quite well from one of his early assignments, and while Ellen was still searching for those elusive words, she found herself whisked onto a *vaporetto*, which carried them down the Grand Canal to their hotel. Frank wanted the very best for their honeymoon and had booked a magnificent suite overlooking the canal.

Ellen closed the book, placed it back on the bedside table and began to conjure up their wedding night in Venice. Recalling it now in light of the last months of uncertainty and disquiet, she realised this was also the first time she saw something in Frank that hinted at a certain turmoil within him. Something deep down which she could not put her finger on. And something she had instantly put to the back of her mind for fear of opening a can of worms. Perhaps that had been her mistake.

She had always had a certain dread of the male body during early adolescence – a sense of foreboding and anxiety born from her strict upbringing and the Catholic girls' school she had attended. A place that had taught her little more than fear and shame. This feeling remained with her in a vestigial form into adulthood, even as she came to appreciate the fascinating nature of manhood in the fullness of time – its immanent power and independence that seemed to invest it with a mind all its own, yet made it such a completely open book at the same time. For Ellen, it was one of nature's wonders. She held it in awe.

When she had seen Frank naked for the first time some months before their wedding, her wonderment was further enhanced by a new discovery that put every earlier enjoyment in the shade. Frank was the first man she had ever seen without that coy sheath of skin which so vainly masquerades as a cloak of male desire. There was an honesty about this one. So neat. So innocent. For Ellen, this had come as a revelation. But then in Venice, on their wedding night, Ellen found that perhaps there was good reason after all for her adolescent sense of foreboding and anxiety.

Frank's first instinct had been to take a shower after their journey, while Ellen unpacked their bags, divested herself of her shoes and curled up on the sofa to flick through all the hotel amenities, the Marco Polo tours on offer and the menu of the hotel restaurant. She became so engrossed that she failed to notice Frank when he emerged from the shower, still drying himself, and then lay down on the bed.

When eventually she looked up and saw him lying there, the sight of him cast an instant spell. He was lying face up, eyes shut, head resting on his hands. He had already dozed off. The towel lay on the floor beside the bed. And in repose, nestling in that tousled charm, lay the substance of Ellen's fascination. Captivating. So unsuspecting. Defenceless and innocent as a sleeping baby. She felt that her excitement was audible as she crept onto the bed and offered up her lingual skills in an act of pure devotion. She was aroused beyond belief in the throes of her worship. And while Frank showed no sign of stirring from his sleep, she caught the soft whispers of his voice as he began to sigh and purr, every so often calling out "pet." It was a name he had not used for her before. She remembered thinking at the time that she was not too pleased, suspecting that perhaps it was a name he had used for some past lover. But she paid it no further attention, as she savoured every second of Frank and offered a train of reverent kisses in thanksgiving.

Then suddenly from nowhere, Frank let out a piercing scream that startled Ellen. She looked up. Any sense of a smile had gone. In its place a strange, unsettling expression that she found hard to describe. Like a symptom of deep distress. An excruciating agony in his eyes and a look of unmitigated disgust on his lips as he cried out "*Scheisse*!" She almost had the feeling he was about to throw up.

Ellen knew he could speak German, but she had never heard him utter a single word of the language before. To hear him speak it at that instant in what seemed to be a moment of such distress hinted at some dark history to which she would never be privy.

But slowly the mood calmed again. He started to run his fingers through her hair. Ellen took this to be a mark of appreciation. And, despite that strange German expletive, this gesture enabled her to put the sense of inner conflict she had witnessed to the back of her mind. Yet vestiges of the shock and concern she had felt that afternoon in Venice never entirely went away.

And the memory of that occasion now put her in mind of his incongruous relish for quoting Sophocles as they lay in bed together. To have a penis, he said, was like being chained to a madman. It was a quotation he frequently repeated. This and the reminder of that expression on his face hinted at a deeper side to him that would be closed to her forever.

There had been so many things in retrospect that should have set alarm bells ringing. And now, between the sombre walls of the hotel in Locarno, her memory of the troubling undercurrent to that brief moment of wedding night bliss seemed all the more concerning. The pain. The distress. That look of rank disgust. Even the innocent name he called her. They all suggested a murky aspect to Frank's history. Some profoundly existential turmoil buried deep in his past.

Was it this, she wondered, this sinister and troubling secret that explained his disappearance?

She let the question sink into the darkness of the room, preferred instead to cling to the memory of their wedding night. It was the reassuring reminiscence of that bliss that eventually caressed her to sleep, allowed her to forget for a time that Frank was no longer with her and that – for some reason she might never understand – he had turned his back on their blissful companionship and chosen to disappear.

Ellen was woken in the morning by a loud knocking sound that drifted up the staircase from the depths of the hotel. In her twilight state of mind, she struggled to get a grip on where she was. Then she recalled Signor Sciarone and his peculiar behaviour the evening before. Rubbing the sleep from her eyes, she wondered what noisy work it was that he felt compelled to do so early in the morning.

She got up and drew back the heavy curtains. The doors onto the balcony were still slightly open. She shivered slightly. But the cool morning air was so refreshing on her skin she felt a new lease of energy. And the morning outside was so inviting that she decided to take a last stroll before leaving the Italian ambience of Locarno behind her and heading back north.

It was quite chilly when Ellen got down to the lake. In the early morning light, the dark mountain facing her looked every bit as menacing as it had the day before. But there was a resonance to the air that promised a warm spring day ahead. It gave her heart. She headed on to the Piazza Grande for a last taste of this strangely ambivalent town and to enjoy a coffee before she left. There was not a lot of activity on the piazza at that hour. While the cafés were open, none of the tables outdoors were occupied, and a restful silence hung over the place, punctuated only now and then by occasional footsteps. Although it was still on the chilly side, Ellen was loath to sit indoors, so she sat at the table she had occupied the day before. As soon as the waiter had taken her order of a cappuccino, the silence gave way to a music from inside the café that was so light it was barely audible. The sound of a keyboard and guitar that strained even to compete with the occasional footsteps on the piazza. Ellen thought she recognised it.

She looked back at the café and saw that the waiter who had taken her order was not the same man as yesterday. This one was older, wore his hair long and sported a five-day shadow that seemed out of keeping with the dress of a Swiss waiter. What looked like a permanent snarl on his lips underlined this impression. It occurred to her that this was probably not a waiter at all, but simply the owner opening up for the morning. And the music perfectly matched the sense of a slow start to the day. As Ellen observed him moving around the bar, she had the sense that he was enjoying the early-morning freedom of doing as he liked. Playing his own music. Not having to concern himself with the clientele. She was grateful for that.

As she continued to watch, the music slowly built into a mysterious, captivating atmosphere. It lent a new dimension to the piazza. The footsteps around her slowly lost their power. It was the emergence of the trumpet that did it for Ellen. The sparing mournful tones gradually eased their way into the music, then skittered into the foreground like a little girl in search of somewhere to belong. 'In a Silent Way'. It instantly put her in mind of Frank. It was his kind of music. He had introduced her to Miles Davis not long before that day he left for Switzerland. The memory evoked by those eerie, almost menacing sounds of the trumpet, guitar and electronic keyboards gave Ellen a strange sense of comfort.

She relaxed into the music, took out her book and started reading where she had left off the night before at the third tale in the collection. 'Don't Look Now'. As the music weaved its mystery and Ellen became engrossed in the story, still waiting for her cappuccino to arrive, she became aware of a figure approaching the table.

"Good morning. May I join you?"

It was the elegant lady from the day before. She was now wearing a coat over her Chanel two-piece, but still clutched the same Louis Vuitton bag emblazoned with the initials P.R. Without waiting for a reply, she sat herself down in the chair next to Ellen. There was a presumptuousness about it that irritated Ellen. But having made up her mind to leave Locarno that day, she felt more at ease with the world this morning.

"I must apologise for being so unfriendly yesterday," Ellen said, overcoming her irritation as the Louis Vuitton lady made herself comfortable.

"I was not aware that you were. But it did seem to me that you were a little troubled."

The words were broken by the man from the café, with the snarl on his lips, placing Ellen's cappuccino on the table. She left the remark to hang in the air, as she contemplated the froth and the dusting of cocoa in silence, listening to the mournful trumpet that encroached increasingly onto the piazza air. She saw the man who put the cappuccino on the table in a different light now. The snarl broke into a smile of casual nonchalance. And he took her uninvited companion's order. Caffè e latte.

"I lost my husband recently," Ellen said, as the man returned to the bar with the order.

The words were intended as an explanation. But the moment she blurted them out, it struck Ellen that she was really speaking them for herself. They provided a release.

"Oh, I'm so sorry. I should not have intruded. Do forgive me."

"It's all right. It was a long process," said Ellen, adding with dubious conviction: "I'm sure it's good for me to talk about it. And probably easier to do so with a stranger."

There followed a long, awkward silence as the two women stared into their coffee cups. Around them, activity on the piazza was beginning to grow. Two more guests arrived and sat down at a table nearby. A delivery van pulled up at the café next door. And the man and woman Ellen had seen the day before admiring each other's dogs were now walking their animals together.

"Where did you say you learned such good English?" Ellen eventually asked.

"A very good friend," the lady said with an enigmatic smile. "I lived with him in South Devon for some years. But when he passed away, I moved back to France."

"Do you know London at all?"

"A little."

"I live in Fulham," said Ellen.

"Oh, I know Fulham. On the few occasions we went to London, my friend would take me to see a polo match there."

"Polo?" said Ellen with a look of surprise. For her, this was a sport that belonged to a bygone age, to the days of the British Empire. Yet looking now at this lady in her stylish clothes with her Louis Vuitton bag, she could well imagine her at the Hurlingham polo club.

"Really? I live just down the road from there. At the less fashionable end."

This unexpected connection between the two women gave Ellen heart to open up a little more. She began to speak of the events leading up to the morning when Frank stepped out of her life just over a year ago:

She was working in Richmond at the time. In a boring secretarial job with the local council, typing letters and minutes of meaningless meetings. There was little work left to do that afternoon, and just as she was about to cook up a story about feeling unwell so she could leave work early and beat the rush hour, Frank phoned. He said he had to leave on an assignment early next morning. That was at 4.30. By quarter to five she was already on the train to Putney.

Putney station was quieter than usual for a Friday afternoon that February. Most of the noise at the entrance to the ticket hall came from the newspaper hoardings that cried out their standard tales of gloom: 'Rolls Royce collapse', 'Government takes on unions' and so on. A nation in a permanent state of decline. But no one was bothered enough to pay much attention. Least of all Ellen as she strode through the ticket hall and out into Putney High Street. She had other news on her mind: the call from Frank; the hurried nature of his words; a certain breathlessness in his voice, similar to the shortness of breath she had heard when he called three weeks earlier to say that his mother had died. But this was different. It was not the Frank she knew.

When she asked him what it was all about, what kind of assignment, he just added a quick "I'll tell you all about it when you get home." Then hung up.

And it was these words that preyed on her mind, reverberated endlessly around her head for the whole journey on the train and pursued her along the street down to the river. By the time she reached Putney Bridge, the early evening mist had already announced its impending arrival in gentle wisps that gathered on the water. Ellen watched as they wrapped spirals around the boats tied up at the water's edge, promising to blanket the Thames in the hours to come. They spelled concealment and mystery. Apprehensive of what awaited her at home, she stopped and contemplated the river and the wisps of early fog.

For a good ten minutes, she pondered the magic they weaved on the water. Eerie shapes and patterns moving along the banks of the river, over the ripples of the Thames – like novice monks assembling in a silent ritual, privy to some arcane knowledge. Seagulls mewing and wailing as they dived and wheeled around the boats and drew erratic circles in the air, resembling cryptic messages that evaporated in the slipstream of their flight.

She normally enjoyed the walk across the bridge – the bustle of the Thames, the endless flow of water beneath her feet, the sound of the gulls. She often liked to stop here and watch the gulls. She found it one of the happiest places on Earth. It was this spot, on this bridge, that marked the start of a new life for Ellen. For it was here that Frank had asked her to marry him.

But every movement on the river now whispered puzzlement. She kept dwelling on Frank's words. For no reason that she could fathom, they troubled her. Gave her a sense of foreboding. Why so enigmatic, she asked herself, and reached into her bag for the comfort of a cigarette – then it dawned on her that she had kicked the habit weeks ago. Her hand hit instead upon the cold metal of the front-door key, reminding her that she was almost home, and she moved on across the bridge.

It was too mild for a February, but as early evening began to draw in, the cold air started to bite. And Ellen felt it now on her cheeks. She pulled up the collar of her coat, tucked her long strawberry-blonde hair into the snug warmth inside and did up the top button as she headed on over the bridge towards Fulham. A flutter of trepidation throbbed in her chest. She caught her breath as she turned into Hurlingham Road and took the key out of her bag. Daylight was already fading as she slid the key into the lock and opened the door into the dark hallway of the old Victorian terraced house where they lived. She switched on the light and made her way upstairs. Their bedsit was on the second floor.

The moment she unlocked the door to the room, she sensed the emptiness. She called out. But there was no response. And there was nowhere to hide in this one room with its forlorn pretensions to be more than it was by virtue only of a niche in the far corner which served as a kitchen. On the coffee table in the middle of the room lay Frank's portable typewriter. Beside it his notebook and a folder with the words 'Bank of England 1920–1944' written on the cover in Frank's spidery hand. Inside she found copies of press cuttings: 'Controlling the masses by Montagu Norman', 'Die Geheimnisse des Mr Norman' from the Frankfurter Zeitung and countless other articles about the governor of the bank. They were the only evidence that Frank existed. That he was not here at this time of day was neither unusual nor unexpected in itself. But that early evening there was an ominous feel to his absence which made her uneasy. Then she heard a voice.

"Ellen?"

It was Frank. She instantly relaxed. And when he appeared in the door of the bedsit carrying a bunch of documents, Ellen ran over and threw her arms around him. The documents tumbled to the floor.

"Whoa, slow down," he said, brushing his hand affectionately over her left cheek. "What's got into you?"

"Sorry, I've just been so worried since you phoned."

Ellen disentangled herself from Frank and stooped to gather up the documents scattered over the floor.

"What's all this stuff? Where have you been?" she asked.

"Just before I phoned you, I had a call and had to dash up to town. Look, why don't I make a cup of tea and I'll tell you all about it."

Frank went to the kitchen niche to boil the kettle, while Ellen tidied the documents, sifting through them with curiosity before she laid them on the coffee table.

As she continued leafing through the papers, she failed to notice Frank emerge from the kitchen niche. He was carrying a pair of kitchen scissors. Half open.

It was the sudden tug on her hair that caught her by surprise:

"Ow! What are you doing?"

Ellen span round to find Frank smiling down at her, scissors in one hand and a lock of her strawberry-blonde hair in the other.

"Do you realise we've never been apart for more than a day since we met?" Frank reached down to the table, removed an envelope from the file of papers and slipped the lock of hair into it. "Surely you wouldn't begrudge me this little souvenir to remember you by while I'm gone?"

Ellen seethed over this assault. She loved her gloriously thick hair. To have it shorn of even a single curl enraged her. But still she found it hard to resist his wicked smile. And she instantly caved in to the romance of Frank's gesture.

"Come on then. The suspense is killing me," she said as he neatly folded the envelope and slipped it into his wallet. With a triumphant smile, he fetched the teapot, set it down on the table, poured the tea and sat down on the sofa beside Ellen.

"You remember Gaynor?"

His question was met with a blank expression.

"She works in Fleet Street. She was assigned to cover a story in Switzerland, where they're holding a referendum on giving women the vote, but..."

"Giving women the vote?" Ellen repeated in disbelief. "What kind of country is it where women don't have the right to vote? In this day and age?"

"That's why they're having the referendum."

"And only the men get to vote in this referendum, I suppose?"

"That's just it," said Frank with a boyish excitement. "It's a really fascinating story."

"Good God, you can be so irritating." Ellen glowered at him. "It's not in the least fascinating. It's grotesque," she added, then paused for a moment as her eyes widened. "You don't actually believe in it, do you?" she asked with a look of horror on her face.

"What do you mean 'believe in it'?" Frank was taken aback by Ellen's truculence. He was not used this side of her. But for Ellen it was as if she felt she had suddenly shone a new light on him and was shocked by what she thought she had found.

"It's not about beliefs or opinions," he said, brushing his hands nervously through his thick brown hair as he spoke. "Anyway, Gaynor was rushed into hospital with appendicitis or something and can't now cover the story. Since she's the only staffer who speaks German, she persuaded her boss to let me cover it instead. They really wanted a woman, but they had no one else, so I jumped at it – not sure how I'll cope with the weird kind of German they speak there though. And of course it means I'll have to put my research on the Bank of England story to one side for a bit. But anyway, I went up to town this afternoon to collect this stuff."

He nodded towards the documents on the table.

"Plane tickets, contacts, background material. Stuff like that. And it will be a chance to reinvent myself."

His flight from Heathrow was booked for early next morning. Ellen was going to miss him. But she tried as best she could to hide her sadness; she wanted them to enjoy their last hours together without any kind of friction. So Ellen spent the rest of the evening attempting to share Frank's excitement, while he studied the documents he had been given and talked endlessly about the trip ahead.

When sadness and excitement eventually gave way to longing, they entered the night entwined together in a communion deeper than she had ever felt before. And lay that way, in each other's arms, until Ellen woke again early next morning. She looked at Frank gently breathing as he slept on in her arms, his smell weaving its way into her senses, his early-morning stubble prickling her shoulder. She stroked every curve of his perfect body. Ran her fingers over the muscular arm half-draped around her waist. Brushing them softly over his neck and face, leaving her thumb at journey's end to explore the intriguing indentation in the buckled bridge of his nose.

She had often wondered whether this feature of his anatomy had anything to do with his sense of smell. Frank had told her of his strange olfactory senses – that some smells he was unable to detect at all and others he was acutely sensitive to – the acrid smell of ammonia in particular. Cordite was also high on his list. Ellen attributed the latter to an overactive imagination fed by a taste for Dashiell Hammett. He put it all down to what he called the landscape of his nose.

As the theodolite of Ellen's thumb now surveyed the territory, Frank slowly roused. His dark eyes a reluctant pair of witnesses to dawn, yet just as fetching as ever in their sleep-entrained effort to open. Frank's arm tightened and he drew it firmly around Ellen's waist to plant an early-morning kiss on her lips. It was a moment that would stay forever in Ellen's memory. She recalled his last words not long after that moment.

"I'll be back before you've even noticed I've gone," he said as he opened the door. And disappeared.

Sitting now on the Piazza Grande in Locarno, Ellen was not inclined to share every little detail of their last brief morning together. She simply said: "That was the last time we spoke."

Her companion took a last sip of her coffee, placed the cup in its saucer and looked across at Ellen. It was a look that contained more than just sympathy – it seemed to convey a kind of knowledge and wisdom that Ellen found both comforting and slightly disconcerting at the same time.

"I'm sorry to bore you with my story," she said.

"It was not at all boring, my dear."

"But I really must be going now," Ellen added. "I'm travelling back to Basel this morning."

"So soon?" asked the elegant lady, looking at Ellen with an expression that bordered on shock, together with what Ellen sensed to be a strange hint of disappointment.

"It was really nice talking to you. This should cover the coffee for both of us," said Ellen, as she got up to leave, handing her companion a ten franc note, which the elderly lady politely refused.

"Please, the pleasure was all mine. I wish you…" the elderly lady paused for a moment as she looked up at Ellen… "a safe journey."

Ellen hesitated, pondering the emphasis her companion placed on those last two words. It was as if the elderly lady knew just how perilous the journey had been over the last twelve months and had some kind of preternatural inkling of further trouble ahead.

Or was it simply that months of talking with Marthe's psychiatrist husband had spawned a paranoid suspicion of the slightest inflection in a person's voice?

These worrisome thoughts hastened Ellen's steps as she headed back through the narrow streets to fetch her bags and settle up with Signor Sciarone.

Chapter 2

Frank flew out of London on Saturday, 6 February 1971. The day was too early, too cold and too empty to enjoy. But it was his first trip to Switzerland and, while the country was known more for dull precision and timekeeping than for any newsworthy stories, he felt an inexplicable buzz of excitement. An odd sense of agitation that surprised him.

Ellen was constantly rebuking him for always being so cool, for the way he never let anything get to him. But Frank was a fence-sitter. He knew it. And he tried to justify this to her by insisting how important it was to remain objective about things. This, after all, was what had attracted him to journalism in the first place. It was this part of his argument that incensed Ellen all the more. And recalling her display of passion now as he sat on the tube to Heathrow airport brought a smile to his face.

His heart was still pounding from the rush to change onto the Piccadilly line at Earl's Court. But it was also racing with a sense of apprehension and expectation. He wondered what Ellen would think about his lack of cool now. Yet it was not so much the prospect of what awaited him in a strange country as the opportunity he felt it offered.

He knew how much Ellen would really like to start a family. In truth, this was not a prospect he relished. He was not ready to commit to the pitter patter of tiny feet. But he also knew that, if it were to happen, there was no way they could contemplate bringing a baby into the world while they were stuck in a Fulham bedsit. So, if this assignment works out, Frank told himself, then maybe it could help pave the way to a staff job, more job security and a bigger flat. It was as much this as the trip itself that set his heart beating nineteen to the dozen.

When Frank arrived at Heathrow, he found that his flight was delayed. He phoned in to tell the newspaper, so they could cancel a meeting that had been set up for him later that morning with a local editor, then took himself off to the bar for a coffee.

Despite the frustration, it was a welcome delay in one sense: ever since depriving Ellen of a lock of her hair, he had been feeling awkward at the thought that the only home he was able to find for it was a shabby envelope. This long wait now gave him time to find something more fitting. He was hoping to find a wallet with a window inside that would allow him to see Ellen's lock of hair every time he opened it. The best he could manage was a wallet with a little pouch for coins. It was not ideal, but at least Ellen's hair would be safe, he told himself as he put a ten-pound note into the outstretched hand of the shop assistant.

When eventually he touched down in Basel, it was mid-afternoon. And the dull gloom of the sky told him the end of the day was already fast approaching. The temperature was several degrees lower than in London. Remnants of snow lay around the edges of the tarmac. The airport itself was on French soil. But to the east loomed the mountains of the Black Forest in Germany and to the south the dark hills that marked the easternmost tip of Switzerland's Jura Mountains.

A state of blurred borders that would come to define his stay. He had wondered, when he was handed his flight tickets, why he was being sent to Basel. He would have expected Zurich or even Geneva. But there were some people they wanted him to meet in Basel before travelling on to Zurich after the vote for some post-referendum coverage.

When Frank was sent on this assignment, it had shocked him to find that there was a country in post-war Europe where women were still denied the right to vote, and he was keen to learn more about this country. But much as he was itching to get his teeth into this mission, he was also deeply frustrated that he had to put his story about the Bank of England's connections with pre-war Nazi Germany on the back burner.

And yet, as the taxi carried Frank into town, this frustration began to ebb away amidst a strange sense of comfort and familiarity that he could not explain. A peculiar hominess. A spirit of belonging. The only discord in this sense of intimacy with the place was the array of posters that decorated almost every street they drove down shouting NO to voting rights for women!

They adorned lamp posts, hoardings, walls and any other space that could accommodate them. Frank was struck by how politely ineffectual the YES posters appeared. And how brutal the opposing posters were: from pictures of women crying "Leave us out of it" to the shock tactics of babies falling out of prams while women were too distracted "playing politics," or of anonymous hands groping a woman in silhouette. One that caught his eye in particular was the picture of a baby's dummy with a fly crawling over it. What kind of country is this? Frank asked himself.

"Are you voting in the referendum tomorrow?" he asked the driver.

"I am Italian," came the reply.

The man at the wheel was the surly, silent type. And he said no more as they drove in the direction of the Centralbahnplatz, along streets that appeared increasingly and curiously known to Frank: past the grand Romanesque church and Jugendstil residences towards the viaduct and the high-rise Rialto that rose up from the road below and peered over the balustrade; the yawning exit from the multistorey Schlotterbeck garage; and the Grand Savoy Hotel, now home to the Bank for International Settlements. All these images tugged oddly at his memory as they headed towards the main railway station.

He had a room booked at the Hotel St. Gotthard. It lay just across from the station. At the desk, Frank was politely welcomed by a fifty-something man at reception, smartly dressed in various shades of grey, except for his gold cuff-links.

In all other respects, there was little to distinguish him from the taxi driver. He was a man of few words.

Once Frank had completed the check-in formalities, the receptionist simply handed him an envelope with his room key and pointed to the lift. Room 202. Frank placed the envelope on the table when he entered the room and went straight over to the window to let in some air. The fuggy mustiness hit him the moment he opened the door. There was a familiarity about the stale atmosphere that he could not put his finger on. It teased him like an afterthought tugging at a synapse buried deep in an untidy archive of souvenirs.

He opened the window. It looked down onto the street that ran past the station. A quiet street that spared the hotel all the traffic noise of a railway station thanks to its location some hundred metres or more from the main entrance. It was effectively a side street that could have been anywhere in Europe.

He had already phoned Ellen from Heathrow to say he had been delayed. But he promised he would call again as soon as he arrived. He dialled 9 for an outside line. The phone rang for some time. But Ellen didn't pick up.

He turned back into the room, took the file of documents he had brought with him out of his suitcase and placed it on the table next to the envelope. He looked pensively at this envelope for a moment, picked it up and found a handwritten note inside. It was from the editor of the local newspaper, Hanspeter Rösti, welcoming Frank to Basel in almost perfect English and inviting him to dinner. He wrote that he would return to the hotel at 7.30 in the evening to pick Frank up.

Frank could not resist a chuckle. Do they really call people Rösti here? And he contemplated the dinner that might be in store for him.

Thinking it best to take a nap and make sure he was fit for this engagement, he lay down on the bed. It was an old and poorly sprung mattress. But after the early start and the long wait at Heathrow, he fell to sleep almost instantly.

How long he slept he could not be sure. But it was a restless sleep. And every time he came anywhere near the boundary line to wakefulness, he found himself dragged back into an endless and disturbing dream:

The musty smell of damp wheat hung in the atmosphere. A fuggy scavenger of the air he breathed. Suffocating. The harvest would come too late this year. He could feel it. The tragedy trying to get a grip on his senses. Banners seemed to fly from the masthead of every tree proclaiming failure. As if this was something to look forward to. He heard them flutter in the wind high above his head. And every now and then the gusting vestiges of the storm that had flattened down the wheat billowed their bleak message that little bit louder, just to reinforce how close he was. Just the other side of the woods. Just beyond the trees.

He knew how near at hand it was. Could hear the knives being sharpened, taste the cold steel whetting its appetite for the plunge. It had been a long year. And he wondered how much longer it would be before it became last year. Time was pressing.

The solitary figure moving down the road between the wheatfields seemed little more than a sad parenthesised remark on the landscape. Lost in a long black fur-collared coat and black homburg hat, and weighted on each side by an oversized suitcase that bracketed his slow progress to the trees, he punctuated his own horizon with dark precision.

A crow cawed and cackled above the trees, before it was tossed to one side by a flurry of wind. It was the only sound to erupt onto the warm, musty atmosphere. Smothered and puffed away again in the stiff breeze. Not enough to distract the traveller. He continued on his way, shuffling ever closer to the dark tunnel created by the archway of dense, leafy boughs across the road. His progress was so slow it was almost imperceptible from a distance. But he kept moving. Had he allowed himself to be roused from his purpose for only a moment – had he looked up – he would have seen that the crow was not alone. Gathering overhead was a whole murder of crows with sinister design. And the sky turned black with their menace.

If only he had looked up…

But he kept moving at the same slow pace, and – just as the black squadrons were making their descent to inflict the first vicious tweaks on the side of his neck, drawing blood – his dogged motion down the road was abruptly swallowed by the tunnel of trees. The hunter crows veered away. For a moment he appeared to be reprieved.

From somewhere in the distance the yapping of a dog became audible.

As Frank surfaced for a brief instant, he eased open his eyes and caught the gloom of the afternoon through the hotel window. Heard a dog barking on the street outside. And fell back into sleep.

The tunnel was short and curved to the right before it began to let in light from the other end. Even at his slow pace it was not long before the silhouette of the man showed up against the blank wall of the customs house at the end of the tunnel. Just the other side of the trees.

The building appeared lifeless. And the traveller paid it no attention as he continued on his path. Past a shutter on the house that swung helplessly in the wind. Every now and then, driven by a sudden gust, the shutter would smash with a crack like gunfire on the wall. Swing back, then smack again against the brick. An unnerving reminder that no storm has respect for borders.

No one challenged him as he passed the barrier. Only the starting drizzle had anything to say. He was already some way past the border when a figure with the look of a customs officer emerged from the doorway of the building, draped in a grey cloak that matched the sombreness of the clouds. Hidden by the foliage of the trees, the yapping dog could still be heard.

The shutter smacked against the wall again, louder this time, and echoed away through the woods. A large patch of the rendering around the window had been pared off by the shutter to reveal naked red brickwork, which glistened slightly where streaks of rain had splashed across its bruised, indurated flesh. The customs man paid no attention to the banging shutter. It was not his concern. It swung its senseless rhythm on the other side of the house. In another country. Across the border. What worried him was the sky

– by now a dark uniform grey above his head, leaden with its imminent deluge. He cocked his head diffidently at the brewing storm. Blinked slightly as a raindrop caught him in the eye. And turned his gaze on the slowly diminishing form of the overdressed pedestrian in the black homburg hat.

The shutter smacked against the wall. Bang. The man in the homburg hat stopped and turned his head. Looked back just briefly at the customs house. Bang. Then again. Bang. In quick succession. But even louder now. The crack this time reverberated through the low-slung clouds, which seemed to take this as their cue. They opened the hatch and let the storm finally run its course.

The black homburg hat, already glistening wet, rolled erratically over the camber of the road and came to a halt in the gutter. The two suitcases had found their rest instantaneously beside the slumped figure. They lay now half-concealed by his coat. A small dark crater between the eyes lay exposed to the downpour. A hole quite unremarkable, except for the trickle of blood that ran a steadily dilute path down the neck and mingled with the rain. The only suggestion of life that remained in the crumpled heap was nothing more than movement created by reflections of light on the blood and rainwater coursing over the blanched skin and the folds and furls of the huge coat, where the water quickly gathered in pathetic small black reservoirs.

From the undergrowth of the trees, a mangy collied mongrel, limping heavily on one of its hind legs, trotted over to the scene and sniffed around the fur collar of the man's coat. The customs officer blinked the rain out of his eyes and cast his gaze towards the amorphous mass that lay some 500 metres down the road. Across the border. On the other side. It had not happened on his patch. It was no concern of his. He stood in the incessant teeming downpour and stared at the body on the side of the road. Only the rain seeped a way into his consciousness. Only the water got through to him. It was cold and wet. He shivered slightly as it made its presence felt down the back of his neck. Was there anything he could have done to prevent this? Could I not go back? Frank asked, briefly surfacing again to wipe the sweat from his brow with the pillow.

That was long past. A trickle of rain ran down the neck. It felt cold. And he glanced again at the crumpled figure, wet and motionless in the road. For an instant, the soaked black bundle appeared in close-up. The right side of the face, where blood had flowed, had taken on the cold white look of marble where it had been washed clean by the rain. The haemorrhage had long since ceased. And the hole now gaped as large as life.

The irony nourished an urge to smile, and brought a sense of relief. It was a dream after all, Frank told himself. But he also knew that the soaking shirt and the trickles of water over his face told another story. He ran his fingers over the buckled bridge of his nose. Explored the unevenness of the dent. Recalled his father's words: "Shot between the eyes at birth". And then another familiar voice:

"Aber was tun?"

Frank was still struggling to free himself from the dream…

Uneasy pangs of conscience gave way to panic. The familiarity of the sheet-white face. Seeing suddenly that it was his mother lying there, her body covered in confetti, laid prostrate and dead by a faceless gunman who could have been prevented filled him with an unspeakable terror.

Exhausted and fearful, Frank lay there for some time not knowing what it all meant or what he should do. His eyes remained firmly shut. He felt a deep, dull throb in the back of his head. Awkwardly he reached out an arm and let his fingers grope their way over the smooth cold marble surface – until they found what they were looking for. Through the streams of wet that still poured over his face he gingerly blinked open an eye and focused it in the direction of his hand. Nearly four. His head ached, the pillow was drenched with sweat, and a peculiar smell filled the room.

He dragged himself up. Reluctant to move an inch, but letting the edge of the bed take the bulk of his weight as he rose, he managed to stumble through the narrow bedroom to the window. His head pounded with every step. Rubbing the remnants of that troubled sleep from his eyes, he parted the net curtains and peered down onto the street. It was dry, and there was no hint of rain in the clouds. The net curtains fell back into place as he turned around and caught a strong smell of time waft from their folds. He wondered how many refugees might have sought asylum here. Was it perhaps the smell of fear and persecution he detected? Or just the pheromones from innumerable steamy encounters on the worn-out springs of the bed? Whatever it was, he had to take a walk and clear his head before his dinner date with Rösti. Tucking the envelope in his wallet and his notebook in his pocket, he ventured out of the hotel.

The street outside the entrance to the railway station was full of activity, people who appeared to have somewhere to go or something important to do. He felt out of place. These were people who categorically belonged. To this extent they gave the street a definition. But the impression he had of the city now was no different from the one he had had when he arrived a few hours ago. It was still plastered with referendum posters, and it occurred to Frank that maybe all the bustle was a reflection of their excitement about the vote next day. But he sensed a profound disquiet. Perhaps it was his throbbing head compounded by the noises of city life in a foreign country. A garbled tongue that bore little relation to the German he knew and the sound of tram wheels meshing with steel track to create a persistent, whining sensation in his head. As the noise swelled, confusion and dizziness threatened to overwhelm him.

In an effort to escape, he dived down some steps outside the railway station and into an underpass that led beneath the tracks. He could hear the dull rumble of a train above him and the muffled voice of an announcer making a vain attempt to communicate. Although it seemed initially safer in this subway, Frank quickly came to realise it was the wrong place to be: his mind became disjointed, spinning with scales of noise he had never encountered before. Everything around him was bedlam. A group of oversized adolescents pushing and shoving each other to shrieks of laughter. A passenger wheeling his screeching trolley of baggage past them in the opposite direction. The cacophony was unbearable and had Frank yelping like a frightened dog. He heard the loud adolescents behind him now turn and laugh mockingly behind him. Still yelping he started to run, almost in panic, and kept going – away from the echoes of the tube he had plunged himself into – until he emerged from the subway on the other side of the station.

The fresh air helped to restore some calm. Standing at the mouth of the underpass he looked about. An utterly normal street. Foreign, but normal. And dull. A typical back-of-the-station area that owed all its character to the appearance of having been ignored for the last fifty years.

Still panting from his panic run, he waited for a tram to pass, then crossed the road. It was at that moment – as he set foot on the opposite pavement – that his sense of confusion finally lifted, as if he had suddenly emerged from a cloud of dense fog. An excited sense of discovery and a secure feeling of familiarity at one and the same time. And this was the curious thing: the shop window that seemed to smile at him as he stepped onto the pavement. It was known to him in a way he could not define. He paused at the window to examine its display of second-hand and antiquarian books in the hope he might find a clue. To his surprise many of the wares on offer were in English – middle to late Victorian illustrated books on exotic fauna and flora. On plants, birds, butterflies and other wonders of nature in far-flung corners of the Earth. But the book which attracted his attention above all others was a German book on physiognomy, whose author was as obscure to him as the subject matter. And yet it caught his eye. No, more than that. It was known to him in an intimate way that had him tingling with a warm yet strange excitement. It put him in mind of Ellen's sister Beth. But he could not remember for the life of him why that should be.

The compulsion to enter the shop, to embrace this knowledge with all the unspent passion usually reserved for an unrequited love in some distant past, was overwhelming.

Breathless with expectation, he climbed the two short steps to the door, pushed it open and was briefly startled from his trance by the insistent jangle of the bell.

An elderly lady sat at a desk in a far corner of the shop. In the dim light, he could just about make out that all her energy was concentrated on a knitting pattern. She was disturbed by Frank's arrival, and her response was automatic.

"*Grüezi*," she said. In the short time he had been in the country, the greeting had already become familiar. Frank smiled as best he could and returned the greeting in a way that plainly betrayed his origins.

"Can I help you?" she asked, instantly switching to English.

"Thank you. I'm just looking."

"We have many English books," she said with obvious excitement at this opportunity to put down her knitting. "Come," she added. Laying her needles and wool carefully on the table, she led him into a narrow back room, where shelves of literature reached from wall to wall and floor to ceiling.

"Here. Some English books for you," she said, an edge of triumph in her frail voice, and left him alone to browse. The books here were of no interest to Frank, but he was disinclined to offend the old lady. So he hung around for a few minutes in her back room, absorbing the dusty atmosphere. It was warm and stuffy. He could feel the heat rising to his head, as the dizziness and throbbing pain began to invade his senses again.

"Oh Achim, what have I done?" He heard the words ring quite distinctly through his mind. In German. Traces of comprehension, like brief clearings in the fog, flashed through his head before a net of fuzziness cast itself over his mind. The tension fastened this net so tight that his neck muscles ached to their deepest nerve cells. Beads of sweat gathered on his upper lip. In the corner of the room was a narrow staircase that led down into the cellar. Should he venture down? He knew full well what to expect. The horror that lay beneath.

No. Mopping away the sweat, he turned and retreated to the front of the shop. The old lady was back at her knitting.

Without really seeing her, he could feel her look up. She was talking to him. He saw the lips move. He heard the sound of her voice. But he could not understand a word. It was impossible for him even to recognise what language she was speaking.

He moved towards the window in a desperate attempt to regain his senses. And rested there. Sweating. Gripped by an unremitting angst. Slowly the fuzziness in his head began to clear. And gradually he became aware of the old lady beside him now, touching his arm.

"Are you needing a doctor?" She was speaking English. This much he could decipher. He pointed to the book in the window display. *Physiognomik* by Rudolf Kassner.

"I'd like that book please," he said. "What does it cost?"

The old woman peered over the partition between the shop and the window display. Looked back at Frank with a quizzical hesitation. Then reached over into the window bay to retrieve it.

"This book?"

Frank nodded, and she opened the front cover.

"Twenty francs."

She could have asked a hundred. A thousand.

"You are reading German?" she asked as she took the volume back to the desk on the far side of the room.

Frank said nothing. He had no energy for any further talk.

"Ah, I understand. It is for a present," she said. And disappeared into the back room. Had she gone down to the cellar? Did she know what was down there? Frank asked himself.

The question was answered a moment later when she returned with a sheet of wrapping paper. And with slow, arthritic fingers she proceeded to gift-wrap the book. Even in his sorely chafed state of nerves, Frank could not help wondering how she could possibly manage to knit a wearable garment when her hands were so disfigured and gnarled.

He pulled a twenty franc note from his wallet. It was only then that he noticed how the palms of his hands were sweating. He sensed the turmoil in his mind begin to stir again. And let the note drop out of his hand and onto the desk before his mind swam totally out of its depth. As he picked up the book, the voice returned, speaking a German that seemed so strange and yet so familiar.

"Oh Achim. Can you ever forgive me?" He could see them all lying there in the cellar. The two baby boys and Gertrude. Barely lit by the single naked lightbulb that hung from the ceiling.

Without another word to the old woman, Frank hurried to the door and out onto the street. Turning right to put some distance between him and the bookshop as quickly as he could, he hoped this would clear his head. After a brisk few minutes' walk, the street opened out at a crossroads in the shadow of a church. He saw a tram approaching from the right. On the front the number 23. It read Barfüsserplatz. He had no idea where that was. But he knew what it meant. It conjured bucolic images of boys and girls romping barefoot on a village green. Intrigued by this thought, he climbed on board and enjoyed the relative calm, the gentle sway of the tram as it negotiated the corners on its journey.

But Frank's quaint picture from a bygone age vanished when the tram reached its destination. The doors opened onto what looked like the very heart of the city. Not a hint of village green. Instead a space dominated by a large white building ahead of him as he alighted onto the pavement. It pointed skywards in a way that spoke of religious fervour and was buttressed by two red sandstone struts – they had the look of skinny legs over which the building spread its white garment like the gigantic habit of a Franciscan monk seated above the square. In the throng around him, he fancied he could still hear the sound of that voice in his head crying "Achim, oh Achim."

The square itself was a teeming mass of people at the tram station, all waiting for their number to come up. Turning left as his feet touched the pavement, in the hope he might escape that voice, Frank followed the tramlines that continued on down a narrow street and headed deeper still into the heart of the city. The street twisted around a monumental sandstone building that instantly cast everything around it – and Frank in particular – into a deep sense of gloom. Cut into the side of the building as he passed was a vast gaping entrance. Perhaps built to let coaches pass in days gone by. Momentarily confused by two words at this gateway that caught his eye – *Passagio proibito* – Frank stopped dead in his tracks. Gaping around him like the jaws of a monster, it had the air of a gateway to Valhalla. Yet those words on the wall hinted more at the threshold to Dante's Inferno. Whatever their provenance, wherever he was, they spoke of gloom and despair. So it came as a huge relief when he got the grim walls of the building behind him after some fifty metres and saw the street open out onto another square.

Frank's vision blurred at the sudden sense of space. He teetered on the edge of the pavement as a gigantic kaleidoscope of shifting patterns from the buildings around the square rolled before him. He leaned against an advertising pillar for support and found himself eyeball to eyeball with a huge insect – that same poster he had seen earlier in the day. A fly crawling over a baby's dummy. In a brief moment of clarity, it reminded him of his mission. The reason he was here. The referendum.

He caught the aroma of roast chestnuts in the air. Then his head began to spin. He sensed the advertising column roll away from him and closed his eyes in an effort to stop the motion. It helped. Slowly the undulating movement receded. And thoughts of that mission called to mind the note from the local newspaper editor. He would be looking for Frank at 7.30 that evening. Gingerly he opened his eyes and squinted at his watch. He needed to find his way back to the Hotel St. Gotthard while it was still light.

Pushing himself from the pillar, Frank turned and crossed the road, then headed into a narrow street off the square. This was not the way back. He knew it.

He knew it only too well. That street. It beckoned him into its clutches. Pulled him into the warren of alleyways behind the square that seemed untouched by time. His world had become completely disjointed since stepping off the plane. But he felt strangely comfortable in this quarter. The homely aroma of roast chestnuts still wafted through the air. The fragrance of street life, spilled beer, restaurant kitchens. Every moment invaded his senses and made itself at home in his muddled mind. Instantly his appointment with Rösti had found its way once again to the back of his thoughts. And sank completely out of reach as his footsteps on the pavement trod what seemed such a cosily familiar path. He knew there would be a place nearby where he could sit and draw his breath for a while over a beer.

But he was not prepared for the deep sense of loss when he turned the next corner and stopped dead in his tracks. In his mind, he had seen a huge advertisement for Persil on the side wall facing him. But there was no wall. And there was no sign of any tavern. There was simply nothing. Just a site fenced off to allow an anonymous new building to take shape.

A sudden sharp slap on the back almost knocked him to the floor. In the shock of the moment he almost missed the crackle of words that came with it.

"*Wir vermissen's auch!*"

"What the fuck!?" Frank swung round and came face to face with a large jovial figure, whose distinguishing feature at that moment was a gut that spilled generously forth beneath an open jacket and overcoat. Restrained by a waistcoat vainly trying to hold it in place, it looked none too comfortable. Frank fancied the garment had lost two buttons already.

"He says we miss it too," came a softer voice the other side of Frank in almost perfect English with shades of an old colonialist or public-school polish to it. This added to the slight oddness about the voice, which carried the strong hint of an accent that Frank was unable to place. Instantly intrigued by the voice, he turned to face its owner – a man some ten years older than him, possibly late thirties, with a strikingly handsome face. Swarthy, with an aquiline nose and dark eyes that would have been sultry and mysterious had it not been for the engaging white smile that came with his words.

"Lisettli's wine tavern," the voice continued. "The jewel of the Spalenberg. She closed down a few years ago. But come along with us old chap."

The two men each put an arm around Frank. Drained by his bewilderment, confusion and the utterly strange familiarity of this city, he meekly submitted to these unlikely Samaritans and let himself be guided down the road. They walked back to the square, past the blood-red building with its kaleidoscopic frescoes, across the bridge over the Rhine and deep into a warren of streets on the other side of the river.

When they reached a corner building that displayed the modest sign of a sheep over the door, the two men led Frank through the doorway into a dingy room. He had the uneasy impression of a lamb being led to slaughter.

"What can we get you?" said the English speaker, as they settled Frank into his seat at the table. Frank looked about him and felt instant comfort in the warmth of the rough but cosy little pub – infused with years of spilled beer and tobacco smoke, the aroma a soothing balm for his confusion. It was the kind of place where he felt instantly at home.

"I must apologise," the man continued, "we have not even introduced ourselves. My name is Jan, but my friends call me Jack."

"And I am Baschi," the jovial one chipped in, offering Frank his hand.

"Thanks, I'll have a beer," he said. Then: "Why Jack? You're not English surely."

"My family name is Hruby. With an H. Jack's the name people called me after Lee Harvey Oswald was shot. And I've been carrying the name around with me ever since. It sounds macabre. But I can live with it. And it's better than Donát."

"That doesn't sound very Swiss either."

"Maybe not. But what does that even mean? My father was originally from Bohemia. My mother is Irish. But I'm as much Swiss as anything. My father wanted to call me Donát. But my mother by her own account hated the name. It sounded too much like a doughnut to her. So they compromised with Jan. And now I'm stuck with Jack."

"He grow up here and go to the school here," added the man called Baschi. "He is Swiss just like me."

"So Frank, what are you doing here in Basel?" asked Jack, as the waitress placed a beer down in front of Frank along with a bottle of red wine and two glasses for his hosts.

"God, I need this," said Frank. He put the beer glass to his mouth with a craving that surprised even him in his slightly unhinged state.

It was a lager. Not his idea of a good beer. But the initial coolness of the liquid was enough to slake his thirst. And the unexpected chink of light that this encounter now shone onto his dark confusion lit up his memory of why he had even come here in the first place.

"Cheers," he said and put down the glass. He pulled the notebook from the inside pocket of his jacket and placed it on the table. "You have a big referendum here tomorrow."

"News travels," Jack said. "At last the country is dragging itself into the twentieth century."

"Will you be voting?" asked Frank. Jack stared into his glass.

"What do you think, Baschi? Will we be voting?"

Baschi shrugged.

"They tried twelve years ago. And failed then. Why will it be any different now? Politics is a dirty business. Not for women. And many women do not even want to vote. They trust their men."

"Baschi doesn't talk to many women," Jack explained, "What he's really trying to say is that women don't have to do military service like men do, so why should they get the vote? Isn't that so, Baschi?"

Baschi just smiled.

"I've been given some names of women I might talk to," said Frank, flicking through his notebook. "Gerhard and Späth-Schweizer, for example."

"Späth-Schweizer", Baschi chuckled. "What kind of a woman is a Späth-Schweizer?" he added slamming his right hand down on the table with a guffaw. His left hand held the buttons of his waistcoat in place just as a precaution.

"Baschi likes his jokes," said Jack indulgently. "It's a name that translates as Late Swiss."

"I know," Frank said, irritated by Jack's assumption of his ignorance.

"I don't know these women myself. Frau Gerhard is very old now, and I know she learned a lot from your suffragettes in England. She also saved many Jewish children before the war. They like to hold her up as a shining example of the great humanist tradition in this city, say it's because of people like her that women have already had the vote in local elections here for some years. But if you want to know what the average Swiss woman thinks about voting in national elections, you'd do better speaking to my wife."

"Most countries gave women the vote years ago. Why's it taken so long for Switzerland? Your women can't be happy with that."

Jack frowned over the table at Frank.

"That sounds a tad like a rebuke old chap. Women are beautiful creatures and they can rejoice in that. As we men can too."

"And that sounds rather like a no vote," Frank reciprocated.

"Let's talk of more interesting things," Jack said, paying no attention to Frank's words. "What do you think of the beer?"

"What you write?" asked Baschi with suspicion, when he saw Frank scribbling in his notebook. Frank ignored the curiosity.

"Lager's not really to my taste."

"You see this place?" Jack asked, as he made a sweeping gesture with his right arm to encompass the entire room. "They were serving wine here 500 years ago. The oldest pub in the city. They have sold many kinds of wine and ale over the centuries. Let me get you something special, which might be more to your taste."

As the sweeping gesture reached the end of its trajectory, he raised his arm again, clicked his fingers and called over the waitress.

Frank was unable to hear what Jack said. But as he was speaking, he cast a sideways glance at Frank, who could not escape the expression in those dark, deep-set eyes. A look that lay somewhere between mischief and villainy. He could not be sure which was closer to the truth. Within a short time, the waitress returned to the table, took the lager from Frank and replaced it with a slender, tulip-shaped glass of cloudy-looking ale that boasted an impressive head.

"*Danke schön, Lisbeth. Und was hältst Du von der Abstimmung morgen?*" Jack said to the waitress, asking her in a clear High German – for Frank's benefit – what she thought of the vote for women. And that look still lingered in the smile on his lips.

The waitress's answer came in an impenetrable dialect that left Frank flummoxed. He looked quizzically at Jack.

"It seems our friend Baschi is right. She said she leaves that kind of thing to her husband."

Baschi laughed. Jack meanwhile pulled a hipflask surreptitiously from the inside pocket of his jacket and poured a shot into the glass while Frank was still gazing at the waitress.

"Now what do you think of this beer?" Jack asked, nodding at the tall glass in front of Frank. Frank caressed the glass with a smile of approval at what looked a little more like the beer he was used to and put it to his lips.

"That's good. It's got a real kick." Smacking his lips, he placed the glass back down in front of him with a look of pure satisfaction.

"It's a speciality I picked up from a friend of mine," Jack said. "Wheat beer with a shot of gin. He calls it dog's nose."

Frank gave a nod of approval. He raised his glass in appreciation to the waitress. She smiled. And the three of them settled into an evening far removed from anything Frank might originally have had in mind. It was several glasses of wine and dog's nose later that the three ventured back out into the night air. The breeze from the river was already making its mark on the street. Frank shivered with the chill and buttoned up his jacket. By now, his date with Rösti had faded into oblivion. And the dog's nose had sniffed its way so deep into his skull that he was glad of the support his companions gave him as first Baschi and then Jack draped an arm around his shoulders with the words "You come along with us old chap."

Frank barely noticed Jack's soft voice. There was certainly no way he could detect whether it still carried any of the mischief or villainy he had sensed earlier. For now, he felt only the succour of those two guiding arms as they steered him back along the street. Where they were taking him, he had no idea. But he knew they were retracing their steps when the cold air from the Rhine hit him in the face as they crossed the bridge.

Perhaps it was the vibration and rumble of the trams over the bridge. Or the sight of the water that flowed beneath. Whatever the reason, Frank felt his gut suddenly heave. He pulled himself free of those guiding arms and leaned over the parapet of the bridge to throw up. Behind him Jack and Baschi laughed, exchanging garbled jokes. Then slapped him on the back.

Frank looked up. Facing him on the far side of the river, a host of lights flickered out across the water. He fancied he could hear their sparkling glitter, as they celebrated the night. Dancing and singing before his eyes. The motion threatened to send his mind into a spin.

"Is that a palace or what is it?" Frank asked. He hoped his words might foil the spin. Jack laughed and slapped him on the back again.

"Quite right," he said. "A palace fit for three kings. The best hotel in town."

"And the most dangerous," Baschi added darkly. And left the words to hang mysteriously, without elaborating further.

Still leaning over the parapet for fear of further heaving, Frank looked up at Baschi. Jack saw the glazed bewilderment in Frank's eyes.

"That was thirty years ago," Jack reassured him. Frank was not reassured.

"The bridges here were packed with explosives back then," he explained. "In case the Germans invaded. The button for this bridge was in that building."

"That's not all," Baschi said in a sinister tone.

"He's not wrong," Jack added in an effort to lighten the darkness. "It's one of the ironies of history that the building was home to Mr Herzl during the first Zionist Congress, while the hotel opposite," he said, gesturing towards a white, neoclassical building behind them on the other side of the river, "was built by the grandfather of Mr Schicklgruber's personal astrologer."

These words only added to the confusion in Frank's head.

"Come on," Jack said, putting an arm around Frank to steady him. "It's time to move."

With his companions either side of him, Frank let himself be guided on across the bridge to the heart of the city. As he found his step and settled into the rhythm dictated by Jack and Baschi, the sounds of the street took over.

It was not until these sounds were shut out by a door closing behind him that Frank regained at least a vague sense of his whereabouts. He caught the creak of boards as Jack and Baschi guided him up two flights of stairs, pushed open a door and escorted him into a dimly lit room. Then he heard Jack call out: "Hello girls. Are you decent? We have a guest tonight."

"Here you are old chap," Jack said, as he and Baschi steered Frank across the room and eased him gently into a sofa. Frank surveyed the scene in the room through the bewilderment wrought by the dog's nose. He sniffed the air and caught the faint trace of ammonia. Mingled with tobacco smoke. He was trying hopelessly to work out where he was. What he was doing here.

Although dimly lit, it was a room made comfortable by heavy dark-green drapes that hung over the windows. On the right of him stood another sofa and opposite him two armchairs that had seen better days. Behind these stood a grand piano.

Jack still stood in the doorway to his right. Baschi alongside him. As Frank was trying to make sense of it all, he became aware of a new fragrance entering the room from behind him. A feminine fragrance that wafted around the sofa as its owner walked over to Jack. She carried a cigarette packet in her left hand. A slim woman, not much shorter than Jack, with long red hair that fell in thick curls over a green velvet, figure-hugging dress. It lent the contrast of the orange cigarette packet in her hand the air of an accessory.

She looked down at Frank with bewitching green eyes that were a perfect match for her outfit, cast a glorious warm smile over him and held out her hand as Jack said: "Frank, meet Esther."

Frank stumbled to his feet and shook her hand.

"Your husband has been kind enough to show me round your city," he mumbled in the best German he could manage with the dog's nose still sniffing at his mind.

The woman called Esther laughed, and the red curls of her hair flew out with wild abandon as she threw back her head.

"Esther's not my wife," Jack explained. "Esther's my muse."

Before Frank had any time to pigeonhole this information, they were joined by a second woman, who followed Esther from around behind the sofa. She was shorter than Esther, with cropped dark hair – a gamine with sparkling dark-brown eyes.

"And this is Vreni," said Jack.

"Your wife?" Frank asked, as he shook her hand.

"My wife's not here."

There was an irritation in Jack's voice. Frank did not pursue the matter any further. He sank back into his sofa. Baschi took one of the armchairs, while Vreni and Esther both settled into the other sofa. Esther pulled out a cigarette, lit it and threw the pack and the lighter over to Frank.

It was then that Frank noticed the only decoration in the room. On the wall behind Esther and Vreni to the right of the window with the heavy green curtains hung a small painting. A portrait of a red-haired woman with dark makeup and bright red lipstick. In her green dress that draped loosely off the shoulder to hint at the curvature of her left breast, the likeness of this woman to Esther was striking.

"Did you paint that?" Frank asked, picking up the lighter and cigarettes with the name Parisienne emblazoned across the pack. A logo with a hint of such warm memories. Yet he could not for the life of him recall exactly what or why.

"You mean Lola?" Jack asked in return, as he walked over to a cupboard behind Frank's sofa, where he took out three glasses and a bottle of wine and placed them at the end of the table in front of Frank. "No. Lola belonged to my mother. She was the one who got me interested in the arts. And painting."

"*Und wer zum Tüfel isch Lola?*" Frank asked. A look of shock etched into his expression by the sense of strangeness in his own voice as he asked: Who the hell is Lola?

He put a cigarette in his mouth and lit up in an effort to feign composure. Jack looked at Frank with suspicion at this sudden fluency in what sounded like the Alemannic dialect spoken just across the border.

"I was told it's Lola Bach," he replied, preferring to conceal his suspicion for the moment. "An erotic dancer from the Twenties. But who knows?"

"Who painted it?" Frank asked.

"No idea. Some unknown expressionist. A woman probably," Jack said and waved a dismissive hand at the painting on the wall. His suspicion had nurtured a growing impatience with Frank and his questions, and he turned to the two women.

"Ladies," he announced," Frank is here to report on how we treat our women in this country. What do you think about that?"

Esther and Vreni giggled.

"Something few people know about this country is that every single canton produces wine," said Jack, turning back to Frank as he filled the glasses on the table. "Even the city of Basel produces wine. But none of it has the class of an Amarone from south of the border. I think you'll like it." He handed both Frank and Baschi a glass of red wine, then sauntered over to the piano.

Frank watched Jack place his own glass on the piano as he sat down to play. Feeling disinclined to add another layer of confusion to his mind, Frank put his glass back down on one of the magazines lying on the table, leaned back in the sofa and drank in the music. He recognised the melody instantly from many years ago. A slow spiritual dirge that he recalled his mother often singing in the kitchen as she prepared the evening meal. And he began to hum along.

In the chair opposite, Baschi's gut quivered and heaved as he chuckled quietly to himself.

"He always like beginning with Dvořák," he said, as if to explain his merriment. Esther and Vreni on the other sofa looked at each other, kissed and then fell into a giggle.

"The largo from Dvořák's Ninth Symphony," Jack called from behind the back of Baschi. "In America, they call it 'Going Home'."

That was it. Frank recalled that his mother had an old 78 of Paul Robeson she used to flog to death on the antiquated record player. It was the tune she always sang as she prepared the scouse for the evening meal. Even Ellen had recognised it when she first heard his mother singing in the kitchen. "You didn't tell me your mum was into Sam Cooke," she said with a look of disbelief. Frank had no idea what she was talking about at the time. It was only later that he learned from her sister Beth how she had secreted one of Beth's favourite EPs from her record collection and claimed it as hers.

As these flashbacks punctuated the music in the background, Jack raised the tempo very slightly, slipping into a mysterious melody full of melancholy tension.

"What's that?" Frank asked, throwing his voice across the room when the change of tempo sent his thoughts scattering suddenly like marbles across the floor. Jack was lost in his music. Esther had already discarded her cigarette and was now locked in Vreni's arms.

"Jack play only Czechish music," said Baschi, as he sipped his wine and contemplated the two women with a satisfied smile.

Their playful frolics matched the release of tension in the music, and the melancholy mist was blown away as if by a sudden gust of wind. The mysterious music continued to entwine itself around Frank's mind. And he watched the kindling embrace of Esther and Vreni gradually begin to catch alight. Their hands explored and wandered over each other's skin with a tenderness he had never witnessed before between two women. The flaming curls of Esther's long red hair emphasised the intensity of their embrace, as she gently slipped the strap of Vreni's dress down over the shoulder and caressed her right breast. Frank could not imagine what Ellen might think if she could see him now. But he found it deeply arousing and was fascinated by the uncanny correspondence between their intertwined devotion to each other and the enigmatic music that became entangled in his senses with every change of meter.

"Janáček," said Jack, glancing over at Frank as his fingers floated nimbly over the keyboard. "I find there is such a beautiful sense of repressed passion in his music. And since the Prague Spring I find it has a special piquancy. So I play it all the more today. Pure magic."

The music stopped. Frank looked over at Jack, who was staring down at the keyboard, and felt he had been torn away from an intensely satisfying dream. As if caught out when a sudden bright light is switched on. The discomfort made him shiver. Slowly, pensively, Jack stood up from the piano and sat in the chair beside Baschi. He took what appeared to be a large sketchpad from the coffee table and rested it on his knees. He said nothing more. Esther and Vreni were still locked in their embrace, oblivious to the loss of music, and they continued their devotional attention to each other. Jack watched with an intensity and a look in those dark eyes of his that Frank was unable to fathom. Not a word was spoken. Finally, Frank felt compelled to reach for the wine on the table.

By now, the two women had shed every last inch of clothing. Vreni lay in raptured abandon on the sofa. Her right leg was wrapped around the waist of Esther, who leaned over her partner and let her flaming red hair gently brush the curvature of Vreni's body.

Frank's head began to spin. He took a large gulp from his glass, topped it up from the bottle on the table and watched as Jack took a pencil from his pocket. His hand swept back and forth across the paper, eyes every so often lifting to gauge the mounting passion on the sofa alongside him. Vreni threw her head back with a smile of the deepest satisfaction as Esther turned to Jack and asked:

"Is this ok for you?"

"It will look wonderful on canvas. What do you think, Frank?"

At that moment, the sound of bells chimed a deep, sepulchral toll from outside, which rumbled its way into the room. A solemn sound. Like the voice of a dark angel chanting a heavy, heavy song.

"Damn the church bells in this country," Jack cursed. And turned to Frank on the sofa opposite. Frank stubbed out his cigarette and held his head in both hands, his eyes shut tight and his face seemingly contorted in pain.

"I said what do you think, Frank?" Jack repeated in an attempt to raise his voice above the sound of the bells.

Baschi continued chuckling quietly to himself. Esther and Vreni wrapped their discarded clothes around them and looked anxiously across at Frank.

"Frank? Are you all right?" Jack shouted, louder this time. There was a hint of concern in the voice. But it was lost on Frank, as his head now flinched with every chime of the bells. They boomed through his skull twelve times. And each time left him trembling a little more.

As the church bells ran through their midnight repertoire, Frank's hosts looked on. Speechless. Awaiting Frank's next move. When eventually the bells fell quiet, what should have been a blissful silence was invaded by the faint sound of the words 'Achim, oh Achim' repeating over and over, as they ricocheted around Frank's head. He clasped his hands over his ears vainly trying to stifle those words. But in time they too faded, and as they did so he became aware of the smell he had noticed when he first entered the room. But now, mingled with the taste of stale nicotine, it had a new edge to it – an odour deeply redolent of a history he could not put his finger on. A troubled history. The odour swirled around his head adding new layers of confusion to his mind. For an instant, it reminded him of the little dachshund his mother adopted for company after he left home. He recalled how his father never seemed to have enough time for his mother; he was often away on business – if not in Berlin or Leipzig, then abroad somewhere. In New York, London or mostly Calcutta.

But Frank could make neither head nor tail of these memories. In an attempt to shake off his confusion, he finally opened his eyes in the hope he might get a grip on reality. Jack, Baschi and the two women fixed their eyes on Frank in expectation. But all he could see was the bottle on the table. He picked it up and gulped down the remainder of the wine straight from the bottle. The haunting odour in the room was quickly dispelled by the Amarone on his tongue. But the memory of the dachshund stayed with him nonetheless. It played with him. Tormented him. He lashed out with his right hand as if to sweep his mind clear of the memories – and swept the bottle to the floor instead. The last dregs of wine splashed their drops of blood-red liquid onto the carpet. The weave of the floor covering was sorely worn away in places. It was old and dirty. But what should that matter?

Without a moment's hesitation, Frank threw himself to the floor and began to lick up the drops before they soaked into the carpet. The taste was abhorrent. And the physical sensation of the dust, the hair and the carpet, as the fine papillated surface of his tongue scraped over them and trapped them in his mouth, made him retch. He was on the brink of vomiting. But still he continued to lick at the carpet as if his life depended on it.

"What the hell are you doing old chap?"

As Frank lay on the floor, licking at the hairs and the weave of the carpet, he was completely oblivious to Jack's words. It was the brutal blow to his ribs that brought him halfway to his senses.

"He takes the dog's nose to heart."

It was Baschi's voice.

"And this is what we do with dogs," Baschi added, as he aimed another boot into Frank's side. "We don't let dogs into this house, do we Jack?"

Frank could not hear Jack's reply. Or even tell if he said anything at all. He only felt Baschi grab the collar of his shirt and jacket, then let himself be dragged across the floor. He heard the door open and felt the pain of Baschi's boot again in his side.

"Out!" Baschi screamed, pushing Frank out onto the landing and giving him one final kick down the stairs before he shut the door behind him.

Frank lay at the bottom of the stairs and listened for some time to the faint sound of raised voices mingled with fits of laughter from the room above. Picking himself up, he rearranged his shirt and jacket, opened the door to the cobbled street and staggered out into the night air.

Out into the familiar street with its familiar worn-out look. He knew instantly where it would lead him. Knew that it was only a short walk from here over the cobbles that he had trodden so often in the past. The place where it all began. In the Hotel Storchen.

Chapter 3

It was just after lunchtime on Sunday when Ellen got the call. She was sitting on the sofa in their Fulham bedsit with the Sunday paper, playing with the tresses of her strawberry-blonde hair and smiling to herself as she thought of Frank stealing a lock of it before he left.

The phone was shared with the other tenants. It hung on the wall outside the bedsit. She ran out onto the landing as soon as it started to ring – certain that it must be Frank. And when she picked up the receiver, she fully expected to hear his voice at the other end. But what startled her was not the strange, high-pitched woman's voice in place of Frank's. It was the words.

"Your husband's had an accident," the woman said. She was calling from the Fleet Street office that had sent Frank to Switzerland. Ellen's heart missed a beat. She felt quite faint and sat back in the stool beside the phone.

"An accident? What happened? What sort of accident?" Ellen asked. By now her heart was racing and she began to gasp for breath.

The woman on the other end did not know the exact details. She had been given to understand that it was nothing life-threatening and that Frank was in good hands, but they wanted to keep him in for observation. The newspaper, she added, would be prepared to fly Ellen out to see her husband.

It was twenty-four hours later – around lunchtime on Monday – that Ellen touched down on Swiss soil. Everything had moved so quickly since the phone call the day before that she felt almost in a daze as she pushed her passport under the glass screen to the immigration officer on the other side of the desk. She was engulfed by a brief sense of panic at the thought that her dazed demeanour must make her look so suspicious that she expected to be called to one side. Ellen reached into her bag for a handkerchief – as if the hint of a cold might explain any oddness of behaviour.

It was not necessary. Once through immigration and customs, Ellen was met by an elegant, middle-aged lady in a black trench coat – she carried a board in front of her that read: Mrs Ellen Goss. At the sight of her name, Ellen instantly felt her entire body relax. It seemed in her fragile state of mind to be a sign she was among people she could trust.

"Good afternoon, Mrs Goss. I hope you had a good journey," said the lady in the trench coat, as she lowered the board and offered Ellen her hand. "Frey. Maria Frey," she added. "I'm Professor Abegg's secretary."

Ellen shook her hand.

"Thank you," she said, before mumbling – almost as an afterthought – "I'm pleased to meet you."

Ellen's new acquaintance gave her a slightly inquisitive look.

"If you follow me, I'll take you to the clinic."

Ellen followed her companion out of the building and across the road to a row of cars. She was slightly taken aback when the elegant Maria Frey in the black trench coat opened the back of a red Austin Healey, took Ellen's suitcase and placed it inside, before opening the door on the passenger's side.

"Please," she said.

Ellen duly ducked down and manoeuvred herself into the bucket seat of the Austin Healey. She was still trying to reconcile the picture of this rather serious, yet elegant middle-aged woman with her flashy choice of car, when they turned off the airport road just a few minutes later and directly into the grounds of what she assumed to be the clinic. A complex of pavilion-style buildings interspersed with trees in a park that lent the scene a slightly desolate feel in their denuded winter state. But as she climbed out of the car, Ellen could well imagine the tranquillity of the setting in a couple of months' time when the trees in the park sprang back into life.

The car had stopped outside the tallest of the buildings in the park – a large grey two-storey edifice from the nineteenth century that put Ellen more in mind of a railway station with its huge arched windows towering above the main entrance. As Maria Frey led her up the stairs to the entrance and in through the door, it was the words on the plaque beside the door that jumped out at Ellen: Psychiatrische Klinik.

"I was told my husband had an accident," she said as she tried to keep up with her escort, who led her up to the second floor and along a rather bleak corridor heavily punctuated with doors on either side.

"Yes, he has had a small accident," said Maria Frey, as she opened one of the doors.

"So why is he in a psychiatric clinic?" asked Ellen.

Maria Frey turned, beckoned Ellen through the doorway and gestured towards a chair just inside the room. "If you take a seat, Professor Abegg will be with you very soon. He will explain everything."

With that, she disappeared through another door, leaving Ellen to ponder what seemed to have the trappings of a sinister mystery behind the events of the last day. Were they even talking about her Frank, she asked herself. Her mind remained so deeply entrained by her thoughts that she failed to hear the door open behind her.

"So you survived the journey in Maria's little sports car. I suppose we must get used to more such whims now that they've won the right to vote."

Ellen turned to find a tall, slim, slightly beaky-looking man in a white coat smiling down at her.

"Abegg," he said, as he offered Ellen his hand and invited her into his office.

He walked around behind his desk and beckoned her to take a seat, modestly apologising for what he insisted was a poor English picked up during several years of research in the United

States. But Ellen found his command of the language nothing short of perfect, albeit betrayed by a thick Swiss accent that made each word sound as if it were being dragged over a cheese grater every time he spoke. Despite the slightly cynical joviality of his opening words, the impression created by this fifty-something man was one of sympathy and understanding. Due undoubtedly to the furrows of fatherly concern etched into his forehead by years of patient listening, Ellen told herself. She could well imagine him as a father of daughters.

"I'm so glad you could answer our call so quickly," he said. "We are faced with a particularly difficult and puzzling case. And I think it is very important that you are here to help us find the root of your husband's problem."

"Look, I'm sorry," said Ellen, "but I'm really confused. What's actually happened to Frank? I was told he'd had an accident. And now I find he's in a psychiatric clinic. What's going on? Where is he? Can I see him?"

"Mr Goss is in good hands," he assured her. Then looked at Ellen with a piercing expression in his eyes that unsettled her when he asked: "Why is your husband in Switzerland?"

"He's a journalist. He came to write about the referendum on women's right to vote. But what's that got do with his accident?"

A wry smile crept across the professor's lips, disconcerting Ellen even further.

"You know, Switzerland's first qualified female lawyer campaigned her entire life to achieve equal rights for women and was eventually committed to this very same institution for her lunacy. It seems a strange irony that your husband who came to report on the referendum should be admitted to this clinic on the very day the country finally accepted that women must be given the vote."

"I wish I could share your sense of humour." Ellen made no attempt to disguise the irritation in her voice. The professor peered across the desk at Ellen with a look of questioning concern, his hands folded across his chest fiddling with a pen.

"Mrs Goss, your husband was found early yesterday morning in great distress. He walked into the road and was hit by a car."

"Oh my God!" Ellen exclaimed. "I was told it was just a minor accident."

"As I said, he's in good hands. You really don't need to worry. Just a few scratches and bruises. But he was in great distress when he was taken to the accident unit. And it was decided to admit him to our clinic."

"Why? What's the matter with him?" Ellen asked. She was growing ever more disturbed by what seemed to her like euphemisms for something sinister. "What do you mean by distress?"

"Your husband speaks very good German," the professor said, ignoring Ellen's questions. "Can I ask where he learned to speak the language so well?"

"He studied it at university in England," Ellen replied. She was growing increasingly impatient. "But he did say before he came here that he was wondering how he would cope with the weird kind of German you speak here."

Professor Abegg smiled.

"Well I can tell you he is coping very well," he said with a tone of reassurance that Ellen felt carried more than a hint of sarcasm. "In fact, he speaks an Alemannic dialect like a native from just across the border in Germany. Yet he has a British passport. So I find that puzzling."

"Why?" Ellen was beginning to feel increasingly defensive, and her question came across almost as a challenge.

"In my experience, Mrs Goss, foreigners do not truly master the dialects of this region unless they've grown up here."

"Well, Frank grew up in London," said Ellen. "So maybe your patient is simply not my husband."

With a vaguely sardonic smile that nourished Ellen's growing impatience, Professor Abegg opened the right-hand top drawer of his desk, took out what she instantly recognised as Frank's worn passport and put it on the desk in front of her.

"Perhaps it was stolen." She was struggling to control her patience. "Do you think I could see him now?"

"In good time, Mrs Goss." The professor put down the pen and flicked open a thin file on the desk in front of him. He sifted through the papers in the file for what seemed to Ellen like an eternity.

"Have you been having problems in your marriage?" he asked, without looking up from the file.

Ellen sensed her irritation was on the verge of tipping into rage.

"Look, I know these are the kinds of questions you doctors like to ask. But our marriage is just fine. We have a great sex life. And zero problems."

"And your mother-in-law?" he asked, fiddling with the pen again as he looked up at Ellen.

"What?"

"Your husband's mother. Do you and she get along?"

"No," Ellen replied bluntly. She was tired of this interrogation.

Professor Abegg leaned back slightly in his chair, his left hand still resting on the open file. He seemed a shade reassured, as if he felt he was finally getting somewhere.

"Tension between a wife and her mother-in-law is quite normal," he said, as if to put her mind at rest.

"Of course," said Ellen. "And it could get quite bad at times. But there was probably far more tension between my husband and his mother than me and his mother."

"Really?" Ellen's words had piqued the psychiatrist's curiosity. "Why was that?" he asked, and instantly stopped fiddling with the pen.

"I don't know," she replied. "They never seemed to have a good relationship. Frank always felt a sense of alienation from his parents. He often used to say that he thought he must have been adopted at a young age, that they couldn't possibly be his parents as they seemed to walk on different planets.

"His mother told me he'd always been a difficult child. Always saying strange things, talking about imaginary places and people. Having nightmares. One story she recalled in particular was about a zoo where people gawped at enclosures full of Black people. Caged like animals. I think she found it quite hard to take. The day we married, she took me to one side and said: 'You take care young lady. I do hope you haven't bitten off more than you can chew.'"

"Interesting," Professor Abegg said, finally laying the pen to rest on the desk. "So there has never been any real tension between you? Over the dog, for example? You don't argue about the dog?"

"What on earth are you talking about?" Ellen was mystified by this odd change of direction. "Yes, all right, I hate dogs. And she loved the little beasts. But fortunately she never owned one when I knew her. So it's not something we ever argued about."

The professor hesitated. Ellen's words plainly concerned him in a way he had not expected. But she could see that he was also quite intrigued. Her words had stopped him in his tracks. Ellen wondered whether he was simply not as confident in English as he appeared. Or did he suspect that he might be about to find himself unravelling something more sinister than a difficult psychiatric case?

"You speak in the past, Mrs Goss," he said at last.

"My mother-in-law is dead."

Just like that it came out. Right to the point. No beating about the bush. He must think I'm a real bitch, she told herself. But she was past caring what he thought.

"She died three weeks ago," Ellen added. "A heart attack."

"I'm sorry to hear that."

He paused again and fiddled with the papers in the folder, as if considering where to go next.

"Only three weeks ago?" he repeated. "Did you know she had a heart condition?"

The professor was becoming increasingly pensive. His expression of condolence was rather less than half-hearted, and his questions betrayed a vaguely accusing tone. But they seemed to be becoming steadily less confident.

"And you say she never had a dog?" he asked.

"I said she never had one when I knew her. A cat yes, but not a dog." It was all Ellen could do not to laugh at this line of questioning.

Ellen felt intimidated by the almost accusing tone of his questions and the pondering hesitation. This only reinforced her anger all the more. She felt the heat begin to rise and a sense of panic start to grow, when suddenly he asked: "Do you know someone called Achim?"

Ellen shook her head. "Should I?"

"He seems to play an important part in your husband's distress," the professor said. "And it puzzles me. It puzzles me very much. Because the pieces of the puzzle don't appear to fit with the picture I have of your husband."

"What do you mean? What picture do you have of Frank?"

"A fragmented picture. Very fragmented. My assistant, Dr Zellweger, was on duty when your husband was admitted. And he picked up the fragments that we have. But this is very little. The picture remains a puzzle full of holes."

At that moment, with all the talk of a dog, someone called Achim and her husband speaking a local dialect, scepticism and disbelief began edging back into Ellen's mind. She became convinced that Professor Abegg could not be talking about Frank. That the person admitted to this clinic had probably stolen Frank's passport or found it somewhere. A warm sense of relief began to grow inside her.

"Your husband wrote this," the professor said, taking a piece of paper from the folder and laying it on the desk in front of Ellen. "And ever since he wrote it, he has remained silent. He has not said another word. It is as if he has nothing more to say."

She stared at the messy scrawl. The handwriting looked familiar, but more erratic and untidier than usual. With a mixture of trepidation and curiosity, she took it in her hand and read the text to herself. Over and over again.

Pneuma, silent susurrus, whispers
ancient legends of what might have been:
tristan in tintagel, for example,
roc healed by holy water
isolde's dark enigma
cascading within
inches of a quiet
arrest

Eine nicht ganz tastbare Gegenwart
ist längst vorbei;
es bleibt nur noch ein Hauch der Legende übrig,
während unser Leben zum langsamen Drift
durch die Dardanellen wird.

Es war doch immer so,
nur die Legende war anders.

Nun wollen wir eine eigene Legende schaffen,
einen eigenen Hauch ausatmen,
um den Spiegel anzufeuchten und die Geschichte
mit dem Finger an dem Glas umschreiben.[1]

But the legend will always speak for itself before it crumbles into the brick dust of Babel.

Und unter den Ruinen
flüstert wortlos der Wind
über die beiden ersten Blätter einer Eiche,
die sich aus den Trümmern schon entfalten.[2]

---

1 A present not quite palpable
is long since past;
leaves only a misty hint of that legend,
while our life becomes a slow drift
through the Dardanelles.

Yet it was always thus,
only the legend was different

Now let us forge a legend of our own,
breathe our own faint mist
on the mirror and rewrite this story
with the tallows of our fingers on the glass

2 And among the ruins
the wind whispers its message without a word
over the first two leaves of an oak
unfolding already from what remains.

Ellen was engrossed and bewildered. The writing was so familiar, and the words so incredibly strange.

"That is your husband's handwriting?" the professor eventually asked.

"Well, it could be." She was still uncertain. "It's very much like his writing. But it seems different." She paused, silenced by a sense of accelerating despair. Close to tears. But too distraught and confused to cry. And all the while she felt the professor watching her with his psychiatrist's eyes.

"But..." Ellen struggled to find the words she needed. "I don't understand. What's this all about?"

"Would you like me to translate the German for you?"

"No. That's not what I meant. The English is just as incomprehensible to me as the German. Look, I just want to know what's happening. I'm completely lost."

Professor Abegg sat impassively on the other side of the desk, his expression somewhere between concern and fascination.

"Doctor, I need to see the man you say is my husband," Ellen insisted. And at last he had the hint of a smile for her. Only a hint. But this at least restored a little of the sympathy and understanding she detected in him when she first entered his office.

"Under the circumstances, Mrs Goss, I think that is a very good idea." He rose from his desk and went over to the door, turning to Ellen as he opened it:

"Please wait here for a moment. I will ask Maria to bring you a cup of coffee." He hesitated. "Or would you prefer tea?" he asked.

"Yes, tea please," said Ellen.

Professor Abegg nodded and closed the door behind him.

***

It was the soreness in the ribs that woke him. A soreness that escalated to a stabbing pain with every breath he took. Frank eased open his eyes. And the brightness of the room instantly closed them down again.

He heard the door open and what sounded like the short, soft steps of a woman approach his bed.

"Mr Goss," the voice whispered.

He felt the gentle touch of her fingers on his cheek. A balm for the soreness of his wounds. And when he opened his eyes again, he now found the brightness of the room replaced by a vision of such sweet angelic beauty he believed himself to be in heaven. A soft, fair face perfectly proportioned with deep blue eyes that sang of the sea. A crown of golden blonde curls arranged around her face like a halo. And a smile that would have melted even the coldest of hearts. He thought for a moment it was Ellen come to see him. And was momentarily confused because she called him Mr Goss and not Frank. Then she spoke again:

"I'm Nurse Esther," she said.

The name flashed up in Frank's mind. Stabbed at him like a dysfunctional neon display on some deserted seafront – just for an instant – as he struggled to recall the events of last night.

"I have some lunch for you, Mr Goss," the nurse added. She pointed to a table on the other side of the room. "Would you like to sit at the table? Or shall I bring it to your bed?"

Frank pushed himself up on his elbows, winced at the pain in his ribs, and slowly eased his legs out of the bed.

"The table?" she asked, taking his right arm to steady him.

"When you have finished your lunch, you take one of these," the nurse said after guiding him to his seat at the table. She placed a small plastic beaker containing a tablet down on the table. Frank took the beaker and tipped the tablet into the palm of his hand. A small blue pill with the number 10 and the name Roche imprinted on it.

"You can take that after you have eaten," the nurse repeated.

"What is it?" Frank wanted to know.

"Valium. To relax you. Later you can sit in the lounge if you wish. You have a nice view of the garden there. And Dr Zellweger will be back to see you later this afternoon."

Frank had no idea where he was or what this woman was talking about. But her manner and the soft cadence of her voice had the effect of water rippling over the pebbles of a stream on a warm spring day. It gave him all the relaxation he needed.

"Would you like me to bring you to the lounge after lunch?" The question came with that same heart-warming smile that greeted him when he woke.

"That would be nice."

Frank watched as she made her exit – enthralled by the divine warmth of her figure, her every movement as she turned, glided towards the door and closed it quietly behind her.

The lounge was a light, expansive place. It was populated by a handful of people, standing or sitting in discrete isolation. Almost like grey shadows in the mist. No one spoke.

One side of the room consisted almost entirely of large windows that extended practically from floor to ceiling. They gave onto a dense garden of birch trees and shrubs around a pond that seemed to cry out for attention. But the benches on the path around the pond remained vacant. Deaf to its cries. It was a garden that gave a depressingly desolate impression in its state of winter undress. An effect underscored by the forbidding white palisade of birch trees. Yet it managed to hold the silent grey shadows around the room in its thrall as they contemplated the scene in a solemn kind of communion. It was not the kind of view that would give Frank any comfort. But submissively he settled into the armchair to which the nurse had guided him.

"This was found in the pocket of your jacket when you had your accident," Nurse Esther said, placing his notebook and pen on the table beside his chair. "We thought you might want to have it while you sit here."

Frank stared blankly at the objects on the table, struggling to recall their significance. He opened the notebook. Save for some incoherent scribbles and a few unfamiliar names on the first page, it was empty.

As the nurse faded out of sight, Frank picked up the pen. In two minds about the puzzling scribble, he let the pen hover over the page for some minutes. Then tore the page out altogether.

"I know that feeling," said a brittle voice.

Immersed in the silence of the room, Frank was startled by the sudden trespass on his thoughts. He was not expecting conversation. Nor seeking it. He looked to his right and found a woman two chairs along watching his every move. She had the anxious eyes of quarry. They peered out from under a luxuriant head of dark shoulder-length hair that hung over her face like a curtain of concealment from any predators. But she had the confidence to smile.

"Are you a writer as well?" she asked. Her hands fidgeted with what looked like a cigarette lighter as she spoke. The smile took the brittle edge from her voice for Frank. He was surprised, too, by the Englishness of her accent.

"Are you English as well?" he asked, mimicking her turn of phrase.

"No. Are you?" Her smile gave way to an expression that Frank found hard to fathom. She appeared to sense his fluster and smiled again, but this time with a curious resignation in her voice. "My husband's mother is Irish. She's been living here for years, but she's still not mastered the language. So we speak in English."

She turned her head and looked out into the winter garden, contemplating its emptiness.

"My name is Anna," she said, turning back to Frank. "I'm a writer as well."

"I'm a journalist. I report things," he replied.

"We all report things in our own way." The quarried expression in Anna's eyes turned back onto the garden. "Do you see those trees?"

Frank watched as she dropped the cigarette lighter on the tray, raised both arms, with hands and fingers outstretched, then slowly lowered them again and let each finger jiggle down in a trickling motion as if to trace the outline of every single birch.

"They plant them there like that especially for us, you know. A perfect scaffold to keep us in our place. Like the bars of a cage. But I love them nonetheless. Especially in winter. There's an honesty about them in the winter. None of the airs and graces of the spring or summer, when they're shrouded in green. And none of the pretentious ways of autumn either."

For the first time, Frank caught the hint of an Irish lilt in Anna's voice that she must have picked up from her mother-in-law. It lent a pleasing warmth to the brittle voice. And while Anna's expression was hidden from Frank beneath the dark curtain of her hair, he sensed a satisfaction in her as she sat now contemplating the garden outside, fidgeting again with the lighter.

Her silent engrossment in the winter scene outside lingered for so long that it became clear to Frank her mind had wandered off along another path altogether. Thankful for this release, he turned his thoughts back to Ellen. Looked again at his notepad and took pen to paper.

He recalled an early spring day together on the north coast of Cornwall. The trees, like these outside now, showed no signs yet of dressing for the spring. But unlike the naked birches, they were at least invested with a little life by the gentle breeze that blew in off the sea. A breeze that whispered its way quietly through their branches – a near-silent susurrus almost drowned out by the surf that swept over the rocks far below them. And he recalled how later in the evening, in the cool night of the cottage they had rented, Ellen breathed on a window pane, then drew a heart in the mist and the letters F and P on either side. Then they watched together as the mist faded.

"But the message never really fades," she said. Frank recalled how captivated he was by the innocent lightness of her voice. "You just have to breathe it back to life," she reassured him. Then she breathed on the pane again and let out a warm chuckle of girlish delight as they watched the heart and letters reappear.

No, that's not right, Frank told himself. The letters are wrong. I'm getting everything mixed up. He threw the pen down on the pad in frustration and ran both hands through his mop of hair.

"It makes you wonder what you're doing here, doesn't it? Who you really are?"

That brittle edge had returned to Anna's voice. It dragged Frank back from his entangled memories. He peered across at her. A look of sad anxiety had returned to her eyes.

"I like to write," she continued. "I like to paint as well. But I'm not allowed to."

"What do you mean you're not allowed to?"

"There's only room for one artist in a man's world. But at least I can write when I'm allowed the time," she said. Then added with a curious tightening of the lips: "What are you on?"

The mystified expression on Frank's face was unable to penetrate the curtain of hair over Anna's eyes.

"Do you know they invented LSD just down the road from here?" she continued. "It wouldn't surprise me if they tested it in this clinic."

Frank smiled. "You don't need to worry. I'm only on Valium."

"You may be. Or maybe not. They don't say what they're giving me. They just keep telling me it's new." Anna chuckled to herself, before adding, "So I suppose it can't be LSD."

"So what prevents you from painting?" Frank asked, guiding Anna back to the original question. She prevaricated.

"My husband's not an easy man. But I think there are many husbands in Switzerland who are not easy," she said and paused to gaze out through the window for a moment, before adding with a grin "I call it '*la condition suisse*'."

It was a grin that spoke of resignation more than amusement.

"I heard there's a referendum to give us the vote," she said, then asked: "Are you an easy husband?"

Frank was momentarily stung by the directness of her question. He struggled for an answer that could be squared with his conscience. But it was an unnecessary struggle. The question was purely rhetorical.

"It was when he brought Esther home for the first time that I realised it was not going to be easy," she continued. "I asked myself if it was simply the artist in him. Or was it the man? Was it this that marked him out as the true artist and me the failed one, since I had no such wish to play the kind of games he wanted me to play?"

This confessional turn had Frank shifting his gaze uncomfortably out of the window through the white scaffold of the birch trees. The light was already beginning to fade, and the background gloom accentuated their white lines.

"It wasn't just the games. She was a nice enough girl."

Frank looked across at Anna. Her lips trembled slightly as she spoke these words, but he could not read any meaning into their tremor. Her eyes remained firmly concealed beneath her hair. The words were spoken for her. Not for Frank.

"'You have to push the boundaries,' he always says. "It's his way to prove that he's alive. I suppose that's why he always invites so many people home. Many of them are not even friends. He doesn't even like most of them. They pretend to adore him, but much of the time they just make fun of him. And I think that's why he does it. It makes him feel better than them. So that's okay. But when Esther moved in to live with us – to share our bed, our kitchen, our entire life together – that was very difficult. It feels almost like a prison sometimes. So I often take the little blue train out into the country and the hills where I grew up. Such happy days. Playing in the woods, making fires and grilling our cervelat in the flames. I still love the climb up to the ruins of the Landskron Castle. Such freedom up there. Standing at the top. The breeze on my face. And that clear view sweeping over the city to the Vosges Mountains in Alsace and the Black Forest in Germany. These are borders I can understand. Frontiers I can cross. Not boundaries to push. Why does he need that?"

Anna's question hung in the air like a dead fly caught in the faintest of webs. In the awkward silence that followed, Frank's attention was attracted by loud whispers in the background. He turned his head. Anna was still immersed in her contemplation. Beyond her, in the far corner of the room stood three white coats, deep in conversation. As they spoke, they cast occasional glances in his direction – until suddenly one of the coats became particularly agitated, turned and walked over towards him.

But Frank was not the point of interest. The coat stopped at Anna. And the other two came running over.

Anna looked up through the dark fronds of her hair. Frank caught the mumbling of voices between them. He saw what looked like smoke rising from Anna's chair. And the commotion of white coats as they fanned the smoke and reached out to lend Anna support as she rose from her chair, chuckling. One of the white coats surreptitiously retrieved the cigarette lighter from the chair as they went.

"Tomorrow, Fredy, I will bring my writing with me and we can share our thoughts," she said before turning to leave on the arms of the white coat.

"Frank," he said, correcting her. But she was already out of earshot. He could now see the scorched patch on the chair where she had been sitting, and watched her shuffle slowly out of sight, before turning his mind to the notepad on his lap. The weekend in Cornwall. The breeze. The near-silent susurrus that whispered in off the sea. And Ellen's sweet expression, which seemed more distant now than it had ever been.

Es war doch immer so. He looked at the page in his notepad. Where did that come from? What does it even mean, he asked himself.

Afternoon turned to early evening. And from somewhere in a remote corner of this large room, a light switch was flicked, accentuating the darkness outside. Anna was right. Standing out from this darkness, the white birch trees resembled ever more the bars of a cage.

***

No sooner had Professor Abegg left the room than Ellen heard a clamour of excited voices in the corridor outside. The professor's voice was clearly audible above all the others. His anger was palpable. But almost as abruptly as the clamour had begun, it suddenly died back into a prolonged muffle of whispers. Then silence. And without warning the door instantly swung open again. The alarm in Professor Abegg's face lent his beaky appearance the look of a startled bird. Standing timorously in the doorway behind him was another white-coated figure.

"Mrs Goss." The professor abruptly stopped at her name. He had to catch his breath. There was a hint of panic in his eyes. But he remained outwardly calm. "I would like you to meet my assistant, Dr Zellweger."

The sheepish man in the doorway behind him took a step closer to Ellen. She was struck by the firmness of his handshake – it completely contradicted her impression of him. Although he was quite tall and must have been some ten years younger than Professor Abegg, his timid manner made him appear rather frail and lined. Was this the price he paid for taking up psychiatry? Or did it have something to do with the news he bore?

"Dr Zellweger admitted your husband," Professor Abegg said, "and he is more familiar with your husband's case than anybody."

Dr Zellweger smiled nervously, but said nothing. His mouth hovered half open in hesitation. Ellen had the impression that he was struggling with the English. Or perhaps he is simply intimidated by the professor, she was thinking, when suddenly he spoke:

"Unfortunately, Mrs Goss, we are in a slightly embarrassing situation."

"Please just tell me what's going on."

Ellen was surprised by her own composure. She really wanted to scream. Her irritation at the caginess of these psychiatrists had already pushed her patience way beyond endurance. Dr Zellweger cleared his throat.

"I'm afraid your husband discharged himself early this morning without informing anyone. We have no idea where he is at the moment."

"What?!"

Ellen stared at the two men in disbelief.

"How is that possible? He's injured, he's confused. How can he just walk out without anyone even noticing?"

Her voice rose in impetuous anger. But it was a temper born of despair. She felt suddenly cast adrift in a vast, empty ocean. Nowhere to go. Nothing to guide her. In her desperation, she still clung to the conviction that this could not be Frank they were talking about.

But then she asked herself: if this was not Frank, then where was he?

Chapter 4

Frank stood on the bridge over the Rhine. It put him in mind of Ellen and Putney Bridge. He recalled the day they stood there watching the seagulls. Enthralled by the dense green of the trees around Fulham Palace with a hint already of colours changing. Intimations of the autumn to come that were carried by the westerly breeze down the Thames. It was the day they decided to get married.

But here on this day, on this bridge, it was a chill northerly breeze that blew off the river. It carried with it a hint of chemicals from the industry downstream that lined the border districts of the city. He shivered. And gazed down at eddies of water as they emerged from under the bridge on their slow journey to the North Sea. The water level was low. The river sluggish. It would not revive until the spring, when the mountains released their snow and ice. But for now, winter still held the river in its grip.

The wind. The water. The drift beneath his feet. This bridge seemed to be all that separated him from oblivion. The way it balanced him precariously on the arch of its back made his head swim. The river skyline began to spin. He sensed himself losing control. And looked about for a marker to latch onto. A secure peg to steady him. He found it in the gleam of a statue. A bronze Amazon that stood at the head of the bridge, leading her horse proudly into the city. It seemed almost as if she was offering her support – inviting him to join her, to escape the dullness that hung over the river beneath the louring sky.

The flatness of the scene was matched by a drab Baroque-style edifice that was trying to be something it was not as it abutted the grand hotel Les Trois Rois. The diffident lettering above the doors – Basler Kantonalbank – that coyly advertised its quintessential Swissness seemed no less out of place. An aloof end-of-terrace loner that no one was inclined to invite to the party. Meanwhile, the sumptuous lights of the hotel next door still flickered out across the water. They spoke of cosy conviviality. And came to him like sharp pinpricks of warmth and comfort that gnawed at his own solitude on that bridge.

Just below him a sudden cacophony of seagulls ripped through his quiet reflection. A momentary shard of pain shot through his left temple. He winced. Instinctively putting his left hand to the side of his head, he looked down at the landing stage by the waterside. A vast squawking flurry of white gulls wheeled erratically around the water. A dense inflating mass that enveloped everything around it and eventually encompassed even the grumbling bowels of the bank that loomed above the landing stage. So dense that he failed to see the focus of their menacing encirclement: a man lost amid the screeching mass. A solitary, slightly hunched figure in a long dark coat and black homburg hat by the water's edge. Rooted to the spot, undismayed, the man paid no attention to the gulls around him. Seemed oblivious to the commotion.

Frank's heart missed a beat. This figure was so familiar to him. The homburg hat, the coat, the posture. He shouted out.

"Achim!" But his voice was instantly drowned by the squawking of the gulls. In a sudden feverish excitement, he turned and dashed to the end of the bridge as best he could with the bruises from his accident. It was a good hundred metres to the strutting Amazon with her horse. Breathless with anticipation, his heart in his throat, he skirted around the bronze statue. Headed for the steps down to the landing stage. And stopped.

As he stood there looking down the steps to the river, his excitement instantly washed away. The sound of a tram navigating the bend onto the bridge behind him squeezed out the squawking of the gulls. The birds had vanished. The landing stage was bereft of life. There was no one there. No Achim. No anyone.

Had he imagined it?

He wandered the streets nagged by this thought for much of the morning. Plagued by the image of his friend. The image of quarry caught like a fish in a dense white net of gulls. A phantom cast adrift at the foot of the bridge.

It was Frank's aching feet that eventually urged him through the doors of a quiet-looking restaurant just off the marketplace in the centre of town. It defied the outwardly quiet impression the moment he opened the door and pushed through the heavy curtain that was keeping out the cold. He recognised it instantly as just the kind of place for him in his present state of mind. It had character ground into the floor by decades of weary, homeless feet. Down-and-outs and drifters, students and labourers, men on benefits, would-be philosophers and armchair revolutionaries. The place was packed – charged with the kind of atmosphere that drags you with it, holding an ostentatious mirror to your detachment. He found an obtuse, uncomfortable sort of security here. Felt at home in a way that he could not quite put his finger on. A deep sense of belonging in the thick smoke of cheap cigarettes and garbled, broken conversations.

He found space on a long bench seat at the window by the door. A waitress pushed through the crowd and placed a menu on the table as he sat down.

"*'ne Stange, bitte*" he said without touching the menu, "-*und Kalbsläberli mit Röschti.*"

The words rolled over his lips with an Alemannic timbre as familiar to him as the beer she placed in front of him a minute or two later.

"*'S chalbsläberli chunnt*", she said to reassure him that his plate of calf's liver and *rösti* was on its way, then turned and vanished back through the crush towards the bar.

He watched her getting swallowed up by the crowd until he found his line of vision was suddenly obscured. A tall dark figure had swept aside the thick curtain over the door and stood in front of him, surveying the scene. The faces in the crowd turned, descended into a low murmur and made space for him. The man strode through the impromptu path to a table at the far end of the room that had been vacated the moment he entered the tavern. He removed his hat and long black leather trench coat, hung them on a peg beside his table and sat down with a newspaper. He looked about the room, and his gaze caught Frank's. He had the look of a predator. Steely lupine eyes beneath a head of black, neatly brilliantined hair. And a pencil-thin moustache that highlighted his cold razor-like lips. They exuded a dark conceit about them as he turned his gaze back to the newspaper, opened it out on the table before him and lit a cigarette.

Frank jumped when the waitress slapped the plate down in front of him. The dark figure with the newspaper momentarily vanished from his thoughts. Frank cast his eyes over the calf's liver and golden, straw-like strands of fried potato. He had heard a lot about *rösti* (it conjured the fleeting memory of a meeting that never was – with a newspaper editor – and in the hubbub of the tavern around him the recollection was washed away as quickly as it had appeared). But he had never tried the dish until now.

And from the casual way the waitress banged the plate down on the table – producing some cutlery from the folds of her apron almost as an afterthought – Frank sensed it was not about to do a lot for him. But after the nightmares of Jack, Baschi and the clinic, his appetite was ready for anything. So it was not the memory of Baschi and the shrinks in the clinic that put him off his meal. What really did it for him was the cluster of short black hairs. Each one cooked into place in the golden strands of fried potato with a true eye for detail. He felt his stomach heave. And pushed the plate to one side. He ordered another beer instead.

The waitress slopped the new glass in front of him. He watched the handsome head of froth spew onto the beermat. When he looked up, she had already moved on to the next table. And his gaze instead met the predatory eyes of the brilliantined stranger. The eyes briefly turned their attention to the ashtray on the table as he tapped the ash from his cigarette.

Then returned their scrutiny to Frank. The conceit on those razor-thin lips had veered now into a new realm of sentiment. It smacked of malice. And instantly set Frank's heart pounding.

Unnerved by the menace, he looked away. His gaze rested instead on a petite Irish-looking lady who had just entered the tavern, dark anxious eyes peering from under a fringe of jet-black hair. She was selling red roses. Someone even greeted her by a name that sounded to him very much like Molly. But this was a long way from the streets of Dublin. And a long way too from Putney Bridge and Ellen. Frank opened the pouch in his wallet and took her lock of hair between his fingers. The only remaining handle on the world as he knew it.

The rose seller's fringe of jet-black hair put him in mind of Anna. The clinic. The white coats. And the Valium. He recalled the endless questions by the doctor. The cage of white birch trees. His head ached with every image. Everything began to spin as the noise in the restaurant began to obtrude. The scraping of knives and clacking of forks that cut through the thick curtains of chatter. The screech of knives across cheap porcelain seared through his head. And the spin refused to let up. The entire room appeared to be in overdrive. The crowd of people, the brown nicotine-stained furniture, everything that had been there just a few seconds before now vanished. Only the image of the white coats stayed with him, taunting his every turn, growing steadily black as the spin accelerated.

"*Oh Achim, bitte.*" The words erupted again. And he reached out for the only anchor in sight that seemed capable of preventing him from being swept away altogether: the coat, now black, around which everything else rotated. He clutched at it. Held it fast. And felt like a lost baby desperately holding on to the only security the little mite thought it knew. He wanted to bawl and yell until the world stopped.

And it did.

He felt the grip on his shirt collar tighten round his neck. Sensed himself reeling through the doorway. And landing face first on the cold hard asphalt of the street outside.

"*Hau ab, huere Schiessdrägg!*" The malicious bellow telling Frank to get the hell out brought the spinning thoughts in his head come crashing to a halt. He caught the outline of a large figure that filled the entire doorway of the tavern. It was the tall dark stranger in his hat and black leather trench coat. The teeth between his razor-thin lips glinted faintly in the light. He flicked his cigarette to the ground, turned and walked on up the street.

The bruising, it seemed, would not let up. Frank surveyed the street around him. It was empty and dimly lit. He recognised it as the street where he had met Jack and Baschi. This recollection, the sense of familiarity, prompted him to head for the only place he knew that was not too far from here. The bridge.

The northerly wind off the river stung his cheeks. His eyes prickled in the cold. He felt a shiver course through his entire body. And standing on the bridge again, contemplating the Rhine on its journey to the North Sea, Frank tried focusing his mind now on the thought that it would not be long before the eddying current of water below his feet met the water from the Thames – that he was not as far from Ellen as he felt. But the north wind on his cheeks was a chill reminder that, even so, this river was not the Thames. The bridge was not their bridge. And the eddies of water below sent his mind into a bewildering spin once more.

In an effort to focus, he looked down at the landing stage where Achim had appeared to him lost in a white flurry of gulls. That seemed like an age ago. Now the embarkation point was a cold and soulless place. The only sense of life here came from the sandstone wall and the relief of a naked, musclebound wharfman tugging on a ship's rope.

This figure put him in mind of his one and only trip to Spain in the summer of '35 and his fascination as he watched the stevedores and other dock workers sweltering in the quayside heat of Malaga. Was that really only eighteen months ago? How they must be suffering now in the cold reality of winter, he muttered to himself, with Franco's fascists beating down the door. Is there nowhere safe these days? Frank wondered. The whole of Europe seems to be in the grip of dangerous fools.

This chilling thought and the biting wind brought it home to him that he was in desperate need of somewhere to stay. He recalled in his bewilderment that he had passed what looked like a hotel and decided to retrace his steps. As he approached the fountain in the old fish market with its elaborately decorated spire, he saw on the far side of the market square the building he had in mind. The huge sign above its doors read Hotel Storchen. And in front of the entrance stood a handsome, spanking-new Maybach Zeppelin with white-walled tyres. It seemed out of place. Yet at the same time the vehicle appeared vaguely familiar. But he paid it no further attention. He was tired, bruised and in need of rest. Tomorrow promised to be a big day.

Achim was due to arrive.

Frank Eigenmann picked up his key from reception and went straight to the room that was to remain his home over the next few weeks. He pushed open the door. The pale light from the street bled its anaemic pallor through the window and across his bed as he entered. It was a chilling welcome, and he went straight over to draw the curtains across the little balcony that looked out over the fish market. But he was distracted. What it was that compelled him to open the window and peer over the balcony he had no idea; perhaps the sound of a door on the Maybach swinging open onto the anxious night. A solid confident sound. He caught sight of a man wearing a hat and black leather trench coat getting into the car. There was a familiarity about them – the vehicle, the man and the leather trench coat. But he was too exhausted to give it any thought. And went to bed.

The prospect of meeting Achim the next day unleashed an endless stream of thoughts that raced around his head and overwhelmed any sense of fatigue. His mind turned constantly on memories of Achim. He had not seen him since a chilly late-spring day eighteen months earlier on the Kurfürstendamm in Berlin. Achim was still there now. And his letters from Berlin painted a picture of life getting ever more difficult for him and his family. Especially in the last few months since the Olympic Games.

The idea of encouraging him to come south occurred to Frank one evening in November. He had just seen a student performance of Aristophanes' *Frogs* in the large restaurant room of the zoological gardens. It seemed to him an odd location for a performance of classical Greek theatre, but the passion of the players and appreciation of the audience were so infectious that the oddness was quickly forgotten. It was not the first event of this kind he had enjoyed since coming to this city, which seemed to be one of the few enclaves of culture left in the German-speaking world. A place where the theatre especially was in full bloom and did not have to suffer the pressures that poor Achim had to face.

Life was difficult enough anyway as a stage designer in Berlin at that time. For any self-respecting artist it must have been intolerable. From the letters Frank received, it was beyond his imagination how Achim was able to stay there. But his friend was so dedicated to his art and so in love with Berlin, he would endure all of these sufferings as long as he had some kind of outlet, however modest, for his creative passion.

Probably the greatest moment in his life came the day when he claimed to have met Gordon Craig, perhaps the only person whose name alone was sufficient to draw an endless litany of accolades and acclaim from Achim. The memory of that night was still quite vivid, how he so rudely dragged Frank from his sleep just after midnight in a bitter-cold January. Achim was utterly elated. He had obviously been drinking and was almost manic in his garrulous urge to talk. He was clearly not going to be leaving in a hurry. So Frank reluctantly accepted his invitation to celebrate the night with a bottle of champagne. It was a luxury he could ill afford. So together they disposed of what turned out to be Sekt rather than the real thing. But at least it did not need chilling. And nor did the second bottle.

By now only half-conscious for other reasons, it was some time before Frank learned what occasion it was they were toasting. In his manic excitement, Achim had omitted to explain that he had become engaged that evening to Gertrude, a girl about whom Frank knew little, except that she was extremely attractive and vivacious. But it was not until the following morning that he learned the true reason for Achim's elation. He had spent the earlier part of the day at the Flechtheim Gallery visiting an exhibition of Gordon Craig's designs for *Hamlet* and had met the master himself. Whether they actually met was uncertain. But Achim came away from the gallery so excited by the event that he could think of no better way to celebrate it than to ask for Gertrude's hand in marriage.

Perhaps the marriage was intended to serve as a constant reminder of this great day in his life. It was certainly the oddest reason for a proposal that Frank had ever known. But it was so typical of Achim and his obtuse unpredictability.

It struck Frank that Achim should have been with him a few days before. Then he would have witnessed a theatrical event that would have really appealed to him. It was a performance at the Stadttheater in Basel of *A Hundred Days* by Benito Mussolini and his mate Forzano. The lead was played by Werner Krauss – the man who had portrayed the brutal butcher in *The Joyless Street* alongside Greta Garbo and who now sat on the Nazi council in Berlin. There was a large contingent of Germans from across the border in the audience. They wore their patriotism on their sleeves. Not least of them was Reichsstatthalter Wagner.

Frank found the atmosphere both fascinating and deeply disturbing. He wondered how this city with a social-democratic government could tolerate such a festival of fascist thuggery. And it was at this moment – as the curtain finally went down, and Krauss came out on stage with the director – that a solitary brave voice from the audience shouted out: "*Raus!*" That single word made his evening. Restored his faith in humanity. If only Achim could be here, he thought, to enjoy these little freedoms with him.

It was around this time that he decided to write to Achim. His friend needed to know what opportunities there were here. The place not only vibrated with ideas and conversation that could give him new inspiration. There were also so many people from the Berlin scene already in the country. If not here, then in Zurich. He could not help but feel at home and, with all his experience, find work in a local theatre. He put all these arguments to Achim in a long letter, without truly expecting him to be quite so enthusiastic in his reply.

So he was surprised to get a very positive letter back. Only the day before, a bunch of Nazi thugs had thoroughly trashed the Jewish newsagent's next door, given the owner a severe beating and dragged him away with his wife. This was the final straw for Achim and Gertrude, who by now had twin baby boys to feed as well. It became clear to them that night that, if they did not leave soon, they would all perish in the very near future. And so it was that Achim's letter of reply came by return, announcing that he and his family would follow very soon. Frank was both surprised and relieved.

When sleep finally overcame him, the dawn light was already beginning to break in over the balcony to his room. And it was not long before his headiness and anticipation of their reunion had brought him back to an exhausted form of life. Frank felt terrible. His head ached. His mouth was drier and rougher than pumice stone. And the bed seemed as hard as a rock. He cautiously opened his eyes. Squinted. And came face to face with a pair of black boots.

Chapter 5

Frank's disappearance from the clinic presented Professor Abegg and Dr Zellweger with a problem. Having dragged Ellen all the way from London only to lose her husband before she even had a chance to see him, they now felt an obligation to look after her while the search for Frank continued. The two men exchanged uncomfortable glances, before the doctor turned to Ellen with an awkward hesitation.

"Perhaps you would you care to stay with me and my wife for the time being?" Dr Zellweger asked, with more than a hint of coercion from his professor. "She would enjoy the company."

"That's very kind," said Ellen.

"But I should warn you," the professor said with a smile on his lips that seemed closer to a smirk, "Dr Zellweger's wife is feeling quite excitable now that she has the right to vote. Quite irrepressible."

His secretary Maria Frey, he added, would drive her to the Zellwegers' place up on Bruderholz. Professor Abegg was clearly keen to banish Ellen from his embarrassment over the loss of Frank as soon as possible.

In Maria's Austin Healey it took little more than ten minutes from the clinic, a drive that culminated in a steep, winding road. This is the smart side of town, Ellen thought, as they climbed past the rows of rather cold and menacing Bauhaus mansions with touches of Jugendstil that looked proudly out over the city. A view dominated by the twin spires of the cathedral. After countless twists and turns that eventually took them away from this view over the city, Maria swung into a drive and stopped the car.

"Here we are."

This was a cosier-looking house than the mansions they had passed on the way up. Still grand enough, but comfortingly modest with its green window shutters, white-washed walls and terracotta roof tiles growing dark with age. Ellen felt relieved.

As she and Maria Frey climbed out of the Austin Healey, the door of the house opened. In the doorway stood a slim woman in her forties, with dark shoulder-length hair and eyes the colour of sapphire that sparkled with a deep emotional intelligence. She wore a navy cardigan and light grey slacks. Casual, but elegant.

"*Salü* Marthe," said Maria as they approached. "This is Mrs Goss."

"Please call me Ellen."

She held out a hand as Marthe Zellweger came down the steps from the house. The doctor's wife took her hand with a limp indecisiveness that bothered Ellen.

"Zellweger, Marthe," she said with an uncertain smile, and looked from Ellen to Maria Frey.

"We're not so free with first names in this country," Maria Frey explained.

"No really, that's perfectly fine," the doctor's wife insisted, instantly abandoning her Swiss formality. "I spent some time in America with my husband when he worked at a clinic in Chicago. I'm quite used to it. Please come in, Ellen."

Once Maria Frey had left to return to the clinic and Ellen had been shown her room, Marthe invited her guest to sit in the lounge that looked out onto the garden, while she made a pot of tea. Ellen was struck by how spotlessly clean and uncluttered the lounge was. The minimalism of the furnishing gave the impression that the room was barely lived in. On the coffee table lay an unopened packet of cigarettes, a magazine with the name *Annabelle* emblazoned across the top, resting on a newspaper, the *National-Zeitung*. Otherwise there was no sign of life here at all. The walls a pristine white were equally uncluttered but for a single painting, hung like a counterpart to the magazine and newspaper.

Ellen moved closer to examine it. There was a sombreness to the scene that was in stark contrast to the theme. The browns and greys of the watercolour depicted a dreary, dingy room furnished only with a chair and a bed. A setting of bleak cheerlessness. Yet on the floor beside the bed lay the forms of two naked women flushed with the pinkish-red passion of an embrace so joyful that it was hard to reconcile with their surroundings.

"That belongs to Urs," said Marthe. Ellen sensed a disapproving smile on her face as she set a tea tray down on the table. "It was painted by a local artist who went to school with my husband. He likes it."

Then after a prolonged silence as she poured the tea: "Urs told me your story. I can imagine it must be very difficult for you right now."

Ellen could hear traces of an American accent she must have picked up when she was in Chicago. But it was softened by another accent Ellen was unable to identify. It was unlike the harsh Swiss accents she had heard in the clinic.

"I hope the tea is all right for you," she said, placing the cup on the table in front of Ellen. "It's Darjeeling. We have a very fine tea house in Basel, where we buy our tea. I'll take you there one day while you're here. I know the English have a special relationship to their tea."

Ellen looked down at the cup and smiled.

"You might be surprised to learn that our relationship with tea is not quite as refined as all that. PG Tips would have been fine." She looked around the tray on the table. "Do you have any milk?"

Her hostess apologised and went back out to the kitchen.

"I don't mean to be rude," said Ellen, as Marthe returned with a small jug of milk. "But I hope I won't be here long enough for visiting tea houses in Basel."

"Of course. I'm sorry," Marthe replied. "I didn't mean to sound like a tourist brochure. But at the same time, this is quite a small city. And your husband knows no one here. So if you spend some time walking around the place, it's quite possible you might see each other."

"Your own husband and the professor seem to think he's quite at home here. So maybe he knows people I'm not aware of. But I'm not even sure they're talking about my Frank."

"If it was not your husband in the clinic, then the question of your husband's whereabouts is as urgent as ever," Marthe said. And then asked: "What is he doing in Switzerland?"

"He came to report on the referendum."

Marthe's eyes briefly lit up, then darkened again. "It's a shame he will not have had a chance to file his report. But perhaps it's more to our shame that we had to wait this long before any such report could be written."

"The professor said you were quite excited about the result," said Ellen, happy for the chance to change the subject. "Irrepressible, he said you were."

"The professor's a fool. Like both my parents, he thinks it a completely stupid idea. So his answer is now to patronise us."

"Even your mother?"

"She doesn't patronise. But yes, even she thinks it stupid. And many other women too. They seem to think that women are not intelligent enough for politics. That they should keep to looking after the household.

"When I met Urs, I wanted to understand something about his field of work, so I started to devour a lot of books about psychoanalysis, especially Lou Salomé's work. And it really worried my mother that I should be reading a woman she saw simply as a temptress to so many great men of her time. I think she thought I would be led astray in some way. She can't seem to understand that women are no longer defined by the men in their lives, that we have views of our own.

"But she's nothing like as bad as my mother-in-law, who said she would refuse to let Urs marry me when I entered her house one day carrying a book called *Women in Playpens* by Iris von Roten. Such a brilliant writer. So inspiring. Even now my husband's mother attacks me for wearing trousers – 'Why do you insist on walking around looking like that awful von Roten woman?' she says."

Marthe's eyes were alight. They sparked with more than a hint of rage. Ellen again recalled the professor's word for Marthe Zellweger: irrepressible.

"It's not as if any of this is really new here. Do you speak French?" she asked.

Ellen shook her head.

"Then you've probably never read Louis Aragon. He wrote a novel called *Les cloches de Bâle* set against the Peace Congress that was held here before the First World War. Everyone was there. Even your own Mr Hardie. And the book closes with Clara Zetkin's rousing speech in the cathedral. *'This is where the romance of chivalry ends'*, she said. *'Here for the first time in the world, room is made for true love'*.

"She was German of course. But that speech inspired a lot of Swiss people here. Can you imagine? A political speech by a Communist woman in the cathedral of this bourgeois city? Nothing like that had ever happened before. And perhaps because of that day, this city has produced so many strong women of its own. In fact, women already won a vote in local elections here a long time before last week's referendum.

"Oh dear, I'm sorry to bore you Ellen," Marthe said, pausing for breath when she noticed Ellen's expression glaze over with this flood of information. "It's a passion of mine. I majored in history. With sociology and psychology."

Aware though she was of how daunted Ellen seemed to be by the monologue, Marthe was not ready to let up just yet.

"You know, when I read in the newspaper what is happening in your country, or even just across the border in Germany or France, I realise we're still a good half century behind the times. It's mostly just a fear of change. If you're here long enough, Ellen, you will find this is a country driven by angst. Let me show you something."

Marthe rose from her chair and beckoned Ellen to follow her out of the lounge. Opening a door on the other side of the hallway, she flicked a light switch and led Ellen down a staircase into the cellar. At the bottom of the steps was a door to the left and a door to the right. But it was the door which greeted Ellen when she turned to follow Marthe back around the bottom of the steps that took her breath away. It stood open. A massive concrete door that must have been a good foot or more thick. And on the other side of this twelve-inch threshold lay another door. Marthe opened this and beckoned Ellen inside.

She shivered at the coldness of the room. The chill was underlined by the spartan, grey concrete walls with piping and equipment on the far side. Only the shelves neatly stacked with cans of food and a large wine rack alongside them offered any sense of comfort.

"This is our bunker," Marthe announced. There was a hint of embarrassed irony in her voice. "All new houses must have one. It's the law. Everyone is terrified that the Soviets could drop a bomb on us any day. It's even worse in the last years since they ordered their tanks onto the streets of Prague." Her dark sapphire eyes appeared to seethe with a frustration that bordered on anger, which then visibly ebbed away when she added: "We're not quite so bad in the French-speaking part of the country, where I come from – or even here in the Basel area. Here they think a little like the French speakers. And often vote the same way."

Marthe paused, letting a smile cross her lips and a sparkle light up her eyes.

"This is one of my favourites," she said, as she reached out to one of the shelves and took a book from behind the cans of food. It was more of a booklet than a book. A red tract emblazoned on the cover with huge white letters that were indecipherable to Ellen.

"Civil defence," explained Marthe. "Our government distributed this to everyone after the Czech crisis. And Urs feels a duty to keep it on the shelf. It's full of such useful information like what to do if Switzerland is invaded. It's unbelievable the fear and anxiety that grips this country sometimes. And when people are not worrying about invasion, then they're feeling alarmed by the vote for women, attacks on Swissair, getting swamped by foreigners or even the *frontaliers*."

Marthe Zellweger's voice quivered slightly with exasperation as she took back the booklet, placed it on the shelf and turned to leave the shelter, guiding Ellen back out to the stairwell. But closing the door behind her seemed to help Marthe regain a sense of composure. And the puzzled expression on Ellen's face was sufficient to restore her wits.

"Sorry. I don't know how you say that in English," Marthe apologised, stopping halfway up the stairs to ponder. "This country is quite schizophrenic about foreigners. They are so important for the economy. But at the same time there are many people who live in fear of being overwhelmed by them. Even the ones who live just across the border in Alsace or Germany and simply cross into Switzerland for work, then go home again in the evening. These are the *frontaliers*. People who cross the border. But in this case, I sometimes wonder if the fear is driven mostly by tax issues. As so many things are in this country."

"So frontier workers I suppose."

"Exactly," said Marthe. Then asked: "Do you work?"

Ellen smiled to herself.

"Why do you laugh?" Marthe's expression betrayed a sense of hurt.

"I'm not laughing," Ellen insisted, following Marthe back into the lounge. "You just reminded me of a play I saw at the theatre recently with Frank. A man asks a woman whether she works, and she replies: 'My arms and legs move'."

The quiet, neatly furnished lounge that exuded gentility and decorum suddenly exploded with a guffaw of laughter that seemed completely out of character from what Ellen had seen of Marthe until now.

"That's very good! It should be our motto!"

There was an inclusive, conspiratorial turn of phrase in Marthe's words that gave Ellen a sense of warmth and belonging.

"But yes," she said. "I work as a secretary. And the professor kindly let me phone England from the clinic. My boss has given me the rest of the week off."

"I hope you won't need more than a week," Marthe said in a tone that left Ellen fearing she almost certainly would.

Dr Zellweger did nothing to dispel this fear when he arrived home in the evening from work. His wife and Ellen were still in the lounge talking. Only the tea tray was missing. Replaced by a bottle of wine.

"*Salü Schatz,*" he said, planting a kiss on his wife's cheek. Then turning to Ellen: "Mrs Goss. I hope my wife has been looking after you?"

Without waiting for an answer, he disappeared into the kitchen, promptly returned with a glass in his hand and poured himself some wine after topping up the other glasses.

"I'm sorry to say, Mrs Goss, that there is still no news of your husband. We shall just have to be patient."

For the rest of the evening, over a light dinner, the conversation remained polite and restrained. Ellen said little more. She felt herself sinking into a morass of despair and felt it better not to sit at the dinner table with her hosts any longer than necessary. She decided to have an early night.

For Ellen it seemed a particularly dark night. Left her in a sleepless turmoil, dwelling on her irritations and deep concern. Irritation over Frank getting himself into this mess in the first place and concern about where he might be at that moment, as she lay in the comfort of a warm bed and the temperature outside fell below zero.

It was before breakfast – before she had even had a chance to wake properly – that her next ray of hope set her heart beating with anticipation. She heard the phone ring from her bedroom. When Marthe called her down and handed her the receiver, Ellen heard the voice of Dr Zellweger on the line. He had long since left for work by the time she rose for breakfast.

He apologised for disturbing her so early, but he wanted her to know that a man answering Frank's description had been picked up that night by the police. He had been found sleeping in the Storchen. This was a multistorey car park, he explained, and by coincidence it lay almost next door to the police station at the Spiegelhof. He had arranged to be at the Spiegelhof at ten that morning and said that Marthe would bring Ellen into town to meet him.

Once again, the doctor insisted that Frank had displayed a native fluency in the Alemannic dialect – even to the extent that, on this occasion, the man who was supposed to be Frank Goss convincingly persuaded the police that he was a German national from just across the border by the name of Eigenmann. Yet Dr Zellweger persisted in speaking of this man as Ellen's husband. His conviction, it seemed, was based entirely on Frank's passport photo, and she had to admit there was no escaping the fact that the photo he had shown her in the clinic was authentic. Yet this very photo, from a British passport, was confirmed by the police as being the exact likeness of their Eigenmann. How this could possibly be, the doctor was unable to explain. But Ellen had the distinct feeling that he saw this simply as evidence of how shaky their marriage must be and how little she knew her husband.

Still, now that the man was in police custody, Ellen was sure they would soon get to the bottom of the mystery, and she would be able to correct everyone's impression of her. For she was certain the professor saw her as a rather unstable woman at the very least. And possibly even a potential patient in his clinic.

It was a short walk to the tram stop. And the tram ride into town took no longer than twenty minutes. But it seemed much longer to Ellen, whose heart raced with a mix of excitement and anxiety for the whole journey.

The Spiegelhof was a long, grey, soulless building from the 1940s. Despite an endless succession of windows on each floor, it gave the impression of a closed, impenetrable garrison. The intimidating air about the place did nothing to dampen Ellen's spirit. She and Marthe arrived just before ten. Dr Zellweger was already outside the main entrance awaiting their arrival.

By now, Ellen's heart was pounding even faster at the prospect of finally seeing Frank. Or the man who was said to be Frank. Her excitement was short-lived.

When Dr Zellweger caught sight of her approaching with Marthe, he hurried towards them.

"Good morning, Mrs Goss," he said, offering her his hand. "I'm afraid we have a problem. When I arrived here a few minutes ago, I was told that your husband somehow managed to slip out and disappear again. No one knows where he is."

Chapter 6

When Frank eased open his eyes, he was confronted by two solid dark table legs, like menacing boots. Uncomfortably close to his head. The hard floor had left his back aching. Must have fallen out in the night, he thought. And dragged himself back into bed feeling bruised and battered. Then recalled that he was due to meet Achim later that day. His mind raced ahead of his discomfort with a buzz of expectation.

By the time he appeared for breakfast, his condition had outwardly improved. The bruising ache in his back remained, but the puffy oedema round the eyes had subsided. And he could now see things with a strained modicum of clarity – something for which he was about to find himself oddly thankful.

He sat at a discreet corner table and waited for breakfast to be served as he took a book from his pocket. *Confession of a Murderer* by Joseph Roth. It was either that or Rilke's *Duino Elegies*. This was the incongruous extent of the library he had with him. And on that bruised and battered morning, murder was a better match for his mood.

Sitting over croissants and coffee a few tables away from Frank were two men in grey suits with a young woman. The two men had their backs to him and were as inconspicuous as the chairs they were sitting in. The young woman told a different story altogether and seemed unlikely company for her faceless companions. She had a natural chic that was captured in the self-assured contrast between the fullness of her raven hair and a silver-white scarf that hung delicately around the collar of a navy-blue jacket. He could not hear what they were saying, but it was obvious that she carried herself with supreme self-confidence. The way in which every so often she threw herself back in her chair. The gentle curvature of her back touching the frame. Teasing it. And tantalising Frank's curiosity. He placed his book to one side and watched. Captivated by the scene.

A feigned expression of surprise or amusement on her lips. Maybe a look of shock in her eyes. It was plain she was in complete control of whatever conversation they were holding. She was not especially attractive in the conventional sense. Yet an aura of quite exceptional, indescribable beauty was described by every movement she made, every expression she conveyed across the table. When she threw her head back, her hair would catch in the corner of her mouth. And as if deliberately to underline this moment, she would discreetly part her lips and sweep away the black strands with her fingers, leaving the lips pouted in a way that was all the more provocative for their fleeting, innocent sensuality.

But Frank's enchantment was suddenly trampled all over by the arrival of a newcomer at their table. For all his frustration over this intrusion, however, it proved an intriguing turn of events. The newcomer was wearing a black hat and long black trench coat. Frank recognised him at once.

It was the man with the Maybach Zeppelin from the night before. And seeing him now in the light of day, he realised that he knew the man. He was, or used to be, the owner of a sleazy cabaret in Berlin. Willi Breitner. An opportunist, a fast talker and a womaniser. The type who wore all the danger signals like a bright red carnation in his buttonhole and still managed to soft-soap anyone into doing whatever he pleased. During Frank's years in Berlin, before the Nazis seized power, he had often seen Breitner strutting around some of the classier establishments, like the White Mouse or the Chat Noir, before setting up in business himself. Frank considered himself fortunate never to have made the man's acquaintance. He knew a number of people who had. And every one of them had come to regret it.

The aversion that Frank felt towards Breitner was nourished all the more as he watched him take the delicate hand of his temptress, raise it to the loathsome curl of his cold razor-like lips and – with all the charm of a cobra – stoop to kiss it. She smiled and discreetly withdrew her hand before getting up to leave. Breitner stepped back slightly. He deliberately allowed her too little space to pass without brushing against his beefy, barrel-chested frame and bade her an ostentatiously regretful farewell. As he lowered himself into the chair she had just vacated, opposite the two faceless men, his lupine eyes followed her across the room to the cloak stand and watched as she slipped on her coat. Even this she managed to do with an innocent allure that teased away all the layers of cold cynicism that Frank had accumulated over the years. The way she moved her arms back, sliding them into the sleeves of the coat and just briefly revealing the white blouse under her jacket – the warm hint of fragile femininity beneath.

Frank's curiosity was uncomfortably divided. Who was this woman? And what was she doing here with a man like Breitner so far from his stamping ground? Whatever it was, Frank's muddled logic told him he would be unlikely to find the answer to the second question here in the breakfast room. So, to satisfy the deeper part of his curiosity, he went after an answer to the first instead.

It was still twilight when he reached the pavement outside. She was already some distance down the street and just turning into a side alley. Frank hurried after her as unobtrusively as his burning eagerness would allow. Once at the alley, he could see her some thirty metres ahead walking almost meditatively, hands in coat pockets, up a steep flight of steps. The higher up she went, the slower her pace became. His eyes never once left the beguiling movement of her slim dark ankles as they flexed effortlessly over the steps, the seam of her stockings tracing the movement with the elegance of a master calligrapher. For all the confidence she had displayed in the company of those two men, these ankles betrayed a poignant vulnerability. Yet paradoxically, the beauty of their movement and the gentle curve of the legs invested her at the same time with an irresistible appeal of strength and independence.

On reaching the top, she disappeared over the horizon of the steps against the looming white wall of a church. Again Frank quickened his stride and arrived at the topmost step just in time to catch sight of her cross the road on the other side of the church. She skipped lightly over the road, up a short flight of steps and into the park on the other side. Bereft of any foliage, the winter trees that lined the park stood like sentinels guarding her passage to the other side. At times, he almost lost her in their shadows.

It was a good five minutes after crossing the park before she eventually entered a tall terraced house in a narrow street the other side of the city's mediaeval gateway of the Spalentor. The late dawn sky had barely penetrated here, and the house was in darkness. It was cold and uninviting. But after a minute or so, a lamp from a garret window lit up and strained to compete with the grey twilight above. Frank needed no second bidding. He tried the door she had entered and found it was not locked. He went in. There was just enough light on the stairwell for him to find his way up the creaking wooden stairs to the top floor. The nameplate on the door that awaited him there read 'P. Roche'. He knocked. The sound reverberated through the chamber of the stairwell, and only then did it occur to Frank that he had no idea what he was going to say when she opened the door. He began to panic. He had allowed myself to be drawn here by her magnetism. And now that he was jolted into considering his actions in the cold light of reason, he felt completely out of his depth.

When the door opened, he stood mesmerised by the sight of her before him. And said nothing. The deep ebony of her eyes sparkled with an eloquent edge of melancholy trying not to be heard. It was camouflaged as suspicion and mistrust, but was visible nonetheless.

"Can I help you?" she whispered.

"Good morning, Mademoiselle Roche. I have a message from Mr Breitenbacher," he replied, misnaming his taskmaster in his agitated haste.

This impromptu creativity came right out of the blue and took him by surprise. He felt slightly ashamed at how easily the lie came out – yet rather pleased by his resourcefulness. He had hidden depths. It was not until sometime later that the folly of his inventiveness was made painfully clear to him.

The long silence that followed Frank's words hollowed out his brief moment of smugness to a thin shell that eventually cracked and disintegrated under its own weight. He felt himself beginning to shuffle from one foot to the other. And almost as a reflex he started rubbing his hands together to disguise his nervousness.

"Who?" she asked.

"Mr Breitenbacher."

"I don't know any Breitenbacher." Her sweet voice had by now taken on a dismissive edge. It left Frank teetering on the edge of dejection.

"The man you were with earlier in the Hotel Storchen," he explained, affecting the sense of a chill on the stairwell as he continued rubbing his hands together.

"You mean Mr Breitner?" she asked. He nodded.

"Could I come in? It's quite cold out here."

She looked nervously over Frank's shoulder in the doorway, as if nervous of eavesdroppers on the stairwell. Then stepped back to open the door a little wider and silently beckoned him in.

"You don't really seem the kind of lady to keep company with a man like that," Frank said as he stepped inside. She ignored the intrusive bluntness of his remark.

"What message?" she asked.

Frank hesitated. He looked about him, uncertain where to go next with his lie. The room was small, but well-furnished. A dining table and chairs, a settee with books strewn over it, a single armchair and beside this chair a table on which there stood a vase with three red roses. And a gramophone. A record lay on the turntable. Vocalion label. *A Fine Romance*.

"You like Billie Holiday," he said.

Close to the table with the gramophone stood a wood-burning stove. He moved over to the stove and warmed his hands while he continued to absorb the scene – the mood of independent womanhood that pervaded the room, the secrets, the longings and the anxieties that lived within those walls.

All the while, she stood in tantalising proximity watching Frank. Still waiting for a reply to her question.

"You have a lot of books," he prevaricated further, trying hopelessly to make conversation.

"I need them for my studies."

"Oh really? What are you studying?"

"Did Mr Breitner not tell you?"

"No, why should he?" Frank sensed he was being tested as he struggled to come up with an explanation for knocking on her door.

"No reason." She smiled in a strangely coquettish way that was both alluring and yet out of place. Then threw in the words "History of Art" like a half-hearted tip she was leaving for the waiter.

Another long silence followed. From the corner of his eye he watched covetously as she swept back the right side of her jacket and rested her hand on the slender curvature of her hip. There was an implicit impatience in her posture. And it brought a certain piquancy to the excitement he was already feeling over the gentle curve so exquisitely accentuated by her hand. Frank was floundering in his agitation.

"All right," he finally admitted. "There is no message."

"So who are you?" she asked, releasing the hand from her hip and letting the jacket fall back into place. "And why are you here?"

A flash of anger lit up her ebony eyes. A look tinged with unease that verged on panic.

"Sorry, I didn't mean to upset you. I saw you in the hotel. And I was wondering." He paused, aware that he was getting onto dangerous terrain. "Would you care to meet this evening for a drink? Or maybe dinner?"

She said nothing. Simply buttoned up the jacket.

Having come this far, Frank was not going to be put off now.

"Do you know Lisettli's wine tavern?" he asked. "On Spalenberg?"

Still she said nothing. But he fancied that he saw a trace of acknowledgment in her expression.

"I'll be there at six this evening," he insisted. "If you'd care to join me, I'd be delighted."

Frank turned and made to leave. Standing in the doorway, he turned back with a nodding gesture towards the nameplate outside: "What does the 'P' stand for?"

"Patricia" came a reluctant reply.

"My name is Eigenmann. Frank Eigenmann." With that, he left. And felt ludicrously fulfilled by this venture. It all seemed worth the effort at the time. But he could not remotely envisage the trouble it would bring.

No reasonable excuses could explain his lateness for the rendezvous with Achim. He had started the day full of expectation and excitement at the prospect of seeing him again. And the reasons for his distraction were only partly to do with Patricia Roche. After leaving her place, he had spent most of that morning wandering aimlessly through the streets of the old town and along the banks of the river recalling her every move, her every hint of injury in those sadly sparkling eyes. But she was not his sole preoccupation. He had other things on his mind. It was the sight of her with Willi Breitner that had brought them to the surface.

Frank lost count of the times he crossed first one bridge, then another, on this planless journey through his thoughts. But every time he did so, he stopped, compelled by the strong current of the water as it swirled and eddied away beneath the bridge. Above him a faint winter sun eased its way through the cirrus clouds for the first time in more than a week. Close to the right bank of the river downstream of Frank, a boat bobbed in the water. A boat beneath a sunny sky, he mused. And time stood still with him as he watched.

He stood mesmerised and confused by the message delivered by this river on its journey to the coldness of the North Sea, taking it through the heart of his homeland. A heart that had long since started to fail. Every eddy round the pillars of the bridge below brought the knowledge home to him: this water would soon be sweeping through the narrowing arteries of his home. Only then did the meaning of that message dawn on him.

Frank was put in mind of a report he had read in the *National-Zeitung*. A student had recently taken his life in this city and left a suicide note describing his vision. The banks of this river would burn, he wrote, and their raging fire would not be put out until the river overflowed with blood. It was a vision that had robbed that student of the inner strength to cope with the senselessness of the coming chaos and the river of blood which he saw. And at that moment, standing on the bridge, Frank felt he could understand his motivation.

Why it was that Willi Breitner brought this deeply depressing vision to the surface was not entirely clear. By all accounts the man was a villain with friends in the SS, someone to steer well clear of. But Frank had no reason to let the racketeer impinge on his life in this way. Perhaps it was due to his sense of disquiet at seeing Breitner in the company of such a fragile beauty as Patricia Roche. Or maybe it was simply the fact that he reminded Frank of Berlin: the smell of the spreading cancer in the streets, the harbingers of death and decay on every corner.

It was these troubling thoughts which made him late that morning. And which presumably also left him so unprepared for the long-awaited reunion when finally he stepped into the restaurant where they had agreed to meet. A place out in the hinterland hard on the frontier between France and Switzerland.

It was mid-week, and he was surprised to find the restaurant in this quiet little village bustling with custom. Frank stood close to the bar, searching through the smoke for a familiar face. The waitress jostled past, cursing under her breath. Or was she just telling him there was no room? It was hard to know. At all events, even allowing for the distortions of the smoke-filled atmosphere, no one looking remotely like Achim was to be seen. Had he run into trouble at the border maybe? One thing was clear. There was no room here to sit and wait.

It occurred to him that a walk up to the castle ruins overlooking the village would not only enable him to kill time. It might also give him a good view of the surrounding area – in particular of the border where Achim would be crossing. He emerged from the restaurant into a long stream of people strolling past up the hill in animated conversation. Once the stream had passed, he followed on behind.

By now, the sun was already beginning to lose the battle with the cumulus clouds gathering to the west. It brought a chill to the air on the steep walk up the hill. And he buttoned up his coat right to the neck. Every so often a pool of sun ran over the valley, lending the grimly naked trees an ephemeral glow that hinted at the capricious beauty of this quiet enclave. Frank could almost sense the perfumes and the resonance of spring as he pictured this place a month or two hence.

When Achim had suggested in his letter that they meet in this village, Frank bought a guidebook of the area. And walking now behind the long trail of people up this road, which was little better than a farm track, he remembered that it was described as a path of pilgrimage. A description that seemed to be confirmed by the dense crowd ahead of him. Yet it was a Wednesday in early February. Frank was mystified as to what possible significance such a day in the calendar could have to attract so many pilgrims to this path.

He slowed his walk to an amble and let the pilgrims move on ahead, stopping now and then to appreciate the setting until they had vanished out of sight and sound around the corner. About halfway up the hill, the castle ruins were now barely visible above the trees and seemed further away than ever. He grew impatient and decided to strike out across the fields. The castle stood on French soil, but there was no clear border to announce the fact, unless the thick undergrowth of the woods could be regarded as a boundary. Even in its state of undress, this belt of forest was forbidding enough with its clinging creepers, brambles and bushes to slow him down. And he began to regret his short-cut. He realised too that the path he had taken was not only much slower, but could also be utterly counterproductive, since he might easily miss Achim by coming this way.

He struggled on as fast as the thicket would allow, cursing his impatience and wishing he had found a corner in the restaurant and waited there. But as soon as he reached the ruins and clambered up through the darkness of what must once have been the keep, his impatience instantly vanished. The moment he came out on top of the castle, and the vista opened around him, he felt the heaviness of his heart begin to lift. It was as if the city that held his memories in its oppressive grip had released him for a brief reprieve. To the north-east in the far distance over the hills of the Black Forest hung an ominous scythe of dark cloud. Other than this, the clarity of the air was magical. The view breath-taking. Aside from the distant dark cloud, everything appeared deceptively peaceful. Frank was almost taken in by its idyllic beauty.

He had often wondered what it was that fascinated him about the lofty views of the world offered by so many of history's building projects. It was a spell that had been cast in early childhood from his very first climb up the steps of Cologne Cathedral during his school holidays, when his mother shipped him north each summer to stay with his aunt. It was an adventure to which he became so addicted that he was soon intimately familiar with the profile of every step. Once at the top, he would happily spend an hour or two transfixed by the miniaturised life displayed below. It all seemed so insignificant. And yet it impressed him deeply. At times he felt such a pull that he was almost compelled to let himself fall into its midst, to plummet headfirst smack into the ground where it traded in its bewitching insignificance.

These castle ruins where he now stood had little to compare with the grandeur of Cologne Cathedral. But the view was still magnificent – and the sense of altitude had the same magical effect, luring him precipitously close to the edge. But on this occasion, when he peered down to the rocks and pathway below, he felt an unaccustomed dizziness surge through his head. Aware of the danger, he quickly stepped back to avoid toppling over. As he stood there holding his head in both hands, his eyes shut tight, the dizziness gave way to a flash of lights and a splitting pain. An ache the like of which he had never experienced in his life before. His skull felt as though it was cracking in two. And from the fissure that seemed to open up in his head, he sensed a peculiar otherness emerge. At that strangest, most alienating moment the headache started to ease, and he sensed this otherness at his side. Only for a brief instant, but very intensely. Just over his shoulder.

Then, all at once, the air was rent by a thunderous roar that had him almost reeling in pain again. A jet airliner soared up in the sky on its take-off path over the Jura hills. It was a BEA plane. With the giveaway T tail of a Trident. The same aircraft he had arrived on. Frank buried his dazed and bewildered head in his hands. What was going on? His mind seemed to be spinning out of control. The sense of otherness had long since evaporated. All he knew was the harrowing roar in his head.

It was some time before he felt able to let his eyes open. The relief to see the landscape around him at peace again, the wooded hills still standing, everything untouched by the thunderous roar, was more immense even than the open sky above him. He took in a vast vital breath of that clean air and stepped over to the edge again to celebrate the release. And there in the distance, on the road leading out beyond the hamlet at the foot of the castle ruins, he saw two people, a man and a woman, each carrying what appeared to be a child in their arms. They were far enough away to enjoy a curious kind of anonymity. Yet despite the distance, Frank's heart leapt with excitement. Though little more than a speck on the landscape, the man was unmistakably known to him. Even with a child in his arms, that gait – with its incongruous coordination of spring-heeled confidence and hunched introversion – could belong to no one else.

"Achim!" he shouted. "Achim!" Again and again at the top of his voice. But the couple were too far off. They continued on their way, over the open unwatched border, completely oblivious to Frank. Charged with a frustrated sense of elation, he swung round, almost slipping over as he went. His flailing foot dislodged a piece of masonry. But the crack that reverberated around the valley when it smashed against the rocks some fifty metres below was drowned in his excitement. As fast as the narrow winding steps of the castle ruins would allow, he went in pursuit.

By the time he caught up with them, they were already installed in the restaurant where they had agreed to meet from the outset. The place was not quite as full as it had been before. But the smoke was just as thick and the cacophonous chatter round the tables almost as dense. His heart sank when he failed to find them in the commotion.

"Frank!" The name strained to reach him through the clatter and hubbub. "Frank!" None of the faces in the room meant anything to him. But the voice was unmistakable. He quickly turned. Even in his eagerness to believe, he felt unable to trust his own eyes. It was difficult to make the link between the Achim he knew so well and the figure who stood before him now. In all the years they had known each other, Frank had never before seen him dressed in the hearty outdoor attire of a hiker. The walking boots, the thick red knee-socks, the breeches – even the rucksack. He was almost unrecognisable.

It was his eyes that gave him away. Slightly bulbous – reminiscent of Peter Lorre's Kürten, the child murderer in Fritz Lang's film *M* – yet paradoxically so warm and affectionate. And now positively sparkling with the electricity of the moment.

The two men both stood for some time between the thronging tables of the restaurant, gazing at each other in disbelief. Frank's immediate impulse was to throw himself into his old friend's arms and embrace him. And it was plain that Achim would have done the same. But they both seemed instinctively to sense the need for caution, for merging with the crowd, perhaps because they were still so close to the border.

Frank surmised that this probably also explained Achim's strange garb. So, trying to keep the lid on their excitement for the moment, they self-consciously shook hands. The gesture struck him as a preposterously formal pantomime. And he instantly abandoned all pretence, putting his left arm around his old friend's shoulder, hugging it tightly. Achim responded. But it seemed a mannered reciprocation, as if playing to the audience, and he discreetly led Frank to a table in the corner. He really did appear a changed person to Frank since they had last seen each other. Worried or anxious in some way.

"Gertrude," he said as they reached the table, "you remember Götz. Likes to call himself Frank."

She smiled and gave him her hand across the table.

"You look as lovely as ever, Gertrude," Frank said, scowling at Achim's introduction and thinking how ashen and drawn she looked against his memory of her. No longer the vivacious young woman, but visibly aged since they had last met. He turned to the two baby boys asleep on the bench seat beside her.

"You two have been busy since I last saw you," he said with a smile in Achim's direction.

"They're very tired," Gertrude replied. "It's been a long journey."

"I can imagine. How was it? Did you meet with any problems?"

"No. Not really,' Achim said wearily. "I'd been told it was becoming ever more difficult to get into Switzerland, and I didn't want to get caught with this," he continued, pointing ponderously to the small rucksack beside him. "So this seemed a good way to come."

They had so much to say to each other. Yet a silence broke over the table which left Frank feeling uncomfortable. There was a furtiveness about his old friend that he had not seen in him before. He fixed his gaze on the rucksack.

"What have you got in there?"

"It's a long story."

The words hung like a fly teetering on the outer strand of a web, wary of entering any further. And the curious silence that followed was drowned out by the cacophony of voices around them.

"But tell me," said Gertrude when the cacophony died down, "why do you insist on being called Frank? Götz is a wonderful name. It has such pedigree."

"Apparently, it was my mother's choice," Frank replied. "She was a great Goethe enthusiast." This was all he offered by way of explanation. It was not a subject he wanted to dwell on. "Achim," he continued, raising his voice again when the crowd around them resumed their cacophony. "You can't imagine how pleased I am you're here. Slowly I feel our dream could be coming true."

Achim looked suspiciously across the table. Frank saw himself confronted with a strange expression on his friend's face that he could not recall ever having seen before – his eyes slightly sad and lips parted just a fraction, as if he was about to say something. Then his face relaxed again, and his lips broke into a smile.

"What dream is that, my old friend?"

"You know exactly what I'm talking about. We've discussed it so often in the past. The day we'd form our own theatre group and take the world by storm." Frank reached over the table and touched his arm with wishfully conspiratorial zeal.

"And there could be no better time or place than right here, right now. The place is teeming with opportunity. They have their theatres and cabarets all right. And attract huge audiences most nights. But a lot of them are quite introverted, all busy examining the Confederation's navel. There's a demand for something else. The interest is there. They want to know what's happening on the other side of the border. And we could do that, Achim, the two of us."

Gertrude looked at Achim. She appeared anxious and worried. But her eyes betrayed more besides. There was the vague hint of some undefined entreaty. Achim said nothing.

The two babies began to stir in the noise around them. This only added to the tension.

"That was all idle talk, Frank. In idle times," Achim said at last. "But times have changed. And when you've had all the sleepless nights that we've been through these last few months, you reach a point where dreams are just a forgotten luxury you can no longer afford."

At that moment, it was as if the whole substance of Frank's life had been knocked out of him. All the meaning that his thoughts had been fixed on those past weeks was suddenly counterfeit and worthless. He reached across the table and placed an imploring hand on his friend's arm. But Achim was unmoved.

"As you said yourself, Frank, there are any number of theatre groups here already. They have everything they need, and more political cabaret than they can cope with. Look at Erika Mann. From what I hear, she had enough to contend with from the local fascist thugs, until they forced her to close and hounded her out of the country. That's why they prefer to examine the Confederation's navel. We have nothing to offer. Even here in Switzerland, the arm of the Third Reich is not far away."

"But what else do you have apart from theatre?" Frank asked forlornly, raising his voice further to compete with the cacophony of the crowd. "What else do you plan to do? What are you going to live on?"

If fanciful dreams could elicit no response, he thought, then perhaps the practicalities of life in exile might.

"I'll find work," he replied with cool matter of fact.

"Just like that?"

Frank grew angry with his friend, whose grasp of reality seemed even weaker and more questionable than his own.

"Do you have any idea how much unemployment there is here? And what about a work permit? You're not even legal. How do you expect to get a job?"

Achim smiled. "We'll manage. I have one or two ideas." He paused briefly, then turned the tables. "But tell me, Frank, how do *you* manage to keep your head above water?"

Frank was all too aware of the implications of this question. And it made him slightly uneasy. He had been living on his unearned inheritance for too long. And he knew that he would soon find himself dipping below the waterline if he failed to change the hotel life to which he had become so comfortably accustomed.

"I'm still living on what my father left me. But you're right. I need to adjust my living habits if I'm to stay afloat."

"That reminds me, Frank." He had the impression that Achim was more than pleased to have an opportunity to change the subject. "Apropos your family, we came via Cologne and took the chance to visit your mother."

"How is she?" Frank asked, trying not to appear too indifferent, as much for his own conscience as for any other reason.

"She's not too well, I'm afraid. She obviously took your father's death very hard. And now that she's lost the dog as well, she hasn't a companion left in the world. Except the dragon of a nurse. It was quite upsetting to see her after all these years. I had always remembered her as a rather cheerful lady."

"What happened to the dog?" Frank asked.

"I don't know. It was hard to get any sense out of her. Some bully-boy thugs by the sound of it, but it was hard to tell."

"I must try and get up to see her soon," Frank said in an unconvincing tone.

"What about somewhere to stay, Achim?" he added, keen to change the subject himself. "From your letter I wasn't sure what your plans were, so I had a look around at a few possibilities, but I don't have anything concrete as yet."

"Don't worry. That's taken care of already," he replied with an air of mystery. "I was recommended to stay in the Hotel St. Gotthard, so we'll be there for a few days at least, until we find something more permanent."

Achim clearly saw the sense of alarm in his friend's expression, because he quickly followed this with: "Why?"

"I just wonder who might have recommended that place to you. You know that was Wesemann's stamping ground?"

"Who?" Achim asked.

"Come on, you must have heard about the Gestapo agent who's just been put away for abducting that journalist? It was a huge story. In all the papers."

Signs of a wakening memory began to show in Achim's eyes.

"Yes, I heard about it," was all he said.

"Heard about it? It caused a major diplomatic row, almost put the country's neutrality at stake, and you just heard about it. Well, just in case you hadn't heard this: the Gotthard is where he used to hang out. And he may still have friends there. So take care."

His expression gave way to a look of concern, and Frank could not escape noticing the way he gave Gertrude a reassuring squeeze of the hand.

"But you don't need to worry," he continued, trying clumsily to put their minds at rest. "I'm sure they wouldn't try anything like that a second time. And anyway, what possible interest could they have in a stage designer?"

Another uneasy silence spread over the table. Achim and Gertrude became submerged in unspoken exchanges with one another. Frank noticed how they had both changed almost beyond recognition since he had last seen them. Gertrude had grown so quiet and timid; her bubbling enthusiasm, her electrifying beauty had all been swallowed up by anxiety. Her eyes resembled those of an animal in captivity, the lids now drawn with depression where once they had displayed her magnificent eyelashes with such pride. Achim for his part had exchanged the carefree excitability he once knew for an almost suffocating, protective concern, continually but silently comforting Gertrude throughout their conversation. But Frank told himself they were probably just suffering the rigours of their long journey. As he was contemplating this idea, Achim looked over the table at him with an oddly pained expression on his face.

"Were you always such a naive optimist, Frank? Of course they'll try it a second time. And a third. And as often as they want. That whole Berthold Jacob affair, and Motta's nauseating two-faced response to it simply reinforced them in their bullying self-esteem."

Achim was starting to get heated again, his voice louder by the second. Frank tried discreetly to signal the need for restraint. It seemed to him unwise to speak so disparagingly of a Swiss politician in such a public place. Especially with a strong Berlin accent.

"You do know they eventually released him again after the Swiss protested?" Frank said.

"Only after they tortured the shit out of the man!" Achim cried and brought a fist down on the table with a thud that brought questioning glances from the table next to them.

It was plain to Frank that Achim had more than heard about the case: he had made himself familiar with every detail of events in Switzerland these past months.

"You only have to look at their arrogance over the trial of that man who shot Gustloff in Davos. The blatant contempt displayed by the propaganda hounds they unleashed on the Swiss courts. Their self-righteous zeal as they bayed like hungry wolves for the head of a man who had the guts to stand up to them."

Then he added with a final, ominous flourish: "Don't you worry, they'll try that kind of thing as many times as it suits them – and as often as they're allowed to get away with it."

Achim's fervour embarrassed Frank into silence. For the first time in their long relationship, he had made Frank feel like an unworldly, ineffectual simpleton – like an empty shell washed up on the beach, rinsed of all emotion and opinion by the salt water. But Achim seemed unaware of the effect his words were having on his friend. At times he appeared almost to be talking to himself. And his impassioned monologue left Frank wondering why he had initially pretended to be so ignorant of the whole story. But his friend gave him no time to call him out on this contradiction as he added almost without pause: "Come on, let's pay for this and get moving."

He gestured to Gertrude that she should see to the two sleeping infants on the bench seat beside her. Then got to his feet, carefully arranging the mysterious rucksack on his shoulders.

"I'll get it," said Frank. He pulled the wallet from his pocket, gave the waitress a ten-franc note and opened the inner pouch for the small change.

"What's this?" asked Achim, reaching down to pick up the lock of strawberry-blonde hair that tumbled out of the wallet. The broad smile that lit up his face was the first sign of cheer that Frank had seen in him since they met. But he hurriedly retrieved the lock of hair and slipped it back into the wallet, ignoring his friend's amusement.

By the time he had brought Achim and his family to their hotel, it was already late in the afternoon.

"You know, there's a Kolping house just the other side of the river," he said as they stood at the entrance to the hotel. "I'm sure you could find lodging there for a time. It's not only cheaper, but you would also find it a whole lot safer than this place."

Achim squeezed his friend's shoulder.

"I'll look into it," he said, as much to reassure his wife as Frank. Gertrude gave him what seemed a worried and imploring glare. He squeezed her hand. Then they turned and disappeared into the hotel lobby.

Frank returned to his own hotel room to wash and brush up. The reunion with his old friend had been deeply dissatisfying. And left him feeling more alone than ever. He needed the promise of that evening with Patricia to keep him from dipping below the water that he felt was slowly flooding the life out of him.

So it was a sense of desperation that had him leave his hotel at five-thirty already to head for the Spalenberg and the wine tavern just around the corner. The huge Persil advertisement covering the entire blind wall of the end building stared down at him as he turned the bend. Perhaps a reminder that everything eventually comes out in the wash, he told himself. And smiled at the idea as he entered Lisettli's wine tavern almost half an hour early. During the next thirty minutes, he marinated his thoughts with half a litre of *pinot gris*, rendering him certainly too carefree to create a serious impression on her when she turned up.

The tavern was almost empty. In the far corner, an elderly couple sipped coffee together exchanging a few quiet words with each other every now and then. Two tables from them sat a slightly dishevelled old man poring over a newspaper, nursing a cigarette in his mouth and a glass of red wine in his right hand – ready to be raised at any moment. Otherwise, there was nothing to dispel the sense of tired early-evening indifference that filled the space between the empty tables and chairs. Frank took up a strategic position two tables away from the door so that Patricia Roche could not miss him the moment she entered.

He recalled the gentle curvature of her back as it touched the frame of the chair. The way she parted her lips every so often to sweep away the strands of her raven hair. These warm memories coupled with the thoughts provoked by his disturbing reunion with Achim occupied Frank almost to the end of his second half-litre of *pinot gris*. The elderly couple had by now been replaced by a succession of other guests. Only the old man poring over the newspaper seemed a permanent fixture. When he got up to go, Frank finally shook the wishful alcoholic haze out of his mind and looked reality in the face. He would not be seeing her tonight. But that was no reason to walk out on a dream that was only just beginning. He ordered a last glass of wine.

As the waitress set the glass down in front of him, another customer sat down at the table next to his. Between him and the door. There was something different about this one. He wore a conspicuous otherness that set him apart from the earlier passers-through. This one did not exude the contentment with his lot in the way the other guests had done. His face displayed a doughy sheen about it with an unhealthy shade of pasty grey. It belied the calm, eager-to-please smile that was fixed into place.

Frank lifted his glass, almost as a kind of reflex response to the anxiety this man instilled in him. He became aware of the man's insistent eyes homing in on him from the other table. Involuntarily Frank turned his gaze towards him. The stranger smiled with thick wet lips that seemed about to pout their message across the room with a blatant, almost unctuous self-assurance that Frank found both disturbing and disgusting.

Inclining his head coquettishly, the stranger raised his glass to Frank, who just about caught the words '*zum Wohl*' distorted slightly by the spittle in his mouth. It was clear to Frank that it was well past time for him to go.

But even this, even his leaving, was not allowed to pass without the stranger insisting himself on Frank's unease. As he edged by the table where the man was sitting, and drew level with him – almost waist to shoulder – the stranger raised his glass again, and wished Frank a pleasant evening. Without so much as a glance in his direction, Frank kept straight on through the doorway but still he could sense the man's expression, his staring eyes, his luscious lips radiating their obsequious smile.

The fresh evening air brought welcome relief. It cleared his head of all this interference and left him space to consider his reunion with Achim and his non-existent rendezvous with Patricia Roche. Two diametric opposites. And both signalled failure.

The way from the wine tavern to the Storchen was short. Too short. Five minutes if he really took his time. And time was a commodity he needed to take in very large measure. So, when he came out into the fresh air, he headed immediately down to the market square. And into the teeth of a cold wind that blew into the square off the river. It reminded me that spring was still a long way off. The market had long since closed and the place was almost empty. He crossed over and headed up the narrow mediaeval street that led to the cathedral square.

After the day's disappointments, he knew that he would not be finding any peace that night. So it came as no great surprise when he realised, as he was climbing the steep cobbled street, that he was being followed. It was not a feeling he was familiar with. To his knowledge he had never been followed in his life before. Yet without turning, stopping, or hesitating in any way, he knew that someone was there in the shadows behind him. Watching.

Frank did his best not to let panic get the upper hand. He persuaded himself that it was merely a fellow stroller who just happened to be on the same path as him. Not without some difficulty he kept his composure and continued on towards the cathedral. But his ears were alerted now. And every hint of movement had his full attention, had him analysing and interpreting the content of each and every sound. When he reached the square, he paused at the large stone fountain under the trees, ran his fingers through the icy water, and turned his gaze back in the direction he had come from. The street and the square were empty, lined only by a mass of shadows from the trees, which whispered suspiciously with each rustle of wind through their branches. A stray scrap of paper scampered across the ground in the darkness. In every meaningful sense of the word, the place appeared to be deserted.

Yet still he could feel the presence. Somewhere not far away. In the black recesses of the night. His heart started to race. A chilling anxiety began to close in on him, threatening to shut out the natural noises of the street in all its emptiness: the cold wind sweeping round the cathedral walls from the river; the ice-cold running water of the fountain; a distant tram. He struggled to keep his grip on these small footholds in reality.

But the stark looming edifice of the minster behind him threw a vast shadow over his unease. He wondered how many scenes of religious intolerance and persecution these cold sandstone walls had already witnessed. What mystery they were being treated to at this very moment. The darkness still whispered shades of menace. And he speculated as to which of the eclipses in the orbit of this building might conceal the threat that was meant for him.

With breathless agitation, he made his way around the cathedral to the terrace overlooking the river. He remembered feeding the pigeons here only a few days before, and now sensed he was throwing himself at the mercy of vultures. But who were they? And what did he have to be frightened of? Nothing. Yet everything. Frank recalled the story of Berthold Jacob and his abduction not far from where he was standing. But Jacob was a journalist – and a Jew into the bargain. A man who had invited trouble through his provocative articles. What was Frank by comparison? A nobody with no secrets and no commitments.

While his paranoid state appeared to dwell on a plural enemy, there was no good reason for assuming that he was being followed by more than one person. Or even that he was being followed at all. The shadows and the mediaeval edifice remained totally loyal to their protégés. Not a single movement out of place did they betray. From the open safety of the terrace, his back to the river, he stood watching these shadows for a single false move. It seemed an eternity until he felt secure enough to start sidling cautiously along the terrace wall. At an opening in this wall he stopped, hesitated a few seconds as he surveyed the darkness one last time, then darted away and down the steps that led to the river.

Once down on the promenade and round the corner he sought the safety of the bushes and trees. And waited, breathless, for his pursuers to appear. He shivered in the breeze blowing off the water when suddenly he heard what sounded like the giggling of a female voice. Through the bushes, he watched a couple arm in arm emerge at the bottom of the steps. She was all over him, a little tipsy judging by her laughter. But he was evidently enjoying the attention and allowed himself to be firmly anchored to the trunk of a tree, where she proceeded to take her pleasure of him.

The extravagance of her enjoyment made Frank feel a shade uncomfortable and more than a little absurd as he stood behind a tree barely two metres from their boisterous passion. And since their exhibition provided him with the kind of cover that would distract anyone who might be on his tail, he considered it a good opportunity to go. So, as silently as the undergrowth would allow, he detached himself from the tree and, confident that he must surely now be alone, made his way back to the safety of his hotel room.

Chapter 7

It was Friday already. Ellen had by now been treated to Marthe's favourite tea house and a whole series of sights and historical landmarks that meant very little to her. To end the tour, she was also keen that Ellen should see the house where C.G. Jung lived – something of "a shrine for my psychiatrist husband," she said. "It's on the other side of town in the harbour area. But Basel's a small city, and we can do the round trip in an hour, just have to change onto the number 8 tram." So off they went.

But the whole time Ellen was out sightseeing with Marthe-cum-travel guide, her mind was elsewhere. Her attention was on the people who passed by. On the men striding ahead of her. On the faces in trams and buses. On the crowds at tram stops and the people on benches. On the vaguest of hopes that Frank might be among them.

When Dr Zellweger arrived home early that Friday evening, he was still unable to give Ellen any further news of Frank. There had been no reports of anyone bearing the slightest resemblance to her missing husband. He seemed to have simply vanished off the face of the Earth.

Ellen stood in the lounge after dinner, contemplating the cheerless ambience of the erotic painting on the wall. And wondered how long her own cheerless situation would continue.

"Do you like the painting?" Dr Zellweger asked. Ellen jumped. She had not heard him follow her into the lounge. And she spun round with a faintly embarrassed smile. It seemed a provocative question, and she was not sure how to respond.

"I find it quite sad."

"My wife doesn't like the picture either. But she tolerates it. She thinks the lounge is not the place for such a picture and believes I hang it here just for the thrill. Simply to shock."

"And do you?" asked Ellen.

"It was painted by an old schoolfriend," he explained, ignoring Ellen's question.

He paused and gazed thoughtfully into the painting with the inquisitive expression of the psychiatrist that he was. He appeared to be carefully mulling over his next words, visibly conscious that his explanation so far was no explanation at all.

"We had lost touch a long time ago. Then a few years back he appeared at the clinic with his wife. A poor soul. She has been in and out of the clinic with depression ever since. I'm not sure why he gave me the painting. He said it was his way of thanking me for looking after his wife. But I'm not so sure. It did not seem quite appropriate at the time, and I didn't want to accept at first. But eventually I agreed because it makes me think of Jack and his wife. Their story. And so it hangs here to remind me not only of them, but of all my patients and the stories they struggle with each day."

He turned his gaze from the painting to look at Ellen, as if considering her own story. And Ellen could not escape the telling concern in his expression. Fortunately, her growing discomfort was interrupted by the intrusion of his wife.

"Is he trying to persuade you of the deeper significance about that picture?"

Like two synchronised swimmers, Dr Zellweger and Ellen turned their heads to see Marthe enter the room behind them.

"I was simply explaining the provenance of the painting to Mrs Goss," said Marthe's husband.

"Urs, why do you still insist on being so formal? I'm sure Ellen would prefer to be addressed by her first name."

Ellen smiled. But said nothing.

"You forget that Mrs Goss's husband is still my patient," Dr Zellweger reminded Marthe. "As long as that remains the case, I think it best that we respect the normal formalities."

"But that shouldn't stop her joining us tomorrow," Marthe insisted.

"Tomorrow?" Ellen asked, and cast a probing look first at Marthe then at her husband.

"Urs has a protégé out in the country and tries to visit on Saturdays whenever possible."

Dr Zellweger did not enjoy his private affairs being placed on display. The smile on his lips betrayed a slight unease. But his words gave nothing away.

"We will be taking a short drive up into the hills," he explained, turning to Ellen. "And of course, if you would like to join us tomorrow, Mrs Goss, you would be very welcome."

Marthe gave Ellen a conspiratorial smile.

"Do you have some sturdy shoes with you?" she asked.

Ellen gave a quizzical shake of the head.

"Never mind. It looks as if we wear the same size, so I can let you have a pair of mine."

The next morning brought patches of blue to a sky that had been relentlessly grey ever since Ellen's arrival a week before.

"The perfect day for a trip to the country," said Marthe, pulling the door of the BMW shut as she climbed into the passenger seat and cast a glance at Ellen behind her.

Driving drove out of the city on that chilly Saturday morning, Ellen was struck by the number of houses that had their windows wide open and bedding draped over the window sills. Even in the depths of winter. They greeted Ellen like welcoming flags, as she rode through the outlying villages and into the rolling forested hills of the Jura. The moment she saw the fields begin to open up around her on either side of the car, Ellen felt her sense of heaviness start to lift. It was as though the city that held Frank somewhere in its oppressive grip had released her for a momentary reprieve.

As if to underscore this feeling of release, Marthe stretched forward to switch on the radio and filled the car with a familiar sound. 'Lola' by the Kinks. Ellen sensed an uncontrollable smile unfold across her face. The song put her in mind of

Putney Bridge, walking arm in arm with Frank, her head on his shoulder, drinking the sweet smell of his body.

"I love this song," Marthe grinned over the back of her seat to Ellen, abruptly breaking up those precious memories.

Ellen was taken aback by the glee in her voice. She had seen Marthe as a woman with a taste for Debussy or Mahler. Something classical at least. It seemed to Ellen strangely out of place, this music that conjured images of London life from Muswell Hill to Soho now blaring out over the quiet, sweeping hills that ran along the border with France. It made her feel oddly uncomfortable. But perhaps this came more from the sense of tension she picked up between Marthe and her husband, when Dr Zellweger reached out his right hand and turned down the volume. Ellen could not see the expression on his face, but she felt that it was one of disapproval.

After some twenty minutes and a winding climb into the hills, they turned into the spacious elongated square of a village. Dr Zellweger brought the car to a halt in the centre of the square opposite a long, low-roofed farmhouse. And Ellen sensed a sigh of relief in the driver's seat when the radio went silent.

The near end of the square, on the left, was dominated by a large three-storey building with late nineteenth-century flair. The words Hotel Jura were emblazoned over the door. Looming over the far end of the square, to their right, stood the gleaming white, neoclassical façade of what was plainly a place of worship. Dropped here amid the forested hills, it seemed oddly out of place and took Ellen by surprise.

Marthe climbed out of the car, exchanging a few words with her husband that Ellen was unable to understand.

"We get out here," Marthe said. "And take a walk while Urs goes to see his protégé."

Ellen dutifully followed and closed the car door behind her. Dr Zellweger gave a smile and waved, before motoring off to see his mysterious protégé.

"Would you like to see the basilica first?" Marthe asked and then, without waiting for an answer: "Afterwards we can take a walk over to the next village and maybe have lunch."

Ellen simply nodded.

"This is a very special place. La Notre Dame de la Pierre," Marthe said, extending an arm in what seemed a demonstrative expression of pride. "It was built originally to mark a miracle that is supposed to have happened here hundreds of years ago. There's a beautiful grotto under the church that was carved out of the rockface to mark the spot where it occurred."

"Who's this protégé of your husband's?" Ellen asked. She felt disinclined to go along with Marthe's attempts to play the travel guide. It irritated her intensely while Frank remained missing somewhere along their sightseeing trail. But she tried not to let it show, and added politely:

"Or would that be an indiscreet question? I have the impression that he doesn't want to talk about it."

"In a sense perhaps the protégé is as much a patient as anything else," said Marthe. "So his silence is probably more a case of professional confidentiality."

There was a long pause as they continued towards the basilica, before Marthe added:

"Patient is not quite the right word either. A few years ago, Urs worked at a clinic in the east of the country. There was a Yenish boy there called Stefan. And Urs took him under his wing."

"Yenish?" Ellen gave Marthe a searching look.

"They're like Roma people. Travellers. There are quite a lot in the east of the country, where Urs comes from. A small town close to Lake Constance. While he was qualifying as a psychiatrist, he gathered a lot of practical experience at a clinic there. That's where he first met Stefan. He found him extremely subdued and apathetic. Over time, he learned more about the boy's background. He had apparently been taken into care for some reason that was not clear. It happened with a lot of Yenish children at the time. Still does occasionally. I don't know the full story. But Urs says the family where he was placed treated him very badly. They worked him extremely hard. And like any boy in that kind of situation, Stefan rebelled. He became difficult to handle. So the family complained, and he was admitted to the clinic for what they called conduct disorder.

"The more he came into contact with Stefan, the more he realised that the boy probably had no place in the clinic at all. He also suspected that his colleagues were using Stefan and other patients to test a new drug. But he was a junior and had no access to any evidence. Later on, Urs moved to the clinic here. But he never forgot Stefan, and often returned at weekends to visit him. Eventually, he became so concerned about the boy that he suggested they stop his treatment and let my husband bring him back here, where he knows a good family that would look after him. So Urs comes out here as often as possible to check and make sure everything is all right."

"That's very noble. My Frank says a lot of very caring, humanitarian things. But it's all talk really. He just sits on the fence most of the time. I'm sure he would never give up so much of his free time for such a noble cause."

"It's just how things work in this country. They try to instil a strong sense of solidarity into you from an early age," Marthe explained with a carping edge to her voice when she added: "But not everyone absorbs these things quite as completely as Urs. He's always so absolutely thorough and precise in everything he does."

"What's Stefan like?" Ellen asked, ignoring this hint of censure.

"I couldn't tell you. I've never met him."

By now, they were walking through a long tunnel of a corridor that led down and under the basilica. The lighting was subdued. And the ambience of the corridor perfumed with frankincense began to claw at Ellen's throat. When they reached the top of a steep and seemingly endless flight of a narrow enclosed wooden staircase down the side of the craggy rock face, she became instantly giddy, sensed her legs begin to give way beneath her. And she reached for the railings to steady herself.

It put her in mind of her Catholic boarding school and the steps leading down to the basement. The punishment room where the nuns would relish doing God's work and locking girls in isolation for twenty-four hours without food or drink. Even the slightest deviation from their bizarre rules was deemed worthy of this torture.

"Marthe," she said, "do you think we could leave this out? I have a real problem with places of religious devotion."

Marthe held her by the arm. A look of concern in her eyes.

"Of course. Let's get some fresh air," she said. Then added with a teasing air of mystery: "As a godless woman, you probably just sensed the spirit of the prayer crusaders."

She was plainly expecting the puzzlement - though perhaps not the slightly wounded look - which etched itself into Ellen's face and, after the briefest of pauses for dramatic effect, she explained:

"Basel was a melting pot of socialists, communists and freethinkers around the turn of the century. And for a long time after. The Catholic Church believed their atheism was such a danger that some of the more conservative priests here decided to fight it with a 'prayer crusade'. So, every first Wednesday of the month, thousands made the pilgrimage here to pray against what they called the 'godless movement' in the city.

"And it's now a tradition," Marthe added. "They still do it today."

"I'm not an atheist," Ellen insisted, as they left the basilica and walked out onto the square. "I just don't like the Catholic Church."

"That's all right," Marthe said, touching Ellen's arm in a gesture of reassurance. "You don't have to justify yourself to me."

Walking out of the village, Ellen was entranced by the way the surrounding fields were peppered every so often with patches of sunlight as gaps opened up in the scudding cloud.

When they reached the top of the hill and Ellen looked back down on the village, her heart leapt at the majestic sight of the basilica against the dull, grey-brown winter background. For all her aversion to the devotional spirit that religion imbues in its followers, she felt quite uplifted by the gleaming whiteness of the church's neoclassical façade. It stamped its presence on the landscape with such beautiful confidence. Ellen sensed a tingling warmth course through her veins at the very sight of it, which surprised her.

"Are you feeling better now?" Marthe asked.

"I'm fine," Ellen replied, taking in a deep breath of fresh air. "It's so beautiful lying there beneath us in the valley. Churches can be so impressive from a distance. As long as I don't get too close."

Marthe smiled. Ellen was not sure whether this was out of understanding or simply tolerance. And the chiaroscuro effect of the light on her face, clouding the expression in her eyes and the definition of her lips, lent an added layer of mystery to the smile that was compounded by the tantalising way in which Marthe stretched out a hand with the words:

"Come on. We're now crossing the border."

Ellen obediently turned and followed.

"Into France," Marthe added.

On the crest of the hill across the border, the ancient ruins of a castle were silhouetted against the sky. A handful of houses sprawled at the foot of the hill beneath the ruins. It was a ten-minute walk down to these dwellings. As they approached, Ellen could see no sign welcoming them to the hamlet with anything that resembled a name. And the street showed no sign of life. The anonymity perversely put her in mind of Frank and underlined her own sense of emptiness. On the packed streets of the city it was possible to imagine that she might bump into Frank at any moment. That he could not be far away. But here, the solitary emptiness of the street merely accentuated his absence. Ellen felt a shudder through her entire body.

"Urs will be meeting us in the village further down the hill," Marthe said as they passed an unpretentious building on the left. "So we can have lunch in here on the way back before we meet."

The only thing indicating to Ellen that it could be an eatery of any kind was a small, slightly shabby sign on the building with the words *au chasseur*. It told her game was likely to be on the menu.

"But first I want to show you the view from up there," she added, pointing to the castle ruins. "But we must take care. It can be quite dangerous."

The danger Marthe referred to lay in the loose stonework of the ruined walls and doorways. So they trod gingerly along the pathways towards what must once have been the keep. But for Ellen, a far greater sense of menace hit her when they climbed the stairs and, reaching the top, entered the central tower, where they were instantly plunged into pitch darkness. She could see nothing ahead of her.

"Take my hand," said Marthe and stretched her right arm back behind her for Ellen to grasp her hand.

Ellen had never been good in the dark. As a child, she had always felt the need to sleep with a light on outside her bedroom, so that at least she would catch a glimmer of light if she woke in the night. But here there was nothing. A complete and absolute absence of any luminescence. Ellen was struck by a brief moment of panic – until she felt Marthe's soft yet reassuring grip. As they moved through the passage, Ellen was totally dependent on the guiding hand of Marthe, who appeared to have some preternatural awareness of any obstacles ahead of them.

So evidently familiar was she with the terrain that she almost moved too fast for Ellen, who preferred to inch very slowly forward, feeling her way cautiously along the wall with her left hand as her right kept threatening to lose touch with Marthe's hand. There was a damp mustiness in the air that clawed at her throat. And made the going even slower. It seemed like an eternity before eventually a faint glow emanated from somewhere on the right. Like the glimmer of light she had been so dependent on at night as a child. It revealed the vague outline of broken stones ahead, making progress easier for Ellen. As Marthe guided her closer to the light, she saw that it shone down a narrow stairway from above. Still holding Ellen by the hand, Marthe led her up these steps.

As they both followed the upward twists and turns of the stairway, the glimmer of light grew steadily brighter, making the steps ever simpler for Ellen to negotiate. And as she let go of Marthe's hand, her companion suddenly leapt the last few steps ahead of her and out onto the very top of the castle ruins. Ellen quickly followed. And felt a staggering sense of release as she surveyed the magnificent vista and breathed in the fresh, clean air.

Behind her to the south, they remained nestled in the forested hills of the Jura, which continued their steep upward trajectory and blocked out any further view. It was plain that this castle must have once been an important defence against marauding hordes from the north, for there before her she had the world at her feet. A panorama that seemed to stretch to infinity.

"It's quite cloudy today, but you can just make out the hills of the Vosges over there," said Marthe, her guiding hand now become the needle of a compass pointing northwest. Then swinging forty-five degrees to the right: "And those dark hills rising behind the city are the Black Forest in Germany."

Ellen paid little attention to the dark hills in the far distance and the grim shadow of cloud that swept over them like a menacing scythe. Her thoughts were on the city below. In the veiled haze, it was barely visible between the rolling hills of the foreground and the bulging highlands on the horizon. But somewhere lost beneath that veil was Frank. She found it so hard to get her head around this idea.

"I can hardly see the city," she said. "It's just swallowed up by the mist and the hills."

"This is Switzerland, Ellen. We don't build high. We carpet the cities with houses, squat apartment blocks, and tunnels," Marthe added. "With all our mountains, we're very good at tunnels. We like to stay close the ground. It's all part of the safety-first mentality. Hundreds of years ago, the city was destroyed by an earthquake. Perhaps that also explains it a little."

"But what I find so hard, Marthe, when I look over at the city devoured by the mist is that Frank is somewhere there, swallowed even deeper, out of sight. I can see the mist, and I know he's there, but I can't see him. And I just can't believe that he can go missing like that."

Marthe took her hand and squeezed it gently. Ellen thrilled at the first tingle of comfort she had felt in what seemed an eternity, until the sudden roar of an aircraft cruelly dashed this sense of respite before it could even take hold. She glanced up to see what she recognised as a BEA plane veering off westwards as it climbed into the sky.

"That's your flight to London," said Marthe. "I'm sure you will be on that plane with Frank very soon."

The image of Frank pulling the door to as he left for the airport just a week ago had etched itself into Ellen's memory. His mop of thick brown hair and those dark brown eyes peering back around the door as he went. Why had she not gone to Heathrow with him to see him off? She had imagined he would be back home in a few days. But was that sufficient reason to make the excuse that his flight was far too early for her to get up just to see him off? Ok, it might have been his suggestion, but she did not have to go along with it.

All these thoughts were now brought to plague her by the memories that the plane evoked. She watched it veer ever further to the north. And caught the flashbacks of Frank that trailed in its wake. So vivid. Like effigies from a lost civilisation that she could touch, but knew they were no longer part of her life. A cold shiver ran through her body, and she felt quite faint.

"Do you think we could go back down now?" Ellen asked. "I'm getting quite dizzy up here."

The prospect of the trek back through the dark filled her with dread. But it was nothing to the harrowing image of Frank at the door that still hovered over her conscience.

"Of course," said Marthe, taking Ellen by the hand. "You'll find it better going back. Return journeys are always easier."

The two of them descended back down into the black interior of the tower. Marthe was right. It was easier going. But as they approached the light that marked their exit from the darkness, she let go of Ellen's hand. Ellen stopped in her tracks. Petrified of moving an inch further. She looked at Marthe now standing in the arched doorway. The silhouette of her figure against the outside light morphed into an image of Frank. He stood there on the threshold, taunting her.

She called out "Marthe!" in the hope it would shake the image from her mind.

Marthe turned, took a few steps back and reached out her hand to Ellen.

"It's all right. You're almost out now."

Holding on to the soothing warmth of this guiding hand, Ellen gingerly followed Marthe out of the tower and down the steps to the safety of ground level. The walls that now rose above them, though crumbling, gave Ellen a sense of comfort. It was a feeling reaffirmed by the surrounding trees and bushes, which seemed to have grown all the closer now – as if to protect her – on the walk back down around the outer walls. She caught the hint of smoke from a log-burning stove that told her the hamlet could not be far off. This added to her growing sense of ease, until she was startled by an almighty crack.

Ellen screamed. And stopped in her tracks. The violence of the impact as the stone smacked against the rock just ahead of Ellen, missing her by inches, left her trembling and breathless.

"My God!" Marthe yelled, flashing a look of shocked concern back at Ellen, then looked up at the tower that now loomed above them to see where the masonry had come from.

"That could have killed you!"

Ellen stood stock still. Unable to speak.

"I did say it was dangerous," Marthe added, "but I've never seen such a huge stone fall here before."

She took Ellen by the hand.

"Come on. You could do with a stiff drink. The *Chasseur* is only a few minutes from here."

"Could we go straight on to the village instead, where Urs is meeting us?" Ellen asked, her voice still breathless. "I would just like to get away from here.

"Of course," Marthe replied. "We're not due to meet until about three. But there's a nice little restaurant there where we can get something to eat."

It was a good fifteen minutes down into the village. When they eventually arrived, Ellen's nerves were still frayed from the falling masonry and the images of Frank still speaking to her from the back of her mind. She looked forward to sitting down with Marthe for a drink. The weekend hikers were out in force for their country walk, so the restaurant was already quite full, but they found a table in a far corner.

"I would recommend a veal sausage in an onion sauce with *rösti*. And a glass of Dôle. Do you like red wine?" Marthe asked.

Ellen nodded.

"Then let's make that a bottle."

"Santé," Marthe added at last, raising her glass once the waitress had poured the wine. "You had quite a shock up there. This should do you good."

She rested a comforting hand on Ellen's as they drank. The gladdening warmth of this gesture both enthralled and disconcerted Ellen in equal measure. A confused blurring of emotions that left her pondering their drift.

Chapter 8

The Hotel St. Gotthard lay in a side street close to the railway station. For an early Monday morning the central square in front of the station seemed especially lively. Frank Eigenmann preferred to avoid stations even at the best of times – but today the throng of travellers reminded him all too vividly of all the other parts of the world he might be in at that moment and of his good fortune to enjoy the safety offered by this station in particular.

Frank had not told Achim he would be calling on him that morning. But his old friend did not seem surprised to see him. After their tense reunion, Frank was a little apprehensive. He wondered how he might be received if he turned up unannounced. But Achim seemed genuinely pleased and welcoming.

Gertrude had taken the two baby boys to the zoo, he explained, while he sorted things out. Maybe it was this brief parole from his responsibilities that made him appear less anxious, less ill at ease. Or perhaps it was Frank's obvious disappointment over their meeting in the restaurant that prompted him now to make a special effort on his behalf.

"Here," he said.

Fishing deep into the same mysterious rucksack which he had carried with him earlier and which he now took from the wardrobe, Achim pulled out a bottle and held it enticingly up for Frank to admire.

"Gerti hates me drinking this stuff, but whenever I'm in Alsace, I feel duty bound to buy a bottle. And since we have something to celebrate, I'm sure she won't object, even at this hour on a Monday morning."

Achim leaned the rucksack against the table, took the two tumblers that stood by the washbasin and poured a measure of the liquid with slow precision into each glass. Then handed one to his old friend.

"Here's to us." He tossed the drink back with infectious enthusiasm. Frank followed suit. And Achim watched his expression intently for every nuance of reaction.

"Don't you find it exquisite?" he asked, when Frank failed to respond. "The very best Mirabelle brandy that money can buy."

"Hmm" was all Frank managed in reply as he concentrated on savouring the elixir. He was impressed, but felt that Achim had misinterpreted the non-committal hum of satisfaction.

"My dear Frank," he said. There was a genuine edge of concern in his voice. "I do hope you didn't get the idea that I wasn't pleased to see you the other day, because nothing could be further from the truth. In fact, nothing's given me so much pleasure for a very long time. But we've been through a lot lately. And then the exhausting journey from Berlin. Even the sight of my dear friend couldn't possibly compete with the promise of a night's peace and quiet in a friendly hotel bed."

"I never had any such impression," Frank lyingly reassured him. "I can quite understand how difficult it must have been."

"How could you even begin to understand?" Achim replied in a tone that came across as a rebuke, but spoke of inconsolable pain. "To start with, you're not Jewish."

The way he said it came almost like a slap in the face. And Frank retaliated.

"So you think Jews have a monopoly on suffering?"

"Today, yes. Absolutely."

Frank was taken aback by the conviction of his friend's reply, but said nothing.

"I sometimes get the feeling that we've come to symbolise the guilty conscience of the entire human race. All man's basest desires. Everything that humankind is unable to come to terms with. That's why we have to suffer."

He turned to the window, looked out onto the street, and appeared to lose himself in his thoughts. It was some time before Frank broke the silence.

"You amaze me, Achim. I've never even thought of you as Jewish before. In fact, in the past you were not even averse to cracking the occasional antisemitic joke. And now here you are talking of 'we'. I had no idea you felt so strongly."

"Nor did I, until those gangsters in government started spouting their hatred and contempt."

He fell into a pensive silence. And before he was able to stir himself from his thoughts, Frank went on to relate his experience in the wine tavern a few evenings earlier.

"You know, I was sinking a large quantity of *pinot gris* the other night. On my own. The place was quite empty. This man comes in and sits down at the table next to mine. Unashamedly queer, probably on the pick-up, and quite obviously Jewish. For me he was the epitome of so many Jews. But you're so utterly different. In many ways you're totally unjewish. So why do you feel so strongly?"

Achim smiled. It was a smile that came with a slight wince in his expression. "You see what's happening to us my friend?"

"Come on, Achim. Don't start these cryptic comments."

He was beginning to irritate Frank. He appeared so strangely smug in a way that did not fit with the Achim he knew.

"All right, Frank. Let me give you an example. I've been reading a book recently, a pseudophilosophical work by Rudolf Kassner. Maybe you know him?"

Frank shook his head.

"He's a writer of essays. A thinker. A culture critic if you like. Much revered by poets. He's published erudite writings on the Romantic poets and painters of England, like William Blake and the Pre-Raphaelites, as well as fascinating pieces on Indian idealism and the morality of music. The man is embarrassingly well-read, well-informed and articulate – a model of our civilisation. This book I've been reading was published a few years ago, just as the mindless masses were sweeping their Führer to power. It's a very learned book and rambles evasively through the author's highly abstruse theories on what he calls 'physiognomics' – something he's constructed as a means of classifying the character of people, for example by the shape of the face. At one point, early in his book, he describes what he calls the 'phallic' face. Let me just quote what he says."

Achim went over to the bedside table and picked up a book lying beneath the light.

"It's incredible. Just listen to this," he said and started to read: "'Another variant of the phallic face is that of the money type (commoner amongst Jews than amongst other races), which is not to be confused with the mean type. The money type with his round, spherical, unfinished, overgrown money-face is not at all mean, or is just as wasteful as he is mean and greedy. This is a very modern face which has developed gradually with modern capitalism, the stock exchange, share prices and so on. A face without substance, like coins or bank notes are without substance…' And so it goes on."

There was a quiet rage in his voice and a hint of disgust drawn on his lips as he threw the book on the bed.

"This man is educated, a writer and intellectual, a man of culture revered by poets, playwrights and professors. A man with sensitivity and an awe-inspiring mind. And yet he writes trash like this. So corrupted is he by the zeitgeist that he's become a mouthpiece of official dogma, disseminating lies for which he's unwittingly helped to contrive a fashionable camouflage with an uncomfortably respectable semblance of truth about it.

"And we, Frank, are no better," he continued. "We're just as corrupt in our own way. We've absorbed all the lies, drawn our conclusions, and – whether we realise it or not – we've all taken sides. It's inevitable, I suppose."

"You're quite wrong, Achim," Frank said, when he finally found a sufficient pause to intervene. "I've definitely not taken sides. And I'm not the only one, I'm sure."

Achim slowly poured himself another Mirabelle brandy, without looking to see whether his old friend was in need of one.

"Then these are sad bloody days for humanity," he muttered, "because it's about time you did. There are moments in life, Götz, when you can't just sit on the fence, but have to decide. There are things about which you can never be in two minds."

He tossed the drink down his throat, leaned his head on the back of the chair, and stared into space.

Achim's words stung and left him smarting all the more by the calculated use of Frank's given name. A name that Frank so loathed. He knew Achim was right. In the uncomfortable silence that ensued, Mirabelle brandy was the only remedy to paper over the cracks they opened up in his conscience. He stood up and walked over to the table, where the half-empty bottle stood. He refilled both glasses. Turning to hand a glass to Achim, he knocked the rucksack that was leaning against the table leg. It gave a thud as it hit the floor.

Frank held out the glass for Achim.

"What else have you got in there?" he asked, nodding at the rucksack. "Apart from Mirabelle brandy?"

"I was sixteen when my uncle Max first introduced me to the stuff," Achim said, ignoring his friend's question. There was a mild sigh in his voice, which Frank was unable to identify. "It was the first real summer after the Great War. I'd been sent off to stay with my uncle in Alsace. An amazing character. One of life's survivors – you had to be, living in Alsace in those days. He had a gammy leg. I was never told why. There were many things about Uncle Max we didn't talk about. But that leg probably saved his life. He would certainly never have volunteered for service, and he would have refused to be conscripted. Not that he was a pacifist. He was just unable to take sides. He had a lot in common with you, Frank."

Achim smiled as he savoured the brandy.

"Actually," Achim continued, "he had very little in common with you. But in that one respect, the way you refuse to take sides, you remind me very much of Uncle Max. In every other detail, he was not like anyone else I've ever known.

"He lived on the edge of a small town in a region near here called the Sundgau, where he eked out a sparse living as a sculptor. You'd be surprised what a fertile breeding ground it is here for sculptors. Did you know that the creator of New York's Statue of Liberty was from this region and that one of his other monuments stands just around the corner from this hotel? Of course, poor old Uncle Max didn't make it to such dizzy heights. But perhaps I loved him all the more for his failures as a sculptor. It just added to his charisma. Certainly, the monolithic shapes that stood sentry in his atelier nurtured an insatiable fascination. Of course, nobody at war is interested in art anyway. By all accounts he suffered unimaginable hardship, until circumstances moulded him into such a master of survival that, by the end of the war, he had become one of his town's wealthiest citizens.

"It had apparently been an open secret that he was involved in smuggling during the war, but most people turned an indulgent blind eye to it. After all, they enjoyed the benefits of what he was able to bring across the border with him from Switzerland. And those who felt unable to ignore his illegal activities were simply too dull to catch him at it. Perhaps if they had realised at the time what a fortune he was amassing, the silent majority would have been less indulgent, because when the war ended and it eventually emerged just how affluent he had become, there was a lot of resentment and envy. Even as an insensitive sixteen-year-old I could feel it in the village when I visited him. Of course, this only heightened my fascination for him. And when he let me into the tales of his smuggling exploits, and even took me with him one weekend on a nostalgic tour of all the crossing points along the frontier, the spell was complete."

"Is this why you picked out that place to meet the other day?" Frank asked.

"Absolutely. The frontier there is a rabbit warren of easy access routes. Almost invisible. And served by a little railway that carries you straight to the anonymous heart of this city. It seemed perfect."

"Why all this cloak-and-dagger stuff, Achim? Why this need for anonymity?"

He looked across at Frank with an intensity that hinted almost at a trace of animosity.

"I can't afford the mistake of being too honest. Otherwise I'd run the risk of being kicked back across the border. And the family with me." He poured another drink. "I came down a few months ago, you know. Before I got your letter. But the Basel police refused me entry. I don't know why. Was never given any explanation. Someone suggested that they'd probably used up their annual quota for Jews and couldn't risk letting any more in for fear of stoking antisemitism. Strange people the Swiss. They like to stay aloof, but they sometimes seem a little too keen on enabling our own gangsters in government."

Achim sipped from his Mirabelle brandy as he contemplated this story. Then added:

"So, I just felt this back door would be safer. And our crossing point is in a different canton, too, so if there had been any checks there, they wouldn't have had any record of the Basel police rejecting me. I learned a lot from Uncle Max. Or maybe it's just in the blood."

At that moment, the phone by the bedside rang. Achim looked nervously at his watch. Then picked up the receiver. The conversation was short and almost monosyllabic. When he put down the receiver as nervously as he had picked it up, Frank's curiosity was suitably primed. But it was not about to be satisfied.

"I'm sorry, Frank, but we'll have to bring this delightful binge down memory lane to a close." He lifted the bottle and held it up against the light of the window. It was already half empty. "Under the circumstances, it's probably just as well," he added, a gleaming smile in his eyes.

He put the bottle back on the table and picked up the rucksack that still leaned against the table leg.

"So, what precious cargo do you have in there?" Frank asked again, gesturing towards the rucksack. "You never did tell me."

Achim gave no reply. He plainly did not want his old friend to know. Nor was he prepared to disclose where the telephone call was taking him. He let Frank accompany him only as far as the square in front of the Central Station. Then insisted they part, saying he needed time to think. But either he had not reckoned on his friend's curiosity or his preoccupations had blinded him to the possibility that his odd behaviour might make Frank suspicious.

The gut of the avenue leading away from the station was lined with bushes and trees. The shrubbery and the archway created by the dense, leafy boughs above formed a dark tunnel that gave Frank the cover he needed, allowing him to avoid any backward glances from Achim. And it occurred to Frank at that moment that there was something disturbingly ludicrous about this whole situation. He asked himself: 'Are we both paranoid? Or does all the madness lie with me?'

When he saw that Achim was approaching an opening on the tree-lined avenue ahead that widened out onto a large square, he quickened his pace so as not to lose him. Until his old friend stopped beside a fountain that stood close to this opening. He looked about. Frank dodged behind a bush. From here he watched as Achim plunged his face and hands into the water as if to freshen up, then looked about again and carried on into the square ahead.

It seemed to Frank an odd thing to do in mid-winter. Was this a signal of some kind? Frank wondered. Or was there something special about the water?

But when he reached the fountain, it revealed nothing of significance – except for the black bronze crow that sat atop a pillar rising from the water basin. It glowered menacingly down on Frank as if feasting mentally on carrion below, pecking at it, drawing blood. He shivered in the sudden coldness of the avenue, turned his back on the bird and followed Achim out onto the square. But his old friend was gone.

It was only by chance that Frank regained sight of him when he tried crossing the square and was brusquely alerted by the bell of a tram approaching from the left. Frank pulled himself back smartly onto the pavement, glancing at the looming tram as he did so. It was then that he caught just a glimpse of Achim drifting off towards the centre of town. Frank promptly changed course, wondering whether Achim knew he was there and was trying to give him the slip. One thing was sure: wherever it was his old friend was heading, he was not taking the most direct route there.

They soon took another turn. This time to the right. And within a few minutes Frank was following him through the courtyard of the Museum of Fine Arts – a modern building of cool simplicity compared with the palatial, neoclassical monuments that passed for museums in other German-speaking cities.

Frank watched as his friend bought an entrance ticket with a fussiness that was unusual for him. When Achim eventually left the desk, ticket in hand, he disappeared into the cloakroom before emerging a short time later without his rucksack and then made his way up the staircase. Frank quickly bought a ticket for himself and followed on behind.

Journey's end proved to be the Holbein collection. Here Achim's stride shortened. He paced slowly along in front of the paintings. Yet it was a pace that was still too fast to absorb the fine detail in the portraits. And together with his frequent glances around the room, it betrayed a restless interest not so much in Holbein, but more in the other visitors to the museum – or perhaps to one particular visitor.

Frank's curiosity by this time was razor sharp, but he had to take great care not to let himself be seen every time his old friend swung a glance in his direction. This inevitably meant that he was unable to observe his every move. So, when Achim left this gallery and moved to the next one, a sinking sense of disappointment told Frank that he had probably missed the crucial moment. But when he entered the next room and regained sight of Achim, his patience was rewarded: in front of a familiar portrait of a man in a large floppy hat stood his old friend. And beside him a man about fifty years old. A tall, slim figure in a light grey fedora and trench coat. The two were engaged in a conversation that clearly had little to do with the painting on the wall. The discussion lasted no more than two or three minutes before Achim handed the stranger what looked like a key, and they then parted company. The tall stranger left through the door at the far end of the room. Achim continued to pace slowly past the Holbein portraits. Then followed through the same doorway a minute or two later.

Frank trailed behind at a discreet distance while his old friend made his way back down the stairs to the entrance, turned right past the ticket office and into the cloakroom. With little cover to conceal himself in the museum foyer, Frank found a pillar in the courtyard just outside, from where he could keep an eye on the cloakroom entrance. Hardly was he in position than he saw Achim emerge and walk out into the courtyard straight past Frank. What struck him as he watched his friend disappear out onto the street was that Achim no longer had his rucksack with him.

He was on the brink of abandoning his cover behind the pillar to follow Achim, when he caught sight of the tall stranger in the trench coat some fifty metres ahead, carrying a large Gladstone bag. Frank abruptly changed the target of his pursuit and followed the stranger out onto the street. For reasons he was unable to explain, he needed to know who the man was. And what was in the bag – especially since Achim now had no rucksack.

It was not clear to him how he would achieve this. He was a total novice in such games and felt utterly miscast. The man turned right towards the river when he reached the street, then crossed the road. Frank kept him in his field of vision while he considered his next move, then briefly lost him when the man turned left into a side street. Beginner that he was, he decided there was only one option and – without fully realising what he was doing – he quickened his pace to catch him up. Then took the plunge.

"Excuse me, sir," Frank said, touching the man's sleeve as he came alongside him. "Could you tell me how I get to the cathedral from here?"

He knew they were already moving in the direction of the cathedral and felt this would give him the opportunity to walk with the stranger and get him into conversation.

The man looked down at the hand on his sleeve. Then examined Frank with a studied expression. There was a coldness in his steely blue eyes and thin lips that Frank found disconcerting. When eventually the man spoke, his firm but gentle voice betrayed the accent of a cultured American.

"I'm going that way myself," he said. "You can come along with me. It's not far."

This was exactly the response that Frank had hoped for. Yet the man's openness unsettled him. It came across not as an invitation, but almost as a command. And lacking the warmth of any kind of a smile, it seemed a little too calculated.

"You're American," Frank said, brushing his disquiet aside. "And yet you know your way around here so well. Do you live here?"

"Yeah," was all that came in reply. Terse. To the point. Giving nothing away.

"Eigenmann," Frank said, offering his hand. "Frank Eigenmann." He knew it was a naive and clumsy move to disclose his identity like that. And he felt all the more stupid when the move was not reciprocated. The stranger's only response was to usher Frank across the street with a prompt of the elbow. Then he turned the tables.

"You're not from these parts yourself."

"You have a good ear," Frank said with an edge of surprise in his voice that an American was able to distinguish his Badisch German from the dialect spoken on the streets of this city. "I come from just over the border," he added.

The stranger processed this information with what seemed to Frank like an excess of care. Or was it suspicion?

As they approached the wall of red sandstone ahead that was the cathedral, the man again took Frank by the arm and nudged him to the right of the building. Manoeuvred into a cul-de-sac beside the minster, Frank instantly found himself thrust against the wall. And before he could catch his breath, he took the full force of a vicious, winding blow to the solar plexus. Pinned to the wall like a crucified dog, he could not even crumple to the ground to relieve his agony. The stranger pressed his face close to Frank.

"Who are you?" he whispered. The menace that came with his soft cultured accent was chilling. Frank gasped for breath. Unable to reply. The man tightened his grip and repeated the question over and over until Frank found the air to reply.

"Frank Eigenmann."

"You already told me that. So, what do you want with me, Frank Eigenmann?" The stranger tightened his grip further.

"I don't know what you mean."

"You don't know a lot of things, buddy. But you seem to know me, otherwise you wouldn't be tailing me. Now, I call that an unfair advantage, and I don't look kindly on people taking advantage of me. So, tell me something about yourself. And make it snappy. Who are you? What do you want from me?"

"I told you. My name is Frank Eigenmann."

"And?" he threw in quickly before Frank had a chance to pause.

"No 'and'," Frank said. "I don't know you from Adam."

At that moment he felt the grip on his left wrist relax just enough to wrench it loose from the American's hand. And with a ferocity that took even Frank by surprise, he propelled his fist into the man's groin. The angle was too narrow to make full impact. But the effect was enough to throw the American on the defensive. And as he released his grip on the right wrist, Frank buried his other fist deep into the solar plexus and brought his right knee up to meet the American's crumpling face. The man sank to the ground.

Time to make myself scarce, Frank told himself. He quickly ran his fingers through the man's pockets, removed a wallet with various papers, and made off around the corner past the cathedral. Estimating that the Gladstone bag would slow him down, he let it lie.

He had never imagined himself capable of common thuggery and theft. And he was surprised to find how much it elated him, how powerful the excitement was that urged him along on his flight through the streets. It was not fear. He had known fear, and it had paralysed him. This was different. This was pure galvanism. A stimulant to act and act fast. But he was in no doubt that the American would soon be hard on his heels. So, racing across the cathedral square and down Augustinergasse, he cut into an alleyway to the left that would take him quickly down into the marketplace and from there to the refuge of his hotel.

Once he reached the market square and – trusting that he had given the American the slip by now – he slowed to a walking pace so as not to attract attention. Turning to the right, he passed a department store that he had passed almost every day since he had been in this city. But at this moment, he was struck by a bill poster advertising the 'Will Hildering Dance Band Gold Stars with Lady Crooner' in the Globus Tea Room. That would be the perfect place to disappear for a while, he thought.

The dance band was not due to start for an hour, so he whiled away the time exploring the department store. Although he had passed it so often, he had never been inside. He had expected it to be full of ladies' fashion, so was surprised to be informed they had a tea room with a dance band. A further discovery that thrilled him once he was inside was the record department. It put him in mind of Patricia Roche's gramophone. With the thought of making a better impression the next time they met, he started browsing through the jazz records. There was an entire section devoted to Vocalion and Brunswick, and amidst the Benny Goodmans and Fletcher Hendersons he found just the thing. Billie Holiday – *These Foolish Things*. With a broad smile on his face, he took the record to the cash desk, paid the cashier and took himself off to the tea room.

He placed his purchase on one of the few tables still vacant, ordered a pot of tea and felt uncomfortably conspicuous as the roomful of prim ladies' eyes homed in on the only man in the room aside from Will Hildering and his band when they emerged onto the stage. But it seemed to him that the American would be unlikely to venture into a tea room full of middle-aged ladies in his search for the man who mugged him. So he remained there, sipping his tea for a good hour, until his pot was empty and cold. Then he made his way to the Hotel Storchen.

It was no more than a few minutes' walk to the hotel. Despite the relaxed interlude of music and tea, the excitement of his crime must have still been burning in his eyes. This at least was the only conclusion he could draw when he collected his key at reception and was greeted with a curious and anxious look from the man on the desk. It was only with the dubious advantage of hindsight that he realised the true reason for that anxious look.

How long the thugs had been waiting for him it was hard to say, but they had plainly made themselves at home in his room: one stretched out on the bed, one in the armchair by the window and another by the door to nail Frank as he entered – a feat the man accomplished with imposing effect. Before he had a chance to appreciate the mess they had already made in the room, Frank was pinned to the floor by a heavy insistent knee in the small of his back, while a rough hand pulled on his hair until he felt his scalp was about to come adrift or his neck about to snap. With the other hand, the man quickly ran through his pockets. If he was looking for a weapon, he was disappointed, but he seemed satisfied with the two wallets he found – Frank's own and the American's – which he tossed over to the ape still draped on the bed.

As if they were now done, the hand and knee withdrew. And Frank was just pulling himself to his feet when a crushing boot swung in from the right and sent him sprawling back on the floor with the words: "On your feet, scumbag. Someone wants to meet you."

No further words were exchanged. The three of them bundled him out of his room, down the corridor, out onto the street and into a car that was standing outside the hotel. The vehicle was all too familiar to Frank. It was the Maybach Zeppelin with those white-walled tyres. He was still a long way from getting the full picture, but some of the pieces in the puzzle were beginning to slot into place. And it was not looking pretty.

Chapter 9

They drove north for about fifteen minutes to a leafy suburb of the city, and must have been a stone's throw from the border with Germany when the car pulled up in front of a large fin-de-siècle house overlooking a park. It seemed to Frank the kind of place you would expect to see a brand-new Maybach in the drive.

It was an impression that left him feeling no less out of place than the evening in Berlin six months earlier, in the late summer of 1936, when a large section of the audience in the cabaret broke into the Horst Wessel song, and the rest of the audience joined in. That was the moment he decided it was time to leave. And here he was now, equally out of place and just arriving. Time appeared to have gone into reverse in a disquieting way.

The sense of unease was not dispelled when his escort led him into a cavernous lounge looking onto the park to meet his host. Quite the contrary: he grew more ill at ease merely at the sight of Willi Breitner in his white suit and two-tone shoes. There was a flash tackiness about the man who greeted Frank from his garish baroque armchair, right leg crossed over his left, as he puffed on a fat cigar. On the table beside him a half-drunk glass of cognac, a bottle of Rémy Martin and a cigar box.

He smiled a leering, supercilious expression in Frank's direction and gestured towards the only other chair in the room, the other side of the table.

"Take a seat Herr Eigenmann," he said. "Or should I call you Mr Silverstone?"

Frank was momentarily puzzled by the question, until he caught sight of his wallet lying on the table behind the cigar box alongside the wallet he had pilfered from the American. He gave no answer, sensing that the uncertainty around his identity gave him a slight edge. So, not wanting to squander this advantage, he said nothing. If this irritated Breitner, it did not show.

"Herr Eigenmann from Berlin or Mr Silverstone from Baltimore. Or possibly neither of those. It makes no difference. I'm not interested in who you are. It's what you do that interests me. Do you get my drift?" He took a puff on his cigar.

"Not exactly, no." Frank had always assumed this man to be German through and through. So he was taken aback by the slight Austrian intonation he detected in Breitner's accent.

"Then let me spell it out for you." He took a deep puff on his cigar. "You've been muscling in. I don't know why. And I don't want to know. It's enough that you do it. You see, I don't like jerks who pretend to be something they're not and then start interfering in my business and pestering my people."

Frank stared blankly at his host. He had no idea what this man was talking about. Willi Breitner leaned forward, stubbed out the cigar and fixed Frank with an almost manic stare that looked disturbingly close to becoming unhinged.

"Mademoiselle Roche, for example," he said almost in a whisper. "She's one of my people, you see. No, she's more than that. She's almost like a daughter to me. Almost," he added with his supercilious smile.

"Now, what's this?" he continued, as he picked up Frank's wallet and pulled out a carefully kept lock of blonde hair. "Do you keep a trophy of all your conquests?" Breitner asked, as he placed it back in the wallet, picked up the cigar box and offered Frank a cigar.

Frank declined, while his host stubbed out his cigar and took another for himself. He licked it, cut it and lit up with a relish that was just a little too studied to be convincing. But what he lacked in style he made up for in words.

"Herr Eigenmann, Mr Silverstone, or whoever you are, you need to understand there are limits. Boundaries you cross at your own risk. Now, I have many friends in very influential places. And they can make life very uncomfortable for people who cross those boundaries. Of course, I don't like to bother them with trivialities and prefer to handle my problems without such assistance."

"I had no idea until now that I *was* one of your problems," Frank interjected.

"You interfere in my life. You're a pest," his host insisted. "Are you a Jew?"

It was a rhetorical question. Not looking for an answer. But it stirred signs of vexation on Breitner's face. He visibly winced as he spoke the words. And grew increasingly agitated.

"Why is it so many of you congregate in this city ever since your Mr Herzl brought his Zionists here?" The grimace in his expression grew into a menacing sneer.

"Vermin like you need to be taught a lesson once in a while. But have no fear," he added ominously. "You are already well acquainted with some of my humbler friends – and you will find they are excellent teachers."

After a pause clearly intended to leave Frank enough time for those last words to be digested, Breitner rose from his chair.

"For the first part of the instruction, however, I intend to take personal responsibility. Come with me," he continued. The twisted menace underlying his host's surface magnanimity sent a chill through Frank that had his heart pounding as he obediently complied.

"I don't know what you've been told about me," Breitner said as he guided Frank out of the lounge. "Nor do I wish to know. Second-hand information is of no interest. It's as worthless as it is no doubt false. So, for the first part of your instruction, allow me to give you the benefit of some first-hand information about me. It will serve as a sign of my generosity, which I hope will sustain you through the second part. If it does not, that would be a pity, because I do feel it's important you know how generous I can be if you stay on the right side of me."

With the barely concealed threat of these words, he ushered Frank into a dining room prepared for a sumptuous feast. The walls were hung with countless paintings and drawings of erotic scenes and orgies that matched the lavish bacchanalian flavour of the food and wine set out on the table.

"I trust you had no plans for lunch today," he said, with a self-satisfied smile as he pulled out a chair for Frank, took a corkscrew in his hand and twisted it into a bottle of red wine. "Chateau Margaux 1926. An excellent year," he said as he poured two glasses and slid one along the table to Frank. "I think you'll find it quite agreeable."

"This of course is only half the pleasure," he added. "To get the best out of a good lunch, it is essential to have the right company."

Breitner moved over to a door at the far end of the room and eased it slightly ajar.

"Helga. Maria. Lunch is about to be served. Would you care to join us?"

His invitation had the tone of a command. And the force of his words was plain from the instantaneous appearance in the doorway of two young women. They displayed an uncanny ingenuity for seeming both overdressed and underdressed at one and the same time.

"Girls," Breitner announced, "I'd like you to meet Herr Eigenmann from Berlin or Mr Silverstone from Baltimore Maryland. We haven't yet made up our minds. But I have no doubt a little lunch and your charming company will help the memory cells."

The girls promptly seized on this chance to exhibit the other main feature of their collective personality and fell into a mildly hysterical giggle. Much to his own shame, Frank found it quite endearing. Maria – dark-haired, dark-eyed, the slightly more voluptuous of the two, with inviting curves and a provocative landscape of flesh rising over the low neck of her white satin dress – was the first to speak.

"Pleased to meet you," was all she said, betraying a twinkle of amusement in her expression as they shook hands.

Helga – red-haired, green-eyed, less curvaceous and less garrulous by nature than her friend, but every bit as sensuous with the sulphurous hint of an active volcano at rest – simply offered Frank her hand and a look that left him with an oddly disquieting thrill of expectation.

The role of Helga and Maria was, as Breitner put it, to provide the "right company" for their lunch. So Frank was not anticipating any contribution to the conversation from this company. And he received none. Conversation in fact proved a misnomer, monopolised as it was by the host. As to be expected from a Willi Breitner, he talked incessantly about himself with a nauseating and entirely unconvincing smugness. He gave Frank the impression of trying to conceal some deep sense of inadequacy by painting a picture of rampant virility and a towering career of achievement. He even claimed acquaintance with his Führer during his teenage years, talked with a chilling nostalgia of his days at school in the Upper Austrian steel town of Steyr – of how he and Adolf would often come out of school at lunchtime on a Saturday, head straight over the bridge to the town square and spend the rest of the afternoon in cafes or bars, drinking the cares of the week away; and as the evening wore on, how they would sometimes take a boat out into the gentle current of the Enns and spend the remaining hours of night-time on the river in communion with nature, a supply of bread and dripping, and a bottle of apricot brandy. It was not uncommon, he said, for one or both of them to be found next morning littering the riverbank or the side of a road leading into town.

It was impossible to say how much truth there was in the stories, but the picture of adolescent depravity that Breitner painted matched the image Frank had of the country's saviour and leader. It was still a complete mystery to him how an entire nation of people, from gardeners to bankers, could give itself with such enthusiasm to a man whose political skills appeared to consist in little more than loud-mouthed lies, self-aggrandisement and bigoted scapegoating. A man who came to power on a wave of intemperate, mendacious bullying and sustained his grip on their worship by systematically isolating the scapegoats and brutally eliminating any rivals. Yet still they adored him. Willi Breitner was no exception and showed every sign of being a model disciple.

Throughout the monologue, both Helga and Maria excelled in their roles as supernumeraries. Maria would contribute appreciative laughter every so often, while Helga cast occasional glances in the direction of Frank with a seductive power that was reinforced all the more by a contrived veneer of shyness.

As lunch drew to a close and they sat over coffee, Breitner suddenly – with a crass non sequitur that suggested it was as carefully planned as the lunch itself – swung the talk away from himself and on to Frank.

"What is your connection to Zimmermann Joachim?"

Frank was initially perplexed by the question, unsure who his host was referring to. He never thought of Achim in terms of his surname. And he could not recall anyone having ever used his given name in all its fullness.

"He's in the art business, I understand," Breitner said. "Are you in the art business?"

"He's an old friend. And he's a stage designer, if that's what you mean."

"Really?" The trace of a leery, dismissive smile spread across Breitner's lips as he studiously wiped the corners of his mouth with a napkin, folded it up very deliberately and set it down with careful precision beside his coffee cup.

"And you have no idea what your friend has done with Lola?" he asked. His voice loitered over the words 'no idea' as if gazing on them in disbelief.

"Who the hell is Lola?"

Frank had never heard the name before. Certainly not among any of the circles Achim moved in.

Breitner watched Frank with an inscrutable smile on his face. And said nothing. He was enjoying the discomfort of his guest, the sight of him shifting nervously in his chair. He was sizing him up. Gauging his resistance.

"No matter," Breitner said, when he eventually broke the anxious silence. "We can discuss it some other time."

He reached for the brandy, poured two glasses and passed one to Frank.

"You know what I fail to understand about you people?" he continued, with an undisguised trace of meanness in his voice as he pushed the glass across the table. "It's the way you gather like ants in this particular corner of the Earth. Do you honestly imagine that the arm of the Third Reich is so short? We showed only recently just how easy it is to reach across the border and bring traitors and enemies of the people back to face justice."

"You're referring to the Berthold Jacob story," Frank said, recalling the conversation with Achim some days before. Breitner beamed a self-satisfied smile in reply.

"So, what sort of person do you think I am?" Frank asked. "Quite frankly, I've never seen myself as the enemy of anyone."

In reply, Breitner simply rose from his chair, the smile on his face now worn thin, and moved around the table to the buffet. His voice betrayed a threatening edge of irritation as he spoke:

"Come here," was all he said. It was sufficient. Frank complied and joined him beside the large Jugendstil sideboard with its beautifully bevelled mirror. He was feeling tense with anticipation of Breitner's next move. Close up, the features of his puffy face betrayed all the signs of dissolution Frank would expect in such a person. The lips pencil-thin. The lupine eyes a heartless stare. Frank almost had the sense that Breitner was reading his thoughts. He stepped back a little, as if to break any subliminal contact.

"I never trust people who insist they are speaking 'quite frankly'," Breitner declared.

Frank began to sense that Willi Breitner was getting down to business.

"Take a look in the mirror."

Frank turned to look at the mirror and saw Breitner's narrow lupine eyes staring back at him.

"What you see before you," he added with unconcealed feeling as he put a heavy hand on Frank's head and turned it to face directly into the mirror, "is one of the more wretched examples of our species."

'How right you are,' thought Frank. For the focus of his attention remained on his adversary, and he affected an uncomfortable smile as he stared back into those narrow eyes.

"You claim to be frank. Yet you're not even honest enough to admit where you stand. Or even what your true name is. You'd sooner crawl under stones and hide in shadows to survive. I don't know whether you pretend to be a socialist, a communist, or just a sympathiser. Maybe you're even a Jew. But we do know some of the people you mix with."

"I don't mix with anyone. I'm not the mixing type."

"You mix with Zimmermann. And that's not the kind of company I would recommend. At the same time you attempt to mix with Mademoiselle Roche. And that's the kind of company that can get you into serious trouble."

Breitner began to study his fingernails with a sinister attention to detail. "You see, you have choices. It's entirely your decision. But one thing is certain: it's a decision you must make sooner or later. I have tried in my own modest way to show you the kind of benefits you can enjoy if you decide to make the right choice," he added with a sweeping gesture over the sumptuous half-eaten feast on the table behind them. "Maria and Helga are rather less modest. But equally compelling."

These words were the cue for the two girls. As Willi Breitner moved back towards the door, they both rose from the table and sidled over to Frank. With a look of mischief in their smiles, they each took an arm.

"But do remember, my dear Mr Silverstone," he added, as he reached the door, "or is it Eigenmann? Take great care to consider these benefits. And weigh them carefully against the disadvantages when you make your choice."

These words, as calculated as the rest of the occasion, prefaced his departure. Without further comment, he left Frank with the menace of his razor-thin smile engraved on his guest's memory. And the dubious charms of Helga and Maria. They had a duty to perform and Frank could be sure they would do it in the thoroughgoing spirit of *Kraft durch Freude*.

They said nothing, just smiled, as they led Frank out of the dining room and up a wide, heavily banistered staircase. Maria on his right giggled now and then as they went, while Helga held rather more tightly onto his left arm as if afraid he might run. But he was sufficiently familiar with the Breitners of the world to know that there was little point in running. And since he was not entirely averse to the pleasures these two girls could offer, he saw no good reason not to let himself be led into the sumptuous bedroom that had been set aside for the occasion. This too was decorated with erotic scenes and orgies similar to those in the dining room.

It was easy to forget the menacing words of Breitner, as he watched the two of them disrobe each other, caressing like lovers as they did so, against the backdrop of these paintings.

"Which of us would you like to try first?" Maria cajoled, as Helga quietly teased her friend's satin lingerie down over her legs. Maria stepped out of this last remaining garment, while Helga sat back gazing up at her in admiration of her naked body.

"Perhaps he's the greedy type," Helga suggested. "Maybe he'd prefer to take both of us at once."

Now, finally divested of any shyness, as if this too was simply an article of clothing, Helga revealed herself as an unabashed lady of pleasure. Frank was enthralled by the transformation, but his excitement was mingled with all the inertia of nervous indecision. He felt like a fifteen-year-old confronted with the opportunity for his first carnal experience, uncertain whether he should seize it or whether – underneath it all – she was just making fun of him. His hesitation evidently amused them.

But this teasing interlude was brought to an ugly close when the bedroom door crashed open. The scene that greeted two of Breitner's gorillas when they crashed into the room brought an instant flicker of mirth to their faces that chilled Frank with their menace. A menace that was in stark contrast to the amusement he saw on the faces of both Helga and Maria, whose nervous giggles distantly echoed the ominous chuckles of Breitner's bullies.

"What do you make of this, Horst?" said the bigger one, throwing his words across the room as if he were tossing fish heads to a hungry cat. Frank fancied he could almost smell the fish on his hands.

"What I make of it? Well, I wouldn't care to say, Wolfgang. But since you ask, I'd say he doesn't much like our girls."

"Maybe he doesn't like girls at all," said the one called Wolfgang. His eyes lit up at this suggestion. And the insinuation brought more nervous giggles from Helga and Maria.

All at once Frank felt an arm around his shoulders.

"Is that right?"

It was the one called Horst. His leery smile could not have been closer to Frank's face. A faint hint of tooth decay filtered through on the warm breath. It made him want to heave. And his whole body tensed at the prospect of what was to come.

"Over here girls," said Horst, keeping his arm firmly round Frank's shoulders. Helga and Maria picked up their giggles from the bed where they had been sitting and moved eagerly in his direction. They were enjoying the sport. Horst removed his arm from Frank's shoulder and stepped aside.

"He's all yours, girls. Let's see what he makes of you."

With giggling deliberation, they set about disrobing Frank, layer by layer, down to the vulnerable quick of utter nakedness. Under any other circumstances he would have found the experience intensely exciting. But the hospitality of Breitner and his friends had successfully instilled a withering fear into his body. And it showed. Helga took his flaccid apology in her hands, stroked it and coaxed it. But it was unmoved. He heard Maria snigger. Then her friend cupped it in her hands, put her mouth to it, teased it with her tongue. And all the while Frank felt like an uncooperative patient waiting with embarrassment for the doctor's examination to end.

"Looks like I was right girls," said Wolfgang. There was a disturbing relish in his voice. "What do you reckon, Horst? You think we might stand a better chance?"

"It's worth a try," replied Horst, who at last appeared to show a genuine interest in his charge, as he gripped Frank's shoulders in a tight embrace. It was an interest that filled Frank with trepidation and disgust. And the demonstrative display that Horst made of his eagerness was met with the audible approval of both Wolfgang and the girls. Maria's squeals of delight were quite distinctive as Horst pushed Frank face down onto the bed and used his knees to force his legs as wide apart as they would go.

"Take a look at this, girls." The lust in Horst's voice turned Frank's stomach, but he was pinned down and utterly helpless. "Clean and fresh as a daisy in spring."

"What are you going to do with it?" Traces of Maria's giggle still lingered in her question. "You're not going to stick that in it, are you?"

Horst gave out a chilling laugh. Frank sensed both curiosity and disbelief in Maria's question.

The disbelief part of her reaction struck a chord in his swelling, swirling desperation, which had him fondly imagine that at least there was someone who was on his side – a pathetic straw in view of the vast flooding tide of humiliation that swept over him. He felt rough fingers run their own excited curiosity along his perineum.

Frank looked up to see Maria still standing over them. The expression of amusement had given way to nervousness, but her eyes continued to betray a lively curiosity in what was being done with him. The incredulity in her voice that he had clung to was nothing as compared with his own. He was on the brink of vomiting. His heart raced out of control. He sensed his entire body moisten with sweat as Horst came down on him, breathing his tooth decay over Frank's shoulder, as he brought the hard, hot flesh of his prick creeping up from beneath. Frank tensed.

"Shit!" Horst suddenly relaxed his designs on Frank and eased back. The sense of reprieve was immense. And premature. "It's too early in the day for deflowering such a tight little cunt. Let's make the virgin do his share of the work."

He stood up, pulling Frank to his feet with the help of Wolfgang. Together they instantly forced him onto his knees and brought him face to face with the ugly expressionless ogre of Horst's warped libido.

"Suck on this, my little virgin."

Utter nausea restrained him from making even the remotest gesture in that direction. He felt painfully mocked by Horst's apparent pride and joy that glared at him in its aggressive silence. He was riveted firmly into place by his disgust. And showed no sign of moving one way or the other – until a sharp blow to the side of his face that sent him reeling to the right.

"You heard what he said," growled Wolfgang, who then kicked him viciously in the thigh as he added: "Get to it."

Frank dragged himself back up onto his knees. He knew there was no way he could avoid their sport with him. He had to get it over with. Spontaneously he took the thing in his right hand – perhaps just to get the feel of it, to test it. The familiarity surprised him. Familiar because it could have been his own. And it was this that enabled him, by closing his eyes, to overcome his deep nausea and repulsion. With his eyes still firmly shut, imagining that – by some impossible contortion – it was his own, he placed it in his mouth and worked on it with all the clumsiness of a novice. The bizarre idea that it might be himself he was playing with triggered a disturbing reciprocation that had him visibly excited.

And the more electrified this reaction, the more real became his fantasy – much to the amusement of the onlookers, who saw in this a vindication of their judgement that, deep down, he preferred Horst to Helga. Not that this spoiled the girls' enjoyment of the sport. Frank caught their giggles clearly through all the foggy haze of the depravity – and the sudden gleeful roar of laughter when Horst's pleasure manifested itself in full. The hot sickly sensation that hit the back of Frank's throat hurled him back from the fantasy with a force that had him coughing and spluttering, choking on the floor, in utter degradation.

"Ach! *Scheisse*!" he cried. The words crawled with abject disgust.

He felt more wretched and tarnished than a disease-ridden dog. And was treated no better: the boot caught him square in the face, instantly washing away the sour pungency of Horst with his own sweet-tasting blood. It was impossible to count the number of teeth swimming around in this bath. And any interest in such detail was quickly kicked out of him by a second heavy boot to the solar plexus.

"No one does that to me and gets away with it." Horst barked. "Come on, Wolf. Let's get this filth out of here."

Frank felt each one grab him under an arm and haul him to his feet. He was barely conscious, but was aware of being dragged out through the door and bundled down the stairs. His battered, naked body slipped headfirst to the bottom and sank in a heap beside the dining-room door through which he had been so cynically ushered about half an hour earlier. His clothes landed on top of him where he lay. A wet pool quickly gathered under his head where the blood continued to pour from his mouth.

"You see what trouble you can get into when you find yourself on the wrong side of us."

All Frank could see through his barely conscious daze were two nameless feet in the doorway, right beside his face. But the two-tone shoes were sharp enough in their vulgarity to pierce even the thickest fog. And the arrogance of the voice that went with them was unmistakable.

"You came off lightly this time, because I asked the boys to treat you with respect. It could have been so much worse."

The two-tone shoes walked back and forth, mocking Frank as he lay immobilised by his pain.

"You find Lola for me, and you will find I can be a very generous man. But for now, you filthy little fairy, get up, get out of here and stay away from Mademoiselle Roche!"

These last venomous words were delivered with the toe of his right shoe propelled sharply into Frank's shoulder. A token gesture. It should have been the head. But Breitner would have wanted to avoid getting blood on his two-tone shoes.

Frank was not afforded the time to dress. Having arrived at the bottom of the stairs the slow way, Breitner's odd-job men now dragged him to the door and kicked him out into the refreshing chill of the afternoon air, tossing his clothes after him once again.

Chapter 10

After Breitner's crash course in compliance, Frank spent the next few days in his hotel room, nursing his injuries. He avoided the mirror for fear of what he might find. When he ran his tongue around the inside of his mouth, he was surprised to find that he still had all his teeth. Loose, but in place. Yet the bruises were slow to heal. And his dignity even slower. He skulked in his room, outraged, scared and vengeful – like a scheming injured rat. The entire negative spectrum of human sentiment occupied his every thought in the four walls of that room from where he had been dragged so rudely into his nightmare. He relieved the lingering pain in his jaw and ribs with a ready supply of wine. But his thoughts remained devoid of any constructive pattern.

His only consolation on getting back to his hotel room was the discovery that the record he had bought for Patricia Roche was still intact. But even this was not enough to lend any meaningful structure to his thoughts. Two strands of thinking preoccupied his mind, each as mystifying as the other: the paradox of why such an obnoxious misogynist as Breitner would insist on always referring to Patricia Roche with such respect as to call her Mademoiselle; and the question who the hell was Lola?

He remained cooped up with these questions wary of venturing out at least until the weekend. His left eye was still swollen, but had become more yellow than black. His mouth too felt misshapen by the multiple contusions and a deep gash in his upper lip. He knew he was not a pretty sight. But after the conversation with Breitner, he sensed that he could not leave it too long before contacting Achim.

It was mid-morning on the Sunday when he called at the hotel. It seemed a reasonable time to catch him in.

"He checked out on Wednesday, sir," the young lady on the desk informed him. "With his family."

Frank was stunned.

'How could he just check out without getting in touch?' he asked himself. 'And only two days after we'd last seen each other. Why didn't he tell me he would be moving on so soon? Maybe Breitner had got to him. Or did it have something to do with the mysterious Silverstone? Or the even more mysterious Lola?'

These thoughts flooded his mind in a torrent made all the fiercer and more urgent by the memory of Breitner's thugs still fresh in his bones.

"Do you know where they went?" he asked the receptionist. "Did they leave a message or a forwarding address?"

She simply shook her head and continued with the paperwork on her desk.

Having persuaded his friend to join him in this strange exile, as he saw it, Frank felt a sense of responsibility for him. Yet from the first moments of Achim's arrival, he had found there was no cause for any such sense of duty. On the contrary, he saw in his old friend a steely independence that both mystified and at the same time slightly irritated him. Irritated probably because he wanted Achim's dependence on him, and found that all along it had been he who was dependent on his old friend. Now, after all the promise Frank had nurtured before his arrival, his old friend was already gone again. And it was he who felt abandoned.

Out on the street, he spent the rest of his Sunday solitude wandering aimlessly through the city trying to fathom Achim's behaviour, wondering where he might have gone, why he might have gone and, above all, why in such secrecy.

The most constructive outcome of that lost day was the decision he made to move out of his hotel surroundings and to look for less extravagant lodgings. His resources were not unlimited. And with the Hotel Storchen clearly a familiar haunt for Breitner, the case in favour of an alternative had become all the more compelling.

It was when he considered crossing the river in the hope that he might find a room at the Kolping house that he was reminded of Achim.

'Perhaps that explains his disappearance,' he thought. 'Maybe he followed my suggestion and has gone to the Kolping house on the other side of the river.' This idea encouraged him all the more to head across the river the next day.

He rose early the next morning and, after breakfast, set off with an unaccustomed zeal in his step. Just in case they had no room at the Kolping house, he decided to stop at the nearest kiosk and buy the local newspapers. He'd be sure to find something in the classified ads for apartments or some offers of lodging. On the way, he passed an inconspicuous grocer's. Outwardly, the premises gave no reason to invite even a passing glance. It was presumably the reflex behaviour of a hunted animal that had him look through the window of the shop as he passed by.

His eyes were instantly greeted by a temptation he was unable to resist. His heart skipped a beat. He caught his breath. A tremor coursed through his body. As he opened the door, the bell above that sounded his entrance rang especially for Frank – and announced not only his excitement, but also the stark warnings of Willi Breitner.

She did not see him as he entered the shop and stood a few short paces behind her. Waiting. He watched while she recited her shopping list to the woman on the counter. A kilogram of Gravensteiner apples, a lettuce, and a camembert cheese. A modest shopping basket. Short and concise. Yet spoken in a voice which came to him like the gentle rippling cascade of a mountain stream and drenched him with the cool bewitching sweetness of its tone.

"That will be three francs seventy, please," said the woman on the counter, bringing Frank briefly down to earth.

Patricia Roche became very busy in her handbag as the humourless woman made no attempt to conceal her impatience. She kept her waiting hand demonstratively outstretched.

"Oh dear, I'm so sorry, I seem to have left my purse at home."

The despair and embarrassment in her voice vexed him. But what pained him more was the rudeness of the woman on the counter.

"And what do you expect me to do about it?" she asked. "Give it to you? I'm not a charity, you know."

"Here," Frank said, moving up to the counter and putting down four one franc pieces. "Let me help you out."

When Patricia Roche turned to identify her Samaritan, she looked both shocked and less than pleased. She hesitated. It was plain that she was about to refuse the offer.

"You can pay me back later," he added in an effort to pre-empt the refusal.

"Er, no. No, thank you," she said. There was a hint of resentment in her voice. She then turned to the woman on the counter:

"Would you put the items to one side, please? I'll be back later for them." With that, she hurried out through the door and did not give Frank so much as a look. He turned back to the woman on the counter.

"I'm sure you will take my money though, won't you?" he said, pointing to the four francs on the counter.

"What?"

"For the apples, cheese and lettuce," he added, pointing now to Patricia Roche's order.

"You can't have those," she said, dry and dour as ever, "they're reserved."

"In that case," Frank rejoined, somewhat baffled, "would you please give me a kilogram of Gravensteiner apples, one camembert cheese and a lettuce."

With a methodical sense of propriety that belied the unreasonable, crotchety impatience of the woman and completely blinded her to the nonsense of the scene, she gathered together the ordered items afresh and handed them to Frank.

"You can put the others back," he said, and left the woman to her ill humour.

"*Sauschwob*," she muttered, as he closed the door behind him. Frank ignored the insult. He had grown used to being called a German pig in this city, where his fatherland was generally held in pretty low regard. And not without reason, he had to admit.

The aim of Willi Breitner's brutal instruction course the previous week was clear. Yet now, as Frank hurried after the enchanting presence of Patricia Roche, it had lost all value. When he reached the address to which he had followed her that fateful early morning, she was just coming back out onto the street. The closeness of her as they virtually collided – the discreet passing touch of their bodies – rendered him almost speechless. She looked up at him, and he saw a new kind fear in her eyes that was disconcerting. Yet when he held up the groceries he had bought for her, the hint of a capitulating smile flickered across her captivatingly clumsy lips.

"I almost didn't recognise you in the shop," she said timidly, "with your rather gruesome makeup."

"That's a memento from your friend Breitner."

The faint spark of concern that showed in the momentary flinch of her eyes made every inch of his suffering worthwhile. So dark, so mysterious – and yet so warm and soothing.

"I'd like you to know," she said at last, "that Mr Breitner is not my friend. Our association is a purely business arrangement."

"What sort of business?" he asked.

"I don't think that's any concern of yours."

"And I have bruises that suggest otherwise."

"Look." Her voice, so soft and mellow, was beginning to crack with exasperation. "I don't know what sort of a game you think you're playing, but you're not very good at it. And you're starting to irritate me. Let me pay you for these groceries, and we can go our separate ways."

Maybe she was right. Whatever he was playing at, he was really not very good. But he was not prepared to throw out this intriguing potion before he had drunk from the cup and tasted the poisoned nectar for himself.

"You know, I took a good deal of beating and humiliation for you. I thought it was because you were Breitner's girl. Now you tell me it's business. So it seems to me the least you could do is tell me what the business is I took that beating for."

She said nothing. But the anxious movement in her eyes told him she was hard at work choosing the right words. Until he added:

"You could tell me all about it over lunch."

To his surprise, the movement in her sparkling eyes became quite still. She hesitated – with a gentle smile that made his heart miss a beat. He had expected outright rejection. And was rewarded for his perseverance. But when eventually she agreed, she did so on condition that she fix the time and place where they would meet.

And it was this, the meeting place for their projected lunch date, which startled him above all. Eleven-thirty, she insisted, at the Holbein collection in the new Museum of Fine Arts.

"There are various restaurants nearby where we can eat," she added. Then turned to take her leave of Frank. The sleekness of her raven hair taunted him with its sensuous motion as she dipped her head slightly to bundle the groceries under her arm. Then she disappeared through the doorway to her flat.

A good three hours remained for him to kill before they were due to meet. Although he partially resumed his original plan for the morning and bought a local newspaper, it was only a token gesture. He was completely unable to focus on his search for new lodgings. His thoughts were fully occupied by the significance of the proposed meeting place. Was it coincidence? Or was it some kind of signal? Did she have some connection with Silverstone, and by extension also with Achim?

The endless unanswered questions sharpened his appetite all the more for his lunch date. And ensured that he would be at the museum with time to spare – and with the gift that he had bought for her in Globus.

The waiting did nothing to help quell his impatience for answers to all those questions. As time dragged on, he recalled his fruitless lingering in the wine tavern some ten days earlier – the first time she had stood him up. Would this be the second? The thought occurred to him that it was after this first futile attempt at a date with Patricia Roche that he had experienced his paranoid trek through the streets, hounded by the conviction that he was being followed. Had she checked with Breitner about the fake date in the tavern, prompting him to put his bullies on Frank's tail? And had Frank now fallen into the same trap again?

It was already a quarter to twelve, and these thoughts trailed endlessly through his mind. She would not be coming now. That was plain. It seemed to him that everything was managing to slip through his fingers or evaporate, as if none of it existed, as if he were dreaming his life away.

The idea both irritated and frightened him. He thought of Breitner, and it struck him that he should make certain this time that he was not being followed when he left. He took a last cautious stroll through the rooms of the Holbein collection, looking about him like a hunted animal. As he turned into the last room of portraits, his heart instantly skipped a beat. There she stood, studying a painting. Her head of silk-black hair slightly inclined. Her delicate frame captured against the gallery wall with the suggestive economy of a line drawing. Yet it was not this which made him catch his breath as much as the portrait she was examining – the very same one that had witnessed the meeting between Achim and Silverstone.

It seemed to Frank that coincidence was being pushed beyond the bounds of credibility. And the questions this begged ran furiously around his brainpan like balls of hot fat, when suddenly she turned and saw him. She smiled.

"I'd almost given you up," she said, the smile still lingering tantalisingly on her lips. "I've been waiting here for ten minutes already."

In dumb silence, he let her words wash over him with all the responsiveness of a lumpfish caught between ebb and flow. He did not even consider how it was that he had managed to miss her while he was waiting round the corner, and how or why it was that she had missed him. He was completely tongue-tied, his brain barely functional. It was not just that he was utterly taken aback to find her standing in front of this portrait – of all the paintings in the museum she could have chosen. It was as if she was baiting him in some way that his befuddled brain was incapable of processing. But there was more to his hopeless inertia than this.

Above all, he was disarmed once again by her strange beauty, by the strong but soft geometry of her cheekbones, the rich lustre of her raven hair toned with a warm hint of mahogany, the dark eyes that appeared paradoxically to sparkle with a perpetual melancholy, and the lips so perversely enticing in a clumsy imperfection that may have been moulded by grief. Once again, she gave him the impression of immense strength coupled with delicate vulnerability. It was a picture that intrigued him to the depths of his soul. For all his reluctance to admit of such feelings, he had to acknowledge that he was dangerously close to something called love. And yet, in spite of all his innocence and willing sacrifice to her charm, he was fully prepared to accept that she was not to be trusted.

"You're probably wondering why I wanted to meet you here," she said.

With great difficulty, he concealed his burning curiosity for fear of forfeiting some undefined advantage. So he said nothing.

"What do you think of it?" she asked, gesturing towards the man in the floppy hat.

"It's a fascinating portrait. The expressiveness of the eyes, the mouth – the face as a whole – even though the rest of the picture is incomplete – he looks anxious, hunted, underneath that calm exterior."

He could see that his affected response amused her. This was apparent from that smile of hers, which was rapidly becoming the cause of such sweet pain.

"I think perhaps you're projecting a lot of yourself into the picture," she observed, with a disturbingly accurate grasp of his condition. "Do you know who it's supposed to be?"

Frank had to admit his ignorance.

"Theophrastus Bombastus von Hohenheim," she said with slow deliberation, showing a cynical edge to her voice that ill-befitted his image of her.

"Poor soul. His parents really didn't like him, did they?"

"Better known," she added, ignoring his attempt at wit, "as Paracelsus. A man who is said to have made a lot of enemies – and a dubious contribution to the advance of medicine. I can't understand why people are still so interested in him here, of all places, where his ideas aroused such indignation. But that's so typical of the people in this place, so petty bourgeois and resistant to change – until they perceive the opportunity for a little reflected glory."

Her voice had changed, become more poignant in its expression, more accusing, but then softened slightly as she added: "So they've talked themselves into believing that this portrait by Holbein represents the great man."

"And you think otherwise?" I asked.

"Let's just say I'm still waiting to be convinced." She paused and studiously contemplated the portrait.

"This is why I suggested meeting here. I wanted you to see the picture. Despite what the experts say, I doubt very much that it's Paracelsus. And for good reason. So, every time I see it, it reminds me not to trust anyone or what anyone tells me until I'm convinced that it's so, until I know for sure that the person or the information can be trusted. It's the only way to survive these days."

Without giving Frank so much as a glance, she then turned to leave the gallery.

"Now let's go and have lunch," she said.

Smart, single-minded and committed. To what he was not sure. But it was here that she derived her strength. And here that she cast her bewitching net over him.

Frank had always found grit and intelligence in a woman highly seductive. And yet, impressed as he was by her knowledge of the artworks on display, he doubted that this was the true reason she wanted to meet right here, exactly where he had witnessed the encounter between Achim and the mysterious Silverstone a few days earlier. It all seemed such a contrived arrangement, not to say a tad pretentious, just to make such a simple point. He was certain that she was conveying another message he was too stupid or too innocent to comprehend.

They exchanged few words as they walked together to the restaurant, Frank pondering the true significance of that moment. Yet right now, as he let Patricia Roche guide him to their appointed lunch, he was more intent on keeping both eyes firmly on what was going on around them and checking to make sure they were not being followed.

But the manner in which she also kept glancing back behind them told him that she was no less wary of stalkers than he was. She guided him around the cathedral towards the terrace overlooking the river that he had come to know so well. Before reaching the thick red sandstone walls of the terrace, however, she tugged Frank by the arm and pulled him around the outer wall of the chancel.

"We wait," was all she said, as they stood pinned against the wall behind the furthermost column of the chancel. The last time Frank had walked this way, late at night, he had been hounded by a sense of shadows in pursuit.

'Is it the church,' he wondered, 'that foments this sense of persecution?'

The answer was carved into the walls above: weird sandstone sculptures of exotic creatures, sciapods threatening to plant a huge foot on anyone who came too close to the walls of the chancel where they stood. They spoke of trouble and menace.

'These buildings are made to intimidate,' Frank mused, and felt the nudge of Patricia's elbow in his side. He looked at her, and followed her gaze as it fixed on a shabbily dressed young man in a cloth cap. The man hurried to the edge of the terrace, peered over its thick sandstone walls, then turned and vanished down the steps to the promenade below.

"Who was that?" Frank asked, as Patricia walked over to the terrace walls and cast a glance down at the promenade.

"I don't know," she replied. "But I don't like the look of him."

They watched as he hurried along the promenade to the ferry. This was moving slowly towards him, carried by the slow winter current of the river. And in its wake a swan gently drifted and bobbed on the ripples created by the boat. It seemed oblivious to the world around it, as if floating in another dimension altogether.

Satisfied that they had shaken off the man in the cloth cap, Patricia tugged at the sleeve of Frank's coat and led him back across the cathedral square, down the weaving side streets of the city and in through the back door of a tavern unknown to Frank. The blast of warm air as they entered spoke instantly of cosiness, a feeling that was reinforced by the interior design. Beneath the low-slung, low-wattage lamps, many of the tables were slotted in between high-backed bench seats that offered cosy séparées for dining. It was clear to him that Patricia had chosen this tavern precisely for its discretion. The kind of place to share secrets without fear of any wider disclosure.

They settled on the table in the farthest corner. She placed a pack of cigarettes and lighter on the table beside her, and Frank ordered half a litre of La Côte, while they studied the menu. But once the order was taken – a *rösti* special for each of them – and they gingerly immersed themselves in conversation, it seemed as if there were no secrets to reveal after all. The conversation rambled through the more anodyne corridors of their histories, as neither of them appeared ready to take off the safety chain. He insisted on guarding secrets that did not seem worth the engrams they were etched in, while she preserved confidences that looked too heavy to carry for much longer, but too important to let go.

And so their lunch became a game of hide and seek. A certain ration of conversational detail was supplied on both sides. But in her case, he sensed it was intended to serve as bait more than anything else. She told him that she was studying the History of Art at the university, which he had already ascertained on their first encounter. He asked her why, of all the temples of misogyny, she should choose this country in which to do her studies, where women were not even allowed to vote.

"My father wanted me to," was her only reply, which went nowhere near satisfying his curiosity. But when he delved further, he got no response. So he tried a different tack.

"Where are you from?" he wanted to know.

She furrowed her brow and feigned a questioning smile across the table: "What do you mean? Biologically? Geographically? Metaphysically perhaps?"

Frank had the feeling she was making fun of him. Or was she merely being evasive again? At all events her caginess began to irritate him. He would have almost been ready to throw in the towel had it not been for those dark, captivating eyes.

"I'm quite serious," she insisted. "I don't understand your question. If you want to know where I was born, then Normandy in France. That's where I spent my childhood. In a small town called Avranches. A pretty place with beautiful views of Mont Saint-Michel rising from the sea like something out of a fairy tale. My parents lived in Metz originally, which was still part of Germany of course. But when war broke out, my father insisted that my mother should move to Normandy and stay with my grandmother. He stayed in Metz because of his job, but travelled to Normandy as often as he could. And that's where I came in."

At this, she took a cigarette from the orange pack beside her, emblazoned with the name Parisienne that could have been created especially for her, and lit up.

How apt, Frank thought, but said: "I didn't know you smoked."

"There are times when it helps," she replied. "Do you want one?"

"I haven't smoked since Berlin," he said, taking one from the pack. "But sharing a Parisienne with a charming French lady is too much of a temptation."

"But I'm not sure any of that answers your question," she continued, ignoring his clumsy attempt at flattery, "because the last dozen years or so I've been in Stuttgart, where my father now lives. Then about a year ago, he sent me to study here, where many people assume from my name that I have something to do with the pharmaceutical company just across the river. So they think I'm Swiss. And if you ask what it all means to me, I really can't tell you. I feel neither German nor the charming French lady you speak of. And certainly not Norman. I have no idea where I belong. But none of that matters. All I need to know is that I'm me. Anything else is quite unimportant. And slightly boring. A little like this Chasselas," she added, as she finished her glass of wine.

"I'm sorry," he said. "They don't seem to have a great range of wine to offer."

And since the restaurant only appeared to have chestnut Vermicelles to follow their main course, she declined his offer of a dessert and insisted on no more than a cup of coffee to complete the lunch.

Frank began to sense their time together slipping away. Already with the bitterness of the coffee serving as a foretaste of regret at his own foolish hesitation, he could feel the threat of failure coursing over his tongue. Here was an opportunity he could not allow to be simply tossed away with all the other forgotten litter of his past. This woman exercised an influence over him that told him she was too important to leave in the limp hands of his indecisiveness. So why mistrust her?

'Why not for once in your life take the bull by the horns?' he asked himself. Yet even then he felt the need to approach the task elliptically, homing in from an obscure angle, in the hope that the bull would not notice – so affording him the opportunity to escape without having to show himself up should he be rejected.

"Would you take me for a thief?" he asked.

This apparent non sequitur had her visibly baffled.

"I would take you more for that swan we saw in the river. But I imagine most of us are capable of stealing," came the philosophical response.

"But would it surprise you to learn that I was no more than a mean street thief?"

"Yes, to be honest it would," she said, and began to look slightly worried in her curiosity.

"But I am," he insisted. And proceeded to relate the story of his encounter with Silverstone. Perhaps it was her apparent concern that seduced him. Or maybe it was simply the exquisite, slender beauty of her wrist as she stirred the cream into her coffee and allowed the sheen of her hair to cascade over the cup like a jet-black waterfall. Whatever the reason for the seduction, he almost unwittingly found himself laying bare the whole history behind his assault on Silverstone. He told her of Achim, their friendship, his dreams, and his recent disappearance. Almost as if seeking absolution, he began to confess every detail of the last few weeks. He appeared to need it – like a novice drinker who sips gingerly from his first brandy and quickly acquires a taste for it, renewing glass after glass with an increasingly intemperate relish. He thought of Achim and his Mirabelle brandy. And it seemed to him that those excerpts of his tale which involved his old friend were followed with particular interest by his temptress and confidante. But he did not let this impression deflect him from his confession. Now, as he unashamedly showed his colours to this woman who evinced such experience of the world in her sweet, sad eyes, he felt as naive as he had done that Monday morning when Achim had recounted the stories of his youth over the Mirabelle brandy. A simpleton with no grasp of the world about him despite his gruelling experience at the hands of Breitner. And the threat of worse if he were to be seen here now with Mademoiselle Roche.

"And the only reason he seemed to have for brutalising me was to warn me against having anything to do with you," said Frank, as he brought his confession to an end.

As he added this rider to his story, he watched her expression for some tell-tale sign of her involvement. Some handpost to an explanation for the whole episode. But she simply raised her beautiful dark eyes from the empty coffee cup in front of her and smiled from a distance in a way that was guaranteed to lend enchantment, but defied any attempt to read its message.

"I was told the same story," she said. "Breitner warned me to stay away from you too. He said you were dangerous." Her smile took on an incongruous warmth as she spoke these words. And the sad sparkle returned to her eyes. "Are you dangerous?" she asked.

He threw the question back at her: "Do you think I am?"

"The way you behave, I think you must be." She saw that her reply had taken him slightly by surprise, and she paused briefly to enjoy the moment. "Why invite me to lunch today if contact with me is such a risky game as you would have me believe?"

"Why accept the invitation if I'm such a danger as Breitner would have you believe?" he countered. "But the question that interests me more is why I was warned off you in the first place. What's your business with Breitner? What's his hold on you?"

"You should be more careful in your choice of words," she said, and he saw the sparkle momentarily vanish from her eyes. "Especially in matters you don't understand. Ill-chosen words have a way of putting things in a false perspective."

"That's really unfair." He felt foolishly stung by this rebuke. "I've spent the last fifteen minutes trying to explain every detail of my situation to you. And I get nothing in return, except a reproach that I don't understand. But how can I, if you tell me nothing?"

"I'm sorry."

She said no more than this. But, as with every other aspect of her, that single word of apology completely disabled him. She could have left him there, powerless as a fledgling pushed out of its nest before its time, and he would not have complained. But instead she followed up her apology with a remark that both intrigued him and gave him a vague hope that perhaps she was beginning to trust him – just as he was feeling compelled to trust her.

"One thing you can be sure of is that Breitner knows very well you are not Silverstone."

"What do you mean?" he asked. But she brushed off his question.

"I'm afraid I have to be going. I'm already late." And she got up to leave, threatening to desert him with an abruptness that nearly threw him into a panic. He rose to his feet and, as she stood by the table preparing to make her exit, took her hand in his. It seemed so soft and slight, so fragile.

"I almost forgot," he said. "I thought you might like this."

Frank reached down to the bag that was leaning against the table leg and placed it on the table. She looked at it with a puzzled smile.

"What is it?"

"Open it and see."

The sweet smile of appreciation in her eyes when she took the record out of the bag was the perfect balm for every one of the bruises he had suffered.

"I couldn't help noticing the record on your gramophone. I hope you don't already have this one?" he asked hopefully.

"No," she replied, and the smile had now taken on a pensiveness that he was unable to fathom. "You're very kind."

"You know, we have so much more to talk about," he said, and hesitated for an instant, before adding: "I'd like to see you again."

"You will," was all she said in reply before slipping out of the restaurant. Evasive and enigmatic as ever.

Chapter 11

After the events of the last days, Frank should have become inured to surprise. But on his return to the hotel later that afternoon, he found the unexpected was still capable of stopping him in his tracks. The tracks in question ran between the reception desk and the staircase up to his room. Past the lobby. Here, relaxing with a newspaper, sat a figure painfully familiar to him. As Frank approached the staircase, the man lowered the newspaper and cast a glaring looked in his direction.

"I believe you have something of mine."

He fixed Frank with a stare that momentarily froze him to the spot. It was Silverstone. He tried desperately to gather his composure, as the American put the newspaper aside and rose up from his chair.

"I was only talking about you just now." Frank put on an unconvincing display of cheerful familiarity. It was more for the man on reception than for Silverstone's benefit.

"Oh yes? And to whom might that have been?"

"But I'm afraid I no longer have what you're looking for," Frank confessed, ignoring the question. "A man called Breitner relieved me of it."

Silverstone continued to fix him with a calculating expression, as if measuring and analysing the words before venturing any closer.

"Can we talk?" he asked.

Frank gestured to the seat from which he had just risen.

"Let's go to your room instead," Silverstone insisted. Frank looked across at reception and saw the man on the desk ostentatiously minding his own business. With an uneasy reluctance, Frank turned and directed the American up the stairs to his room. With a sense of trepidation, he contrived to lead Silverstone from behind.

Ushering him into his room, he offered him the armchair on the far side near the window. Silverstone seemed surprisingly content with this perfunctory show of hospitality. Frank preferred to stand next to the door, from where he could keep an eye on him. For some time Silverstone said nothing, but simply observed Frank with his cold, analysing stare. His lips betrayed the trace of a smirk. The supercilious manner put Frank in mind of Breitner. He was more elegant than Breitner, more tasteful in his dress, more stylish – an East Coast American version – but he gave the impression there was little to choose between the two.

"Was it Breitner that fixed your makeup for you?" the American asked with a smile.

The coincidence of the question with Frank's own thoughts left him momentarily perplexed. Silverstone ran a finger around the corner of his right eye to underline his question. Frank nodded.

"Nasty, isn't he?" Silverstone added.

"Do you know him?" Frank asked. He was thinking of what Patricia had said earlier.

The American smiled. He considered the question carefully, seeming to test the options on his thin lips, which moved almost imperceptibly, as if rehearsing a response. It never came.

"You know what Scott Fitzgerald said about Switzerland?" Silverstone asked in turn. "It doesn't so much draw people as accept them without inconvenient questions. That's Breitner." His smile thickened. "So what does he have against you? He surely didn't do that just for a souvenir of my ID?"

"Well, he wasn't too clear about that. He seemed to think I'd been messing around with his girl."

It was Frank's turn to be evasive. His answer did at least have the virtue of corresponding to a certain version of the truth. And since he was somewhat in the dark anyway as to the full truth behind his meeting with Breitner, it seemed as satisfactory a response as any other. But Silverstone was not satisfied.

"I didn't know he had a girl."

The distrust in his voice prickled and put Frank on the defensive.

"As I said, he was not entirely clear about the whys and wherefores. He was more interested in the sport. And, of course, he threw me into the usual fascist spittoon of socialists, communists, Jews and the rest."

"Why do you think that was?"

"I guess it suited him," Frank conjectured. "You know how it is with fascists if you don't fit with their view of the world."

"In what way don't you fit?"

And so the interrogation continued. One lazy noncommittal remark succeeded another, and was instantly followed up each time by a relentless probing question. Frank's initial discomfort and mistrust of this enigmatic American rapidly gave way to impatience.

"So what precisely did you want to talk about?" he eventually asked, "because I'm pretty sure you didn't come here for a political discussion?"

Silverstone considered the question with the studious care of a chemist assaying for some obscure substance close to the limit of detection.

"You," he said at last.

"I thought we'd been doing that. What more do you want to know?"

"I understand you're planning to visit your mother in Cologne soon."

The presumptuous intimacy of this man with Frank's private life instantly hit a nerve. It heightened his dislike of the man to a pitch of near repugnance. And the fact that his understanding was not entirely accurate didn't help. It simply added to a sense of betrayal that edged its way into Frank's mood. It was clear that Achim had been talking to this man about him. And this hurt.

"What else has Achim been telling you about me?" he asked, feeling instantly irked by his failure to conceal the anger in his voice.

But Silverstone ignored the question.

"I'd like you to do me a favour," he said.

"Really?" Again he had succeeded in taking Frank completely by surprise. "What sort of favour?"

"I'd like you to deliver a package for me."

"And what would be in the package?"

"This kind of thing."

Silverstone pulled a small booklet out of his coat pocket and threw it on the bed. It was little more than a slim primer on the rudiments of chess. Unimaginative in design and cheap in quality, but it looked harmless enough. Yet it didn't fit with the image Frank had of Silverstone. Or with the man's supercilious manner. But, above all, it seemed an odd request.

"Just supposing for a moment you were correct, and I were going to Cologne, what reason could I have for doing you a favour?"

"I figure you owe me," came the self-assured response.

"And where does Achim come into this?" Frank persisted. "Was this his idea?"

Again the American ignored his question. He slipped the book back into his overcoat pocket, rose from his chair and turned to gaze pensively out of the window.

'Was this really the stranger I had beaten to the ground and robbed only a few days earlier?' Frank asked himself.

He found it difficult to square this whole scene – the expectation of favours, the careful deliberation – with the history of violence and assault. At length, Silverstone turned back from the window, a thin smile on his lips, but worry in his eyes.

"Perhaps you should come along with me. It might simplify matters."

"Where to?"

"I'd like you to meet someone," the American insisted, his right hand already reaching out for the door.

"Who?" Frank asked.

By now the door was open, and Frank saw Silverstone raise his left arm like the wing of Roc stretched in readiness to carry off its prey. The man's propensity for ignoring questions irritated Frank intensely. And the invitation reminded him all too vividly of the last occasion when he was abducted from his hotel room. But Silverstone took a more subtle approach, and although Frank was disinclined to have anything to do with the man – let alone accept this invitation – he was sufficiently intrigued by the tight-lipped nature of his coaxing to follow him.

Out on the street, the air was filled with the tantalising aroma of roasting chestnuts, and Frank was sorely tempted to stop at one of the street vendors to buy a bag. But Silverstone was not for lingering. He gave the impression of not wanting to be seen. And lost no time leading Frank to the market square, where he leapt onto the very first tram that passed, dragging Frank with him as he went. They stood in silence, side by side, watching the anonymous shop facades slip by outside. It was already late in the afternoon, and the trams were beginning to fill with the wage-slaves and factory workers savouring the tired freedom of their journey home. In no time, the tram was opening its doors to the next wave of languid faces. Frank wanted to move further into the carriage to make space for them, but Silverstone placed a vicelike grip on his arm and kept him close to the door. The sudden brachial pain and the seething masses around him set his head spinning; perhaps the beating by Breitner and his friends was taking its toll. As the tram doors were drawing to, and a stabbing pain shot from behind his eyes, he heard Silverstone mutter something and became aware of being tugged through the closing doors back onto the street. He caught the words 'Just to be on the safe side', but the significance of this caution escaped him as his head felt ready to split.

It was as if a curtain had suddenly gone up and lifted the dizzy fog, just momentarily, just long enough to be struck by an acrid smell in the air and the sight of empty fast-food containers littering the pavement. The sound of a distantly familiar glamrock melody wafted from some unseen recess nearby: 'Ride a White Swan'.

It conjured images of water. Mud. And a strange Exakta camera. In this muzzy confusion and dissonance, he sensed the remote memory of his experience on the castle ruins waiting for Achim. A distant sense of otherness. And then he was wrenched up steps he couldn't see into another tram, the vicelike grip even tighter on his arm.

"You feeling okay?"

Frank could hear the words, but was unable to give a remotely coherent reply, not least because he was uncertain of the answer. His head ached from the cleavage of his skull. His mind was clouded with turmoil and battered by a farrago of images and sounds. Like a blind man in helpless innocence, he allowed himself to be led out of the second tram and across the road.

It was not until the fresh air of the street washed over his face that he began to regain some semblance of meaning and order. Silverstone had loosened his grip on Frank's arm and directed him now along a forsaken-looking street to a shop that was already known to him from somewhere. As they entered, the American left him hovering by the entrance to engage the shopkeeper behind the counter in a furtive conversation. Throughout the exchange, his fellow conspirator cast suspicious glances in Frank's direction. It gave him the impression that the shopkeeper was no less distrustful of Silverstone than he was of Frank. But since this appeared to be a national characteristic, he paid it no further thought. And when Silverstone eventually appeared to receive a nod of approval, he beckoned Frank to follow him out into a back corridor.

They climbed what seemed in his washed-out state to be endless flights of stairs, which were only dimly defined by the fading daylight admitted through occasional modest windows in the stairwell. When they ran out of steps to climb, Silverstone stopped at the door ahead of them and turned briefly as he put his hand on the doorknob.

"Feeling okay now?" he asked.

Frank nodded. But he felt oddly discomforted by the concern implicit in the question. His dislike of Silverstone had firmly taken root and was not easily reconciled by intimations of kindness or consideration.

Silverstone opened the door and stood aside to let him in. The room was even gloomier than the stairwell. And seemed as empty. Silverstone followed him in, closed the door behind him and strode over to the far side of the room, where he knocked with curious deliberation on another door. Frank had the impression this knock constituted some carefully observed code.

Perhaps he should have anticipated it, but nonetheless the sight of Achim's familiar face greeting him in this dingy garret made Frank's heart leap.

"Frank!" he said. There was a sense of alarm in his voice. "You look terrible. What have you been up to?"

He stood back, gesturing Frank into the room.

"He's been giving me a real hard time," Silverstone added as he followed him in.

"Did you do this to him?" Achim asked, flashing a look of concern at the American.

"Hell no!" Silverstone protested.

"Here, you could do with some of this, Frank."

Achim poured two glasses of his favourite Mirabelle brandy, passed one to his friend and lifted the other to the light.

"Such sweet golden nectar," he said. "You can almost see the fruit on the trees, gleaming in the sunshine. But tell me what the hell you've been getting up to. How did you get that face?"

"Pretty, isn't it?"

Frank evaded his friend's questions. He felt it best not to make any mention of Breitner just yet. What interested him more was to know what Achim had been getting up to and what his connection was with Silverstone. Why had he suddenly vanished from the Gotthard, he wanted to know. What was he getting involved in? And why was Frank being dragged into clandestine adventures of hide and seek?

"But Frank, remember it was you who dragged me down to this part of the world in the first place."

"Well, you didn't take much persuading."

"No, but you gave me the tip, and I'm grateful to you for that."

"What tip? What are you talking about?" Frank asked. He detected shades of the flippancy he had always so appreciated in Achim. But on this occasion it irritated him, because he sensed that his friend was using it as a kind of subterfuge. "When I suggested you join me here, it was because I thought you could do some real work again. Maybe even join a theatre group. And instead you start playing Bo Peep with foreign thugs."

"Look, Zimmermann," Silverstone complained, "I wasn't even happy about bringing this guy here. But you said he could be trusted, so I took the risk. I thought maybe you could explain things better than I can – like you said in the first place. But I don't have to take these insults. And when I think of the trouble he gave me coming here..."

Although Silverstone appeared to be offended by his choice of words, Frank had the impression he was simply playing some elaborate game. And when the American meekly acceded to Achim's suggestion that he go down to the basement and give Gertrude a helping hand, he began to wonder whether this whole scene had been carefully rehearsed.

"How are Gertrude and the kids settling in?" Frank asked.

He had imagined that, once Silverstone had gone, the conversation with Achim would assume contours he could identify. But he was mistaken. His old friend shook off the question like a dead leaf clinging to his shoe. He preferred to return to less easy pastures.

"Your innocence and naivety amaze me, Frank. Do you honestly think I came down here in search of artistic freedom and all that crap? How long have you been here now? Six weeks? Eight? Two months of self-indulgent fantasy can be extremely ruinous to your health, you know. And meanwhile there's a whole world outside falling apart at the seams. There comes a time when you have to grow up, Frank. When you need to put aside the existential poetry of Rilke or the nonsense verse of Morgenstern or whatever poet captures your attention at any given moment. And just leave the pleasures of self-absorption behind."

"Did you know that Rilke's first name was René?" Frank said, ignoring his friend's diatribe. "It was Lou Salomé who gave him the name Rainer."

"Have you even heard what I've been saying, Götz?" Achim gasped with exasperation. "Just quit the evasion and listen to me."

"But it's interesting, isn't it?" Frank said with a smile that made plain he had heard every word – and his friend's intended irony – despite the persistent evasion. "It's interesting the way people like to substitute given names. It's as if they want to blank out the attributes they don't like in someone and assign a new identity to that person."

"Like you, Götz."

Frank smiled now with a hint of awkwardness.

"What's more interesting about Lou Salomé," Achim continued with an unaccustomed harshness in his voice, "and more germane, is that when she died a few weeks ago, they confiscated her entire library because it was tainted with 'Jewish science' and was full of books by Jewish authors. Did you know that?"

"Look, I'm not quite the innocent you imagine me to be, Achim. I know what these people are like." Frank pointed to the injuries on his face. "I didn't get this walking into a lamp post."

And for the second time that day, Frank went into the details of his encounter with Breitner. But for Achim's ears, the motives behind the storytelling were rather different. The story was very much a service stripe, a badge of honour to impress. And Frank did not spare his friend's sensibilities, as he had done Patricia's. Achim was presented with a complete tapestry of the violence committed against him.

"So that's why Silverstone was persuaded to bring you here," said Achim.

"I don't follow."

"I may only have been here a week or so, Frank, but one thing I've learned is that anyone Breitner takes a dislike to is a friend of Silverstone's."

"A dubious privilege. I wouldn't trust him any further than I could throw him. And besides, after nicking his papers off him, I wouldn't be so sure you're right about his judgement of me."

"You couldn't be more wrong, Frank. But then you don't know him yet."

"That sounds ominous. You mean I'm going to get to know him better?" The words drew a smile from Achim. "But since you seem to know him so well, tell me about him. Who is he?" Frank asked.

"I don't know him well. But I know what he stands for, and that's probably more important these days." He broke off for a moment to pour himself another brandy, as if this would help concentrate his mind. Frank allowed him to fill his glass, too, as he watched the tension playing on his old friend's face.

"Some people in Berlin put me in touch with him." His voice cracked almost imperceptibly with a hint of self-mockery as he continued painting in the background to his picture. "You know, Frank, you would hardly have recognised me these last few months in Berlin. I've been moving in very mixed company."

Achim rose from his chair, and Frank's eyes followed as he poured himself another glass and moved over to the window.

"You're hitting it pretty hard these days, Achim. Is that down to the mixed company you keep?"

"It all goes back to an insignificant landlord of an insignificant bar somewhere in Kreuzberg. And you know, it's the insignificance of it all that appals and haunts me most of all."

"You're talking in riddles, Achim."

"You remember our bar on the Ku'damm?" said Achim.

"Of course," Frank nodded, recalling their intoxicated evenings in the garishly decorated blues and golds of the bar room and the ladies of the night entertaining their clients on the dance floor.

"I dropped in one evening for a beer on my way home," Achim went on. "The place was quite full, but seemed oddly quiet. The band had stopped playing. I must have been very tired, because it took some time for it to click, before I realised what was happening. There were a few brown uniforms among the clientele, but that was a sight I'd grown used to, so I paid them no special attention. I walked over to the bar. Two of them were standing there and seemed to be in conversation with the barman. It was not until I interrupted them to order a beer that I could see this was not a normal conversation.

"The barman was expecting payment for the drinks he'd just served them, and they were faking amazement at his chutzpah. Suggested he should be paying them for drinking such 'piss'. And they greeted my intervention with some comment like 'if it's good beer you want, you'd better try somewhere else'.

"And as I was still trying to process the ugliness of it all, one of the thugs threw himself over the bar, grabbed the barman round the neck and dragged him to the floor. What then followed took place under cover of the bar, so the visual impact was thankfully lost on me. But the crunch of boot against bone and the lifeless silence of the victim with every savage kick made up for anything I might have otherwise missed. You know, that thug was enjoying himself so much that he began to laugh and chuckle at his footwork and the lump of senseless flesh he was creating at his feet. It was not until his euphoric frenzy had taken him to the point of exhaustion, and he had to lean on the bar for support, that he eventually stopped. Draped over the bar, he smiled, looked down at the floor, and spat out the mouthful of phlegm generated by what was probably the only kind of exercise he knew. 'Filthy Jew' he scowled, then left.

The other brownshirts followed, looking well pleased with the entertainment. One of them muttered something to the effect that I could help myself now if I was really so keen on the beer.

"And do you know what I did? Nothing. Just stood there and did nothing. One of the other customers ran over behind the bar as soon as they'd gone. And I did nothing – until my dumb inertia was wrenched apart by a deafening crash that made me duck for cover. Suddenly we were all pinned to the floor in terror as all the tables around us were showered with splinters of glass. The mindless animals had taken it into their boneheads to leave a visiting card. They hurled bricks and bottles from the street outside through every pane of glass in the building. When the cacophony of breaking glass eventually subsided, the hush that fell on that house was deafening. I've never known a silence like it. And I hear it to this day."

Achim's eyes moistened with the memory of that night. And Frank had nothing of value to offer in the way of sympathy or commiseration.

"Ever since then, I've given up what you would probably call gainful employment and devoted my energy to a more meaningful life. Away from all that dumb inertia. I had to do something, Frank. And it was your letter that eventually gave me the idea."

"So this is where Silverstone comes in?" Frank asked.

"I was told that a lot of counterpropaganda is being produced down here on some of the friendlier Swiss printing presses. And I thought that might be something for me. I could even put my graphic talents to use designing posters. And as I say, some people I know gave me Silverstone's name."

"Well, if that little book he showed me on how to win at chess in three easy moves is an example of his propaganda, I think you're barking up the wrong tree."

Achim hesitated, and shed the trace of a smile as he pondered his friend's words.

"That's just for a dummy run, Frank." He poured another brandy for each of them. "And this is where you come in.

I remembered you saying that you would be going to visit your mother soon. So it seemed like the perfect opportunity. You see, we need someone to test the run to Cologne. We're slowly exhausting all the courier options. A lot of the stuff doesn't reach its destination. Much of it is delivered haphazardly, thrown almost at random onto trains that pass through by night from Italy. And we thought a brazen daylight run would not only stand a good chance of success. It could also get the stuff delivered straight to its target."

"So you want me to play courier for you?" Frank asked.

"No, I want you to do a dummy run. We just need to know if it's viable. And since you're going to visit your mother anyway, you seem the obvious choice."

"Can I remind you, Achim, that it was you who suggested I visit my mother in the first place?"

"But you are going to, aren't you?" his friend asked. There was an audible uncertainty in his voice. For a moment he seemed to lose his composure.

"I'm not sure," Frank replied.

"Look, why don't you stay for dinner. Gertrude would love to talk more with you. And we can discuss the detail in a more convivial atmosphere."

Without warning, Achim got up and left the room. Frank listened to the fading rhythm of his footsteps down through the stairwell. When he returned a few minutes later, Gertrude was with him. She seemed genuinely pleased to see Frank again. Nonetheless, the entire choreography of the way she welcomed him and invited him to dine with them made him suspect that this, like the whole meeting, had been well rehearsed beforehand. The suspicion chafed at his efforts to appear calm and composed. In reality, Achim's whole manner had ruffled him. But at least Silverstone had gone, so that was one irritation less to contend with.

As the evening progressed, and they sat over the modest fare that Gertrude was able to provide for them, Frank's unease sank little by little into the sea of nostalgia that inevitably flooded their conversation. Gertrude remained conspicuously in the background the whole time, and Frank found himself thinking once again how she had changed from the vivacious and carefree person he had known. She devoted most of her attention to the two baby boys, even long after they were tucked up in bed. The earnestness with which she took her role as a mother surprised Frank. It seemed to exclude every other aspect of life, and he wondered whether she was unusual in this respect. He had no yardstick. She was the only woman among his contemporaries who had chosen to go forth and multiply. Everyone else he knew had found the patriotic calls to breed for the fatherland too repugnant. To this extent, then, she was certainly unusual within his limited circle. But in the broader population, she was probably excruciatingly normal. With the benefit of hindsight, it now seemed almost as if her carefree nature had been an ill-fitting mask that she had struggled to keep on in order to conceal the real and painfully conventional ambitions for her life. It made him wonder whether this made her a poor match for his old friend after all – and whether maybe he regretted it. Or was she perhaps just what Achim needed?

At all events, Frank was happy to let her retreat into the shadows of their conversation, as he and his old friend wandered through the history of the days and nights they had shared in Berlin – down the avenues of their friendship to a time when that city breathed the kind of excitement which made you hungry for the next day. From lively cabarets to some of the most exciting playhouses in Europe.

He recalled the time they attended the premiere of *The Threepenny Opera*. It was late one summer evening, and Achim had already got wind from some of his theatre friends that this was going to be something special. So they were already full of boyish expectation as they headed off to the theatre, calling on the way at their favourite Hungarian restaurant Zur Csarda – the best goulash he had ever tasted, evoking shades of the *puszta* and the flavour of gypsy music. The atmosphere that evening was as merry as he had ever remembered it. Many of the guests, like them, were plainly on their way to the theatre.

As Frank and Achim quaffed their second bottle of Tokay and let their merry abandon run loose like dogs off the leash, they failed to notice that the other theatregoers had long since left. When eventually they felt compelled by the emptiness of the second bottle to settle up and head off to the theatre, the fact that they were late arriving for the performance was a triviality. More important was the mood. And this was as much imbued with the late-August merriment of a city humming with excitement as it was with the Tokay. It was a city of gaiety and bright new ideas. A city for falling in love, not for timekeeping.

So primed were they by this mood, and so captivated by the cabaret atmosphere as soon as they got into the theatre, that they barely noticed they had missed half the play. They arrived just before the duet between Lucy Brown and Polly Peachum. And Frank fell instantly for Roma Bahn's Polly. He found the sexual jealousy of women always such a fascinating and intensely arousing spectacle, and this duet accommodated all his deepest fantasies. He could not help feeling a certain envy for Macheath.

It was a feeling he recalled with particular irritation now because, with the benefit of hindsight, he reminded Frank in many ways of Willi Breitner. It was an association he preferred to suppress so as not to burst the bubble of his nostalgia too soon. But he could not suppress the nagging question that this reminder brought to the surface: who the hell was Lola?

Achim did not betray a hint of recognition when Frank mentioned this name.

But the way he derided what he called Frank's superficial enjoyment of the play with such exaggeration, dismissing him as a licentious romantic, gave Frank the impression he knew exactly who Lola was and was simply trying to change the subject. He and Gertrude exchanged smiles that suggested a private joke at Frank's expense.

Frank let the question lie and pointed out that he had not been alone in his enjoyment of the performance, that the theatre had fairly bubbled with entertainment that evening and that it was probably the biggest stage success they had ever witnessed in Germany – or were ever likely to witness there again.

"That just goes to prove my point," said Achim. "Germany is now dead to culture. And no one wants to visit the theatre only to be reminded of just how dead it is."

This return to the darker reaches of their shared memory brought them back to the real reason for his being there. Achim was not slow to pick up the thread. He tilted the bottle towards Frank and refilled his glass.

"Achim, your methods are both crude and unnecessary."

His old friend seemed to weigh each one of those words with painstaking scrutiny, frowning sceptically as he put the last one on the balance and repeated it with the questioning care of an archaeologist as he pieced together a priceless vase not believing he had all the fragments.

"Unnecessary? Does mean you might help us?"

Frank signalled his agreement with the merest hint of a nod as he sipped from the glass and muttered something under his breath to the effect that this was surely what friends were for. Frank was aware that his assent was demonstratively weak in conviction – almost as if born of the sheepishness of knowing that it could be construed as a step over the fence into the realms of commitment. So, perhaps by way of insurance cover, he reiterated Achim's insistence that this would only be a test run, and that he would not be carrying any incriminating material with him through Germany.

Achim's enthusiastic endorsement of this condition set the seal on the contract.

"Here," he said, pulling a hip flask out of his back pocket, pouring the remains of the Mirabelle brandy bottle into it and handing it to Frank. "This will give you some company on your trip."

Frank took the bottle and slid it into the inside pocket of his coat, as Achim opened another bottle. And they spent the rest of the evening lubricating their taste for nostalgia with a little more of his friend's elixir.

But after Gertrude politely departed for bed and left them to become hopelessly lost in their nostalgia for the pulsating young arteries of a city that had long since ceased to exist, nagging questions continued to chip away at the back of Frank's mind. He could still not completely bury his more recent, painful memories of the last few days. And the shock on his friend's face when he interrupted their reminiscences was plain to see.

"So what was in that rucksack you gave to Silverstone?" Frank asked.

"What?" Achim was taken aback, his lips unable to form another word while his eyes darted from side to side, as if speedreading through all the implications of the question. "Have you been following me?"

"Breitner said you're in what he called the art business. What did he mean by that?"

"Breitner?" The scampering movement of Achim's eyes betrayed the deep disquiet of a quarry at bay. "Did he elaborate?"

"He also wondered what you'd done with Lola."

Achim cast a nervous glance in his friend's direction. Sipped anxiously from his glass. And said nothing.

Frank simply watched. The furtiveness irritated him, and he was enjoying the obvious discomfort of his friend as Achim struggled to retain not only his composure, but presumably also a deeper secret. Yet Achim remained evasive.

"Silverstone has a position at the Bank for International Settlements. He has a lot of interesting connections. Can put you in touch with the right people," he said. It was all he was prepared to offer by way of explanation. And it did nothing to allay Frank's suspicions.

"You do realise what a Nazi-friendly organisation that is?" he asked. "One of the founding members was awarded the Golden Badge of the NSDAP only last month. He's also great buddies with another keen enabler of the Nazis: the Governor of the Bank of England no less. And they both sit on the board."

Frank paused to let his words sink in.

"Do you think it's just possible that the right people Silverstone knows could be entirely the wrong people?"

Achim cast a worried look at Frank. But said nothing.

It was plain to Frank that his friend had no inkling of the hornet's nest in which Silverstone plied whatever trade it was he pretended to be engaged in.

Chapter 12

Uncomfortably at ease with his rash agreement to go along with Achim's plans, Frank took his imprudence back to the hotel room with him. Like a ticket he had been given for a concert that held no interest for him, it lay crumpled and forgotten in a pocket of his tipsy tired mind. The lubricated nostalgia they had enjoyed together still had him too firmly in its warm embrace. And the effects of the rapture were slow to wear off. But once they did, the implications of his agreement to attend that fast-approaching 'concert' began to seep through. He shivered at the chilling thought of his folly.

For the first time in years, he felt a profound need to talk to someone about the fundaments of his life. To the only person he was interested in talking to right then.

As he stood in the dark stairwell that led up to Patricia's flat, he sensed a growing apprehension. And when eventually he knocked on her door, disappointment instantly rose from his stomach in a sour mix that smacked of heartburn. Furtive noises escaped from behind the door. But the door itself failed to open for a length of time which, in his impatience, seemed far too long for any comfortable explanation.

Frank began to wish he had not come. And he was about to turn back down the stairs, when suddenly a narrow chink of light appeared in the doorway to be instantly blotted out by the tantalising nuance of her figure. His appearance at her door failed to elicit the welcome he had been hoping for. Indeed, her soft gasp at the sight of him struggled to avoid betraying a slight irritation.

"What do you want?" she asked. "It's far too risky for you to be seen coming here."

With these words, she pulled him in through the door by his sleeve. Beside the stove, where he remembered warming his hands not so long ago, there stood a young man he had not seen before. On the table beside the gramophone, in place of the record he had bought for Patricia, lay a camera with the name Exakta inscribed on its brow. Frank recognised it as one of Germany's hottest-selling cameras. And the three red roses in the vase had been replaced now by a single rose.

With his tousled ginger hair, lean figure and a pale, hungry expression in his eyes, this stranger did not give the impression he might have anything to do with Breitner.

"Frank, this is Léandre. Léandre, Frank."

They shook hands, but said nothing. Léandre cast a questioning eye at Patricia.

"You can trust him," she said.

Although Léandre gave a sickly impression – pale and unshaven, tired red eyes, shabby clothes – he carried himself with a self-assurance that bordered on arrogance. It quickly dispelled any feelings of charity or sympathy that may have been lurking in Frank's mind. He was wondering why she had been so slow to open the door – it was hard to imagine that she might have been enjoying any kind of intimacy with such a picture of ill-health. Yet perhaps it was precisely the knowledge of intimacy that imbued the sickly looking stranger with such overweening confidence. Frank was not sorry when Léandre picked up the camera and announced that he would have to be going. But he was surprised to find this Exakta belonged to the shabbily dressed Léandre. How could he even afford a camera at all? Frank asked himself. And he wondered whether it might have been a gift from Patricia.

"I'll see you tomorrow," Léandre added. The words came with an emphasis that Frank felt was intended for him. And he saw his worst suspicions confirmed when Patricia gently kissed him and bade him "Take care" as he left.

With the delicate frame of her body, she pushed the door to and turned back towards Frank. A pensive smile played between her exquisite eyes and the conflict zone of her inviting lips. It was hard for Frank to judge whether the smile was meant for the just departed or for him the uninvited. For the time being, he preferred not to know.

"Who was that?" he asked.

"I told you. His name's Léandre. I've known him since primary school in Avranches. He's a very dear friend."

Those last three words dug a deep trench through the pit of his stomach. He clammed up to stem the pain. And they sat watching each other, not saying a word, for some minutes. The pensive smile still lingered tantalisingly on her lips. But in her eyes it had given way to a disquieting expression that he could not identify.

"Why should he feel the need to trust me?" he asked at last.

For an answer she offered him some soup that was keeping warm on the stove and a glass of wine. Frank accepted, but he felt ill at ease, a sense of having been let down by the brief passage of time. When they had lunched together what seemed like just a short while ago, he had the impression that confidences had been shared – however small. Now it appeared that he was back at square one and having to work all the harder. But in the short time they had known each other, he had already come to realise that appearances can be deceptive when fashioned by the unpredictability of this beautiful sphinx.

As she returned from the cooking niche, she was carrying a tray that contained not only two bowls of soup and two glasses of wine, but also a small yet deliberate display of camembert cheese and two apples. She put the tray with studied care on the table in front of Frank.

"I'm afraid it's Maggi soup," she said apologetically.

"I've no quarrel with Maggi. Their soup may not be great, but they're a socially minded corporation. Even Frank Wedekind worked for Maggi. He wrote advertising copy for them before he made his name in the theatre. So we're in good company."

"I didn't know that," said Patricia, raising her glass with a "santé." And savoured a modest sip of the wine, looking over her glass at Frank with those mysteriously sparkling ebony eyes that had so captivated him the very first time they met.

"A Riesling from across the border," she said. "A little more interesting than the Chasselas we had at lunch the other day."

Frank was not used to a knowledge of wine being expressed by a woman, especially one who exuded such uncompromisingly feminine charm. He watched every subtlety of expression, every nuance of movement on her lips as she sipped her wine, as she spoke her words. He was not listening to what she had to say. It was her curiously melancholic beauty that enthralled him. And he was not willing to sacrifice the piquancy of the moment for the dullness of small talk. But she insisted, and once again she succeeded in surprising him.

"I was born in January 1913. Quite a good year I've been told. My father has a whole crate of 1913 Chateau Haut-Brion at home, which he says he's keeping for the day I get married." She smiled. "How long do you think a good Bordeaux will keep?"

Her question had a strangely prismatic quality about it – a simple statement that her beguiling smile managed to break down into a whole spectrum of possible meanings. She was like a traveller passing through customs and immigration, her only item of luggage a suitcase with a false bottom, and when she opens up the case with a smile, she appears to be laying bare every intimacy that she carries with her on her journey. But in truth, all her secrets remain as well concealed as they ever were.

This careless image reminded him of the half-hearted bargain he had struck with Achim and his initial motivation in seeking out Patricia's company. But her manner left him uncertain how to broach the subject. And the existence of Léandre had created a new dimension of insecurity to cope with. He approached the situation cagily, skirting the issue with an ineptitude that did not escape her attention. He should have read the label on the display of camembert and apples. It was clear enough. But instead he allowed his unease to continue until these had long been digested by the acid in his stomach. And eventually he had to rely on her to save him from his own awkward clumsiness.

"What did you come here for, Frank?" she asked at last.

A simple enough question. But it was the way she wrapped her sensuous lips around the words that did it. And the way she used his first name. It was the cue he had been waiting for. As so often with seduction, the moment came unsuspectedly, leaving no space for cautious manoeuvres. And he jumped in with both feet, willing and easy prey, to deliver a basket of detail that seemed to capture her imagination and instil in her expression an intentness and energy that he had not seen in her before. And she seized on the story of his involvement with Achim with the eagerness of a hungry child. He had the impression that her estimation of him was growing with every mouthful. When at length he reached the announcement of his intention to play courier for Achim, the spell was complete – as if this was what she had been waiting for since they first met.

She leaned the slightness of her body towards him, took his hand, and pressed her lips gently to his cheek. The seducer was seduced.

"I'm glad," was all she said.

From here to a final consummation of her regard for him was only a short distance. But he was not yet ready to go down that path.

She was too important. He needed to know more about her. About why his decision made her glad. But everything remained securely locked away, and he had no idea where he should start looking for the key. She seemed so rootless in every way. So hard to pin down.

"You know, when I was a little boy," he said at last, "I had dreams of growing a huge oak tree at the bottom of our garden that would get as tall as our house and outlive me by hundreds of years. It would be my gift to posterity."

"I can just imagine you as a little boy. You must have been very sweet," she laughed with a gentle sparkle in her voice. It was a laugh that appeared to be born of the purest affection. And it left him with an exquisite tingling sensation. Like bubbles of the finest champagne.

"Every spring for about three years," he continued, "I would plant acorns in pots and watch them strike root, pushing out the first two leaves on their way to heaven. Then, when they were big enough to survive on their own, I would secretly put the seedlings in the ground in a distant corner of the garden. But every time my mother found them, she pulled them up. 'We don't want these growing in the garden, they'll destroy the foundations of the house before too long' she used to say. Goodness knows how long she was hoping to live. But I never gave up, and every spring I tried again, until my dream faded."

"Is that why you decided to go to Cologne for your friend? So you can finally plant your oak tree?"

He sensed she was mocking him.

"You remind me of those acorns I was always trying to plant," he said. "The way I kept hopelessly trying to help them strike root and was constantly being thwarted."

Patricia broke into a new kind of laugh.

"That's the first time anyone has likened me to an acorn. What does that make you? A squirrel come to sneak me off to your lair?"

"You mean my nest. Foxes have lairs."

She was making fun of him. But she did it with such magic that he found it impossible to take offence. He lifted his empty glass.

"Is there any more wine?" he repeated.

"I think I'll call you my squirrel from now on," she said.

The sense of possession implicit in these words sent a ripple of excitement through his chest. Bewitched by her mysterious beauty – which was all the richer for its modesty – he followed the line of her body with an impatient eye as she rose, still laughing to herself, and fetched the bottle from the cooking niche.

She bent forward slightly to pour the wine. Frank watched with rapt attention, drinking in the beauty of her slender wrist and her straight black hair as it cascaded over her face and concealed for a moment the enigma of her smile. The way her fingers flexed around the stem as they chinked glasses reflected the tantalising amalgam of vulnerability and strength of purpose – a paradox that teased his desire for her. He leaned forward and, before she could put the glass to her mouth, took it in his left hand to savour the soft sweet flesh of her lips on his.

Her response was not so much reciprocation, more a passive lingering. This encouraged him in the belief that it signalled at least a mild appreciation of his advances. Until his hands travelled down to the curvature of her waist and started slowly working back up the buttons of her blouse.

"What are you doing?"

Her words did not wholly convince him of the surprised innocence in the inflection of her voice. An impression that was reaffirmed when his continued unveiling of her slender body failed to elicit any further words of protest or bewilderment. On the contrary, as she let her blouse drop to the floor, a shy smile of acceptance flickered over her face. He took her in his arms, carried her over to the bed and laid her on the quilt cover as carefully as he might set down an injured dragonfly on a lily pad.

For a moment, which lost all shape of time, not a word was spoken.

Frank ran his fingers gently over the flesh of her lips. He let his middle finger lie in the exquisitely deep furrow of her philtrum.

"We call it the mark of an angel in French," she whispered. "Placed there by Lailah according to Jewish tradition."

"I can believe it," he said.

In a gesture of sweet surrender, her eyes followed the movement of his arm as his fingers explored further, gently skimming over the contours of her body. He sensed a frisson of tension as he did so – like a gentle pulse of lightning between the touch receptors of their skin – from the dainty, perfectly proportioned anatomy of her feet, over the soft black fleece protecting her virtue, to the muted ridges of bone that adorned her neck and put him in mind of the delicate collar worn by a certain kind of dove that he could not put a name to. The faint trace of a flush came into her cheeks, and she smiled.

"It seems to me that you have an unfair advantage."

She reached over and began to unbutton his shirt. He allowed the gentle touch of her fingers to work his garments loose and watched in silent passion. But not without a certain discomfort.

"I thought we were on a pretty equal footing already. After all, until I set eyes on you in all your nakedness, you knew far more about me than I did about you. I've simply redressed the balance. And now you're trying to tip the scales back in your favour."

"No," she said playfully. "Simply undressing the redressed balance."

Her immodesty, the way in which she made no secret of her appetite, took him by surprise. Yet it was not this, but the indescribable beauty of her that made him hesitate.

"How I'd like to stretch this moment to the end of time," he said. The remark appeared to please her. But Frank sensed that she did not fully grasp his meaning, and he tried hopelessly to expand on his words.

"There's something so pure and exciting about the erotic line of a woman's body. And when it shows this kind of perfection," he continued, as he ran his fingers the full length of her delicate frame, "then I just want to keep that moment of purity open for as long as possible."

"You mean you don't want to make love to me."

The bluntness hurt. And was compounded further by a sudden, fierce pounding on the door.

"Mademoiselle Roche!"

The voice from the other side of the door was ugly, but ineffectual. It repeated Patricia's name several times before eventually conceding defeat. They remained motionless on the bed and listened to the footsteps disappearing down the stairs. Then lay in complete silence. Like laboratory mice in an anechoic chamber.

"That was Lutz," Patricia whispered at last. This remained the extent of her words, until she saw that the name failed to make any impression on him.

"Didn't you meet him when you were at Breitner's place?" she asked. "He's what Breitner likes to regard as his private secretary. I've never been quite sure whether Lutz is his first name or his family name. Everyone just calls him Lutz. But it's certainly not a term of endearment. He's smarmy and thoroughly unlikeable."

"What do you think he wanted?"

"What he usually wants at this hour."

"Which is what?"

"To take me to Breitner." A cold despondency came into her expression with these words, and a blankness clouded the melancholy sparkle of her eyes.

"Why? To sleep with him?"

"You know, my first-ever acting role was a terrific success."

Was this another of her evasions, Frank asked himself. Or was it a relevant digression? He was rankled by the studied avoidance of his question.

"It was in my last year at school," she added. "We put on a stage play of *Tristan and Isolde*, which our teacher had adapted especially for the occasion. I was asked to play Isolde. By all accounts I did it quite well. My teacher said I had a natural talent. But I think my performance had more to do with the fact that I was madly in love with the boy who played Tristan. And I found the whole story so beautifully sad, so full of love and betrayal, just the kind of thing an adolescent girl adores."

Patricia smiled wistfully through her private reminiscence. It was a smile that seemed to shut Frank out entirely.

"Isolde taught me a lot about life and betrayal. Sometimes I think that life is just one long series of betrayals. But you know, it's not the big betrayals that are important. They can be excused by the schemes of history. The ones that matter are the small betrayals – the ones we commit in the course of a day without really giving them very much thought. It's those that gnaw away at our fibre and slowly destroy us."

"What happened to your Tristan?"

"Oh, I went off him shortly after that, when I saw him with a gang of his friends all in lederhosen. I can't abide lederhosen."

"And where does Breitner fit in?"

It was a clumsy question, but having brought her back to earth with Tristan's lederhosen, Frank felt the timing, if not the wording, was quite apt.

"He doesn't fit. He just forces his way in."

Frank sensed anger in these words as she slipped out of bed, tiptoed over to the door and opened it just a crack. He saw her crouch down and pick something off the floor outside. It was a single red rose. She closed the door, walked over to the table, put the flower in the vase with the other rose and crept back into bed.

Lying back into her pillow, pensive and unapproachable, Patricia left Frank to hang like a bat at dawn waiting for night to fall.

He regretted his earlier clumsiness. And, intrigued though he was by the significance of the scene he had just witnessed, he said nothing. Simply waited patiently for her to continue. When at last she appeared ready to admit him to her thoughts again, she spoke with a flatness and detachment that only served to underline his regret.

"My father has no time for all the talk we hear about race and religion these days. The woman he fell in love with and married, my mother, is classed a Gentile. But that makes him no less of a Jew. And Breitner has some useful connections. In exchange for certain favours, he promised to see that my father would be all right."

"What sort of favours?"

Frank's indiscretion was met with a partly worried, partly disparaging look which he found hard to fathom.

"Breitner sees himself as a businessman with interests in every corner of the city. He has a lot of contacts in the Swiss chemical companies here, for example, and other organisations that do business in Germany. And he keeps an eye on the students here as well. Especially German students. All for his masters in the party over the border. So I feed him with useless information about student activities."

"And where does he take his meals? In bed?"

"You know, it seems to me that you're very inquisitive when it comes to things that don't concern you. And not nearly curious enough about the things that really matter."

Her words were right on target. And they stung. The two of them fell into silent contemplation. Frank could sense the tension in the slight touch of their bodies as they lay side by side on her bed.

"Where do the roses come in?" Frank asked at last, unable to let his urge for interrogation lie still for any longer.

"Ah, *les fleurs du mal*." A wry smile crossed her lips as Patricia whispered these words. They came with a deep sadness in their tone that accentuated her French accent in a way Frank had not heard in her before. "Lutz leaves a rose outside the door whenever Breitner wants to see me."

Frank bristled at her words. They sent a shiver through his spine.

"It's a dangerous game you're playing, Patricia."

She smiled, and ran her fingers over his chest.

"No more so than yours," she rejoined, and punctuated this statement with a kiss on his right nipple, which she teased with her tongue and tugged at with her teeth. The way in which she could suddenly banish her sadness sent a pulse of excitement coursing through his veins.

"Frank, I have an idea. If you want to move out of your hotel and find somewhere else to live, why don't you come and stay here? I have to go away next week, and will be gone for some time. So, when you get back from Cologne, you could come and stay here until my return. You would be safe from Breitner for a time. He would never think of looking for you here while I'm away."

Frank was not so sure that his tormentor would be so easily duped. But in his erotic enchantment he had put any threat from Breitner to the back of his mind. And had even forgotten about the promised trip to Cologne. Yet Patricia's unexpected invitation now lent a new urgency to his plans.

He vowed to himself that he would make his preparations the following morning.

They did not make love on this their first night together, but lay in each other's arms enjoying the beauty of the moment. The exquisite touch of skin upon skin. The perfumes that gather around the triangles of the neck. A sense of deep tenderness that Frank took with him into the timeless reaches of sleep.

It was close to dawn when a rude hand fetched him back from this paradise. His immediate impression of that waking instant was of a fierce ache tearing his head apart. No matter how his head was positioned on the pillow, he felt that his brain was being dragged from the comfort of his skull and pummelled beyond recognition. But he sensed it was not this so much as the noise that woke him from his sweet dreams – a deafening, repetitive clanging above his head that seemed to fill the entire room.

"What the hell is that?"

"Only bells. Just damned church bells."

He looked down at the face on the pillow beside him, and caught the scent of a familiar perfume in the air. The flame-red curls of her hair draped over the green polyester satin. And her lips still moved vaguely in the wake of her words. But her eyes remained firmly shut. Who was she? The scene threw him into the tangled arms of a dream state that he struggled to unravel, until eventually sleep returned to save him from the clutches of his desperation.

By the time the full brunt of wakefulness finally forced itself upon him, this discordant interlude in the night had already faded. He gazed on the delicate, sleep-entrained features of Patricia's face on the pillow beside him: her long dark lashes keeping the seductive charm of her eyes still firmly closed to the morning light; her lips in a beguiling, asymmetric pose, as if forming words that wanted to be spoken; and her raven hair curled around her ear in a way that accentuated the fleshy fullness of the lobe. He had never realised until that moment what beautiful perfection there was to be found in the earlobe. Even the perforation made in the tender flesh of the lobe to accommodate an earring displayed an impeccably neat precision.

It occurred to him at that moment that he had never actually seen Patricia wearing earrings. He wondered what special occasions she reserved them for. Were they perhaps another part of her life that was set aside for Breitner?

He watched spellbound by the sight of her beginning to surface, the way she extended first her left arm and then the left leg from under the sheets, as if instinctively testing the air before she woke. Enthralled by the unfolding splendour of her stirring, he instantly set aside any thoughts or feelings about Breitner. And by the time she was fully awake, the picture of her smile on the pillow had not only put to flight any memory of the bully from Berlin. It ensured also that he had completely forgotten the intrusion of the brief, but disturbing dream of church bells, that familiar perfume and the blonde curls on the pillow. They had lost any meaning they might have had for him.

But disappointment soon set in when Patricia – now fully awake – announced that she had lectures to attend that morning. And brought home to Frank that, before his day with her had even started, it was already practically at an end.

Before he left, however, she promised to get a second key to her flat made that afternoon and to drop it by at his hotel. So he would get to see her again that day. A promise that imbued him now with a sense of ambition and allowed him to take the rest of the day in his stride. More easily than any other day he could remember. Patricia had given him a purpose, however vague in its definition.

When he got back to his hotel room later in the day, he found this purpose had already acquired a certain cutting edge.

Chapter 13

The suitcase lay on the bed, looking harmless but heavy. It would probably have been cumbersome enough to carry even without its contents. But when Frank opened it up to find all the bundles of literature that his friend wanted him to hump across Germany, it was plain that his journey was not going to be easy. It was a large leather case, and it was crammed full of the little handbooks on chess that Achim had shown him, together with some small pocketbook collections of Grimm's fairy tales. It occurred to him that the tram would not be the most convenient means of transport for the laden beast he was about to become. So he ordered a taxi to get him to the station.

It was a good feeling to check out of the hotel that had been his home for so long. It had become a dispiriting place to live in, especially in the last three weeks or so, when his privacy had been so rudely and so regularly interrupted – right down to the unannounced appearance of this suitcase. He wondered how Achim had managed to get into his room in the first place. And why he had not waited. Was it perhaps Silverstone who had put it there, he asked himself. But however it had come to be there, it told him one thing: the space he moved in today really had no borders to defend him against life's invasions.

Sadly, Patricia proved not so indiscreet in delivering the key she had made to her flat, but had simply left it in an envelope at reception with a message inside: 'Bon voyage'.

Had the envelope not contained the key to her flat, he would have instantly seen this message as the final brush-off. Instead it left him wondering why she could not find the time to deliver it in person. Recalling now the sound of the man called Lutz knocking on her door the night before made him wonder whether perhaps she had another appointment with Breitner.

Accompanied by the disappointment of not seeing Patricia again before he left, all these thoughts rode with Frank on the short taxi ride over the river to the city's German station. This disturbing oddity of German property on Swiss soil was where travellers came face to face each day with the chilling evidence which proved to him that his obsessive thoughts about the bully from Berlin were not the meanderings of a paranoid schizophrenic.

The station tower rose above this German station like a finger up the arse of Switzerland, mocking the quiet, disinterested streets of Frank's refuge as it let the swastika billow from its large, stubby digit. It came as a shock every time he saw that frightening symbol of hatred flying over Swiss soil. And it reminded him now of Breitner's words when he tried to impress on Frank that the arm of the Third Reich was more than long enough to reach across the border as and when it pleased. There really was no safe refuge from its arrogance.

In the station itself, on the far side of the booking hall, the uniforms and the ominous leather coats and wide-brimmed hats at the customs barrier underlined the menace with fearsome effect. A menace that was enhanced all the more for Frank by the knowledge that the local Swiss branch of the NSDAP had their offices in this station building.

Tucking away the threat as comfortably as he could, he walked over to the ticket office to buy a first-class return to Cologne. With his back to the customs barrier, he felt wide open to everything he had been running from these past months. The feeling chilled him to the bone. After taking his ticket, he remained at the counter for some time, bracing himself to pick up the suitcase and turn with composure towards that guarded gateway to purgatory. He had nothing to fear, he kept telling himself, so why act so guilty?

When he reached the barrier and handed over his passport at immigration, it was taken from him with officious brusqueness and examined in painstaking detail.

"You have been living in Switzerland for almost three months."

The observation came without so much as a glance from the immigration officer. He might have been talking to himself. But it was hard to argue with the truth of the statement.

"Why?" he asked. "What do you have against your Fatherland?"

"On the contrary. I love my country," Frank replied. "If I had something against it, I wouldn't feel the need to return."

The man disappeared into an office with his passport, giving Frank the impression he was less than satisfied with this half-hearted declaration of patriotism. The struggle to retain his composure was becoming desperate. And the sweat was starting to gather. But he was keenly conscious of the need to keep calm. He was aware of the wide-brimmed hats and leather coats watching everyone who passed through the gate. And he sensed their prying eyes wander down to his suitcase. He tried to throw a casual look in their direction. Their eyes met. The looks that pierced Frank with a force that made his stomach churn appeared to be saying: 'Frank Eigenmann, your number's up', and he had to keep telling himself not to be so foolish, that he had nothing to fear – he was an innocent traveller with nothing more incriminating than a suitcase full of Grimm's fairy tales that he was delivering to a bookseller friend in Cologne.

The waiting seemed interminable. To his relief, the two Gestapo men turned their attention to another target of interest: a younger, more shabbily dressed traveller with rucksack, who had just arrived at the gate further back down the line. At that same moment, the immigration officer returned with his passport, thrust it into his hand and wished him "*Gute Reise*". It did not have quite the same appeal as Patricia's 'Bon voyage', but it was no less welcome. Indeed, he found it hard to conceal his sense of relief, and his expression of thanks was perhaps a little too effusive. But he was through. And it struck him as he walked through the gate that anyone seriously considering this as a route for smuggling propaganda into the country must need his head examined. He was thankful that this was a dummy run.

The real advantage of travelling first class, Frank told himself, was that you can usually find a compartment to yourself. And this train was no exception. At one point, a shabby figure in a cloth cap appeared in the doorway and gave him a curious look, as though he wanted to join Frank. He recognised the man at once as the target of interest behind him who had aroused the attention of the Gestapo. But the familiarity went deeper, when he realised this was the man who had followed him and Patricia after their meeting at the museum. Frank's heart sank. But the man passed. He did not appear the type who would travel in comfort.

The luxury of travelling first class was more than matched by the sense of being able to draw breath again after the last few weeks of harassment. He smiled at the irony that the city of light – his refuge from darkness and oppression – had become such a troubling place to live that he should find comfort on a train ride through the very heart of that darkness he had been seeking to escape. And he began to ponder the nature of this journey.

His funk hole in Switzerland had become a snake pit, which he had only chosen to leave with a view to getting back as quickly as possible. And he was already forging plans, imagining life within the four walls of Patricia's flat as he awaited her return. He was looking forward to introducing her to Achim when she got back. Although his old friend had turned away from his vocation as an artist, Frank was certain he would approve of her and appreciate her impressive knowledge of art.

But why was he even taking this journey. Was it to help Achim? Or was it to salve his own conscience? For he knew that deep down Achim was right, that sweet dreams belong to the luxury of a peaceful night's sleep. That when that luxury is not on offer, there comes a time when you have to take sides.

Then there was the question of his mother, the ostensible motive for his journey. But she was surely not the true reason for his going to Cologne? He disliked the woman almost as much as she resented him. She had never completely forgiven him for being a boy. She rarely missed an opportunity to remind him of her regret that he was not a girl, someone who would be a real companion for her during his father's frequent absences. As an engineer of some renown, his father would often spend months at a time in India, Persia or some other distant part of the world.

Bitter were the memories of his early childhood, when he was not yet independent enough to resist the pressures of his mother, who would invariably dress him up as a girl. She would even take him out for walks in the neighbourhood and pretend to all the world that he was her little niece come to stay. He still remembered those occasions with vivid embarrassment. Fortunately, she was sufficiently in awe of his father to allow him a respite from her fantasies whenever he was home. As Frank grew older, it gradually dawned on him that his mother had a serious psychological problem, and he became more tolerant of her on the surface. But by then the damage had been done, and his antipathy was indelibly etched into their relationship.

So the trip to Cologne did not promise to be a pleasant occasion. And it was hard to imagine that his mother might be an important motivation behind this journey. Yet, when all was said and done, it was still a mother/child relationship, so a sense of guilt inevitably stalked his thoughts. And perhaps hers too, he told himself, if she was not already too senile for moral reflection.

Whichever way he turned, it seemed that bad conscience was the crucial agency driving him on this journey, that Patricia was nothing more than the spice to camouflage its flavour. The atmosphere in the carriage was beginning to oppress him.

When the train rolled into Freiburg, he opened a window. He was pleased to see that more people were leaving the train here than were getting on, so he felt confident that his first-class isolation would remain secure at least until Karlsruhe. But when he turned his attention up the platform in the other direction, he could not fail to notice – leaning from the carriage just a few windows removed from him – the pockmarked face of the man in the cloth cap. Frank had the uncomfortable impression that the man was watching him.

This feeling lingered with him all the way to Karlsruhe and beyond. He began to wish he had brought more than the daily newspaper to distract him from his unsettling thoughts. Then it occurred to him that he had a suitcase full of literature with him, however dull, so he opened up his baggage. He opted for a refresher course in chess rather than a fairy tale, and leaned back in his seat with one of Achim's booklets. As he leafed through it, he was instantly put in mind of what Patricia had told him, when she said he was not inquisitive about the things that really matter. Those words had stung him far more than she had intended, because they were even closer to the truth than she suspected. Certainly, if he had been more inquisitive, he would have given these booklets more than a cursory glance and seen them at once for what they really were – not the primers on chess that they professed to be. No kings, queens or bishops here. Only pawns. From the very first page they preached unashamed, hard-selling, communist propaganda. Slogans of Bolshevist extremism for the working man.

He took a copy of Grimm's fairy tales from the suitcase. And found the story was the same. The same message, the same words. The cruelty of childhood fantasies replaced by the tyranny of collectivist adult dreams.

Was this what Achim meant when he said he had been moving in mixed company? That he had joined the red side of the political spectrum? Had life in Berlin driven him so far as to abandon his dignity? Frank asked himself. The thought appalled him, but far worse was the realisation that he had been so deceived and used by his old friend. A dummy run, he had said. Well, the only dummy was me, Frank told himself. Like Patricia, Achim knew that he was not inquisitive about the things that really matter. And he had exploited that to the full. He even sowed the seed in Frank's mind that he should visit his mother. Presumably, this whole absurd trip he was making had been planned by him and his cronies back in Berlin before he had even left.

The disappointment and anger that seethed in his head blinded him to the full implications of the situation he was in. But one thing was clear: he was not going to be used by Bolshevists fighting to replace one kind of oppression with another. If these were the only sides on offer, he would prefer to stay on the fence.

What was less clear to him was the immediate danger he was in, put there by his own naivety. It was not until the train began slowing down on its approach into Mannheim that it dawned on him how urgently he needed to act. He could be stopped and searched at any time on this journey, and almost had been before even getting on the train. Of course, he realised this when he agreed to accept the suitcase. What he had not realised was the true nature of the luggage he would be carrying – and that it might be exchanged anywhere along the line for a ticket to Dachau, if he was lucky.

He returned the books to the suitcase and lowered the window of his compartment. Already the station of Mannheim was looming down the line like a huge mouth slowly opening to swallow a tasty morsel. He saw two options: either move to another part of the train and leave the suitcase here or break his journey at Mannheim and leave the suitcase to travel on alone. He was certainly in no doubt that Achim's betrayal of their friendship deserved no more than this. And since the latter alternative seemed the less risky, he decided to get out.

Relief. Disappointment. Anger. Fear. All these emotions carried him along the platform. And when he looked back anxiously at the train before merging with the throng, he saw at the window of the compartment he had just vacated a familiar face.

It was the cloth-capped man who had been watching his every move. As ever. Only now he was watching from an intimate recess of his own most recent history – with a direct line to his conscience.

Frank did not let his gaze linger too long in this direction, but he had the impression that the man was reaching for the suitcase as if about to open it. And at that moment he could not escape the feeling that he had made a fatal error.

The thought that this man might be an informer in the pay of the Gestapo pursued him relentlessly into the passageway that led under the railway lines. His mind began feverishly to look for a way out of this trap he seemed to have laid for himself. It was no use leaving the station, since he had a ticket all the way to Cologne and would only draw attention to himself if he was checked at the gate.

He found an inconspicuous vantage point from which he could observe activities on the platform and look out for signs that anyone might have been alerted about the abandoned suitcase. The minutes dragged endlessly by as people passed through the gateway out of the station to the arms of their friends or family – or simply to the welcoming embrace of freedom from the kind of anxiety he was compelled to endure. How he envied every one of those travellers. What he would have given to leave his secret behind on this station and pass through that barrier as easily as they, without let or hindrance.

His own train had already long since continued on its journey north, and he had seen no signs of menacing suspicion apart from those to which the last few years in the Third Reich had inured him. Slowly the possibility crept up on him that the man in the train may be a fellow traveller in the truest sense of the word – and that, when he found the suitcase, probably took it with him to distribute among his own people. The cloth-capped stranger would doubtless be grateful for the find.

As this more comfortable scenario began to take root, he started to breathe more easily. Could he perhaps pass unhindered after all? Frank asked himself.

The next train to Cologne did not leave for a good two hours. Since it was time for lunch, he therefore found a table in a dark, sequestered corner of the station buffet. The palpitations of his earlier panic still lingered as he took his seat. He eyed every diner with suspicion. He was still far from comfortable, but fear was in abeyance. And it gave way gradually to the anger and disappointment he still felt towards Achim. These feelings kept Frank company for the rest of that day, feeding his thoughts throughout the onward journey.

When eventually he arrived in Cologne, he booked into a hotel close to the station. He needed a night's rest before he could summon anything approaching enthusiasm to see his mother. And once he had done so, it was a strange melancholy that he carried with him along the avenue to his mother's house.

The smart row of early Wilhelminian residences that lined the street mocked his coming with their grand, standoffish elegance. The scene was punctuated here and there by the garish patterns of the swastika fluttering from some of the grander houses. He shivered at the sight, which only served to underline the cold disquiet of the nostalgia he was beginning to feel. While it was not the street he had grown up in, the architecture of the buildings and their opulent gardens were very similar to where he used to play, the trees he used to climb. It brought back memories of the friends he used to call on. One he remembered in particular was Volker Schmidt. He was a year older than Frank, and very bright.

He recalled that they would often play together in his garden just like those he was passing now. The tangled overgrown shrubbery always impressed Frank with its neglect and provided them with the perfect setting for constructing all kinds of secret hideaway and indulging every manner of fantasy. It was a place that established a special bond with Volker, but sadly the tie was very quickly severed just a few weeks later when he was taken off to a psychiatric clinic.

Volker had had something of a scientific bent. At the time, he showed a deep passion for chemistry. During one of their afternoons in the secrecy of his garden, he demonstrated how to make a simple, but very effective explosive device by packing a jar with equal measures of sugar and sodium chlorate, which he had found in his neighbour's garden shed. As he lit the fuse and impressively proved the blasting power of his bomb, Volker's eyes displayed a proud look of achievement.

"You just wait till Wassermann crosses my path again," he muttered, a hint of gleeful vengeance in his eyes.

Heinz Wassermann was the local neighbourhood bully, a large and exceptionally dull-witted animal who resented the vast intellectual distance between him and Volker. And he made Volker suffer – until that explosive discovery, when Volker saw the opportunity for a real counterblast to end Wassermann's bullying once and for all. In the event, Wassermann was badly injured. He lost the sight of one eye and gained the dubious honour of a permanently scarred face. But he knew instinctively how to turn his disfigurement to advantage, and he paraded his scars as trophies of his manhood – to great effect. Frank could well imagine that he had joined the ranks of the SS by now.

Volker on the other hand, who had initially seen his achievement as a triumph of science over ignorance, was quickly disabused of this idea. Once again, it was he who was made to suffer, betrayed by the stupidity of his intellect. Frank never saw him again after he was admitted to psychiatric care. But he heard some years later that he had been diagnosed with schizophrenia and gone steadily downhill since his admission.

Frank dwelled on the history of these two as he walked now along the avenue towards his mother's house. And the disquieting nostalgia that was trailed before him by this train of thought remained with him as he stood at the door and rang the bell.

When eventually the door was opened, he was greeted by a woman in her fifties who was a complete stranger to him. Severe, surly and spinsterish in appearance. Her manner and the very presence of foreignness about her drew a curtain of silence around Frank, until she finally gave way to her impatience.

"Well?"

"Götz Eigenmann," he said, aware that the name Frank would mean nothing to her. "Mrs Eigenmann's son."

She looked him up and down with a suspicion that would not have been out of place at the station where he had boarded the train.

"She's never talked to me of a son."

"Has she not? And who are you if I may ask?"

"I'm the nurse," she said, as if every home should have one. And she punctuated this assertion with a firmness that claimed supreme authority. At best, he was an unwelcome intruder; at worst, a contemptible wretch who deserved all manner of vilification for daring to arrogate special privileges for himself as the son of the household, when he could obviously not even be bothered to keep himself informed about his mother's health. However she saw him, she made no secret of her desire to shut the door in his face. But Frank persisted.

"Well, if you would be kind enough to take me to my mother, I think you will find that she will confirm who I am."

"An identity card would be sufficient."

When he handed her his passport, she examined it with the careful suspicion that reminded him once again of the immigration officer at the border. It seemed to him that fear and suspicion had become cherished commodities. And reminded him of all the reasons why he had left.

At length, she handed it back to him with the words "Follow me" and led him into a room that he instantly recognised as his father's study. He had only been admitted to the sanctum of his father's study on the rarest of occasions. And although this room was not that very same study, it was immediately identifiable as his father's by its design.

When his father died a few years after Frank left home to study in Berlin, his mother sold the family house in Freiburg and moved to Cologne to be close to her sister. And she had taken his father's study with her. Every book, every item of furniture and even the curtains were installed in an almost identical room of her new house in Cologne. Frank was able to recollect every detail of the heavy, learned inventory. Everything still in its place, as if in memoriam to his father's achievements.

Only on his desk did he see a change, where the nurse had lined a row of what he presumed to be her own books, behind which she now took her seat. And she beckoned him to make himself comfortable on the opposite side of the desk.

"I think it would be wise, Mr Eigenmann, if we had a talk before I take you to see your mother."

She gave Frank the impression that she was trying to catch up on what she saw as a missed vocation by playing physician.

"As I say, your mother has never mentioned a son to me. She spoke often of her daughter, but never a son."

"Daughter? What daughter?" he asked.

"She died at a young age I believe."

"She never had a daughter."

Frank was growing impatient with the woman. He had not wanted to come here in the first place. And now that he was here, all the reasons for his not wanting to come were being aggravated beyond endurance. Achim had plainly felt disinclined to warn him of the need for dragon-slaying. He had not even intimated just how serious his mother's condition appeared to be, which made Frank wonder whether he had visited her at all. All of which nourished the idea in his mind that the whole story was part of his old friend's plan to make Frank play courier for him.

"Would you please tell me what it is that's ailing my mother?" he asked the nurse. "The last time I saw her was about six months ago. And apart from the usual debilities of old age she seemed to be in reasonably good health. I had no idea that she was in need of a housekeeper."

"I am not a housekeeper, Mr Eigenmann. I am a nurse."

Her voice betrayed the insecure edge of wounded pride. This pleased his sense of irritation with the woman.

"If it was six months ago, then probably it was not long after you last saw her that it happened," she continued, her professional pride restored by a sharp intake of breath and a composure probably learned in some Prussian finishing school. "She was out walking her dog not very far from here when she was accosted by a gang of youths who for some reason took it into their heads that she was Jewish. So they decided to teach her a lesson. It's disgusting what the young people get up to nowadays."

"And what *did* they get up to?"

"It's too horrible."

She was drawing again on the strength of her well-tutored composure and spoke with a flat calmness that seemed completely at odds with the scene she now described.

"They swooped on her like carrion crows and snatched up the dog. Then they hung it from a tree by its lead and slowly tortured the innocent creature to death before her very eyes, pecking at it with sticks and knives. The poor woman was admitted to the clinic in the most appalling state of shock. She was quite beside herself. And she has never really recovered.

"After a few weeks it was decided that she should be discharged in the hope that she might improve in the familiarity of her home surroundings. And so she was entrusted to my care – thus far to no avail. Let us hope," she added, with little sign of conviction in her voice, "that your coming will prove to be of some help."

Her words breathed a miasma of expectant, unfulfilled duty into his face, which mingled with the acrid memories of the house and stuck in his throat, teasing him with a certain bitterness. This was his mother she was talking about. Yet it was difficult to feel more than a passing sympathy for someone who had been such a dire reference point in his life. He was more inclined to be moved by newspaper reports of some calamitous event in the life of a perfect stranger.

His mother's keeper led him out of the study and up the heavy staircase with a solemnness that seemed to be born more of an obtuse reluctance than of any concern for her charge. Then suddenly she stopped and turned to him with new life in her voice.

"She called her dog Götz."

Frank had the impression she expected a response. But he kept his counsel. And they continued up the stairs.

His mother appeared to be dozing when he entered the room. Propped up in bed, her eyes closed and her long grey hair untidy with sleep, she could have been any old woman. She bore little resemblance to the person he had known as his mother. Her teeth had been removed and lay poised in a glass of water like a hungry clam. It was the first time he had ever seen her without teeth, and their absence changed the shape of her face in a way that gnawed at his own identity. Yet it was not only this that made her seem so different. It was the age that had been carved into her face with such savage disrespect for the governance of time. Not months, but years – a lifetime – lay between this encounter and the last occasion when they had met.

An irresistible urge pressed him to leave now while there was still time. But he hesitated. In disbelief, he stood watching her sleep. Her bed was bedecked with a brown, chenille drape that he recalled having always been used to cover the dining-room table. It seemed oddly out of place here. An evidently bewildered look on his face prompted the nurse to explain that his mother had insisted on using this instead of an eiderdown.

Frank remembered spilling some red paint on it as a child and being severely scolded. In its new role as bed cover, the brown fabric still sported the vestiges of this clumsy blemish, albeit less obviously. And he wondered what on earth could be the significance of taking this drape onto the bed.

The room, too, was not at all as he recollected the way it was when he was last here. The fusty narrow darkness remained. But the mahogany furnishings had been rearranged and – apart from the ectopic chenille table cover – betrayed the fussy touch of the Prussian nurse, who by now had at least shown sufficient discretion to withdraw from the painfully strange intimacy of this scene.

On the large dresser beside the window hung with heavy velvet curtains, which admitted only the minimum of light, stood an arc of photographs in elaborate art nouveau frames. In the dimness, one photo in particular stood out as being vaguely familiar to him. He moved closer to examine it. Taking it in his hand, he flinched as a shock of light from the window brought all the memories flooding back. In the picture, a girl of about six in a long pinafore dress and bonnet, sitting on her mother's knee, was clutching a china doll. She might have looked quite sweet, had it not been for the expression of fear in her eyes. How vividly, after all these years, Frank recalled being dressed up for the occasion and being taken to the photographer's studio in town for the portrait to be done. They had taken the tram into Freiburg, and no sooner had they alighted and he set foot on the pavement than he took to his heels, struggling desperately to cope with the unaccustomed folds of cloth that twisted around his ankles in his futile efforts to escape the cruel games of his mother. She of course was not only used to coping with the hindrances of women's attire. She also had longer legs and quickly got the better of him. In no time at all, Frank was being dragged back down the street screaming:

"No, Mama, please. Not today. Please, Mama. I'll go tomorrow. I promise."

His appeals were in vain, to which this photograph now bore poignant testimony. It opened up a wound in the deeper recesses of his memory that he had fondly imagined was long since healed beyond all possibility of pain. It was soon after this incident that his mother gave up her dressing games with him. But seeing the framed photo for the first time now after all these years imbued his memory of the shame with an unpalatable freshness and immediacy.

It occurred to him that it was probably this photo that the nurse had in mind when she talked of his mother's "daughter". And he wondered what fantastic tales his mother must have been spinning around this irrefutable photographic evidence.

"What are you doing over there, young man?"

The voice startled him with its abrasive crackle. He turned and saw the woman who was his mother still propped in the same position against the pillow – her eyes now open. They gave her face a mild quality of expression that allowed him at least very vaguely to relate to her as the woman for whom he had been a living disappointment.

"Hello mother. It's me, Götz."

Those simple words did not come easily to him. And they were rewarded with a bafflement and frustration which he almost welcomed.

"Götz?"

The lips of her flaccid, involuted mouth began to quiver. And the crackle of her voice intensified as she reinforced the dismay in her words: "Who are you? What do you want?"

He could give his mother no satisfactory answer, and in her growing consternation she called for her keeper.

"Nurse! Nurse!"

She could not repeat this desperate, crackling cry often enough. Her words rang in his ears like the sound of a sadly loose violin string in the hands of a frantic novice who imagined that – if he kept plucking at it – then in time it would ring true. Frank pre-empted the arrival of the Prussian matron by leaving the room and met her on the stairs outside. She paused briefly to pierce him with her steely expression.

"I suggest you wait in my office," she said, then resumed her rise to the call of duty. He could hear the incongruously mollifying tones of her harsh and jagged voice attempting to comfort his mother as he continued downstairs to the study.

This visit to discharge his filial duties had developed into a depressing and irritating affair. He had come to say farewell to his mother, only to find she had already gone – and been replaced by a demented product of her own fantasies, complete with supporting vulture eager for the pickings. The way this particular connoisseur of decomposing carrion claimed possession already of territories that were hard pressed even to tolerate the arrogance, let alone smile upon it, drove his indignation to new heights.

It was only a taste for schadenfreude that compelled him to follow the woman's instructions and wait for her in the study. A malevolent desire to see the disappointment on her face when he told her that his mother was in no position to bequeath this property to the first Samaritan who chanced along and that this study in which she had already staked her claim was not hers but his.

In many respects, his father might not have been the model parent. By the nature of his job, which took him away from home for long periods, he had been very distant. And their relationship had consequently been very business-like. But he was nothing if not correct, and he knew his duties as a father. So, when he knew he was about to die, as if preparing to set off on his last great voyage – this time never to return – he saw to it that his son should at least be in a position to enjoy the fruits of his father's years of labour. And he did not rest until every loose end of legal necessity had been tied up.

Frank often wondered why it was he had felt compelled to spend so much of his time in the far-flung outposts of civilisation. Whether it had been a reflection of his relationship with the woman who now lay helpless and demented in her bedroom upstairs. Whether they had never really loved each other. And perhaps he found the answer in that study among the various items on the shelves, which he browsed through now in casual, unconscious search of a clue to his father.

One clue in particular attracted his attention. It was a large, beautifully bound and gilt-edged volume on the fauna and flora of India – a Victorian tome in English from the days of the British Raj. The elaborate colour engravings of peacocks, jambu trees and rose-ringed parakeets were striking enough and hinted at a romantic side to his father's character which Frank had never even suspected. But what especially caught his eye were some loose leaves in the book that became dislodged by his thumbing of the pages and, on closer inspection, revealed a large sepia brown photograph of an attractive Indian girl fetchingly attired in her traditional sari. On the back of the photo he found the words: With regards to you and your family, Neeti.

This intriguing discovery begged so many questions that Frank would never be in a position to answer. But the very thought that his father might possibly have had some kind of a liaison with this Neeti woman filled him with a curious gladness. Was this perhaps the true reason for his father's many travels? Was this his escape from the straitjacket of his mother's regime, which he was certain must have been as harsh for his father as it was for him?

Frank searched the shelves for more clues. But of his other books – which appeared to be mostly dry tracts on the art of building bridges and the like – none surrendered any further glimpses of his father's romantic nature. Nonetheless, he began to feel that his journey had not been entirely in vain after all. He tucked the photograph carefully back inside the book, wrote a brief note to the nurse, giving her Patricia's flat as his contact address, then left. He had no desire and saw no reason to speak with the dragon again. And he felt sure that she had nothing of any consequence to report about his mother that he had not already seen with his own eyes. The book he took with him under his arm. Whether this was out of sentiment or curiosity he was not certain, but he felt in some inexplicable way that it belonged with him. And it was presumably this possession of his mind by thoughts of the unsuspected love knots of his father that blurred his mental faculties and obscured the stupidity of this last act of leaving behind his address.

After the original purpose of his journey to Cologne had been so rudely blanched by betrayal, the enjoyment of this discovery in his father's study now imbued the journey with a certain colour. And punctuated his stay in this city with such pleasing neatness that he was now eager to return. The knowledge that Patricia would no longer be there when he got back slightly took the edge off his appetite. But he was nonetheless still sufficiently motivated by the uneasy feeling that he had a score to settle with Achim.

What he was not prepared for was the reception that appeared to be waiting for him when he arrived at the railway station to start his journey back. The cloth cap and shabby attire stopped him in his tracks before he had even crossed the street to the station entrance. He recognised the figure at once as the man on the train who had shown such a keen interest in the suitcase of betrayal he abandoned when he got out at Mannheim. 'What's he doing here?' Frank asked himself.

From the concealment of an advertising pillar some distance from the station entrance, Frank watched the man for a good fifteen minutes. He appeared to be looking out for the arrival of someone, but gave the impression of having all the time in the world. If Frank did not move soon, he would miss his train. But he felt unable to risk being seen by this man, who remained an unexplained threat to his existence.

Frank's sense of caution told him that his journey south should be postponed for at least another few hours. Taking care to ensure that he was not followed, he took himself off to a cafe from where he could observe the comings and goings at the station.

The permanence of the man's presence convinced Frank all the more that he must be in the pay of the police. Anyone who lurked for so long in one place would inevitably draw suspicion upon himself and be quietly moved on – unless he enjoyed the benefits of some special kind of patronage. There could be no other explanation for the stubborn vigil of this shabby man who had watched his every move so keenly on the train up to Cologne.

It seemed more than likely to Frank that, having found the incriminating evidence in the suitcase left behind in the carriage, the man would have felt compelled to keep a watch for him at the station. They would have established his destination with a quick phone call to the office where his passport and ticket had been so assiduously checked before he got on the train. How they could have known that he would be returning to Switzerland on this particular day remained a mystery to Frank. But he was confident enough of their intelligence to believe that it was distinctly possible.

As he sat in the coffee house, his eye on the station traffic, the bitterness of the coffee on his tongue reminded him of the first time he had drunk coffee with Patricia. It recalled the growing sense of fear that he was going to lose her even before they had become close enough to have anything to lose. How he wanted her at this moment. How desperately he needed her company. And how far away she seemed.

She had not confided in him precisely where it was she was disappearing to for so long. And he had been unwilling to drive a wedge between them by pressing too hard for information. But the coincidence of her departure with the appearance of the mysterious Léandre made him suspect at least a tenuous connection. Yet strangely his suspicions did not unduly disturb him. He did not feel the pangs of jealousy or disappointment. She had left him the freedom of her flat, after all. And he saw this as a commitment that bestowed a special kind of meaning on their ill-defined relationship.

These thoughts further inflamed his eagerness to get back to the comfort of her flat as soon as he could. It was plain to him that he would not achieve this by sipping coffee and watching the departures and arrivals at Cologne railway station forever. And the imagination had long since talked him into believing beyond any doubt that the vigil across the road could only be intended for him.

He considered the alternatives. The most attractive of these was not without its risks, but they were certainly less than the cloth-capped hazard that awaited him in front of the station. And it occurred to him that, if they were watching for him here, then they would doubtless be waiting at the other end of the line as well.

Shielded by the traffic and crowds between him and the station, he slipped onto a tram that would eventually bring him to the harbour, where he was confident of finding a boat that would take him upstream. If not all the way to Switzerland, then at least some distance from Cologne, so that he could safely resume his journey by rail from a station that was not under such scrutiny.

On the assumption that more heavily laden barges would be heading south than less heavily laden ones, he looked for a vessel that lay low in the water. Only two presented themselves as possible candidates. But he was optimistic that more would arrive as night drew in, so he resolved to resume his waiting game – this time from what seemed to him the more seductive comfort of a bargee's pub near the river, where he could enjoy a beer or two. He was mistaken. The place was empty when he entered. Dark, uninviting and – for a stranger not wanting to draw attention to himself – conspicuously bare of custom.

"Heil Hitler!"

The landlord – large, rugged and churlish – merged with the gloom cast by the beams and rafters of the bar. And his greeting caught Frank momentarily off guard. Fortunately, he had the presence of mind to reciprocate before suspicion could take root. It was a necessity he had become accustomed to, but one he never observed without a deep, flinching reluctance. It had always struck him as a particularly juvenile automatism. He had had difficulty enough coming to terms with the infantile stupidities of gang behaviour at school. Now it was as if the world about him had become an extended third-form classroom with all the petty jealousies and herding ethos of adolescence. Only nastier by far.

As Frank sat in the corner, slowly but uncomfortably sipping from his beer, he sensed the barman's unerring gaze on his every move. It remained fixed on Frank even after he had finished the first glass and defiantly settled into another. Only when he was almost at the end of this second glass did the barman look away, at the motion of the opening door. Another customer walked in. And the landlord's expression instantly changed, assuming a more affable tone.

"Hansruedi, where've you been keeping yourself?" he asked. Haven't seen you in here for months."

The two shook hands, and the large barrel of a man addressed as Hansruedi ordered a beer. He wore a reefer jacket and navy peaked cap that told Frank he was probably once used to plying the waterways around Hamburg. But he was plainly not a native of that city. His origins were inescapably betrayed by his accent and his name. This man was Swiss.

The landlord pulled himself a beer, and the two of them sank into a muffled exchange depriving Frank of any further information that might have been of value. Frustrated, but hopeful that he had as much detail as he needed, Frank supped the last dregs from his beer glass and got up to leave.

"Heil Hitler."

Again the landlord baited him. And again Frank acquiesced in the dumb stupidity of his words, as he walked out into the early evening air. It was already dark, and he felt the stringent freshness of raindrops on his face. As he was beginning to wonder how he might identify Hansruedi's barge, his attention was caught by a sight that made this question redundant. Moored just a stone's throw downstream from the bar was a magnificent vessel that could only belong to a bargeman as imposing as Hansruedi: a twin-funnelled steamboat with two barges in tow that was clearly built to cope with every possible challenge thrown at it by old Father Rhine. And to confirm its provenance, a tell-tale red flag with its white cross fluttered from the stern of each boat. This was the vessel for him.

What especially caught his eye were the two small lifeboats suspended one on each side of the vessel between the bow and the paddlebox amidships. Here was the perfect cover for his unseen passage back to Patricia.

Although it was far from clear to him how he would gain access to one of these lifeboats, he knew he needed to act quickly. The black looks of the landlord and his absurd, yet menacing valediction still hung heavily on his shoulders, successfully chipping away the veneer on his fragile sense of security. So he took rash comfort in the quiet, unmanned appearance of the ship and stole on board, trying at once to be both inconspicuous and at the same time suggestive of having business there. It was an impossible act to carry off, but luck proved to be with him as he made his way past the cabins over the paddle-box to one of the lifeboats. He had little difficulty loosening the ropes sufficiently to work his way under the canvas and into the hollow, cold asylum of the boat's shell. Rough and hard, no comforts, but it offered shelter. And he leaned back into the relief and safety of knowing he could not be seen. The prospect of being cooped up in the small boat, cold and hungry, for the next few days gave him little cheer. But it seemed to him an eminently worthwhile hardship when he considered the likely alternative that awaited him at the railway station.

He settled back as best he could into his unsprung sanctum, waiting for that precious moment when the ship's engines would start up and the paddles would begin to turn. But his exhausted body denied him the pleasure of that moment. Despite the discomfort of his bedding, he dropped almost instantly into a deep sleep. And when eventually he was roused from this welcome recess, his mind had no time to pay any heed to the boat's engines, the paddles or the direction of his journey. He found himself face to bewildered face with the vaguely familiar features of Hansruedi holding back the canvas over his shelter. The bargeman peered in with a quietly severe expression in his eyes.

"*Raus aus dem Boot!*" were his only words. Frank's heart sank. As he was dragged out of the lifeboat, he felt the thud of Achim's hip flask in his coat pocket. It knocked against the oarlock, reminding him instantly of his old friend and that suitcase of betrayal. But above all he thought of Patricia. Would he ever see her again, he wondered. And cursed every inch of his stupidity.

Chapter 14

"Ever since I started thinking out loud about Frank, raking over the last few months in search of clues, I've begun to wonder whether I ever really knew him," Ellen said as she placed her empty tea cup on the table. "You probably think I'm daft. But when I think about it now, he often startled me in one way or another. Something he did or something he said, which seemed so out of character. And when I add them all up now, I begin to ask myself whether I ever knew who he really was. You see, I'm even talking of him in the past tense now, as if he was just a passing stranger I once knew."

As Marthe poured another cup of tea, a smile fixed itself on her face. It unsettled Ellen. She was aware that Marthe had a little background in psychology. And she could not help sensing that, as Marthe poured the tea, she was listening to Ellen with the ears not of a woman, but of an examiner drilled to look at every conversation as a cryptogram. Until now, speaking with her had been a completely different experience from conversations with Dr Zellweger. It was woman to woman, and it gave her confidence. Even the way she had gone to such lengths to make Ellen feel at home by getting Darjeeling from the special tea shop in town, and made sure she found some ginger biscuits to go with it, showed such consideration. But this afternoon, Marthe succeeded in making her feel distinctly uncomfortable.

"You think I'm silly, don't you?"

"No, of course not." Marthe put the teapot down. Ellen's remark made her appear self-conscious. But she was not about to be side-tracked.

"What sort of things did you feel were out of character?" she asked.

For the first time since Ellen had been here, she started to wonder whether Marthe's primary purpose was to report back on their conversations to her husband.

"Marthe, I've been here for almost three weeks. And while my employer is becoming slowly intolerant of my long absence, you and your husband have been very kind and hospitable. And very patient. I really am very grateful to you for that. I've no doubt it's mainly professional curiosity on your husband's part. But I'm still very grateful."

"You know that you're welcome to stay for as long as you wish. And not for reasons of professional curiosity as you say."

She continued to pour the tea. For some reason she looked slightly less ill at ease now as she passed the cup of tea to Ellen. Ellen wondered what was going through her mind, why she seemed so strange that afternoon.

"You haven't answered my question," Marthe insisted. "Tell me about the things which were out of character."

"There are so many. Mostly little things. It's hard to remember any one thing in particular," she said, not feeling entirely comfortable with this lie. "It's funny because, most of the time, Frank was so predictable. In every way. It was all a part of what I liked about him. He was so dependable. Not that he was boring. On the contrary. He introduced me to some fascinating things – poetry readings by weird and wonderful people I'd never heard of before, strange music that was completely new to me. And he'd often take me mudlarking along the banks of the Thames when the tide was out."

A look of blank bewilderment crossed Marthe's face, before Ellen added how much "Frank loved the thrill of digging up what he called 'little pieces of the past' – and just being by the waterside, amid the occasional swans on the water and 'the boats laid out like rats in ritual style by the cat tide' he used to say."

The memory brought a smile to Ellen's face.

"He could get quite lyrical at times," she continued, recalling "one day in particular when he pulled an old camera from the mud. He picked it up, wiped it clean and – as he held it staring back up at him in his hands – let out an excited cry of 'Exakta!'

"I had no idea what he was talking about. But apparently it was one of the first single-lens reflex cameras. Made in Germany in the 1930s and 40s. 'Just imagine who might have thrown it in the Thames. And why,' he said. He was almost breathless with the speculation, and his eyes flashed with the innocent wonder of a child as he panned the camera along the river bank until he hit on a solitary bedraggled swan that floated past him in the water. I remember his words quite clearly even now, as he said 'a swan no longer spotless white passes like the times, where the headline reads of chaos and confusion'. And he began to sing that Marc Bolan song to himself. 'Ride a White Swan'. Do you know it?

Marthe shook her head, lifted her tea cup from the table and took a sip.

"He had a strange way with words," Ellen added. "But that's what fascinated me about him from the first moment we met."

"Where *did* you meet?" Marthe asked.

"At a music festival in a little place you will never have heard of called Shepton Mallet. Quite small, but lots of big names. Like Led Zeppelin, Colosseum, Pink Floyd."

"I've heard of Pink Floyd," Marthe said with a spark of recognition in her eyes as she took another sip of her tea.

"Oh, they were fantastic!" Ellen's eyes sparked with the memory. "The whole event was great, of course. Not just the music. I was there with some friends. And out of nowhere this gorgeous man with dark, gentle eyes framed by a mop of dark-brown curly hair rode up on his Triumph motorbike. I was hooked. That was just last summer. It was a whirlwind romance. Within a few months we married, and he moved down to London. He even ditched his motorbike for me.

"That was a big sacrifice," Ellen continued, mulling over the words as she spoke. "He loved his Triumph bike. German engineering at its best, he used to say. Which I found strange, until he explained to me that the company was founded by immigrants from Germany. I didn't know that.

"But actually I don't think he regretted giving up the bike. It didn't really fit. It was almost like a mask he felt he had to wear. He seemed more than happy to throw it off and settle into what was quite a humdrum life in some ways. We were both happy with it, and I was just looking forward to the day when we would hear the pitter-patter of tiny feet in the house.

"Then he started to do these funny things. Mostly little things, as I said. Like the day he came home with an LP of Bartok, all nicely giftwrapped for me. But he knows that's not my sort of music. Nor his.

"Or the time we were walking along this street together in London. We were passing a second-hand bookshop, and he suddenly stopped, transfixed by a drab, dusty old window display. Not that this was unusual in itself: he often browses through second-hand books. If it's not poetry, then it's something to do with the Third Reich."

"An intriguing combination of interests," Marthe said in the manner of someone taking notes. Ellen could almost picture her mentally putting pencil to paper.

"He's become fascinated by that period since he started researching for an article about the Bank of England and its links to Nazi Germany before the war," Ellen explained.

"So anyway, when he disappeared inside this shop, I automatically assumed it must be for one of the few books he hadn't read on the subject. But when he eventually emerged from the place, he came out proudly carrying a dusty copy of Collins Handguide to the Birds of the Indian Sub-Continent. It was probably quite interesting in its way, and the illustrations were beautiful. But it was just not the sort of thing that would normally have interested Frank.

"'I saw it and thought that's just the thing,' was all he said. And he carried on up the street as if it was the most natural thing in the world. It was the first time I had ever known him buy anything on impulse like that. Then a few weeks later came the Bartok LP. 'Heard it on the radio the other night,' he said. 'I thought that's just the thing for pet'.

"And that's another thing," Ellen added. "The way he started calling me pet. It wasn't his kind of word. It's a Geordie word. From the north-east. Not something Frank would use. When I think of it now, it's almost as if he was living a lie."

"How did you react?" Marthe asked.

"What? To being called pet?"

Ellen became aware of herself flushing again at the memory of the first time she heard Frank use this name for her. On their honeymoon in Venice.

"I suppose I got a bit irritated sometimes, that's all. But it didn't really bother me that much," said Ellen, wincing inwardly at the discomfort of another lie.

She sensed her face colour all the more. But Marthe appeared to ignore it. Or perhaps she was enjoying the psychiatrist's couch routine too much to interrupt the flow.

"Did you ever talk to him about his strange behaviour?" she asked.

"I tried. Once."

Ellen's words became involuntarily muted by her recollection of that attempt.

"Tell me about it."

Ellen would have preferred not to, but she knew Marthe would not let her off that easily. And deep down, she also sensed the need to get it off her chest.

"Do you know Cornwall?" Ellen asked. Marthe shook her head with a slightly mystified expression. But Ellen could see that she had her full attention.

"It's very beautiful. Full of myths and legends. I always spent my holidays there as a child. Loved the place. Then, one day, I persuaded Frank to take me back for a long weekend. You must have heard of King Arthur?"

Marthe nodded.

"Well, he's supposed to have held court in a place called Tintagel. And every year, when we went on holiday to Cornwall, I was always dying to visit the place. But I never did. My parents never took me. So Frank made it an extra-long weekend and booked a lovely little cottage just outside Tintagel, because he said he'd never been there either. Actually, I think he was probably lying just to please me – he was a bit like that. Well, to tell the truth, Tintagel itself proved rather disappointing. And much smaller than in my childhood dreams.

"But the landscape is magical. It was late autumn. A damp Saturday afternoon. And we were the only people there, except for a solitary figure sitting on a rock overlooking the ruins. I found it depressingly desolate, but this man above us seemed strangely absorbed by it. He appeared to be lost in his thoughts as he stared at the sea crashing on the rocks below. Then he caught sight of us. And instantly switched his attention. He couldn't take his eyes off us. It made me feel very uneasy. He just sat there, watching our every move.

"Eventually I just couldn't stand it any longer, so I persuaded Frank we should leave and find the nearest pub for a bite to eat. Then, about ten minutes after we'd sat down in the pub with our ploughman's lunch, in he walked. He seemed much larger at ground level, as he stood in the doorway. He wasn't tall, but he was well-built and muscular. Quite good looking in a sinister sort of way, even though he was prematurely bald. He smiled over at us as he came in, looked enquiringly at our table, then walked over to the bar. He appeared to be talking to the barman about us, pointing and looking in our direction. And when the barman pulled a pint of beer and put it down in front of him, he picked up the glass and came to sit at the table next to ours.

"'Wonderful country this, isn't it?' he said in a broad accent from the other side of the Atlantic that took me aback. I remember wondering what on earth an American was doing in those parts. But I didn't need to ask. He was one of those very forthcoming Americans who heap all kinds of information and worldly wisdom on you without stopping for a moment to consider whether you actually want to hear it or not.

"'I'm looking for inspiration,' he said. And he stared profoundly into the ploughman's lunch that the barman had brought over, as if he wanted to reassure us that their conversation at the bar had been nothing more than an innocent discussion of the menu. Without waiting any longer for an invitation, our new-found American friend then proceeded to let us into the whole history behind his visit to Cornwall.

"He reached a large workman's hand across the table and introduced himself as Bill Plattner. He was an artist, he said. Or a sculptor to be precise.

"'You might not think it,' he went on, 'but I used to be a puny little runt at one time.'

"Actually, I have to admit that he had quite an engaging personality on the surface, as Americans so often do. But I was slightly disturbed by the way he couldn't take his eyes off Frank. Well, in the time it took us to finish our ploughman's lunches, we came to know practically everything there was to know about Bill Plattner – at least regarding what he considered the meaningful part of his life.

"He said he had studied art in California. And on his way into art school in San Diego every day, he said, he always passed a gym. One day, one of the men who worked there was standing on the door and started to make fun of him, told him he should take more pride in his own body, it was God's gift, and all that kind of thing. And the taunting got to him so much that he was eventually persuaded to go inside one day and take a look.

"And he never looked back, or so he said. Apparently, he started working out every day, and took such pleasure in the fruits of his bodybuilding that it influenced the whole direction of his studies. And so he became a sculptor. He rambled on about the 'unique interaction between my bodybuilding and my art'," Ellen said attempting to imitate an American accent. "I had difficulty following him sometimes. But Frank seemed engrossed. And that surprised me, because he's usually so dismissive of people like that.

"Anyway, to cut a long story short, he had spent a year of his studies in Europe, 'doing Florence' and that sort of thing. And on what he called a pilgrimage to the south-west of England (he was into Barbara Hepworth and wanted to 'soak up some of the ambience that had inspired that wonderful lady' as he put it), he'd been completely knocked out by the bleakness of the moors. Especially by the granite rocks that jut out of the hills. And the weird shapes they make – 'born of fire and yet so cold' he kept saying.

"In fact, he was so taken by the place that he decided to invest the proceeds of his first big commission in a small cottage on the edge of Dartmoor. I suppose he must have been quite a successful artist to afford that. And he turned it into a studio, where he worked for at least two or three months every year with the local granite.

"'You must come over and see it some time,' he kept saying. And his invitation always seemed to be addressed more to Frank than to me. 'It's another world,' he said, 'right on the edge of the moor. Bleak, depressingly beautiful. The west winds breathe this curious, almost silent susurrus through the grass, not a tree to be seen for miles.' I remember those words to this day. Not so much strange as pretentious, I felt. As if he was trying to impress, trying to prove something."

At that moment, Ellen recalled the peculiar verse that Frank was supposed to have written in the clinic – *Pneuma, silent susurrus, whispers ancient legends of what might have been: Tristan in Tintagel for example.* The words were etched indelibly on her mind. Not a day went by without her wondering what they could possibly mean.

"Would you excuse me for a moment? There's something I must show you," she said. And she left Marthe hanging in mid-story, as she went to fetch a copy of the piece of paper that Professor Abegg had shown her when she met him for the first time in the clinic.

"Here, maybe you can make sense of it." Ellen handed it to Marthe when she returned and resumed the story while Marthe digested the words.

"Well, eventually Frank persuaded me that we should accept his invitation. I have to admit that I was very curious. But also a little apprehensive."

"Why?" Marthe asked, looking up from the piece of paper with a quizzical expression in her eyes.

"I'm not sure. There was just something about the man that disturbed me, but I couldn't put my finger on it at the time. And he could actually be quite entertaining. The setting for his studio was certainly just as he had described it. Bleak and depressingly beautiful.

"And for all his pretentious posing, he was really quite modest. I don't think he genuinely saw himself as a very talented artist.

"'No one can come anywhere near the talents of Nature,' he used to say. 'Nature will always be the only sculptor of any note. She can do anything – from the human body to the Bowerman's Nose.' That was one of his favourite rocks on the moor. 'What can we hope to achieve against that? We're nothing more than poor copyists,' he used to say.

"Well, some weeks after that trip, Frank suddenly announced, quite out of the blue, that he had arranged to visit Bill Plattner again at the weekend. I didn't even know they had kept in touch. And I was very much against him going. Apart from anything else, I already had plans for that weekend.

"'Fine. Then you won't be bored if I'm not here,' he said.

"That got me so angry. I think it was the only really serious argument we had. We hardly spoke for the rest of that week, except to heap abuse on each other. So anyway, despite my protests, he went. And I stayed behind – that is, until I could stand it no longer. Much against my better judgement, the thought of a Saturday night alone drove me to follow him. It wasn't easy to find the place on my own through the rambling lanes of Devon. When eventually I got there, it was already quite late, and I was exhausted. The door was open. I remembered Bill saying he never locked it, so I just walked in. The place seemed cold and deserted, but I could hear voices coming from the studio.

"The studio was actually a converted barn directly adjoining the cottage. And when I went through the passageway that Bill had created between the living area and what he liked to call his workshop, the sight that greeted me was so comical I don't know why I didn't split my sides. Bill was sitting beside a huge lump of his favourite granite, making sketches. Around him and at his feet lay dozens of discarded sheets of paper containing what looked like unfinished sketches of the same model. And the model in question was my Frank. Stark naked. Stretched out on a sofa. I couldn't believe my eyes.

"'Hi Ell,' Bill said, friendly as ever and completely unabashed. 'I thought Frank was coming down alone this trip.' Bill insisted on calling me Ell from the very first time we met, and I hated it. But I didn't bother to make my feelings known the first time since I didn't even remotely imagine we would be seeing him ever again. Let alone under such circumstances. So the name stuck, along with a growing antipathy towards him.

"Well, Frank very sheepishly pulled his clothes on, and it became one of the strangest weekends I'd ever experienced. Frank and Bill spent a lot of time alone together, and on the few occasions they were with me they behaved like two giggly schoolgirls. I'd never seen Frank behave in such a silly way before. In retrospect, I suppose it was embarrassment."

"You say you tried talking to Frank about his behaviour."

"Yes, that was when I tried talking to him – after we got home. Before that, we spent the time either in silence or skirting the issue with meaningless chatter. Or in Frank's case, silliness."

"Which issue were you trying to skirt?"

"Well, there was only one. That cosy little scene on the sofa."

Ellen detected in her own voice an involuntary disbelief that Marthe even felt the need to ask such a question.

"I mean, how would you feel suddenly finding you were married to a queer?" Ellen asked.

"Is that how you put it to him?"

"More or less."

"And what was his reaction?" Marthe asked. "You know, just because he was posing naked for an artist doesn't mean that he's homosexual."

"That's what he said. Those very words. And when I calmed down and thought about it, I managed to convince myself that he was right, that I had probably been exaggerating. A bit like that Geordie girlfriend I dreamed up. But don't you see? He was acting so strangely. I had to find explanations for his behaviour."

"You didn't try to ask Frank for explanations?"

"Of course, but none of them made much sense. And when I pressed him on his 'modelling scene'" (Ellen sensed each syllable breathe contempt as she spoke the words) "all he said was 'Ask my mother. She never liked the clothes I wore'. I mean, what a strange thing to say."

"Do you often press him for explanations?" The way Marthe borrowed her word 'press' – and lingered on it – bothered Ellen. Was it an uncertain command of the language? she asked herself. Or did it betray an implicit reproach?

Marthe appeared to glean a certain satisfaction from Ellen's hesitation. And she promptly followed up with another line of questioning before Ellen had time to consider her reply.

"What was his mother like?"

"A bitch."

Ellen's response this time could not have been swifter. But the eagerness of her reply concealed a reluctance to continue what had become a rather tiresome interview.

"Marthe," she said. There was a new firmness in her voice, "I was lying in bed this morning, thinking things over. And I came to the conclusion it would probably be a good idea if I disappeared for a week or two. My sister lives in North Germany. Her husband's in the army. So I thought it might be a good idea to go up and visit her. It would give you a break from me. And maybe if I come back in a week or two, your husband might have some news for me."

Marthe still had the piece of paper in her hand that Ellen had given her. She appeared to be too engrossed in it to absorb what Ellen had just said.

"And I need to speak to my employer again, as well," Ellen added. "They've extended my leave until the end of the month.

But I'm not sure how much longer they'll be prepared to wait for me to return."

"Did your husband write this?" Marthe said, ignoring Ellen's words. "It's very beautiful in a way. But very personal. Not easy to understand. Quite fascinating really," and she handed it back to Ellen. "Why don't you show it to your sister? Maybe she can help throw some light on it."

Ellen could not imagine how Beth might be in a position to throw even the merest hint of a light on the situation. But Marthe's words at least showed she had been listening. And Ellen took them as a sign that her plan had met with approval.

"Madame Doll will be pleased," Marthe said.

"Pardon?"

"Madame Doll. My cleaning lady. Since you're here, she's been complaining of the extra work."

"I'm sorry. I didn't realise."

"Please!" implored Marthe. "You must not apologise." She leaned over with a smile and touched Ellen's arm. But Ellen caught a hint of reproach under this camouflage. Or was she being oversensitive?

"These *frontaliers* are all the same," Marthe added, sensing the need for some kind of explanation. "Either we are making too many demands or we are not trusting them. They're never satisfied."

"Who?" asked Ellen, confused by this sudden digression.

"The *frontaliers*. I'm sorry, 'frontier workers' was the expression I think you used. The people who cross the border for work."

Ellen nodded. She welcomed this trivial departure, which allowed her to avoid talking any more about Frank. Looking back on this confessional kind of atmosphere with Marthe, she had to concede that the relationship had its strange moments. To an outsider like Marthe, the strangeness must have been even more apparent. So Ellen was pleased to have the opportunity to make her excuses and go upstairs to begin preparations for her journey north.

The following day, Ellen left. Marthe had kindly let her use the phone to warn her sister she would be coming. The call from Switzerland came as something of a surprise to her sister. Ellen had not even told Beth about Frank's disappearance in the first place. And although she did not seem overjoyed at the prospect of her sister's visit, she was clearly burning with curiosity to know what was going on – so much so that Ellen was even able to convince herself that, deep down, her sister cared and was really looking forward to seeing her.

Dr Zellweger appeared genuinely disappointed when Ellen told him of her intention to leave at such short notice, and not only because he had obviously come to look on her as a companion for his wife.

"What a shame," he said, "I have become so accustomed to see you around the house."

She found the remark rather odd since he was so often in the clinic that they rarely ever saw each other. Even at the weekends he was out in the country looking after his mysterious protégé. Ellen therefore assumed he was simply trying to be excruciatingly polite.

Although he could only have been about forty, Dr Zellweger seemed to come from another age. It was not simply the clothes he wore – the bow tie, waistcoat and watchchain, or the moustache so neatly trimmed and slightly stained with nicotine from years of pipe-smoking. Most of all perhaps it was his attitudes, his behaviour, the way he kept his wife at home. And it irritated Ellen that Marthe seemed happy to put up with this. She wondered whether this might change now that women had been given the vote.

But Dr Zellweger was always very correct and courteous. And, of course, it went without saying that he would see Ellen safely to the railway station.

"It can be a little confusing," he explained as they drove to the station. "It's not a big city, but we have three big stations here. There is one for Switzerland and one for each country that has a border with the city."

So he drove her to the German station. And in his impeccably considerate way, Dr Zellweger insisted on accompanying her to the ticket office and waving her off. Ellen could not put her finger on it, but the station interior gave off a feel and a mood that was at odds with the city outside.

"It's different."

Ellen spoke these words almost under her breath. They were not intended for conversation. But Dr Zellweger was quick to pick up on them.

"As I said, it's the German station. It's owned by Germany. Even the track is owned by Germany. And the customs post is here in the station." He pointed over to the far end of the ticket hall, where two official-looking men stood in uniform, complete with peaked caps.

Perhaps Ellen was feeling particularly paranoid after the events of the weeks just passed, but she found the station here strangely threatening. She tried to imagine what it must have been like before and during the war. All those poor Jewish refugees trying to flee the country into Switzerland.

"They were dark times," Dr Zellweger said, as if responding to her thoughts. "And it was especially dark at this border. Of course, most people were horrified when the railway company raised the Nazi flag above the building. It was like an insult to the city. But they preferred to ignore the fact that the industry here also profited very nicely from its German neighbours. In fact, it was the city's chemical industry that supplied the blood-red dye for that flag and those Nazi uniforms."

The wry smile that crossed Dr Zellweger's lips as he spoke these words was quickly replaced by a darker expression.

"You know, Basel has a long social-democratic tradition, but there were also some people here at that time who supported Germany. Some even joined the German army. And many of the business leaders were also happy to sack the Jews in their company to satisfy their business partners north of the border."

After buying her ticket, Ellen walked over to customs in pensive silence, the image of refugees still preying on her mind. Dr Zellweger walked beside her, carrying her suitcase.

"They were difficult times," he repeated at last, as he waved her off through the customs barrier, but not before making a note of her sister's phone number and promising to call as soon as he had any news of Frank.

Why he should assume that Frank would still be roaming the streets of this fascinating city, she had no idea. It had long since dawned on her that, if this man really was Frank, he would almost certainly have already gone. He had no ties to this place, so what would keep him? But on the other hand, where would he have gone? What would he be doing there?

These questions were of no interest to Dr Zellweger, and why should they be? Ellen asked herself. His interest was in the patient. And the patient had discharged himself, as had the patient's wife. So when he waved Ellen off across the border into Germany, she detected a sense of relief in the way he moved his arm hastily through the air and turned back to face his day's clinical duties. It left her with a disquieting sense of vulnerability.

Chapter 15

Ellen's journey north to her sister Beth proved tediously uneventful, until she had to change trains in Cologne. It was the first time she had ever been to Cologne, and since she faced a long wait before her connection, she decided to spend the time down on the riverside enjoying the fresh air and the views. But the air proved a little too fresh to enjoy, while the views were dominated by the cathedral. And the forbidding darkness of the building that rose into the grey afternoon sky gave her no comfort. Ellen found it so oppressively imposing that she would almost certainly have missed the object of far greater interest across the street had it not been for a yapping dog that drew her attention in that direction. It was an irate and lost-looking dachshund, which stood outside a café barking at nothing in particular, as far as she could see.

Then out of the café emerged a figure she knew at once. The mop of thick brown hair. The walk. It could only be him. It was Frank. Her heart missed a beat. Was this a dream? Ellen asked herself. There could surely be no other explanation. She felt she could not trust her own eyes. She wanted to shout to him across the street. She wanted to wave.

But she was transfixed. Could do nothing but gape in disbelief. Was it really Frank? It seemed impossible. What could he be doing here? And by the time she had collected herself, it was already too late. He was stepping onto a tram and moving off out of Ellen's life again as abruptly as he had re-entered it. She was confused. Was it a dream? Was she going mad? Was this really happening?

Ellen was barely aware of the strange impression she must have created, rooted to the spot, gaping into the empty space across the street where Frank had been. A few people approached her and made noises of concern. But she was unable to understand. Each one moved on with a shake of the head when Ellen made no response. When eventually she regained her composure, she returned to the station and found a place to sit. A place where she could gather her thoughts.

She was uncertain what to do. She could not go to the police. Even supposing she would be able to overcome the language barrier, they would simply think they had a raving lunatic on their hands.

Ellen remained totally distraught and bewildered, yet overjoyed at the same time, by the knowledge that Frank was here in Cologne. So close and yet still out of reach. She decided to check into a hotel near the station.

After phoning her sister to let her know she had been delayed, Ellen returned the next morning to the place where she had spotted him. And each day for the next three days, she sat in the café he had emerged from and drank cup after cup of what passed for tea – a bag in lukewarm water with a slice of lemon – and watched the comings and goings: the middle-aged women who gathered for coffee and cakes; the single women with their poodles or terriers, which sat patiently beside their mistresses drinking from a water bowl; and the occasional business types, briefcase in hand, who stopped by for a quick espresso. None sat for as long as Ellen, who stared in growing despair also at every passer-by who walked past on the street outside. Not one of them even remotely resembled Frank.

Ellen became conscious of the strange looks and whispers from the café staff even before the end of the first day. By the third day, she had the feeling that the tolerance in those looks had turned to hostility. It became clear to her that this was no way to find her husband and she would do best to resume her journey.

She checked out of her hotel, comforting herself with the thought that perhaps she could persuade her sister Beth to return to Cologne with her and help in the search for Frank. But the slight solace provided by this idea was in stark contrast to the reception that awaited her when eventually she arrived at Beth's.

Although she was more than six years older than Ellen, the two had been very close at one time and shared every secret and every little intimacy – until Malcolm appeared on the scene. Malcolm was everything Ellen disliked in a man: smug, self-satisfied, unintelligent, opinionated and in the army. And as if trying deliberately to highlight all these flaws in his character, he wore a salesman's moustache on his upper lip and white socks in black slip-on shoes on his feet. The fate of Ellen's relationship with him was sealed the moment she set eyes on him.

Sadly, Beth fell so firmly under his influence that, every time Ellen saw her, she became less and less like the sister of old. Or maybe Malcolm was just bringing out the real Beth. It was hard to know. Certainly, she grew embarrassingly defensive of him in Ellen's presence and always accused her of extreme intolerance. Said she was never satisfied with anything less than perfection.

Beth put this down to the Catholic boarding school her sister attended. In truth, it was the day Ellen was sent off to school that the closeness between them began to wane. Malcolm simply applied the finishing touches. While Ellen saw this school as punishment for being what her parents called a difficult child with an unhealthy interest in boys, Beth resented her for what she saw as the special treatment her younger sister was being given and mocked her incessantly with jibes that, with her pretty looks, she must have plenty of admirers among the girls.

"But it didn't do you much good," she would say. "You were a changed person by the time you finished at that school, that's for sure."

Ellen had never enlightened her sister on the suffering endured at the school, the sanctions for the slightest lapse, the punishments meted out even for sleeping with their hands under the bed covers. She knew Beth would simply turn every word of confidence against her.

The more Ellen mulled over these thoughts, the more she wondered what she expected to gain from going to see her.

She supposed a part of her still clung to the memories of her childhood and fondly imagined they were as close as ever, because even now she felt compelled by a girlish urge to see her sister every so often to giggle and gossip over old times. An urge that was invariably deflated by the anti-climax and disappointment of finding that the Beth she had once known was only a distant memory. This journey proved an exception only insofar as it was even worse than usual.

Ellen had been looking for some kind of sympathy or understanding. From Malcolm, of course, she got no more than the gross insensitivity and callousness that she expected from the lips of a man-sized inferiority complex trying to hide its inadequacy under a military moustache. But she did not expect it from her own sister.

"Walked out on you I gather?" were Malcolm's very first words, before Ellen had even sat down in the little box of a lounge in their army house. It could have been anywhere in Britain, yet here it was – a little corner of England – in Germany. Even this, it seemed to Ellen, was trying to be something it was not.

"Well, you're probably better off without him," Malcolm added. "Never did take to him."

He was enjoying every twinge of despair in Ellen's behaviour. And then, to her horror, Beth joined in as well. At least she had the decency to make a pot of tea first. Not the kind of refined Darjeeling that Marthe so thoughtfully bought in for her. But something coarser. It perfectly matched their attitude towards Ellen.

And then she started, mercilessly digging into Ellen's relationship with Frank, "which was never built on very firm foundations when you think about," she said. Her words hurt.

"I have, Beth. I've done a lot of thinking about it. That's all I've been doing these last weeks."

She sensed anger and frustration coming to the boil. What am I doing here? Ellen asked herself.

"My God, Beth. I don't think you can even begin to imagine what I've been going through. Suddenly Frank disappears, then starts turning up and vanishing again on the other side of Europe. If it is him. You know, I even thought I saw him on my way here in Cologne. You haven't got a clue, Beth. I really don't know what you're talking about, but for your information I was always quite happy with the 'foundations' as you call them. Just because they're not built into the dense rock of the British army..."

Her sister ignored the dig and took a turn that Ellen had not seen coming.

"You don't suppose he's coming here, do you?" she asked.

Perhaps Ellen just imagined the slightly rising colour in her sister's face. But the way Beth hurriedly followed up this question by returning to an earlier remark of Ellen's without waiting for a reply suggested the colour in her Beth's cheeks was real. The burning sense of a blunder that needed to be covered up.

"What did you mean earlier when you said 'if it is him', this bloke in the clinic?" Beth asked.

"I just can't believe it is. It doesn't sound like Frank. Apart from anything else, this man apparently speaks a local dialect like a native. How could it be him?"

"Nothing would surprise me about Frank after the last conversation I had with him," said Beth.

"What do you mean?"

The blush this time was unmistakable. Beth had backed into a corner now that she could not simply escape with a smooth change of tack. Not without some clever explaining first. She put down her cup of tea. Ellen watched as Beth got up to shut the door, her mind almost visibly working overtime. For Ellen, it was a scene reminiscent of someone trying to sneak into the confessional unnoticed. Malcolm had by now taken himself off to some other part of the house. He had more important things to do than talk to his sister-in-law. Beth returned to her chair looking slightly sheepish. She was plainly struggling to find the words.

"The last time we spoke on the phone," she said at length, "he asked if I could get hold of a book for him. A German book. He thought it would be easier for me to get since I live here."

"What book?"

"Oh, I don't know," said Beth. "I told him I couldn't help anyway. It was an old book published decades ago. Probably out of print. And he was getting really weird. Talking about phallic faces and Jews. I assumed it was something to do with this Nazi obsession of his."

Ellen felt as if the ground was suddenly slipping from under her. Her stomach turned over. She could not believe what she was hearing.

"You mean you and Frank have been having secrets from me?" she asked. Her voice quivered slightly.

"Come on, it's not like that."

"What is it like then, Beth? Are you in the habit of phoning each other?" Ellen asked, her anger chiselling out a desperate space around the word 'habit' and all that it implied. She was incensed.

"Look," said Beth. She was insistent. "It really wasn't like that. It was some weeks ago, when I tried phoning you and you weren't there. Frank answered, we got talking, and he just started getting really weird about this book. He asked me not to tell you, because you wouldn't understand. I remember now," she added, "it was by someone called Costner or Kastner. Something like that."

"And what is it I wouldn't understand?"

"Search me. For some reason he seemed to think you wouldn't approve, said you didn't like him reading all this stuff."

"Well, he does tend to go over the top when he gets interested in something."

The corroboration implicit in Ellen's words eased the tension. But she could sense a continuing discomfort in Beth, the way she shuffled about in her chair and her slightly podgy fingers played nervously with her teacup. They had always been like chalk and cheese. Ellen the fine-featured one, slim and blonde, while Beth was not only much older, but also the coarse-featured one with a freckled face, frizzy ginger hair and slightly overweight.

Being keen on astrology in her younger years, Ellen was also very aware that their sibship never really stood much of a chance from the outset, since she was Cancer and Beth was Libra. So it had always surprised everyone in the family that they got on so well when they were younger. How happy they would be to see their preconceived notions substantiated now, Ellen said to herself.

But she could not enjoy her sister's discomfort. It had implications that gnawed at her own self-esteem as they shared what seemed to be the same bed of nails.

Beth had managed to manoeuvre a way out of her corner. But could she be trusted? Ellen asked herself. She did not really want to know. She was not feeling strong enough for the answer. So she let her sister guide them back to the conversation.

"I suppose we all do. And you especially perhaps. But we love you for it," she continued with what sounded to Ellen very much like a backhanded compliment. "We wouldn't have you any other way."

"Everyone except Frank, you mean," Ellen said, pausing briefly to let her irritation settle. "Beth, you're incredibly unfair. Maybe I do expect a lot from people, especially from Frank – he's my husband, for God's sake. But I don't demand anything from him that I wouldn't expect of myself. Hell, I sacrifice a lot for him as well."

"Do you?" was all Beth said, leaving the tension of a meaningful lull to fill the silence between them, before she resumed the assault. "Are you sure they're really sacrifices, what you give him? I mean, have you ever stopped to ask yourself whether he actually wants what you see as your sacrifices?"

"What do you mean?" She felt close to tears, but her sister had no mercy.

Ellen had the feeling Beth had been waiting years for this opportunity to offload all her grudges and jealousies. She was enjoying every moment. But at the same time, her words were carefully wrapped up with such deliberation, they suggested a content that – once fully unfurled before her – might come painfully close to the truth. And it was this more than anything which made Ellen uncomfortably defensive.

"He can't complain. He does all right," she insisted. "In fact, he does just about what he wants."

"Does he? Then why does he feel the need to do things behind your back?" Beth asked. She saw the gaping wound she had left with her earlier revelation and sprinkled salt over it now with heartless relish. But it must have been an exquisite pain that was written on Ellen's face, because her sister instantly tried softening the attack, as if she had finally realised she had gone too far and was beginning to regret her hostility. It was as though she wanted to turn the cutting edge away from Ellen as she struck her with the blade of her knife.

But Beth would not have been Beth if she had not taken a double-edged knife with her into combat. Ellen was going to get hurt whichever way she put it.

"Why was there a post mortem anyway?" she asked.

"What do you mean? What are you on about now?"

"Your mother-in-law," said Beth. "Why did they need to do a post mortem?"

"She was on her own when she died. Lay there for two or three days before she was found. So they had to. It's the law."

"You don't suppose Frank had anything to do with her death, do you?"

"Beth! Don't be absurd! It was a heart attack."

"Well, it seems a bit odd Frank disappearing like that a couple of weeks later," said Beth. She paused, as if for effect, then added mysteriously: "Nervous breakdowns make people do very strange things, you know."

"Who said anything about a nervous breakdown?"

"Well it stands to reason, doesn't it? How else would you explain his being found on the streets of a foreign city, where he's carted off to the funny farm?"

"It's bad enough already, Beth. You don't have to exaggerate."

"Well, he was, wasn't he?" Beth insisted. "You can't really blame him. He's probably had enough of living up to your perfectionist standards. Not that you're a paragon of virtue yourself. I'm still waiting for the return of all my records you pilfered from me."

"Why are you intent on making me suffer even more than I already am, Beth? Is it some kind of cruel compensation to make up for your marriage to Malcolm?"

"You don't need to take it to heart so, Maud." This was a signal, a clear sign that Ellen's words had missed their target and that Beth's ego was still firmly intact. She always used Ellen's middle name when she wanted to drive home what she saw as her superiority over her sister. It went back to when Ellen was five years old and discovered for the first time that she had a second name. Maud. She left no one in the family with any doubt how much she hated the name. And Beth pounced on it with the eager malice of an elevenyear-old girl trying to cope with five years of unmitigated jealousy.

"Presumably having his mother move in just down the road added to the strain. I can quite imagine how these things can happen."

"For goodness sake, Beth. What are you talking about? What strain?"

Ellen had by now been seized with the desperation that must take hold of a rape victim when she's made to feel that she's the guilty party. That she must have been asking for it.

"Anyway, his mother moving into the area was his idea," she added in her defence. "And if that was a strain for anyone, then more for me than for him. Do you remember how I was always allergic to animals as a child?"

"You must be joking. How could I forget the hassle you gave us? We had to get rid of my dear little dog because of my precious little sister."

"You make me sound like a spoilt hypochondriac. God, I was suffering Beth! I was suffering! And so I did when Frank's mother came calling, cat and all. Which was just about every day. She wasn't there for long, bless her soul. But it was hard."

"Come on, Maud," Beth continued. "Don't be such a hypocrite."

"No, I mean it. I don't like to speak ill of the dead. But her animal obsession really got to me. It was horrendous, Beth. She would bring it with her on a lead and let the creature sit at the table so she could spoon-feed it its milk. I tolerated it. But it was quite disgusting. I think she much preferred animals to people. Even her own husband."

"What was he like?"

"I don't know," Ellen said, thankful that at last they seemed to be getting away from the rebukes and insults. "I never knew him. He must have been an odd father, though, because I remember Frank telling me how he would always tease him cruelly about the indentation in the bridge of his nose – 'as if he'd been shot between the eyes at birth' he used to say apparently.

"But Frank also spoke very fondly of him – how he had once brought a lovely ivory bracelet back from one of his business trips for Frank's mother and she flatly refused to wear it. She wouldn't have anything to do with ivory. In fact, she wouldn't have anything to do with her own husband for months apparently. Wouldn't go near him."

"Sounds to me as though you and he would have got on like a house on fire," said Beth.

And so the barbed exchanges continued for the next few days – until the phone call. Beth spent most of her time sniping at Ellen, who felt exhausted having constantly to dive for cover. But she could at least be thankful that Malcolm had to go off playing war games soon after she arrived, so she did not have to suffer his smug, smart-aleck sarcasm beyond the first evening. By the second day, she found herself trying as far as possible to avoid the company of her sister by taking long walks around the neighbourhood.

It was the kind of housing estate that manages to combine a soulless, comatose anonymity with the atmosphere of nosy curiosity. As if the whole place had been picked up lock, stock and barrel somewhere in England and dropped in the middle of Germany, complete with shops, pub, G plan furnishings and all the other accessories of Britishness. Even the classic red telephone boxes. Nothing fitted. After her stay in Switzerland, she found it especially strange to hear her native language being spoken all around her again in this foreign country even on the streets – a paradox that was made complete when the ill-fitting Britishness of the scene, the sense of being back home and yet not, underlined the alienation she felt from her own sister. She asked herself why on earth she had decided to visit Beth. What she could possibly have expected to gain?

Beth herself seemed unable or unwilling to show any understanding. Ellen assumed now that what she had seen as their earlier closeness had probably just been some image-boosting charade on her part. In fact, her recriminations and aspersions showed that the resentment of her baby sister ran far deeper than any sibling bond. What hurt most of all was the understanding she professed, to an almost exaggerated degree, for Frank. And then there were the secrets she shared with him. Her thoughts latched on to the apprehension Beth had expressed, whether feigned or real, when she suggested that maybe Frank was on his way to see her. It was beginning to look increasingly plausible.

How else was she to interpret his being in Cologne? He did not know anyone else within a hundred miles of the place. But why would he want to see her? They hardly knew each other really. And all they had in common was Ellen. It was this thought that had her wonder whether Beth could have been right after all, whether Ellen really was the cause of Frank's disappearance in some way.

They had married in some haste, after all. And Frank was a fence-sitter. Not the type to rush into any decision, let alone a marriage. Perhaps he had already started to regret it, she wondered.

'But was I really so difficult to live with?' Ellen asked herself.

Then she remembered the phone call Beth said she had had with Frank. And the secrets they shared. And a darker thought edged its way into her mind: since Beth had chosen to take sides and clearly opted against her own sister, was it possible that Frank had already been here and discussed everything with her? Or even that they were having an affair?

Ellen recalled the embarrassment on her face when she realised she had said too much. The very idea sent a dull pain to the pit of Ellen's stomach. It drilled through to every nerve in her body as the suggestion took hold and refused to be dislodged.

Although she was forced to run the gauntlet of her sister's wounding remarks and not-so-covert hostility for the entire time she spent in Beth's house, Ellen decided to stay on. Perhaps Frank would appear at the door, she thought. Or maybe her sister would reveal some even darker secret that she shared with him. Suddenly anything seemed possible. So, despite her hurtful attitude, Ellen felt a compelling need to stay with her a little longer. Until the phone call.

"It's for you," Beth said, handing her the receiver. "Sounds like your friend from Switzerland. So women are allowed to make phone calls abroad as well now that they have the vote, are they?"

Ellen ignored the facetious remark as she took the receiver.

"Hello Ellen. I have some good news."

She recognised the voice at once as Marthe's. After the torment of her sister's company, it was such a comfort to hear her Swiss accent again. So pleased was Ellen to hear her voice that the words themselves did not immediately register, and Marthe had to repeat herself.

"I have good news for you," she said, with characteristic patience for what she took to be Ellen's excitement. "We've found your husband."

Chapter 16

Hansruedi was a large, barrel-chested man with a beard that reached almost to his chest. His ship was his castle. Unannounced visitors were not welcome. Especially German visitors. While the Alemannic German that Frank spoke helped soften the bargee's resistance, the air remained clouded with suspicion. And it would take more than the tenuous bond of a vaguely shared dialect to dispel the suspicion any further.

It was the heavy thud as he was dragged out of the lifeboat that did it. Frank had forgotten about his father's book on Indian fauna and flora. He had buried it deep in the inside pocket of his coat on top of the hipflask Achim had presented him with for the journey. He was reminded of it by that heavy thud against the oarlock. When he eventually pulled the flask out from under the book and shared his friend's golden elixir with the bargeman, the affinity between them was sealed.

Frank was granted the privilege of travelling in a guest cabin on condition that he could provide Hansruedi with a supply of Achim's Mirabelle nectar once they reached Basel. The deal was struck. For the rest of the journey, Hansruedi proved a moody, but accommodating companion. A card-carrying member of his local socialist party who was glad of any opportunity to make his own personal mark in the struggle against fascism.

"Take care when you get to Basel," he warned, as he took a final sip of the Mirabelle brandy. "It's a great city. I was at the Peace Congress there before the war, you know. Can you imagine the 'Internationale' and the 'Marseillaise' echoing around the cathedral square against a background of red flags? And the cathedral echoing with the sound of socialist speeches? But you need to be on your guard there today. The place is teeming with fascists and Nazi spies. Take care who you speak to."

Hansruedi was not to know that such warnings were unnecessary. In the telling of his story, Frank had focused on Achim. He saw no need to feature Breitner in the narrative.

The journey up the Rhine took the best part of four days. It was an uneventful voyage. And Frank remained in his cabin most of the time until they reached their destination. The sense of relief he felt when he finally stepped back onto Swiss soil was liberating. He was surprised by the exhilaration he felt at that moment.

The number 8 tram from the harbour area was well frequented with the grey, sullen faces of workers heading home at the end of their shift. But the face that boarded a few stops down the line and planted itself at the far end of the carriage shone through the cloud of early-evening travellers with uncomfortable familiarity. It was not a pleasant light. An awkward and slightly overweight figure, which seemed to have been put together by the clumsy hand of an architect with no eye for the elegance of symmetry or proportion. It also clashed shamelessly with the ingratiating smile that the owner of the face wore with such insistence among the other features of his unctuous manner: the vulgar twinkle in his eyes and the greased black hair. Although Frank could not recall where or when their paths had crossed before, his memory was still sufficiently loyal to him to suggest that it had not been an agreeable experience.

Unfortunately for Frank, the man's powers of recollection were sharper than his. As soon as he caught sight of the weary traveller from Cologne, he moved up the aisle of the tram in Frank's direction.

"Mr Eigenmann, what a fortunate coincidence," he said, sibilating the last syllable with particular effect and causing Frank to squirm inwardly as the man lowered himself into the empty seat beside him.

"I'm sorry. Have we met somewhere before?" Frank asked. While the man's presence nauseated him, he saw no good reason to drop his guard and make his feelings felt. He preferred to know who he was dealing with first.

"We have a mutual acquaintance," was all he offered.

The way he inclined his head as he spoke, like a self-satisfied hen, instantly put Frank in mind of that fruitless evening in the wine tavern, where he had waited in vain for Patricia. It was not enough to identify the man by name, but it told Frank where he had seen him before.

It was on that evening – after the man had raised his glass to Frank as he was leaving the tavern – that he had been pursued so mysteriously through the streets and become embroiled in the dealings of Breitner and his cronies. And it was this sequence of events which led him to assume now that the mutual acquaintance he spoke of was Breitner.

"Why fortunate?" Frank asked.

"Fortunate for you at least, Mr Eigenmann." The man's smile spread even wider across his face with particularly sinister smarm. "You see, I'm in a position to give you some advice which you would find very much to your benefit."

"And why would you want to do that?"

"Let us say because I like you, Mr Eigenmann. Quite simply because I like you."

He knew that Frank did not trust him an inch, and this clearly pleased him, adding an even bolder contour to his self-satisfied smile. But he was also shrewd, and he knew too that Frank's curiosity would compel him to seek a way into his confidence. That all he had to do was wait.

"Well? What's the advice?"

Frank's response was clumsy in its abruptness. He was suddenly impatient for that confidence. The man sensed his hunger and preened himself on it with the manicured nails of a usurer exacting every ounce of advantage from his position.

"Mr Breitner is looking for you, Mr Eigenmann."

"That's no great surprise," Frank said. "Nor am I sure it qualifies as advice."

The man's eyes narrowed as he fixed Frank with a sideways gaze. "If you value your skin, Mr Eigenmann, I would strongly recommend you stay away from the apartment of Mademoiselle Roche."

All at once a light went on in Frank's memory. And the tired rehearsals of his brain were rewarded with a flash of inspiration. Those words had put him in mind of the last time he was with Patricia in her flat, of the fierce banging on the door that had so rudely trespassed on the early alpenglow of their lovemaking.

"Are you Lutz?" he asked.

The man answered with a hint of fabrication in his smile. It gave Frank the impression the question had unnerved him.

"This is my stop," he said as the wheels of the tram ground to a halt. "It was a pleasure meeting you again, Mr Eigenmann." Whereupon the man Frank took to be Lutz rose and melted away into the anonymous crowd behind him.

He felt the cold air of the city sweep in through the doors of the tram as they opened to let his greasy counsellor out. The man was instantly lost in the busy exchange of commuters. And when the doors closed again on the draught, Frank appreciated the cocoon of warmth that he knew he could count on until the next stop. But his slippery, self-appointed saviour had left him with a sense of apprehension. A foreboding that only served to heighten his awareness that the next stop would not be long in coming, that he would soon be treated to another blast of the wintry Bise which blew right across central Europe from the steppes of Siberia and so forcefully drove his need for shelter.

Frank now regretted his decision to take the tram into town. There were taxis. He could even have walked. It was not so far. Had he done so, he would have avoided the misfortune of running into Lutz and would now be happily on his way to Patricia's flat. As it was, he found himself caught in a tangled web of doubt that held him fast in his seat, uncertain as to his next move.

The tram seemed full to bursting as more passengers climbed on board the further it continued into town. The air was becoming thick with the body heat. Hemmed in now by the standing passengers who crowded around him, he felt impotently small. Coats towered densely into the space above him, which narrowed a little more with inexorable malice at every stop of the tram. He sensed the heat of this confined space apply a pressure that came perilously close to his limits of endurance. The needle was in the red zone and still moving. His skull ached with the heat and the noise. He was aware of nothing else. The heat, the noise and the growing pressure in his head, which felt about to split open and gush its hot serous fluid on the spark of anxiety that Lutz had left behind.

In the havoc of this suffocating tension, his mind craved the deliverance of fresh air. He struggled to his feet through the thicket of anonymous coats, and forced a way to the doors of the tram. Crazed panic scored a line through the expression in his eyes so ferocious that a path spontaneously cleared through the dense wall of people around him, and he reached the doors in time to see the river speeding past. The tram slowed down as it reached the other side of the bridge, and when the doors opened, it was a caged and desperate animal they released onto the pavement.

Gasping at the sweetness of the night air, he made his way back to the bridge. From the parapet of a small watchtower halfway across, he sucked in the cool refreshment that blew down over the water. The swirls and eddies of the current below appeared to mirror his own confusion – yet the river displayed a purpose and determination in its chaos that plainly had the edge over his own behaviour.

Lulled into a new composure by this movement of the water, his thoughts returned to Lutz. Why should he offer his unsolicited advice and set himself so clearly at odds with his sadistic employer? So, was his advice even to be trusted? Or was it some devious trick set up by Breitner himself? Every question begged a host of other doubts, and his head was not equal to the task of finding any sensible answers. Nor was he feeling in the mood for empty-headed displays of valour. So he opted against going to Patricia's flat that night and decided to head for the Kolping house a little further upstream in the hope of finding cheap lodgings there.

His head was still throbbing as he checked in at reception, and the elderly woman on the desk promised to send some aspirin up to his room. He had imagined that, in the privacy of his room, he would have a chance to relax. He was mistaken. He threw his coat on the bed, laid the book he had carried with him all the way from his father's study on the bedside table and flopped into an easy chair that stood beside the window. Relentlessly the pain returned. What felt like a deep fissure seemed to open in his skull. Once again, like that day on the castle ruins, watching a scythe of black cloud sweep over Germany and waiting for his old friend to arrive, he sensed an unquiet presence, a peculiar otherness over his shoulder that seemed undefinably a part of him. More than sensed it. Became it. And watched his own discomfort with a strange detachment, as the fissure widened to accommodate the tumescent folds of brain tissue that appeared to feed off the hot, dry air of the room, like bread dough rising in the oven. For an instant, this swelling flesh of his brain appeared to magnify before his eyes, as if it had been slipped under the eye of a powerful microscope to reveal a complex tangle of neurons: dendrites hooking up like the tentacles of an octopus to bewildered tissue; astrocytes like starfish swimming in their element. In panic, he got to his feet in a desperate effort to shake off the vision. But it clung like a stubborn leech.

In a pitiless sweat and stifled by the unrelenting grip of chaos, he flung open the window and willed the traffic noise and coldness of the evening river air to come to his aid. The blue light of an ambulance flashed over what was little more than the blurred screen of his consciousness. He watched the vehicle silently and, almost in slow motion, circle Wettsteinplatz and disappear around the corner to the sleazier end of town. 'No doubt come to pick up another overdose victim,' he told himself, confusing his mind with the speculation – until a banging on the door stirred him from this emotional farrago. His head instantly cleared.

He spun round to face the door. Seconds that may have been minutes passed before he drove himself to open it. By the time he did so, the doorway was empty.

It was not until he was closing the door again that he saw a piece of paper lying at his feet. Crumpled and folded in half, the note was not even given the dignity of an envelope.

'You have not chosen well. Be that as it may, stay in your room now until you receive word from me. The streets are not safe for you.' It was signed 'Your friend', which he took to mean Lutz. What was he playing at? And how does he know I'm here? Frank asked himself.

His head was still sore, and this new bafflement did nothing to help. As he flopped back into the chair with the note in his hand and a horde of questions pressed on his bruised mind, there came a second knock. Lighter this time. But it jolted him into action more quickly than the first. He opened up almost before the knocking had stopped. He expected to see Lutz. It was the elderly woman from the reception desk.

"Your aspirin, sir," she said. He found another piece of folded paper being pushed into his hand with grudging force, this one containing what felt to be half a dozen tablets.

He was still too washed out to express his gratitude verbally, but managed what must have appeared a very thin and sickly smile. She waited. Was it the slowness of an ageing mind or the weight bearing down on her arthritic knees which kept her at his door? Probably neither. He dug his hands into his pockets and gave her a handful of coins. She looked at the coins, shrugged and shuffled uneasily away down the corridor, her progress muffled by her slippers on the carpet.

Eight tablets she had given him. The first two brought almost instant relief, helping him to banish the reminder of his earlier torment and to focus on trying to fathom the motives of Lutz. What was he playing at? Why suddenly change direction and put himself at such risk? He knows what Breitner is capable of. And he gives the impression of being anything but a spunky lionheart. So why should he want to help? Frank asked himself. He doesn't even know me. These questions occupied his mind for the rest of the evening, and kept him awake for most of the night.

Whatever Lutz's game, Frank resolved the following morning to ignore the advice at all costs. But perhaps it was not so much resolve as the ill-reason and woolly wisdom born of a restless night that drove him onto those unsafe streets. It was a sleepy, bleary-eyed city. Sleepier even than he was feeling. But unpredictable. This had always been plain to him. And on this particular morning, the air seemed thick with its perfidy.

The mediaeval streets and the half-timbered houses – so spotlessly maintained – boasted a certain homely charm and suggested the place felt smugly comfortable with its history. It was an irritating comfort, caressed by the occasional aroma of roast chestnuts that still clung to the odd street corner from the night before. Yet no one smiled in the streets this morning. An odd disquiet hung in the air.

After breakfast in one of the town's sleazier restaurants, where he imagined his unshaven unslept appearance might be less conspicuous, he decided it was time for his confrontation with Achim. His recollection of how to get to Achim's place was hazy, but he was able to recall Silverstone leading him along a tired street behind the station. And a search in this area quickly brought him to that strange shop, where the sour, suspicious shopkeeper had stood sentry for Achim. Only today it appeared to be closed. The door was locked, and the place was in darkness. Yet he caught a hint of movement in the shadows through the door. He knocked, and knocked again. But the place remained stubbornly quiet.

He was not a curious person – Patricia had put that on record – so perhaps it was his determination to confront Achim that drove him. At all events, a certain curiosity had been aroused, and an alley to the side of the block obligingly led round to a back entrance, which he found to be open. A dead silence filled the house. The movement must have been the reflection of traffic in the window. But it was not simply the silence that told him there was no one here. A fetid stench filled the dark passageway, which smothered the lungs and threatened to suffocate him with its rancid miasma. Cautiously he made his way up through the half-light of the stairwell to Achim's attic flat. He knocked on the door. But there was no response. And the door was firmly locked.

He recalled that, when Silverstone had brought him here, Gertrude had been in the basement below, that this was where Achim had made his workshop. The basement steps brought him back into the noxious reek that had confronted him when he first entered. An acrid smell of ammonia mingled with decay. It clawed at the back of his throat. He covered his face with a handkerchief and eased open the basement door with a calmness and steadiness that surprised him in view of his fear as to what he might find there.

He let the door go, and it swung slowly back, allowing the stench to blast a way into every pore of his face. He caught the sound of rats scurrying for cover, and ran his hand down the wall beside the doorframe groping for the light switch. The grim horror of the scene lit by a single naked lightbulb was too repulsive to be real. A solitary surviving rat – perhaps the dimwit of the community, or just plain hungry – remained unimpressed by the intrusion and continued to gnaw at the heap of meat that lay draped over the two smaller cadavers. The clothes of each body had been torn away and hung now in sporadic tatters from the congealed crevices of flesh, which in places had been chewed right down to the bone. The bodies had been devoured away beyond any hope of recognition, but he knew instinctively that he was looking at Gertrude and her two baby boys. He remembered the vivacious beauty that he had met in Berlin all those years back. Recalled the pale anxious creature he had seen with Achim just a short time ago. And the two little faces, so full of future, so precious to their mother. Three once fragile souls now nothing more than rat fodder.

Light from the solitary naked bulb was reflected in the twisting bodies of the maggots which breathed ironic life into a nightmare that would stay with him for as long as he lived.

Frank sobbed into the handkerchief over his face. He could stay there no longer. He needed to breathe. But the fresh sweetness of the cold outdoor air was not enough to prevent him throwing up – it seemed to hurry the event – as he came out onto the steps of the back entrance. And as he watched the last mucous remnants of breakfast swim into the gutter, his thoughts began to spin. What was going on? Who could have let this happen? And where was Achim?

His mind was a mess, teeming with unanswered questions. And nowhere to go for an answer. Frank thought of the note from Lutz – the unsafe streets – he must have known about the nightmare that lay here. But the truth of his warning did not make the man any more trustworthy for him – on the contrary. So, rather than return to the Kolping house, he decided to take refuge out of town. Somewhere he could think and consider his next move without trouble breathing down his neck. But he was not prepared for the new shock that was waiting for him round the corner.

The cloth cap, the beard and the unkempt appearance were unmistakable. The last time Frank had seen him was in Cologne. Now here he was keeping vigil at the newsstand of another station entrance, ostensibly buying his morning newspaper. By a stroke of good fortune, a tram obscured the cloth cap's view of Frank on the other side of the street, opened its doors for his escape and obligingly carried him away under cover of the passengers standing on the station side of the tram.

'Did he see me?' Frank asked himself. It was impossible to know. So he kept a cautious eye out for him when he alighted from the tram just a few minutes later and switched to the narrow-gauge railway that would take him out of town. The little station house at the city end of the line in what was once the hay market gave him all the cover he needed to keep an inconspicuous watch while he waited for his train.

He saw no further sign of the familiar, cloth-capped stranger. But his distress gnawed at him too deeply for this knowledge to fill him with any sense of security. The hunter may be anywhere. So, when he alighted from the train at the last stop before the frontier, he took every precaution that a running fox might take.

Only two other passengers got out at his stop – a man and a woman, both rheumy-eyed and plainly on the pilgrim's path to the basilica that lay at the top of the hill. His cautiousness had evidently been unnecessary. He strode on ahead of these two timidly slow pensioners, up the hill past the restaurant where he had met Gertrude and her two baby boys with Achim. Three lives full of history, full of dreams, full of hope. Three futures that had just ceased to be. Smiles that were no more. The memory pierced his heart to the quick and filled it with a huge, painful sense of loss that was out of all proportion to his fleeting knowledge of them. He tried to banish the images from his mind as he continued up the hill to the castle ruins. To no avail. Perhaps this was the wrong place to be at such a time, but he needed the fresh air and the altitude. He needed that clear vista over the trees, over the city, across the border.

If the demise of Gertrude and her two boys was not down to Breitner, then it was presumably the work of his friends. Maybe the cloth cap. At all events, he was convinced that Breitner had played some part in the butchery. But why? Why such innocence? And what had happened to Achim? He cursed his stupidity for ever having suggested to his friend that he join him in what had seemed such a peaceful haven. They might all be safe and well if he had kept his naive ideas to himself.

As he approached the castle ruins, his thoughts were momentarily distracted by a sound in the undergrowth that startled him.

The cloth cap had found him after all, he thought. Instinctively, he sought cover behind the nearest bush. But when he looked in the direction of the noise, he was made sheepishly aware of his foolishness. Just off a side path some twenty metres to the left of him stood a rather stocky man busily tending what looked like a grave, digging out the few remaining weeds of winter with a trowel and arranging a bouquet of snowdrops in their place.

It struck him as an odd site for a grave and left him feeling uncomfortable, like an intruder at a stranger's funeral. But the man was deeply enwrapped in his devotional work and did not seem to notice him. Frank was about to leave the man in the privacy of his ritual, to continue up the pathway to the castle, when something held him back. A loud cracking sound that tore through the valley. The sound of gunfire.

The grave tender paid it no attention, as if gunfire was one of life's everyday sounds which belonged as much to the backdrop of this valley as the birdsong in spring or the wind in the trees.

Frank wondered whether it might be the local huntsman shooting game. Then it occurred to him that the people in this country had a penchant for firearms which was nourished by their fierce sense of independence. He recalled often seeing young men off on their bicycles to do some shooting practice, or military service, with rifles strapped to their backs. Everyone seemed to keep a weapon at home. 'They're going to need them if the Nazis ever march across the border,' he muttered to himself.

Recalling also that every community had at least one shooting range for their marksmen to practise on, he assumed the sound of gunfire that reverberated through the valley now, invading its rustic charm, was a sign that just such a practice session was in full swing. This could be the opportunity he was looking for. He turned and headed back the way he had come, passing the two pensioner pilgrims who were still making their way patiently up the hill.

The continuing crack of gunfire as he reached the other side of the valley told him that the practice session was not yet over. The shooting range was discreetly concealed in the woods, unmarked and not signposted. It was for the initiated only. So every shot served as an acoustic beacon for him to home in on.

Eventually he found the long barrack-like hut at the foot of the limestone rocks that jut out of the landscape in this part of the world like badly kept teeth. And as he stole around the building in search of a door, he felt as small and as mean as the bacteria that bring caries to the impoverished and the ignorant.

He was in luck. When he gently eased open the door, he saw that the marksman was alone and looked to be in the process of getting ready to leave. Pushing the crack of the door gently to again, he hastily took a log from a pile of firewood that was stacked against the building, pinned his body to the wall and waited. His heart pounded so fiercely he was sure that the pulse of his tensed frame must be audible on the wooden boards of the hut. Just as he was beginning to wonder whether the shooter might have slipped out through another exit of the building, the door creaked open. From his insecure vantage point, he could see that the man was carrying a large leather bag over his shoulder, which he let slip to the ground as he locked up behind him.

This was Frank's moment. Emerging from around the corner, he brought the log down on the crown of the man's skull before he had a chance to turn. Frank was struck by the almost spongy softness of the bone beneath the wood and prayed that he had not done this poor unsuspecting stranger any serious damage. Frank found himself apologising to the spreadeagled body for this violence, but his need – he told himself – was more urgent and more real than the marksman's.

In the leather bag, he found two handguns. Not wanting to overstate his case, he took just one. Together with some rounds of ammunition. And tucked them into his overcoat pocket. He then dragged the man's body back into the building, locked the door on him, and quickly considered his retreat. Since he needed to vanish into thin air without anyone seeing him, the village was plainly the wrong direction to turn. So he took a path that led up around the limestone rocks and over the hill that lay parallel with the railway line running back into town. By keeping to the grey-brown blanket of trees that covered this last dorsal outcrop of rock on the north-east tip of the Jura, he knew that he would eventually reach one of the sleepy villages further up the line, where he could take the little blue train back to Lutz's unsafe streets.

The light of day was already beginning to fade, hastened by the path that carried him away down the eastern flank of the hill, where it lost all trace of the setting sun. The spreading gloom in the forest around him, the silence of the undergrowth broken only by his own footsteps, and the lights coming on in the distance celebrated his isolation. He gazed down at the lights of the village as he ran his fingers over the weapon in his pocket. Taking it in his hand and fishing the ammunition out of the box he had pilfered, he decided to load it before continuing his trek. Best to be prepared, he told himself. If Breitner's friends or the cloth cap ran across his path, he would be ready for them.

Chapter 17

"I'm so happy you could return so soon."

This was all Dr Zellweger said as he shook Ellen's hand and – flustered, but correct as ever – politely took her luggage when he met her at the station. There was concern written all over his face. Ellen sensed that he wanted to say more. But she knew he was not inclined to discuss his patients outside the clinic, so he was certainly not going to attempt it in the hall of a railway station. It was not until they were in his car that he spoke again.

"Your husband seems to have entered an extremely labile phase," he said. "I'm very worried about him."

"You've found him then?"

He started the engine and focused on the traffic around him as he drove out of the station car park. Ellen was left teetering on the edge of expectation until he eventually found the words.

"In a manner of speaking, yes."

Again he fell silent and left Ellen waiting for him to elaborate further. While anxious to know more, she was also fearful of where her own curiosity might lead her. And asked no further questions. When eventually Dr Zellweger did speak, he also had no further answers for her. Only more questions. Guarded ones. The cautious, considered questions of a psychiatrist.

"My wife tells me you have seen your husband in Cologne?'

"Yes. I told her when we spoke on the phone yesterday that I'd seen him the very day I left here. When I changed trains in Cologne. He was getting on a tram just outside the station."

"Are you sure it was your husband?"

"Of course I am."

"This is very interesting," he said rather mysteriously. Ellen almost had the impression he was talking to himself more than to her. "You see, we have evidence that your husband was here two or three days after you left." He paused, ostensibly for reflection. But Ellen had the feeling it was more for effect, especially the way he threw the next question at her. "Why do you think he has been there?" he asked.

"I have no idea. But I know it was him."

Generally, the polite correctness of Dr Zellweger had a calming influence on Ellen. She appreciated it. But today his manner irritated her. And she had no wish to share her suspicions about why Frank might have been in Cologne.

"What do you mean by 'evidence'?" she asked. "You sound more like a policeman than a psychiatrist."

He smiled.

"Like any science, psychiatry must also rely very often on evidence."

"I thought you focused on facial expression and body language." Ellen's irritation made her a little too bold perhaps, but she felt she had a point to make, and was certainly not going to be taken for the fool he seemed to think she was. "Is that why you're talking round in circles?" she added. "Because you have to keep your eyes on the road and haven't got time to watch me?"

His smile now broke into a laugh, and although his amusement seemed genuine enough, she felt it was driven by embarrassment rather than a sense of humour. But at least it gave her the feeling that she had scored some kind of a point.

"My wife says the same thing," he said. "And maybe it's true, because I don't like to talk much when I drive." And so the remainder of the journey to the Zellwegers' house continued in silence.

Marthe welcomed Ellen back with an air of concern and affection that was infinitely more sisterly than the reception she had received from Beth. She instantly felt at home again. Marthe had even made a pot of tea for her arrival. Dr Zellweger evidently felt it best to leave his wife alone with Ellen to break the story and withdrew to his study.

"You must forgive me," she said. "I could find no ginger biscuits." (Ellen was touched by the way she always considered every little detail, like the good Swiss hostess she was.) "But try these. They're a local speciality called *Läckerli*. Made with honey and spices, *à la cannelle*."

Ellen tried one.

"They're delicious. With cinnamon," she said, savouring the biscuit with particular relish after the long journey back from Cologne. "I love honey and cinnamon and all those gingerbread spices."

It was when they were sitting there over tea and *Läckerli* – as if this was the most natural thing to do when someone's life had gone haywire – that the story came out. Such as it was.

A man answering Frank's description, the same man the police had identified earlier as Frank Eigenmann, had apparently been found in the Kolping house. As Dr Zellweger had already intimated, 'found' was not quite the right word: although the man had checked into the house, he had since disappeared again; he had not checked out, his things were still in his room, but no one knew where he was. The man had apparently been behaving very strangely, and the concierge at the Kolping house called the police – whether this was because of his strange behaviour or because she was afraid he had done a bunk without paying his rent was not quite clear.

Most worrying of all, when they searched the room, they found things which they had reason to believe were stolen. And it was this latest twist that particularly disturbed Dr Zellweger. Apparently, a man had gained access to the home of a disabled old woman a few days earlier, had entered her bedroom, scared the living daylights out of her and walked off with things that have now turned up in the hotel room.

"Ellen, your husband is in a very unstable condition. And it is important that we find him before he does damage to himself, or to someone else. If there is anything you know which can help us, please tell Urs before it's too late." She paused, hopeful for a clue from Ellen. And Ellen sensed that Marthe was waiting for something very particular.

"What can I say?" Ellen asked in desperation. "I've already told you our entire history."

"You know, this Kolping house is located close to what you might call the less wholesome part of town. Is it possible your husband may be taking drugs?"

"That's absurd. He keeps fit. He plays squash. You don't do that if you take drugs."

"Perhaps if we knew why he went to Cologne...."

But Ellen's thoughts were already moving in a different direction and had long since left Marthe and her husband's interrogations far behind. Other questions were occupying her mind. The place where Frank was supposed to be staying had caught her imagination. At last something concrete, a physical contact of sorts.

Ellen needed to get inside the place, to see the things he left behind. She was sure that if she could get into that room, she would somehow be able to prove once and for all that it was not her Frank they were talking about. When she suggested this to Dr Zellweger, he took to the idea with a bubbling enthusiasm.

"I'm surprised the police didn't suggest it themselves," he said. "Of course, we must get permission from them first, but I'm sure it can be arranged. Naturally they are wanting to speak with you anyway."

Dr Zellweger managed to get the necessary permission the very next day. So, together with a rather sour-faced policeman who was introduced to Ellen as Kommissar Staehelin and reminded her of Malcolm with his pencil-thin moustache, Dr Zellweger and Marthe took Ellen to the Kolping house to see where Frank was said to have lodged. It lay on the other side of the river. The streets they walked through to get there from the police station had a deeply uncomfortable feel about them. Ellen could not help noticing the used syringes that lay in the gutter, the run-down bars and groups of shady-looking people loitering outside. This was not the Switzerland she had been expecting.

The house itself lay the other side of this less wholesome part of town, close to a church and a square surrounded by large late nineteenth-century townhouses. It was so at odds with the unsavoury streets they had just walked through that Ellen could not help feeling this was a special tour put on especially for her benefit – that they wanted to drive home the message that Frank was probably on drugs. It was an absurd idea. But the seamy streets they had taken her through gave it a plausibility that stuck in Ellen's mind.

As Kommissar Staehelin explained to the concierge on the desk who they were, the elderly lady became carried away by an increasingly crotchety impatience. She began to lay into him with a barrage of words that were completely incomprehensible to Ellen. But the message was clear enough, as Dr Zellweger confirmed afterwards.

Her huffy outburst, he explained, was the umbrage of a woman worried about who was going to pay the money that was owing to her. Even with Kommissar Staehelin's presence, they would have been no match for this piqued old dragon had it not been for Marthe. With the winning way that Ellen had come to appreciate in her, she managed to placate the old dear sufficiently to invest her with the human features she was no doubt born with, but which she obviously preferred to suppress for the purposes of her job. And once Marthe had extracted the key from her, the four of them took the stairs up to the second floor.

"You must not think badly about her," Marthe said defensively, as if she felt the old lady was letting her country down. "She surely has many problems with the drug addicts on the streets around here."

It was a strange sensation for Ellen entering a room known to be occupied by a man who was said to be her husband – but was fast becoming a complete stranger to her. It was like invading the privacy of someone who bore no relation to her, and she found it slightly distasteful. The bed was neatly made. A small suitcase lay half-unpacked on a chair. And the bedside table was occupied almost entirely by an old book.

"The room is in the condition how we found it. We wait on your man," the Kommissar explained in his broken English.

"He's not my 'man'," Ellen insisted. She sensed an involuntary anger in her voice. But more than that, she was giving vent to her relief, because she was finally convinced beyond all doubt that this room was not inhabited by her Frank. Nothing in the room was familiar to her. She looked in the bathroom – the shaving set, the toothbrush, the toilet bag: they were all completely foreign. Ellen let out an almost hysterical laugh. She could barely contain herself. Tears of both joy and despair ran down her cheeks as she leafed through the book beside the bed – a gilt-edged Victorian tome filled with beautiful illustrations of exotic fauna and flora.

"This book has been stolen," said Kommissar Staehelin.

His eyes were on her every move. He made her feel she was the culprit, that she was responsible for this whole absurd situation. She tried to ignore his cold, insensitive presence and directed her attention at the suitcase that lay on the chair beside the bed. This too was as unknown to her as every other item in the room. And the clothes she rummaged through were things she had never set eyes on in her life. She examined the labels and found they were not even English – except for one pair of underpants; these she had to admit did bring a flicker of life into her battered dog-weary memory.

But so what? Underpants like these were probably worn by thousands of men all over Europe, she told herself. They did not even have the distinction of a pattern, but were simply brief black crotch holders. A pouch just large enough to carry the substance of its wearer's pride and joy. Yet here was the familiarity that disturbed her. It did not strike her at first when she looked at the label. It was only as she put the pants down and her hand slipped for an instant under the black cotton cloth of the pouch that she noticed it. A hole about a quarter of an inch in diameter where the cloth had been worn through. She knew that hole so well. How often she had teased Frank about it, and joked about what on earth he had been doing to make a hole in a place like that. What were the chances of another man walking around the city at this very moment with a hole a quarter of an inch wide in the pouch of their black English-labelled briefs? She rummaged further. And at the very bottom of the case, she came across two pairs of socks that also looked familiar. No, not familiar – she knew them intimately. It was not only the design, but the pattern of wear; day in day out she had put his socks in the washing machine, taken them out again, hung them up to dry, and tucked them away in his drawer – she knew every worn thread like she knew the lines on her hand.

At that moment, she became more aware than ever of the vast gap that had opened up between them, as she gazed at these socks and underpants. Garments that she had known so intimately now lying in a strange suitcase with a lot of strange clothes in a strange room in a foreign country. It was as though she had years of divorce behind her, and all the pain and emotion of the separation were still there, fresh as ever. She sat on the edge of the bed, a sock still in one hand, and finally submitted to an uncontrollable deluge of tears. The despair was echoed in the doleful bawling of her words.

"Where is he? I can't stand this any longer. Please just tell me where my Frank is."

She sensed Marthe's comforting arms around her shoulders and heard her voice. But the words laboured in vain to get through. Ellen was hopelessly at sea in her distress.

Her recollection of what followed was very vague. Even fainter and more garbled than a half-remembered dream on the edge of sleep. It was not until she was woken the next morning by Marthe bringing her a cup of tea in bed that she learned how Marthe and her husband had taken her home, completely overwrought, after assuring Kommissar Staehelin that she would be in good hands and that he could interview her as soon as she had recovered. The Kommissar had apparently proved to be completely out of his depth and was hopelessly embarrassed by her outburst. Like two overgrown schoolgirls, Ellen and Marthe both giggled at the poor man's ineptitude, as if they had caught him with his trousers down.

"Marthe, you've been so kind. I don't know what I would have done without you."

"Please." Marthe place a reassuring hand on Ellen's arm. So warm. So tender. Her affection sent a thrill coursing through Ellen's veins – a closeness she had not felt in months. Then, leaving her smile with Ellen as she went over to the window, Marthe pulled back the heavy curtains.

"Look. Today we have the sun. Urs has clinical duties today. So we will go for a daytrip into the country, have lunch together somewhere, and forget all our problems for a few hours."

Ellen suspected where the journey into the country was taking her soon after their car left the city boundaries. They were on the same road as before on that day when Dr Zellweger drove out to visit his mysterious protégé in the country and left Marthe and Ellen in a little village up in the hills. Ellen fell in love with these hills the first time she was here. A little sombre in its winter coat perhaps. But it was a coat with promise in its pockets and the contentment of knowing the promise would be kept. So elegant and peaceful the brown wooded hills and limestone rocks against the blue sky. Nature at her tidiest and most reassuring. Ellen had no choice but to put everything to the back of her mind and to forget. If only for a few hours.

Marthe was right. This trip was just what she needed. Ellen's newfound friend, who showed such an uncanny sense of timing and offered the sisterly affection that she had found so lacking when she most needed it, exuded a mood that Ellen had never seen in her before. She had always been incredibly accommodating and friendly. But today she seemed to Ellen especially carefree and light-hearted. So full of life.

Almost as if wanting to put the flourish of a signature to her vivacious mood, she accelerated the car out from the sombre light of a narrow treelined gorge that Ellen recognised from her earlier trip out here and into the bright expansiveness of the plateau where they had walked before.

"You're not Catholic, are you?' Marthe Zellweger asked as she swung the car to a standstill under one of the trees in the village square.

"I'm not into religion at all," Ellen replied.

"Yes, I remember you felt uncomfortable when we were here last. You said you didn't like churches."

Ellen nodded.

"I went to a Catholic boarding school," she said. "And that told me all I needed to know about religion."

"But I would like you to try once more," Marthe insisted. "There are not many people here during the week, so I think you will not find it so uncomfortable. You must see this. For me it is one of the most beautiful places in this part of Switzerland."

There was a trace of reverence in Marthe's voice that Ellen found oddly unlike the woman she had come to know.

This place had been a holy site for hundreds of years, she explained – ever since a child fell from the rocks into the gorge below and was caught in mid-flight by the Virgin Mary. A chapel of mercy was carved out of the rock to celebrate the miracle, which eventually led to a whole industry of religious construction – a Benedictine monastery, a convent.

Marthe giggled quietly, speculating on what the nuns and monks got up to together in the cold winter nights, as she led Ellen into the church.

When Marthe now led her through the door off the side of the building and into the long windowless passageway, Ellen sensed her pulse quicken. She remembered the dimly lit walls, showing pious inscriptions in all kinds of languages that she was only partly able to decipher. And the coolness of the air, as it wafted off the marble walls with a hint of incense. The powerful atmosphere of mysticism in the passageway was overwhelming. But – unlike before –she did not feel the same light-headedness when they came to the top of the steep staircase.

"We're lucky," Marthe said in a whisper that restored that reverential tone after her brief foray into titillating speculation.

"If you would come at a weekend, there would be very many people here," she explained, before leading Ellen down the long staircase into the bowels of the rock on which the church stood. From a window halfway down, Ellen saw that the stairs were actually cut into the face of the rock. She judged that they were now about fifty or sixty feet below the abbey. At the bottom of the steps, Marthe took her arm and guided her through an iron gateway into a small dark grotto lit in one corner by the flicker of candles.

"On a Sunday, you would find this whole chapel lit by candles," she said, adding a quietly earnest "Excuse me" as she left Ellen standing just inside the iron gateway to the chapel and went to light a candle herself. For a moment, Marthe had returned to her more serious mode. And although it was true to the character Ellen had come to know, it surprised her, because she had never imagined that Marthe would entertain religious leanings in any direction.

"Oh, I think it's in the blood since a very early age," Marthe explained, as they came back along the passageway and up the last flight of steps into the fresh winter air. "Most of my school years I spent at a Catholic boarding school in the French-speaking part of Switzerland. A very strict education which you never forget. Perhaps that explains why I have never taken my husband's psychiatry as seriously as he does."

"Well, you certainly talk like a psychiatrist sometimes," Ellen said, as she recalled the grilling Marthe had given her at times about her relationship with Frank.

"Do I? How awful." She laughed with a hint of embarrassment.

"That's because I live with one," Marthe added. "I also considered studying it at one time. It seemed so intriguing. But I could never really believe in it like Urs. He could not live without it. He believes it has the key to all our problems. It has an explanation for everything. Even the things it cannot explain at the moment, he is confident to find an explanation soon. It began with sex and psychoanalysis, but now it has become more complicated. Now everyone is talking about biological psychiatry and neurotransmitters. In a way, I think it is worse than it has ever been. We seem to have forgotten that psychiatry has to do with people, individuals.

"But it still fascinates me. Like the Catholic religion. It makes all the same mistakes. Catholics have an explanation for everything also. Like why that little boy survived his fall from the rocks 500 years ago. It has its dogma. But it still fascinates me. Not because of its explanations. But the things which it is trying to explain. That's what fascinates me.

"Urs is very sweet," Marthe continued, "but he has no imagination. For him, a life after death is unthinkable, because it cannot be scientifically demonstrated. He is just like the Catholic priests who have studied their dogma. I think this is why he finds your husband's case so irritating."

"What do you mean?" Ellen felt oddly offended by this last remark.

"He talks about your husband almost every night when he comes into bed. He cannot understand it. And this annoys him, because it does not correspond to any of his explanations."

"And what do you think?" Ellen asked.

"I? What I think about your husband's case?"

The bells above them began to chime, and Marthe was compelled to pause for reflection before committing herself to a reply. Ellen had the impression she welcomed this reprieve.

The bells grew fainter as they walked, but still they were loud enough to keep the two of them locked in the privacy of their own thoughts, until a few minutes later the chiming stopped altogether, and she admitted: "It fascinates me for the same reason it irritates my husband. I have no explanation for what has happened with Frank. Maybe psychiatry can help, but we need to find him first."

"I just wish I knew what the problem was. I know Bill Plattner had a funny influence on him, but I can't believe he's into drugs. And I can't believe he's capable of burglary either, let alone murder. I just wish I knew what's going on, and where he is. I just wish. Every morning I wake up and I just wish."

Marthe detected the despair in Ellen's voice – it would have been palpable even over the deafening noise of the bells – and she touched her arm in her incomparably gentle way.

"Let's walk," she said, suddenly switching back to her earlier vivacious mood. Taking Ellen's hand, she led her up the hill overlooking the plateau where the abbey fitted so much more naturally into the landscape now that Ellen knew it better. When they reached the brow of the hill and the road into France that was nothing more than a farm track, Ellen was struck by the beauty of the scene before her, which she had not fully appreciated on her first visit here. Just beneath, on a kind of saddle between them and the hill opposite, lay the same hamlet of half a dozen half-timbered houses, dwarfed by the same castle ruins that rose above them, lit up by the low midday sun almost white against the smoky blue backdrop of the sky.

"On the left of the castle, in the distance," Marthe said with a certain breathless excitement in her voice which Ellen put down to the climb up the hill in the cold winter air, "you can just see the snow on the Vosges Mountains through the mist. On the right, not so far, the buildings of the chemical industry and the city.

"But that's another world," Marthe added. "We're standing in France now. So much more space. So emptier. I find it so beautifully peaceful up here. But depressing in a way – it reminds me how alone we all are."

She stood in silence for some time, looking out over the dark green forest of the foreground that fell away into the mists between them and the snowy peaks of the Vosges. She seemed to be lost in the disturbing pregnancy of her own words. She appeared concerned.

"Ellen," said Marthe, turning to Ellen as if suddenly struck by a momentous thought. "We must find Frank soon. Urs is perhaps lacking imagination, but if he believes that Frank could be in danger, he may be right. We must find him soon."

"What do you mean?"

"I don't know. We need to keep an open mind."

Marthe's words unsettled Ellen. She did not fully understand, but Ellen almost had the feeling Marthe was struggling with a personal problem of her own, that what she was saying had nothing to do with Frank at all.

'Perhaps this accounts for the mistakes she's suddenly making in her English', Ellen speculated. 'It seems absurd to think that Frank could be a danger to anyone.'

"But for now, we will walk to the castle and enjoy the view from there," Marthe said, suddenly changing tack. "Until then we have an appetite for lunch."

She had an uncanny ability to manipulate the mood without irritating Ellen. Whatever she said, Ellen felt safe in her company. It was not simply that Ellen was a hapless foreigner who needed the guiding hand of a native. Marthe seemed to be interested in her and Frank as people and not simply as a case of psychiatric interest. And yet, her unsettling words stayed with Ellen all the way to the castle ruins.

As they were approaching the woods that surrounded the castle, Ellen's eye fell on a narrow path leading off to the right. A path to which she would not normally have paid any attention, but the sound of gardening, a hoe against stony ground, caught her ear. When she stopped and looked a little closer, she could see a short, stocky man in a small clearing a few yards down the path busily working the soil. It was obviously a well-tended patch. In the earth around where he was hard at work removing the last few weeds of winter, there stood a cross.

For some inexplicable reason Ellen was reminded at that moment of Frank. At any other time, she would have been uncontrollably curious to know what this incongruous scene in the middle of nowhere meant. And she was curious now. Nosy, Frank used to call it, and he did his best to get her out of the habit, which she found slightly sanctimonious coming from a journalist. But so successful was he in controlling her natural instincts that, on this occasion, the struggle to overcome her nosiness reached such an intensity that she began to feel acutely uncomfortable. As if she was trespassing on private property. She wanted to go. In some strange way, she almost felt as though Frank's reproachful eye was on her.

"Marthe," Ellen said, "would you mind if we skip lunch? I think I've had enough fresh air for one day."

Marthe smiled. She could not possibly have known what was going through Ellen's mind, but it seemed to Ellen that she understood in some puzzling way.

It was a long walk back to the car in the shadows of the abbey. And the journey home to Marthe's house became even longer when they were held up on the road down the valley into the next village. It was a sleepy little community, which nestled inconspicuously between the steep, forested slopes either side of it. Only a single road ran through the village, and the police were stopping every vehicle travelling on it, questioning the occupants and searching the contents of the vehicles with quiet fussiness. This was the first time Ellen had ever encountered a roadblock, and she sensed an instant chill of guilt run through her body. In a foreign country, in a foreign car on the wrong side of the road being interrogated by police in a language that sounded more like an obscure eastern European tongue than anything she had ever learned in school, she suddenly felt she had been dumped in a police state.

"A man has been attacked at the shooting range here," Marthe explained, when eventually the police were satisfied of their innocence and let them pass. "And his guns have been stolen."

"In such a quiet little place," Ellen said.

"You would not believe some of the things which happen in these quiet towns and villages on the frontier," Marthe replied with an ominous sideways glance that disturbed Ellen all the more.

As she lay in bed that night, Ellen's mind returned to the incident with the police and the story of the man being attacked and robbed. All at once, this comfortable little country, which had started its acquaintance with her from the outset as a source of mystery, had now acquired an air of menace. She thought of Frank. And Marthe's words. And she wondered whether he was also feeling the menace at that moment, wherever he was.

As Ellen was pondering these thoughts, there was a knock at her bedroom door. Marthe discreetly pushed it open.

That morning, she said, there had been a terrible fire at a clinic in Zurich, where Urs spent some time in practice. So he had gone there to meet with colleagues and see if he could help in any way. He would not be back until tomorrow evening, so she had come to say goodnight – and look for some company – she explained as she sat down on the side of Ellen's bed.

Ellen was equally glad of her company, and felt instantly at peace when Marthe took her hands in hers. Like she wished Beth had done a few days earlier.

"Marthe, what did you mean when you spoke about the danger Frank might be in?" Ellen asked. In the back of her mind, she was still troubled by the incident with the roadblock. "What sort of danger?"

Marthe smiled and ran her fingers through Ellen's hair, brushing it off her forehead with a gesture that reminded her of the way Beth used to be so many years ago – on the occasions when she took the responsibilities of sisterly affection seriously. It made her sad to realise how often she had missed this affection, but happy to enjoy it now with Marthe, whose only words in reply to her question were: "You know, we Swiss have an exaggerated idea about danger and risk. We insure ourselves against everything. But don't think of such things now. You must relax, and we will talk some more tomorrow."

As if to reinforce her words she took Ellen in her arms and held her tightly as she continued stroking her hair. To feel the warmth of Marthe's embrace and the gentle comforting strength of her body was like sinking back deep into a feather-down pillow, eyes closed, and drifting into a dream world.

Under any other circumstances Ellen might have been shocked by her own behaviour. But when Marthe slipped out of her nightdress a few moments later and slid in between the sheets with Ellen, she did not bat an eyelid. It seemed the most obvious and natural thing to do. The slight intake of breath as they touched was not of outrage or surprise, but excitement at the softness of her skin and the sweet curvature of her body. Ellen had never held a woman in this way. It lent an entirely new dimension to the sense of touch.

With a new kind of ecstasy dispelling any sense of inhibition, she gladly let Marthe's hands explore beneath her own nightdress, which triggered an indescribably pleasant thrill at every stroke. Not a word was spoken as together they lifted the last remaining barrier between them, pulled her nightdress with a final flourish from her body and sank back into each other's arms. It was a curious, electrifying feeling that had her completely at Marthe's mercy.

The strange familiarity of her body intrigued Ellen. As her fingertips explored its sweetly feminine peculiarities with an eagerness every bit as charged as her own, it occurred to Ellen how similar to her Marthe was in shape and feel. 'Now I know what it's like for Frank to hold me in his arms,' she thought. It brought a smile to her face. 'I almost envy him,' she told herself.

"I never thought of myself as having any lesbian leanings."

Marthe laughed.

"Just because you enjoy the embrace of a woman does not mean you are a lesbian."

"Doesn't it?'

"Any more than Frank posing naked for a male sculptor means that he is homosexual. You must keep an open mind. Life is full of doors to be opened and boundaries to be crossed, not a place for closed compartments."

"I always wanted to have babies. I wouldn't if I was a lesbian, would I?" Ellen asked in an attempt to reassure herself.

"A lesbian is also a woman. But, as I say, you don't have to be a lesbian to enjoy the comfort of another woman."

"One thing puzzles me, Marthe. You have a very prominent painting in your lounge of two women in an erotic embrace. I'm surprised you don't like it."

"What makes you think I don't like it?" Marthe asked. "I like it very much. But I don't like the way Urs likes it. He looks at it as a psychiatrist. Not as a man."

"I'm so confused," Ellen said. She wanted to cry, and felt Marthe tighten her embrace as if sensing her despair. She was grateful for the affection and nestled her head under the gentle sweep of Marthe's chin – no stubble, no hint of aftershave, but smooth and soft, the smells of a woman. Such surprising, unaccustomed comfort in her arms.

Marthe ran her fingers over Ellen's lips and rested her thumb in the deep furrow that ran from her upper lip to the lower reaches of her nose. It reminded Ellen of the way Frank liked to stroke her upper lip.

"You have a beautifully deep philtrum," Marthe said. "That's a good sign. We call it a love charm in German. The deeper the better."

"A bit like Cupid's bow," Ellen said with an embarrassed smile. She was keen to change the subject. "Have you never wanted to have babies?" she asked.

It was an innocent question. But Marthe gave no immediate reply. And when Ellen looked up, she was gazing into space, a vague smile on her lips, but sadness hidden in her eyes. She felt for a moment that she had lost her, that her words had stirred an unwanted memory. She was desperate to say something, to bring her back, but was afraid of what further damage she might do.

They remained in this uncomfortable silence beside each other, touching, until Marthe judged the time was right for a reply. And when eventually she did speak, she gave the impression at first of having returned from some internal struggle which she needed to put behind her.

"Do you remember that man we saw this morning who tidied the grave in the woods?" she asked, taking Ellen briefly by surprise with this digression. "That's the local gravedigger. He is looking after that grave all his life, and his father before, and *his* father before him. According to legend, a nun from the convent was walking through the forest and suddenly stopped when she reached that place. She could not go any further, and was overcome by such a fit that she fell on the ground. When they tried to help her, she refused to move. She said that she could feel the spirit of a body buried there which was not consecrated. And she would not move until the body had been dug up and given a proper burial. When at last they dug the ground, they really did find a body – or better, a skeleton. It was very old, and a strange leather bag was lying beside the body, which contained only a few stones. Many stories have been invented to explain the meaning of these stones, but nobody knows for certain what happened. So they made a new grave for the skeleton and consecrated the burial. Since then, the gravedigger from the next village always looked after the grave and brought new flowers for it. So it became a tradition, which was passed through the family – the gravedigger's son became the new gravedigger and took on this duty, like his son after him."

Marthe paused. She ran the painted nail of her index finger pensively along the midline from Ellen's belly to her sternum. And left her hand to lie there on Ellen's chest.

"Such continuity." She paused again. Ellen smouldered under the gentle friction of her caresses. But there was a sense of disquiet in Marthe's words, as if she was struggling to come to terms with a troubled past. "This is the reason why we have children. So that we can pass on our traditions. Perhaps I never had any which I wanted to pass on. But what about Frank? I have this picture of a man with a very strong sense of tradition."

"I don't think so. Not really." Ellen said. "We only seriously discussed having a family once, just a few weeks before he disappeared. Well, it wasn't even a discussion, really."

"And?"

Ellen paused for thought, before finding the words to reply.

"He's just not ready yet."

"Do you think this had something to do with Frank leaving?" asked Marthe.

"He hasn't left. He's gone missing," Ellen insisted. She was ruffled, yet irritated at the same time by her own oversensitivity. "Oh please Marthe, don't spoil everything. I was so enjoying this." She let her hand skate over Marthe's silky body to emphasise her pleasure – so free and so understanding, not tied by the demands of the male body, or at least of Frank's.

"Have you ever slept with a woman before?" Ellen asked.

Preferring to respond to Ellen's caresses rather than to her words, Marthe resumed her own exploration, running the fingers of her hand back down over Ellen's belly, a finger poised teasingly on the edge of her desire.

"The first time was in the boarding school, when I was fifteen. This is the second time."

"Does your husband know?"

"Why should he? It was a long time ago. Anyway, he has a very open mind. He may seem conservative in many ways. But he was the one who encouraged me to help campaign for the women's vote in the referendum."

This prosaic turn in the conversation threatened to pull the rug from under Ellen's longing. To counter the looming change of mood, she lifted her right leg and draped it over Marthe's left thigh, inviting Marthe's hand to explore more deeply. Fingers deliciously poised. And as they lingered, seeming to hesitate, they transported Ellen back to memories of Frank.

"If a white sweating bull of a poet told us our cunts are ugly," she whispered, "why didn't we admit we have thought so too?"

"What?"

The sound of shock in that one brief word and the puzzlement in Marthe's eyes brought Ellen back from her trancelike dream of Frank. With sheepish awkwardness, she tried to explain. And sensed Marthe's hand inching away.

"I'm sorry," Ellen said and placed a hand on the retreating fingers. "I got carried away by memories of Frank. He's a bit of a poetry freak and loves quoting those words at me when we're in bed. They're by a poet called Denise Levertov. He does it just to tease me. But there's a certain truth to the words, isn't there?"

"You surprise me," Marthe said. "For all the rights you've enjoyed as a woman for so much longer than me, I would expect a greater sense of confidence."

She peered through the strawberry-blonde curls that flowed over Ellen's eyes, brushed them aside and smiled.

"Why are you laughing?" Ellen asked.

"I'm sorry. I wasn't laughing," Marthe explained. "I was just reminded of something."

Ellen's mood had suddenly taken on an edge of insecurity as she looked into Marthe's eyes.

"During the time around the vote," Marthe continued, "women's groups began to organise some strange events. I remember one led by a very serious woman who was keen that we should understand our bodies. 'Embrace' was the word she used I believe." Marthe's smile instantly broke into a chuckle. "At one session, she handed a mirror to each of us and instructed us all to examine our vulva and describe it in detail to each other. And how we felt about it."

Marthe paused again. The smile still lingered over the memory. Then out of the blue she asked: "Why do you think Frank is not ready?"

By now, any arousal had long since been deflated.

"I don't know. But it has nothing to do with his disappearance. You say it as if I might be to blame for everything – just because I want to have babies."

"Oh Ellen. I was not meaning it in this way." Marthe moved closer again and tightened her embrace. But the comfort Ellen had felt earlier was no longer there. What had seemed like boundless rapture just a moment before had now evaporated. Its place taken by an ill-defined disquiet. And Marthe was about to provide some definition.

"But I do wonder whether he was upset by something that happened," she added "Or something that was said."

By now, Ellen's carefree sensuality was completely banished. She sensed that Marthe was attempting to frame a further probing question for her.

"Do you think his mother's death might have something to do with his disappearance?" she asked. Ellen was at least grateful that Marthe was no longer persisting with the idea that Frank had left her. But the idea that he might have been upset by his mother's death in such dramatic fashion seemed far-fetched at best.

"I should not really tell you this, Ellen," Marthe continued. "In fact, I should not even know it myself. Urs has made a great mistake when he told it to me. But he was worried, and I think he needed advice."

Ellen remained in Marthe's loose embrace. But said nothing.

"I think you should know that when Frank was first found and admitted to the clinic, he has said something very disturbing. He said that he killed his mother."

Ellen instantly freed herself from Marthe's arms and stared at her.

"That's ridiculous," she protested. "He was speaking metaphorically."

Marthe's words put her in mind of Beth. But her sister was simply being spiteful when she asked the same question. Ellen knew that Marthe was genuinely concerned. Yet the suggestion implicit in those words did nothing to allay her disquiet.

Suddenly a blue light flashed through the window onto the ceiling above them.

"What's that?" Ellen asked.

"It's only an ambulance," Marthe reassured her. She got out of bed and walked over to the window. Ellen watched the silhouette of her breasts as she drew the curtains to and sensed a rekindling of her pleasure at the sight of Marthe's body. But her enjoyment was interrupted by a sharp squeal of brakes outside.

"What's going on, Marthe?"

"The ambulance had to stop suddenly for someone crossing the road. He looks as if he's had too much to drink." And she got back into bed.

Ellen fell asleep in her arms, thinking about Frank, knowing that – like the drunk crossing the road – he was also out there somewhere.

Chapter 18

The firearm weighed reassuringly heavy in Frank's coat pocket. Cradling the cold iron of the chamber in his hand as if it held the key to his existence, he took the precaution of walking a circuitous route into town rather than pick up the train further down the line. So it was well past midnight by the time he reached the city centre. The streets were already fast asleep. The Kolping house held no magnetism for his tired aching feet, especially since Lutz now knew he had a room there. And he did not trust Lutz as far as he could throw him. But he was in desperate need of somewhere to sleep.

So, keen to absorb what he could of Patricia's life, Frank made his way to her flat. The iron in his pocket invested him with the confidence to cope with any trouble, should Lutz's advice prove to be well-founded.

The street had impressed itself firmly on his memory when he first saw Patricia open the door that led to the privacy of her flat – a privacy which he had envied so deeply for its intimacy with her and which he had wanted so much to be a part of. Now it looked empty and abandoned in the early hours of this cold morning. He had been captivated by the street because it was Patricia's, but now that he could sense she was not here, its emptiness saddened him.

Ever since she had made a copy of her door key for him and sent it so invitingly with a note wishing him 'Bon voyage', he had been burning with impatience to use it. Uncertain what might be waiting for him inside, his pulse quickened as he inserted it into the lock. The emptiness he felt when the door opened hit him with a quiet brutality. It came as no surprise, since he was not expecting her back for at least two weeks. Yet it draped a leaden chill over his mood.

The room had been left immaculately tidy, as only a woman with Patricia's style could leave it. On the table stood the telling vase of roses, now multiplied to three. Three flowers of evil, wilted in the intervening weeks and its petals fallen. Frank refused to contemplate the favours they might have involved. Drew a protective shield down against any thoughts in that direction. It was a stratagem made so much easier by the table companion of that vase.

There, on the gramophone beside the vase, lay *These Foolish Things*. Instantly a warm flutter coursed through every muscle of his heart. He smiled at the thought of her laying the record on the turntable for him before she left. Had it not been for this and the books on a corner shelf, the room would have given the air of permanence about her departure. All but two of the books were heavy tomes on the Renaissance, Romanticism, Symbolism and other periods of art that meant little to him. These two books piqued his curiosity for the clues they gave to the private side of Patricia. One was by Lou Salomé, *Ruth*, which instantly put him in mind of his conversation with Achim – and gnawed at his conscience for cravenly abandoning the mission he had taken on. The other book in this otherwise dry and dusty collection, which appeared to be annotated in the margins, was a dog-eared paperback of *Les fleurs du mal* by Baudelaire.

It was plain that this had been often and passionately read. This paperback gave him an uncomfortable feeling because, not only did its association with the flowers in the vase leap out at him, but there was also something about the dog-eared copy of the book that did not fit with what he knew of Patricia. And this drove home to him just how little he did know about her, and how much more privileged others were in this respect. When he opened the book, he saw at once a deeper reason for him to feel so unsettled. Like the other works on the shelf, it was heavily annotated. But by a different hand. Plainly not hers. The scrawl was that of a bold male hand. And it boasted an intimacy with her which Frank was still far from achieving. The page he was looking at appeared to be a particularly important one to judge by the natural ease with which the book opened there. Certain lines of verse showed pencil marks. He suspected they had been made by Patricia, since they bore such a strong similarity to the style of markings in her books on art. Frank wondered why they might be so important to her.

Je pense à mon grand cygne, avec ses gestes fous,
Comme les exilés, ridicule et sublime,
Et rongé d'un, désir sans trêve! et puis à vous[3]

His French was adequate to grasp the meaning of the words, but what was their significance? What was it in her life that warranted giving them such importance? Was it Léandre? Or could it be him the words referred to, Frank wondered in his vanity. It was already one o'clock in the morning. He had committed robbery with violence, and dragged his aching body endless miles through strange territory. He was too exhausted to cope with these questions, however much they intrigued him and teased his vanity. So he took Baudelaire onto the bed with him, where this troubling verse carried him off to sleep with his coat and shoes still keeping him warm.

When he woke, the light was already shining confidently through the garret window. The poet lay on the floor staring up at him like a sad old bitch waiting for its morning walk. Still fully clothed and with stubble on his chin, Frank was aware of the staleness and dirt of his body. He recalled the last time he had woken here and watched the light break through the window. The cool white cubit of her arm thrown carelessly across his chest in her sleep, like an ivory bracelet half open at the clasp. It had reminded him of a bracelet which his father had brought home

3 I think of my great swan, with his crazy gestures,
like all the exiles, foolish yet sublime,
consumed by unremitting desire! and then of you

from India for his mother and which had always lain half open on the dresser, never worn, almost as a symbol of their relationship. It irritated Frank that his memory of Patricia triggered this association. On two counts now he felt that he was sullying the purity of what little intimacy there was between them.

Tucking the secrets of Baudelaire safely away in the coat pocket that was not already occupied by the gun, he got up to wash. The washbasin held no soap. And no towel hung from the rail. So, after splashing his face with some cold water to freshen up, he looked into the cooking niche for evidence of food or drink while his face dried in the chill of the unheated room. He had hoped at least for a trace of stale coffee beans, but there was nothing.

From above, through the garret window, the street looked quiet and harmless; an elderly woman sweeping out her doorway on the opposite side of the narrow, cobbled road; a group of children, satchels strapped to their backs, on their way to school. Only the hint of rain in the clouds that hung over the rooftops gave any suggestion of menace in the air. Frank decided to call Lutz's bluff again and risk the streets by daylight.

It was a short walk past the Spalentor, across the park and down the steps that tapered like a long funnel into the market place. No sinister figures lurked in the doorways. No strange faces crossed his path, except for the occasional woman dutifully heaving the day's shopping home from the market. The square itself was peacefully attending to the routine of the city's housewives under the watchful presence of the mediaeval town hall that dominated the area with the same heavy sandstone of the cathedral. Apart from the stallholders or the chestnut seller on the corner, few men were to be seen at that time. Those who were took no part in the business of the day, but shuffled through their morning in retirement, a stick in one hand and cigar stump in the mouth. He found it hard to imagine the violence that was taking place on the fringes of this ordinary humdrum world, although he had witnessed it himself. Even had a part in it. Would the women buying their cauliflowers and carrots believe him if he interrupted their transactions to tell them of the slaughter he had seen and the putrefying cadavers that lay at that very moment just a short tram-ride from where they stood? More likely they would think him completely mad, he told himself.

The everyday normality of the scene in the market place had the curious effect of heightening his unease and sharpening his sense of menace. So, having purchased the essentials he needed to get him through the next few days, he made his way cautiously back over the river to tie up the loose ends that remained hanging in his room at the Kolping house. With the added security of the gun in his pocket, he was ready for most eventualities, but the welcome waiting for him was one for which he was not prepared.

Having taken the precaution of using the back street to the building, he was stopped in his tracks by a disagreeably familiar figure: the ugly face of the cloth-capped man, leaning on the railings, his concentration seemingly focused on the newspaper that he held in front of him. Frank cautiously retraced his steps and walked around the building to the front of the house. It appeared to be clear.

The fist that drove itself viciously into his solar plexus as he turned into the doorway told him otherwise.

"We've been looking for you, runt."

He knew the American accent instantly. It went with the fist. But above all it was the way the man pinned him to the wall before he could see straight or even take air that told him it was Silverstone. He had been here before.

"You got some explaining to do, friend. So why don't we take a walk?"

Putting Frank's left arm in the vice of a grip that Frank had got to know when Silverstone dragged him off to Achim's all those lifetimes ago, the American marched him back out of the building and down to the promenade beside the river. The cloth cap was still lurking. And when he saw the two walking down to the river in what must have looked a rather comical tandem, he discarded the newspaper and let a smile open up like a deep scar across his face as he approached them. It was the first time Frank had seen any light of humanity in the man's expression, but it seemed fitting that it should shine so darkly. The man said nothing, and his silence disturbed Frank. It was a dumb kind of muteness that suggested he had no power of speech. As if to compensate for the affliction, he hissed slightly through his bearded smile when Silverstone spoke.

"I found him. Says he was just stepping out for some fresh air and why don't we join him. I call that real neighbourly. What do you think, Bert?"

The cloth cap now had a name, and the cicatricial grin looked ready to split his face wide open in response. But still he remained mute and just followed Silverstone, who guided Frank with the brachial force of his grip along the river promenade. In the half-light of the archway beneath the bridge was the inconspicuous door to a public convenience. Frank had never noticed it before. And he recalled with a sense of irony all the times he had searched in vain for a place to relieve himself in this vicinity, as Silverstone kicked open the door and bundled him inside. Bert, the cloth cap, stood back in the doorway. Frank caught him in the corner of his eye grinning with perverse pleasure at the sight of Silverstone pushing him back against the porcelain so that he was forced to stand as best he could in the slippery glazed gutter of the urinal.

"I thought we had a deal, Eigenmann. So what went wrong?"

Silverstone thrust his face into Frank's. It was the first time he had noticed a thin line on the American's upper lip masquerading as a moustache.

"I agreed to do a favour for my old friend, Achim," Frank said, tightening his grip on the gun in his pocket. "I don't recall making any deals with you."

"Achim. Yes, of course. Your friend Achim." There was a menacing mockery in his tone now. "That brings me to the other little matter we need to talk about."

As if taking out a pen to make a note in his diary, he drew a knife from his inside pocket and flicked it open in Frank's face. The cloth cap looked on, still beaming his inane smile from the doorway – until it was wiped from his primitive face by the gun that Frank pushed into Silverstone's belly.

"Just drop the knife and back off."

His speech contorted to the most threatening growl he could muster as his lips were palsied by agitation. But the delivery was immaterial. It was the message that counted. This was a refreshing new experience for Frank, and he enjoyed every inch of the authority this simple instrument suddenly invested in him. A curious expression found a place in Silverstone's eyes. His top lip curled to show the crude untidiness of his large teeth as he stepped back towards the cubicle door. It was the first time Frank had seen him looking so unsure of himself. He was getting a taste for this new power.

"Bert." Frank spoke with growing self-assurance. He sensed his agitation lifting. "Keep your hat on, go join your friend, and get undressed."

Meek as a lamb, the cloth cap complied, only the slightest trace of a snarl where his smile had been.

"And you, Silverstone. Clothes off. Lay your coats on the floor and throw everything on top. Everything," Frank repeated, moving back to the door and wedging his foot against it to discourage any visitors following the call of nature. The sight of them finally removing their underpants made him almost feel sorry for them in the shrivelled despair of their manhood, their bodies pale, flabby and slightly deformed. The pigeon chest of Silverstone especially surprised him: the American had always looked so burly in his coat.

"What exactly do you do at your Nazi-friendly bank?" Frank asked. He was savouring the thought of what his colleagues at work would make of him now. "Okay. Now tie them up with the arms of the coat to make a bundle, then step back into the cubicle and lock the door."

As soon as the lock clicked into place, Frank moved over to the two bundles of clothes and was just picking them up when the door to the street swung open. A tall man in a trench coat and hat filled the doorway, concern written in his eyes. He guided in a little boy with the desperate, inconsolable face of someone who was having the greatest difficulty adopting anything remotely like a normal walk. Frank smiled sympathetically at what he assumed to be the father of this poor little wretch and heaved the two bundles out through the door with as much discretion as he could muster.

To see those two bundles floating downstream from the bridge brought him a malicious kind of pleasure he had not known since the time he watched Heinz Wassermann being carried off to hospital, his face lacerated and bleeding from Volker's revenge.

But the enjoyment of the moment could not smooth away the questions that still gnawed at his newfound confidence. The cloth cap and Silverstone made an unlikely alliance and cast a further layer of mystery over the role of the American. Frank kicked himself for being so ready to cut and run without grilling them when he had the chance. All at once, he pictured Silverstone as an associate of Breitner's, maybe even the chief architect behind the betrayal of Achim and the carnage of his family. These thoughts chipped away at his conscience all the way back to Patricia's flat.

The signs of intrusion initially escaped him when he opened the door. It was not until he had washed, shaved and rinsed away the last vestiges of the urinal that he noticed it. The shelf where the weighty tomes on the history of art had stood was now empty. And no amount of searching brought them to light. They had evidently been removed. A warm thrill coursed through his body at the thought that she might have already returned – but he had overlooked the piece of paper which lay under the table, presumably swept onto the floor as he blustered into the room still heady with the acrid reek of ammonia on his coat.

"You are most unwise to ignore my advice. But perhaps you will listen to Mademoiselle Roche. She wishes to see you."

These words leapt off the page at Frank. Set his heart racing with a frenzy that had him overlook the disquieting fact that Lutz appeared to know his every move. Although unsigned, it was plainly his hand behind the note, which continued with fussily detailed instructions to explain where Frank should be at ten o'clock the following morning. Since Lutz was for once the bearer of good tidings, Frank told himself the murkier side of his involvement could be happily ignored. And for the rest of the day, he warmed himself on the glow of knowing she was back and wanted to see him.

It was already five to ten when he stepped off the tram at the end of the line in a village on the outskirts of town. But rather than draw attention to himself by racing too fast, he walked slowly in the direction instructed. He was halfway up the hill leading out of the village, when the black, low-slung chassis of a black Citroen pulled up beside him. The sight of Lutz behind the wheel took him by surprise. He had not imagined Lutz as a driver. To see him now in charge of a fashionable new 7S Traction Avant gave a new dimension to the man. Lutz leaned over and opened the door.

"Good morning, Mr Eigenmann," he said, instantly dispelling any sense of this new quality with his familiar, unctuous smarm. "Please get in."

Frank hesitated, but Lutz did not let his greasy smile weaken for a moment. He was supremely confident. He knew that Patricia was too much of an inducement to resist. Was this what Breitner was counting on? Frank kept his fingers crossed and clambered in.

"I hope you remembered to bring your passport," Lutz said, as he settled uneasily into the leather upholstery. Frank nodded.

"Please," Lutz said, opening an outstretched hand towards his passenger.

Frank pulled out his passport and placed it in the outstretched hand, nervously recalling stories about the recent abduction of the journalist Jacob as he did so. Am I now to be the protagonist in a rerun of that scene and become a diplomatic incident? Frank asked himself. But no, no one would give a damn – and why should they? He was a German citizen of good Aryan stock. Apart from his brief spell as a failed courier, he offered no history to arouse the interest of those who make it their life's work sniffing out causes for persecution. He was a negligible quantity.

Breitner knew it. Yet it was precisely this that made Frank feel especially uneasy. Breitner knew he was not the stuff that diplomatic incidents are made of – an insignificance he would delight in exploiting. He would take the utmost pleasure in repatriating Frank to stand trial for treason as a courier of anti-government propaganda. Not only would it help to ingratiate him with the people of influence in Berlin (it did not matter to them how small the fish were as long as they filled their nets). It would also rid him of a rival for Patricia's attention.

He looked across at Lutz. His driver was still smiling. Were his thoughts moving in the same direction? Frank wondered. If there was even the slightest possibility of seeing Patricia, it was a risk he felt compelled to take. But this was presumably what they were counting on. These dark thoughts focused his attention on the cold chamber of destruction in his pocket. It had already served him well, and he had not even had to use it. He tightened his grip on the gun for reassurance while the car sped on, curving through a tunnel of trees, to the border with France. The forest on either side was suffused with a curious grey light that made the trees loom like a vast neglected paling erected haphazardly across a wasteland for some long-forgotten purpose. On the other side of the woods at the crossing stood a small customs house. They stopped.

When Lutz wound down the window and let in the cold Bise that gusted through the trees behind them, Frank caught the sound of a shutter flapping on the side of the house. The French customs officer appeared in the doorway. He was alone, and wore the stern expression of a man looking for distraction, anything to chase away the boredom. He walked over to the car and peered suspiciously at its occupants. Lutz gave him the passports, but the officer cast only a cursory glance inside. He was more interested in the car. What was in the boot, he wanted to know. Lutz duly climbed out and opened up both the boot and the bonnet to satisfy the man's undernourished curiosity. The butt of Frank's gun became moist with the sweat from his palm. He prayed that the officer would not see the nervousness in his eyes when he returned to the car. But it was Lutz, not the customs man, who came back to the car door and leaned through the window.

"Would you happen to have ten francs with you, Mr Eigenmann? It seems we have to pay for the privilege of driving into this delightful country." Frank sensed himself scowling at the thought of paying good money for his own abduction. "On the other hand," Lutz reflected, without waiting for him to reach into his wallet, "we don't have far to go. It's only a few hundred metres from here. And it would seem a shame paying good money to avoid a little healthy exercise, so I suggest we leave the car and walk from here."

The way Lutz used the self-same expression that had gone through his own mind only a few seconds earlier irritated Frank intensely. It was as if he were arrogating some kind of intimacy with him. But he pocketed the insult and climbed out of the car while Lutz backed up and parked it on the side of the road under the trees. The customs man had lost interest by now and ambled around to the side of his office to fix the flapping shutter before returning to his isolation.

Walking side by side with Lutz along that lane into France was not a comfortable exercise. Once again it seemed to him that the world at large was being treated to a declaration of intimacy between them by the very fact of their togetherness, and he kept defiantly quiet in an effort to correct the image.

For all Frank's distrust of Lutz, however, the man proved to have been reliable at least when he said it was not far. After a thankfully short walk from the border, they soon found themselves descending a dip into a sleepy hamlet with no obvious character to it beyond the fact that it sat on a border. It gave the impression of not really knowing where it belonged. While it was nominally in France, the few houses Frank could see, and the church in the distance, yielded no clue to their affiliations; they could just as well have been in Switzerland, or then again in Germany. This was a part of what Achim had called the Sundgau, stamping ground of his uncle Max and scene of misspent summers. This thought had Frank wondering where Achim was at that moment, what had become of him. If he had fallen victim to Breitner's evil, then probably Lutz knew what had happened. But Frank hesitated to grill him for fear of the answers he might get.

"Please, Mr Eigenmann," Lutz said, interrupting the uneasy drift of Frank's thoughts, as he opened a door to one of the few buildings in the hamlet and ushered him inside. It was an anonymous-looking *auberge*, and the dark bistre of the restaurant inside was neither inviting nor warm. The red-and-white gingham tablecloths tried to conceal the grimness of the stuffy, burnt sienna atmosphere, but their efforts were thwarted by the hostile emptiness of the place.

"Please, Mr Eigenmann. Take a seat. Is there anything I can get you?" Lutz asked.

Frank said he would gladly take a cup of coffee, at which Lutz disappeared into a back room behind the bar. Meanwhile Frank sat himself at a discreet table in a darker part of the restaurant, trying to estimate the significance of his driver's nauseatingly attentive behaviour.

"Hello squirrel."

The voice caught Frank unawares. Such sweet cadence that had played on the edge of his impatient memory for so long. And now he trembled to hear it – and to hear the affection in that ludicrous pet name she had chosen for him. He was angry at his foolishness, almost afraid of his own desire. And at the pitch of his agitation, he hesitated to turn. But he had no need to: as she spoke, she moved around from behind him and sat down on the opposite side of the table.

"Patricia," was all he managed in response. The melancholy sparkle in her eyes and the sensual parting of the lips pursed in a deeply seductive smile. Yet the smile was deceptive. It blew like the Föhn, melting down the Alpine snow, but too fickle to break the hold of winter. He sensed the same cool distance between them that he had felt when they first met. But it seemed different now, mingled indefinably with a certain reluctance. She seemed sadder and colder than ever before. Yet simmered with the passion of a sleeping volcano.

Her hands were like marble to the touch. He recalled the last time he had enjoyed the pleasure of their searching path across his body. So warm and so inquisitive. But that was just another brief chapter in the history books. Something had happened in the meantime to deepen her sorrow, and it disturbed him.

"When did you get back?" he asked.

It seemed a simple question, but she plainly had difficulty finding the right words in answer. While she was still searching, an elderly man with the look of arthritis in his walk and one too many glasses of *marc* in his cheeks shuffled up to their table with two cups of coffee, then withdrew again without uttering a sound. Frank gave up on his first question and tried another approach.

"Where's Lutz disappeared to?"

This time the ice broke.

"He's waiting back at the car," she said, after testing the coffee with her lips. Her words tugged on his heart like a lead weight. Set an undefined time limit, hovered like the writer's hand impatient to pencil in the full stop on their meeting.

"Patricia." He touched her hand as she put down her cup. The coffee already seemed to have added a hint of warmth to her skin. "Patricia, I have so many questions I want to ask. Too many. About Lutz. About you. About what on earth we're doing here. About so many things I don't understand."

Her eyes sparkled faintly with a smile of amusement. "In that order?"

"You think I might be more interested in Lutz than in you?"

For an instant her self-control evaporated, and she broke into a laugh so exquisitely fragile he wanted to take her in his arms, to preserve every atom of her curious beauty. But now was not the time. The table lay between them and they needed to talk. He suggested they start from the moment they last said goodbye – he wanted to know what had been happening to her in the intervening weeks to make her so indescribably sad. But she remained characteristically obtuse.

"I'd prefer to start from the moment we just said hello."

These few words of contradiction breathed a bewitching hint of affection. But this was plainly not her purpose. From her guarded manner, it was clear that, while there were certain things she wanted him to know, she was keen at the same time to withhold secrets that were not for his ears. And he had the impression she found it easier to manage the disclosure process by working back carefully step by step from the moment she had Lutz bring him here across the border.

"You know, Patricia, while we were on the way here in his car, I was beginning to wonder whether Lutz and Breitner were doing a Berthold Jacob with me."

"You can trust Lutz," she said, dismissing his remark with an impatience he found hard to accept. He recalled how she had used that same phrase when she introduced him to her mysterious friend Léandre. Did this testimonial cast him in the same role as Lutz? Frank wondered.

"You had rather less flattering things to say of him the last time I saw you," he replied.

"Times change."

Lutz had always been a reluctant accomplice to Breitner's business affairs, she explained, but he was basically a decent man. And over the last few weeks, he had been an indirect party to things that left him no choice but to cross over and saddle a worthier horse – even at the risk of his own skin.

"What sort of things?"

"You know yourself the very least that Breitner is capable of," she said, and left him briefly to his unquiet memories. "That's partly why you have Lutz working on your behalf."

"What do you mean 'partly'?"

She ignored his question.

"Tell me about your trip to Cologne. What happened?" she asked instead, feigning an interest which he felt was not there. But, with some reluctance, he gave her an outline of his abortive journey north: the betrayal of friendship and trust by Achim, his abandonment of the false mission that was left in his hands, the boat ride back up the Rhine and – without going into every gruesome detail – the disgusting carnage he had found on his return.

"There was no sign of Achim. Do you suppose Lutz knows what happened to him?" he asked. "I had the impression Silverstone thinks I have something to do with this and wants me dead as a result."

She left him again to pause for reflection, letting him know that she was there only by the touch of her hand on his.

"But it occurs to me," he continued. "Could he have had something to do with it? You know Breitner a lot better than I do. Is it possible that Silverstone is a traitor to his cause and is really working for Breitner?"

A peculiar look of hurt and reproach came into her eyes, which he was unable to explain.

"It's very easy, when you're sitting on the fence, to see betrayal lurking on every corner. It makes your own position so much more comfortable, doesn't it? But you should take care, Frank. The worst betrayals are those we commit without even realising, without even moving an inch no matter where we sit. Just because we're too dumb. Or too naive. And they go unnoticed until it's too late."

"Well, I feel my position is anything but comfortable just now," he assured her.

It was not only her thinly disguised criticism that unsettled him – as it was certainly intended to – but the realisation that he was completely out of his depth. And she did nothing to ease his disquiet when she brought her philosophy of betrayal back to the trust he should put in Lutz. That was an investment of faith that called for emotional gymnastics in which he had had little training.

"It's mainly thanks to him that I found somewhere else to live so quickly," she insisted. He has some very useful connections."

Her last words reminded him of the way Achim had described Silverstone, a memory that had him ponder further on Breitner's interest in Achim.

"You've spent a lot of time with Breitner. Did he ever mention anyone called Lola?" he asked.

Patricia's melancholy lifted for a moment. She smiled with a genuine sparkle of amusement at the question.

"You've been to Breitner's villa," she said. "So the erotic paintings and drawings on the walls can hardly have escaped you."

It was a memory Frank would have preferred not to be reminded of.

"He's vulgar of course," Patricia continued, "but he likes to think of himself as an art lover. Édouard-Henri Avril is a favourite of his. Not the finest art that France has ever produced. But it feeds his fantasies. Like Lola Bach. She was an erotic dancer in Berlin who Breitner became obsessed with. So, when he saw a painting of her, he was determined to get his hands on it, as were many other people. Your friend was bringing it to Switzerland for safekeeping."

"And that's where Silverstone comes in?" he asked, recalling now the rucksack which Achim had with him when they met and which he took with him when he met with Silverstone.

"I have no idea what Silverstone does," she shrugged.

"Apparently he works at that hornet's nest they call the Bank for International Settlements."

Again she smiled with wry amusement. But said nothing. Growing impatient with the dead ends into which his questions kept sailing, he changed tack.

"Why find somewhere else to live?" he asked.

"Breitner," she replied. "You're not the only one he's looking for."

"Well, if it's such a safe house that Lutz has found you, why didn't we meet there?"

"It's not safe. There's no such thing. Especially for you," she added ominously. As if to accentuate the concern expressed in these last three words, she squeezed his hand. "That's why I want you to stay across the border here in France for the time being, while we consider what to do."

"What do you mean 'what to do'?"

She took a last sip from her coffee as only she could – a sparkle in her melancholy eyes and a touch of irony on her lips.

"For one so lacking in curiosity, little squirrel, you ask far too many questions. I shall get Lutz to bring your things out to you from the Kolping house."

"No," he interjected. "They're watching the house. I just have a few things in your old flat. Razor and so on. That's all I need. Or perhaps I should just grow a beard."

She laughed.

"Oh no. I couldn't stand that. Lutz will bring a razor out to you this afternoon."

Her mock horror at the prospect of him with hair on his chin teased his male vanity. That she was sufficiently interested in him to express such preference pleased him, and robbed him of the strength to contradict her. She was in control, and he was happy to submit.

But the finality with which she put down her coffee cup and got up from the table threw him into a premature despair made all the more acute by her words:

"I shall come out and see you every so often, when I can. But I won't be able to come for a few days."

"Please don't go yet, Patricia," he begged her. "We've hardly spoken. There's so much I want to say. And so much I want to hear."

But he knew she had long since reached the limit of what she was ready to tell him. And she was insistent.

"I'm sorry squirrel. I have things to do."

"What sort of things?"

"Work. Somehow in all this mess I still have to study. And on Thursday there's a concert at the Stadtcasino – a friend has given me a couple of tickets, and I have to go. I'll try to get out here on Friday."

"I'd like to meet some of your friends someday."

"You will," was all she said. But she could not disguise a certain amusement in the smile that came with those two words. It chipped away at his self-esteem. 'That smile will be the death of me,' he told himself – like a dark inviting destiny shining out across the water from its unlit world.

"What's the concert?"

"Bartok. It's a world premiere. I can't afford to miss it."

Nor did she miss his desperation. She sensed it in the drift of his questions.

"But it's much too dangerous for you, Frank. Breitner's looking for you, and if he sees you with me…"

"I believe I'm right in saying the Stadtcasino was the venue for a Zionist Congress," he interrupted her. "It's hard to imagine Breitner setting foot inside the place unless it's been fumigated first. And since you have an extra ticket, it would seem a shame to waste it. Unless you have someone else in mind," he added fearfully.

"No."

"Good. Then I'll come."

"No, Frank."

Patricia was smiling, but she remained insistent. It was only the delicate kiss she left on his lips before taking her leave that finally silenced him. And set the sweetest seal on his decision to stay put. For the time being.

The man with arthritis in his hips who had served them coffee proved to be the owner of the *auberge*. When Patricia had gone, he led his guest limping up a dingy staircase to a room that appeared to have already been prepared for him. Patricia plainly had everything well thought out and under control.

"The restaurant opens for lunch at twelve," the landlord mumbled grudgingly as he turned to go, clearly satisfied that his duty was done with these words. And Frank was left to ponder his brief reunion with Patricia from the window of a cell that looked forlornly onto the rolling hills of this strange frontier to nowhere. He wondered what on earth might possess anyone to open a hotel and restaurant here. Certainly his landlord was not enjoying the experience. And neither the functional ambience of Frank's bolthole nor the curious circumstances of his meeting with Patricia gave much meat for reflection. Their reunion had not been at all as he had so often imagined in rehearsal. It left him with too many questions. But without the prospect of any answers at least until Friday, he made an effort to put all the problems to the back of his mind. On balance, he had to consider himself fortunate that he had seen her earlier than originally anticipated.

It occurred to him that he had forgotten in his excitement to return her book of Baudelaire. So he took this out of his coat pocket and let it open spontaneously at the well-used page of underlined and annotated verse. Although this had no solutions to offer, and even prompted further unsettling questions of its own, it gave him the sense of being closer to her, of having a part of her still with him. A small comfort. But it kept him going. It went with him also when he ventured out into the still, sleepy air of this borderland the following morning. But by Thursday, the verse had acquired a hollowness with its constant repetition, which rendered the words as much in need of renovation and a coat of paint as the empty sadness of the restaurant. And come the afternoon, his patience was finally at an end.

Whatever the danger. However thin the ice he was about tread on. Whatever the risk of running into Breitner, he could not pass up the chance of sharing the concert with Patricia.

Chapter 19

It was a long trek back across the border and down into the village on the outskirts of town to pick up the tram. By the time he arrived in the city centre, daylight was already beginning to fade. There was just enough time to buy a suit and new pair of shoes suitable for a fancy concert and bundle up his old clothes to leave in the left luggage at the station. 'If I hurry,' he told himself, 'I might even manage a light dinner at the Gambrinushalle,' where he had eaten with Patricia on their first date.

When eventually he reached the concert hall, there was no sign of anyone starting to arrive, so he could be certain Patricia was not already inside. He surreptitiously removed the gun from his coat pocket and slipped it into the side of his smart new dinner jacket. But this was too bulky and conspicuous for such refinement, so he tried slipping it under the waistband at the back of his trousers, where his jacket would cover it more discreetly. As a temporary measure, it would have to do. At all events, he felt safer having it about his person. And handed his coat in at the cloakroom.

Within half an hour, the foyer was thronging with concertgoers in their gowns and finery. Everything that there was to dislike about the middle and upper classes was on display that evening – the smug self-satisfaction, the airs and graces of the semieducated snob, the demonstratively loud handshake announcing to the hall at large its owner's presence, but above all its acquaintanceships and by extension its culture. Had it not been for the sheer lack of taste, he might have missed her in the crowd. But her style shone through like the evening star as soon as she entered the foyer. She was not alone, however. A man in the early evening of his years, rather fresh-faced with a windswept, wispy look about his white hair, was deep in conversation with her. The moment she caught sight of Frank, she broke into a nervous, almost angry smile.

"I told you I'd come."

"Yes, you did," she said, keeping her composure. Then turning to her companion, she added: "Professor Imhof, may I introduce you to a friend of mine, Mr Eigenmann. Frank, this is my professor."

Professor Imhof extended a hand that seemed far too large and workman-like for academic pursuit. "I'm very pleased to meet you Mr Eigenmann. Are you also a lover of Bartok?"

"No, I'm a lover of Mademoiselle Roche."

"Er, I see. Yes, quite. I understand." The professor was plainly lost for words and, rather than make the effort of a tiresome search, he discreetly withdrew.

"I do hope you enjoy the concert."

Frank took her hands apologetically in his as the professor disappeared into the throng.

"Do forgive me. I just couldn't resist it."

"Don't worry. He actually has quite a sense of humour. I'm much more concerned that you're here at all."

As the last traces of a nervous smile on her lips flickered away, an ineffably warm radiance still remained in the sparkle of her eyes. Even in her most anxious or melancholic of moments, it rarely deserted her. He would have gladly spent the remainder of that evening in the foyer, for whatever Bartok had to offer him it could not possibly surpass the obtuse beauty of Patricia. But his attention was caught by a movement over her shoulder, and she instantly saw his expression change.

"Damn it," he said. The irritation was driven by an anxiety he found hard to conceal from her watchful eyes. "That's just like Silverstone to spoil a beautiful evening."

"Where?"

"Don't turn round. He's over by the door."

She was examining Frank with one of her analytical gazes. "I shouldn't worry. He'll never recognise you in that get-up."

"Maybe." Frank was less than convinced. "But he certainly will when I leave here in my old coat. He'll recognise the smell a mile off." And he gave her a brief résumé of their last encounter in the public convenience.

"Give me your cloakroom ticket and go and stand over in the crowd by the stairs," she said. Again Patricia took control, and again he submitted unquestioningly to her quick thinking. She appeared so slight and defenceless as she vanished amidst the forest of gowns and evening dress that towered around her. But his concern was superfluous. Within a few minutes she was back at his side, thrusting his cloakroom ticket into his hand. "Here, you've just got a new hat and coat."

"I don't like hats," he protested, quietly excited to find that Patricia was capable of such misdemeanours.

"Tonight, squirrel, you love hats. But we must be sure to leave early. Come on, let's go and find our seats."

And he let her lead him into the auditorium, both thrilled and intrigued by this new dimension to her character.

"You knew I'd come tonight," he said as they squeezed along to the only two seats still unoccupied in their row. "Didn't you?"

"It's fortunate we're some way back," she observed, ignoring his question. "That way we can leave early without attracting too much attention."

"Didn't you?" he persisted. But she said nothing, just smiled with her body as she settled the delicate line of her frame into the seat and ran her fingers through the dense cascade of her hair. He was easily seduced and conceded defeat: "Have you seen where Silverstone is sitting?"

She shook her head.

"Maybe he saw you and is lurking outside for the concert to finish."

He felt the comfort of her hand on his, but it did not come without a certain chilling cynicism: "I'm afraid, squirrel, you have to accept that the bird who sits for too long on the fence is liable to get shot at from either side."

"Thank you for those comforting words."

"Look, Frank, I told you not to come – for your own safety." The impatience in her voice stung, seasoning her charm with a pungency that only added to his disquiet and threatened to nurture a disturbing distance between them, until she added: "Even so, I'm glad you're here. So let's enjoy the music and worry about your problems afterwards, shall we?"

It was her utter coolness in face of all the menace that completely disarmed him before he had a chance to say a word in reply. And he sat back in defeated silence to watch her soak up the concert atmosphere. Perched on the edge of her seat, she studied the scene with a girlish wonder he had not seen in her before as she looked out for the slightest hint of activity on the stage. Suddenly he could see her as Isolde, wide-eyed and devoted to her Tristan, and he was pained by a foolish jealousy of this childhood sweetheart she had told him about. Sensed a preposterous sadness that he had not known her then. Yet there were so many impenetrable shadows to her life that he wondered whether he even knew her now. And, as if in answer, she waved to someone from this unlit world of hers. It was her professor, who had just found his seat with what was presumably his wife and was looking almost girlish himself in his anticipation of the evening's cultural treat.

"This is going to be a wonderful evening, squirrel. I can feel it," she whispered, as the orchestra came out on stage. "I'm so glad you're here to enjoy it with me, after all," and she squeezed his hand. She had crossed so effortlessly into another world. No guilt, no complications, no quarrel with reality. Transported from darkness into a make-believe where Silverstone and Breitner no longer existed, and Achim's family might be playing somersaults with Max and Moritz for all she knew. Perhaps she was right, he told himself. Maybe this was the way to handle the situation. At all events, he was glad she had taken him along with her, even if he did not feel entirely at home in this fantasy world.

His knowledge of music was limited, but the symmetry of the players, the way the strings were arranged into two small orchestras either side of the podium, with celesta and drums taking up the centre, pleased his eye for harmony, and helped him relax into the journey Patricia was taking him on as a hush came down on the house to let the gentle fugue-like introduction carry them away. He sensed Patricia become instantly riveted by its mysterious haunting quality. And he knew he had already lost her as the slowly surging repetition of its theme began to build a tension into the ambience of sound which perfectly matched the anxiety that had been hounding his every move. Each new entry of strings brought an added strain on his nerves, conjured a fresh image of his persecution. First Breitner, then Silverstone, the cloth cap, Achim, his family, his mother, the carnivorous nurse all assumed a deliberate relentless edge to their features as they lined up before him in judgement, fixing him with the same steady glare. And when the theme began its slow return to the keynote, each one of them began to move pitilessly towards him.

Desperation seized hold of Frank. He felt a burning need to leave, but there was no way out. When he looked at Patricia, he saw a peaceful serenity that only heightened the loneliness of his despair. Although he saw the audience around him, and the orchestra on stage, the images would not release him from their obsessional grip. They pursued him into every corner of this unrelenting trial. Hunted him down in the merciless allegro of the second movement, running, dragging a net behind them that danced with the flapping wings of a thousand birds in panic, a net that was his destiny. His future a silhouette against the light that shone behind the ghostly architects of this chase and cast its shadow directly through their midst. Back and forth they darted in the remorselessly receding arm of this shadow, his destiny, approaching ever closer, until eventually they faded with the exhaustion of the music.

The landscape went flat, and the sound of a pin dropping on the floor would have echoed through the hall. But it was the faint tinkling of a bell that announced their return to the haunting quality of the opening theme and restored perspective to the bleak landscape. The movement of a solitary figure, larger than life, now grinned through the half-light with the look of a vengeance in its bloodshot eyes. Breitner had eliminated all his rivals in judgement. He dominated Frank now with an obsessional urge to shape his future. Inched steadily closer, shedding an article of clothing with every bar, until he stood over him stripped to the waist, looking awesomely muscular, with an ugly hammer in his hand. Frank was caught on the edge of a precipice and had no choice but down or have his skull fashioned to the art of Breitner's whims. His tormentor grinned. Frank opted for down. Over the edge, forever through the briny air, to the granite rocks below, smoothly sculpted artefacts of nature's hand, washed with salt and the blood of his poor mother, her carcass split open by the impact. He lay in the cold, bloodless embrace of her arms, weeping as the water lapped over his own battered corpse and rinsed the poison from his ravaged skull. Above him, Breitner continued to grin atop his cliff, like a towering granite sculpture, an Aryan statue of tyranny wielding a hammer for a torch. And this he tossed now into the sea, jettisoned with disinterest as if it was nothing more than a smoked-out cigarette butt. Frank watched it sink down slowly through the clarity of the water and slithered after it off his blood-drenched boulder as it assumed an immeasurable significance for him. It drew him down with an irresistible magnetism. He had to have it. But only when it was too late, when it had lodged in the sand, did he see it for what it was: a baby barely old enough to swim. He wanted to gasp for air and began to take in water. But seeing his distress, the baby cradled him in its arms and swam with him to the shore. The waves swirled over them in a contemptuous dance – frolicking, laughing, joyful at his rescue – and dragged them into their dance, pulling them this way and that. And still Breitner stood there watching, laughing from the clifftop, until the waves pushed them ragged and beaten into the pebblewash. The baby still held him tight in its arms, his saviour now become a straitjacket. Now demanding attention. It gurgled as it lay on his chest, pinning him to the ground, trying to suck at his nipple, as the sea washed over them, washed the pebbles over them, gashed a deep crevice through its back, and washed it clean of blood. Through the ebb and flow of water rushing in his ears, he caught Patricia's voice.

"What's the matter?" she asked. "You look terrible. You're sweating profusely."

She was still sitting on the edge of her seat like a little girl, adding her own measure of approval to the rushing applause of the audience.

"Come on. We'd better go, before everyone else starts to move," and she carefully guided Frank along their enraptured row of concert-goers still celebrating their enjoyment and out towards the fresh air of the foyer.

"Give me your ticket," she said with an air of command when they reached the cloakroom. He was thankful for her presence of mind. It was not until they were out in the cool air of the street that he became aware of the unaccustomed sensation of a hat on his head and the feel of a plush new coat on his shoulders. He touched the waistband of his trousers through the coat. The gun was still in place. He surreptitiously tried to remove it and put it in his coat pocket, where it could be in his hand at all times. But she spotted it.

"What on earth do you have there?"

"My insurance policy." He sensed her silent conflict between disapproval and understanding, but he said nothing more and waited for her to break the silence.

"Squirrel," she said at length, "you look as dreadful as ever. Are you sure you're feeling all right?"

His assurances that he was fine, that his *auberge* bed was just a little inhospitable, and all he needed was a good night's sleep carried little conviction. And they failed to forestall the sweet concern and care she showed when she took him under her wing. He was not about to complain, especially at the point where he realised she was not dutifully putting him on the tram out to limbo, but was taking him back with her into the tender confidence of her own exquisitely private world.

"Are you sure we're not being followed?" It was a redundant question.

"Just relax and let me do the worrying," she said.

Patricia was in control. She held him like an injured fledgling in the hollow of her hand, letting him lie back and enjoy the ride. He recalled the first time he had seen her, how impressed he had been by the strength that emanated with such paradox through her fragile vulnerability. An impression that was confirmed that evening. She smiled, almost as if she knew what he was thinking.

"You look very fetching in your hat and coat," she said. Her words put him in mind of the shabby old coat he had abandoned to its unsuspecting new owner.

"I have an apology to make, Patricia."

"Don't speak of it now."

What does she mean? Frank wondered.

"No," he insisted. "Just while I think of it. That book of Baudelaire. *Les fleurs du mal.* It was in the pocket of my old coat."

"I was wondering where that had got to."

"I'm sorry. I'll buy you a new copy," he promised.

"Don't be silly," she said. "It was only something I picked up at a flea market."

An instant sense of relief swept over him. A sense of comfort in the knowledge that the annotations were not some private code of intimacy for her, but came with the second-hand grime and dog-eared corners.

"Nonetheless, it meant something to you," he insisted. "Otherwise you wouldn't have underlined all those passages."

He recited the one that had impressed itself on him with particular effect, as he had done to himself every idle moment of the last three days in his limbo across the border.

"You see," she laughed, "I don't need the book. I have my squirrel."

Vanity convinced him there was affection in her mockery.

"Don't laugh, Patricia. I know my French is appalling. But I remember the words so well because I find them very beautiful, but also because they surprise me. They don't seem like you at all."

"Oh, but they most definitely are. Dreams, little squirrel. They remind me of my dreams. And if I didn't have these, if I couldn't forget this mess every now and then, I'd go insane."

They did not speak again until they reached the new accommodation that Lutz had found for her not far from the zoological gardens. Her words disturbed him, because they seemed to echo a profound disquiet that he would never fathom.

As they closed the door on the menace outside, he recalled her bewitching reverie in the concert hall even before the strings had made their haunting entrance. Now, as she took his coat, the coincidence of their thoughts excited him with its implicit hint of intimacy between them when she asked: "What did you think of the music? Didn't you find it just marvellous?"

The words came with a special sparkle in her eyes. But what captivated him above all was the way she could so easily embrace Bartok and Billie Holiday with equal passion.

"I don't understand classical music well enough to offer a verdict," he confessed, preferring to hide behind his ignorance rather than disclose the truth of his emotional whereabouts during the concert.

"But you must have an opinion. You must know whether you liked it or not," she insisted. "That first movement for example. Didn't you find it absolutely beautiful? The way it slowly opened out like a fan – and then closed again, just as slowly, just as deliberately."'

"Just like you," he said.

"What do you mean?"

The tone of her voice signalled mock offence. It was plain to him from the coquettish way she loosened his tie that she was flattered by his remark – obtusely so, he thought, since the layers of meaning in those three words spoke of an opaque secrecy as much as approval. But he was enjoying the moment and was not about to spell it out any further. They did not speak with any substance again that night, but left their bodies to converse, and enjoyed the mingling of their perfumes.

Before getting into bed, however, he took the precaution of putting the gun under the pillow while Patricia was attending to her evening toiletries. Even in her caring hands, he did not feel entirely secure. And although the touch of her sleek and slender warmth against his body kindled a flame that would never die, and gave him all the strength he needed, it was nonetheless an unquiet night he spent in her arms. The darkness would not allow his eyes to close for a minute. The slightest unfamiliar sound nurtured fear and suspicion of every shadow. Every so often the clouds would draw back their curtain over the moon and let the night light play on the wall beside the window. It shone through the scudding clouds above and cast their shadows in ominous designs sketched out especially for him: every movement spoke of the intentions which the night still had on him, warned him not to drop his guard for a moment – advice he took to heart.

Patricia meanwhile slept peacefully by his side, her hair on his shoulder blacker than the night, an arm draped in carefree nonchalance across his chest. Such sweet innocence in the asylum of her precious dreams, he thought. The contrast between them was immense. How he wished he could sleep with such abandon.

"I was thinking last night," he announced while she prepared the morning coffee. But sleep still swam in her eyes, the fragility of early morning hung in her every move. She was plainly up too early for new ideas, so he did not return to the subject until they were sitting together at the breakfast table with a dose of caffeine already coursing through their veins.

"I was thinking last night, Patricia. Why don't we take a holiday? A couple of weeks in the mountains while things cool off here."

"I can't, squirrel," she said and poured herself another cup of coffee. "And things aren't going to just cool off, as you put it. You just have to learn to accommodate unpleasant truths. Make a few concessions to reality and learn to live with it."

"Can you ski?" he persisted, ignoring her advice. His change of tack elicited what he sensed to be the slight trace of a willing submission.

"Can you?"

Those two words came with a sweet challenging smile in her eyes. They hinted at confirmation. And he could already see her thoughts busily packing her suitcase.

They agreed to meet at the central railway station later that afternoon. This gave him time enough to return to his lodging across the border, settle the bill and fetch his few belongings. But the anxieties of the night still trailed through the cold morning air as he made his way to the tram and back to his *auberge*. Although he checked his tracks continually, he could not escape the feeling that he was being followed. Shadowed by some dark unseen presence, some undefined shape of things to come. When he alighted from the tram at the end of the line, the smell of wood smoke hung in the gentle breeze that blew between the half-timbered houses of the village. He stopped, and looked cautiously down the length of the bottle-green carriages. Only three other people got out with him, all elderly pensioners who appeared quietly content in the twilight of their lives. They plainly had no interest in Frank's fortunes. He was comfortably alone.

Yet the walk up the hill towards the border crossing refused to let him shake off the unease and enjoy the prospect of two weeks alone in the mountains with Patricia. The breeze blew up colder and more harshly as he reached the brow of the hill and started his approach towards the ghostly pale of trees that was the frontier. Alone on the landscape of ploughed fields that swept down to this border, he saw himself as little more than a misplaced apostrophe on someone else's horizon. A clumsy punctuation mark to be erased. Caught unawares, he almost jumped out of his skin when a flock of rooks were startled into flight from their winter foraging. Noisy and menacing, they circled up and over the trees ahead of him like a jackboot army with wings. The dendritic weave of branches drawn against the sky that they vacated reminded him of the nerve cells which run their paths of organised confusion beneath the skullcap and spoke of the chaos in his own mind.

The customs house looked more desolate than ever as he passed. The shutter still flapped in the wind. Only today no one seemed about to fasten it and quell the boring repetition of its noise. It smacked each time against the wall with the sudden crack, as of gunfire, and unnerved him with each strike. He hurried his step, eager to re-join Patricia and begin their escape from reality together, however brief it may be. The overcast sky as he crossed the frontier darkened his path with a message he was unable to decipher. But an uncomfortable feeling told him he was in danger of not seeing her again.

Chapter 20

The laughter came skipping up the stairs to meet Ellen on her way down for breakfast. It instantly dispelled the dreams of Frank that still lingered in the sleepy corners of her mind. Marthe had assumed such an effortless way of helping her forget all her trials, especially since they had come to know each other more intimately. Often it was enough just to hear the sound of her voice from another room or feel the warmth she radiated when she smiled.

Ellen half-expected to find Dr Zellweger still breakfasting with her when she walked into the kitchen, and was surprised to find she was alone.

"Good morning Ellen. Have you slept well?" Marthe asked.

The amusement Ellen had heard from the stairs still showed in the corners of her mouth as Marthe handed her the newspaper.

"You must read this. It's so funny."

Ellen passed it back without even attempting to read it. So often these past weeks she had been made to feel so stupidly dependent at times.

"Oh, I'm sorry, Ellen. I'm forgetting you can't read German yet. But it's so funny, I must read it for you."

Ellen's train of thought caught on the word 'yet'. It excited her in a way she was unable to explain, and she pondered its significance as Marthe took the newspaper in her hands, brushing some flaky crumbs of croissant from her blouse as she did so. The outline of her breasts that she revealed as the crumbs scattered on the table in front of her aroused Ellen. Above all it was the secret that excited her – the knowledge she now had of

Marthe. Only a short time ago, she never would have thought it possible. Marthe either failed to notice her arousal or preferred to ignore it. She was more interested in her newspaper article.

"It is standing here that two men have been found last night walking through the town completely naked."

Ellen was struck by the way Marthe's command of English seized up when she had to translate directly from the printed page. She was normally so fluent when she spoke.

"It says they have been attacked by a gunman who was forcing them to undress," she continued. "He then threw their clothes in the river and ran off. No explanations. No demands for money. He has ordered them just to take off their clothes. Can you imagine what a sight this must have been? I wish I could have seen that. The man deserves a medal."

Ellen smiled.

"Don't you think the male body is very comical?" Marthe asked.

Ellen was slightly surprised by the streak of feminism in Marthe.

"All male bodies?" she asked. "Even your husband's?"

"Especially my husband's!" Marthe laughed.

"I always rather liked my Frank's body," Ellen said. She found the disloyalty a little distasteful, but secretly she flattered herself that she knew what Marthe was talking about.

"I don't speak about like or not like. I just find them comical. Men are so protective about their virility. Can you imagine what these two men looked like? That little difference shrivelled up to nothing in the cold?"

Marthe sniggered at the thought, and the ludicrous image she conjured prompted Ellen to join in the girlish giggles. She almost choked on the breakfast tea that Marthe so thoughtfully made for her every morning.

"The problem is," she went on, "they think they're so wonderful they can't imagine that we don't think so too."

"They are in a way though, aren't they?" Ellen said. And her words brought the disturbing memory of their honeymoon in

Venice back to the surface once again. The pain. The cry. The rank disgust on Frank's face. She sensed herself colour slightly at her own words and felt a little foolish.

Marthe failed to see the embarrassment in Ellen's cheeks.

"But you must agree, Ellen, they are rather messy instruments. We women need more than that. Warmth and tenderness, compassion, understanding. Love. For men, this seems to mean the privilege of leaving their mess all over you and expecting you to be grateful."

"Perhaps you look at it like that because you're not interested in having children?" Ellen suggested. And regretted the words the moment they came out. Marthe glared at her with an expression she was unable to read. But Ellen could see that her words had hurt.

"Don't get me wrong, Ellen. Urs and I have a good relationship. He's very good to me. And very understanding. I'm so much luckier than my sister in that way."

"You also have a sister?"

"She's some years older than me. And I don't see her much these days," Marthe said. "She lives in Berne with her accountant husband. Poor soul. He doesn't even let her have her own bank account, makes sure she keeps a cash book for everything she buys and expects her to present every receipt for him to check. He's quite typical of many Swiss men."

"He sounds a lot like my own brother-in-law."

"I'm sure that's not possible," Marthe insisted. "You know, I first met him when I was going through my 'Women in Playpens' phase. I'm not sure whether it was thanks to Iris von Roten or my sister's husband. Maybe it was a combination of the two. But it was around then that I decided to take a job with the school psychological service in the hope that I could help some of the children to avoid the traps men like to lay in this country."

Marthe paused for a moment. The expression in her eyes spoke of a reminiscence she preferred to keep to herself.

"That was before I went to America with Urs. But you're right, Ellen," Marthe added, reviving Ellen's allusion to her lack of children. Men can certainly be useful."

There was a thinly veiled rebuke in Marthe's voice, but she allowed Ellen to ignore it as she continued in the warmer tone that Ellen had come to appreciate in her.

"How important is it to you really?" she asked. "To have children?"

"Very." It was all Ellen needed to say. It expressed everything. But Marthe was not satisfied.

"I know many people who find children very fulfilling," she said, "but children can also hamper a woman. During the referendum, the campaign against the women's vote was quite nasty. They produced some unbelievably unpleasant posters showing babies falling out of prams or flies crawling over a baby's *Nuggi*, er," she hesitated, looking for the English word. "Pacifier," she said at last, curling her tongue around the r.

"Do you mean a dummy?" Ellen asked, mildly irritated by the American ways Marthe would throw into the conversation now and then.

"Is that the word?" Marthe asked. "Can you imagine? These were the posters they put up to persuade people that women should stay at home, look after their babies and not concern themselves with politics. Voting on issues that affect women's lives was a man's job. Really I didn't need any encouragement to join the campaign against ideas like that. There's more to a woman's life than looking after babies. But let me put this another way," Marthe added in an effort to get them back to the point of her original question, "suppose we never find Frank, and you never meet anybody to take his place. What would you do?" Marthe asked.

"It's funny. If you'd asked that a few weeks ago I'd have died at the thought. Now I can talk about it without any problem. It's frightening really."

Marthe put her hand on Ellen's, as if to demonstrate the warmth and understanding she spoke of earlier. Her touch made Ellen feel strangely at ease with the world. But Marthe was not prepared to leave it at that.

"You haven't answered my question," she persisted.

"I just don't see that as a problem these days. You don't have to have a mate to make babies nowadays."

"It means that much to you?"

"Yes, it does." Ellen failed to understand the disbelief in Marthe's eyes. And sensing the demand for some explanation, she added: "I want to show I can do it better than my parents, who thought it was enough to bring me into the world and then packed me off to boarding school."

"It's interesting that we share the experience of a Catholic boarding school, but come to such different conclusions," Marthe said. Her look of incomprehension deepened, as she paused, then added: "And you wouldn't mind whose sperm you had, as long as it was fertile?"

"I didn't say that. And in fact the question wouldn't arise, because I still have Frank's sperm. We've read a few reports recently about the advances they've been making in donor insemination. We discussed it a few times. And then one day, a few weeks ago, Frank just sprang the news on me that he's banked some of his sperm in a donor insemination centre."

Marthe's mouth dropped. Had she not already finished her coffee, it would have doubtless been spluttered all over the table. Ellen had never seen her lost for words before and was surprised by the reaction. She had always seen Marthe as such a woman of the world, so difficult to shock – yet Ellen appeared to have done just that. Marthe's expression wavered between amusement and incredulity.

"You know, Ellen," Marthe said at last, her hand still reassuringly rested on Ellen's arm, "the science is not nearly as advanced as people would like it to be. And these insemination services can be very questionable."

Ignoring Marthe's words of caution, Ellen felt compelled to justify herself.

"We discussed it a few times after he made it plain that he wasn't keen on having babies just yet. You can't believe what a shock that was. It made me very depressed to begin with. I even thought of stopping the pill and not telling him. But

I couldn't just trick him like that. So, when I read about donor insemination, we talked a bit about it, and I sold it to him like an insurance policy. Only it was my insurance, in case something happened to him before he could make up his mind."

"And he was buying this insurance for you, just like that, without any questions?"

"Yes. I was quite surprised. He really took to the idea. Perhaps it appealed to his male vanity having his seed put aside for posterity."

"He did not feel threatened?" Marthe asked. "I mean, in the end he was selling his power over you."

"On the contrary, it seemed to come as a great relief. It took the decision out of his hands as far as he was concerned. He appeared so much more relaxed about everything. It was as if he had suddenly been set free. He's always been terrible about committing himself in any way. I think that was probably his mother's fault. She was such a domineering bitch, had poor Frank right under her thumb.

"She was constantly going on about how difficult he was as a child. Always talking about imaginary places and people. Always telling wild stories, insisting that he didn't belong there, that his other home was much different. And he was always having nightmares as well. Maybe it was this that made her lose patience with him. According to Frank, his mother had scolded him for as long as he could remember. For every tiniest little thing. So I suppose he just caved in eventually. Anything for a quiet life. And so he did everything she told him to. Even after we married, he was never allowed to be himself when she was around. It was awful. I felt so sorry for him sometimes. Then so angry and irritated.

"He actually suggested buying a house so she could live with us, although we didn't even have the money for a down-payment. He put the whole idea across as a business venture, with his mother putting up the capital that would enable us to invest in a more valuable property later. I knew all along she'd put him up to the idea. It had her stamp all over it. Fortunately, Frank realised it would probably mean the end of our marriage, so it never came to anything. But it didn't stop her moving into a house not far away. She was such a scheming bitch. Still, she was the one to suffer in the end."

"What do you mean?"

"When she died. It wasn't long after she moved in. I've heard it's quite common for elderly people to give up the ghost when they suddenly find themselves uprooted from their familiar surroundings and dumped in a strange place where they have no roots. A bit like plants, I suppose."

Ellen was not sure what part of her rambling response the affirmative nod was intended for, since Marthe's thoughts were clearly elsewhere:

"That reminds me, Ellen. You have a busy day before you. The police telephoned just before you came to breakfast. They want you to go and see them."

What reminded her? Ellen wondered. Marthe was not about to elaborate, but poured another cup of tea for her instead. It fascinated Ellen to watch this elegant Swiss woman with whom she had been intimate the night before. Ellen coloured slightly at the memory, while Marthe poured the tea as if it was the most natural thing in the world for her. She had learned a lot of trivialities to accommodate Ellen – even buying a proper teapot to make it as nearly English as she could. It was hard for Ellen to imagine she might be hiding anything from her. But then she recalled what Marthe had told her that night, about Frank confessing to have killed his mother.

"When do they want to see me?" Ellen asked. Already she could feel her heart beginning to race. She sensed it showed in her voice. But Marthe either failed to notice her apprehension or chose to ignore it.

"Whenever you have time. They said there's no hurry, but if you like I can bring you there later this morning. Then we could have lunch together. There's a nice restaurant round the corner near the police presidium, overlooking the river. And this afternoon I will drive you to the clinic to see Urs. He wants to talk with you at four-thirty."

"Why four-thirty?"

"He doesn't get back from Zurich until four. But he's blocked his appointment book for the rest of the afternoon so he can talk with you in depth."

"What are we talking about Marthe? And why the talk of appointment books? He can talk to me when he gets home."

"You know how correct he is. He thinks it is not ethical to speak about a patient outside the clinic."

However ordinary and matter-of-fact her manner, Marthe dressed up this announcement in a way that had Ellen firmly hooked on its unspoken mystery. She could not imagine what Dr Zellweger might have to say to her within the cold, scientific walls of his clinic that he could not say in the comfort of his own home. The speculation that grew out of her bafflement kept her mind occupied for the rest of the morning. She tingled with a dark, reluctant curiosity throughout her interview at the police station and was unable to concentrate on all the repetitive well-worn questions they threw at her.

The police had apparently long since abandoned any prospect of Frank returning to his room at the Kolping house and had fetched all his belongings over to the police station. They now wanted her to make a formal identification of the items.

It was the same dour Malcolm lookalike who had accompanied them to the Kolping house. And he now seemed to Ellen incapable of seeing the absurdity of the scene or appreciating the smile that she sensed spread over her face as she picked out the two pairs of socks and the quaintly worn-out underpants. He took them from her as if they were crucial evidence by which the case for the prosecution would stand or fall. But he wanted more. He wanted to build a picture of Frank, he said. In fact it emerged that he was playing with the same idea Marthe had thrown up at Ellen, that maybe Frank was involved in drug-trafficking – a notion so ludicrous that her interest in it paled away to nothing in the shadow of her impending appointment at the clinic.

After withstanding this first trial of the day, Ellen hoped the lunch with Marthe would help distract her preoccupied mind. But it was not to be – despite Marthe's company and the delightful setting of the restaurant, where they sat overlooking the Rhine, watching the water flow beneath the bridge. Occasionally, a barge would pass low down in the water, struggling to compete with the downstream current. It was a scene that only nurtured the apprehension in Ellen's curiosity all the more, since across the water – almost directly opposite where they were sitting – she could not help but notice the throng of people, mostly young men and women, shabby and stooped with all the homemade sorrows of the world heaped upon their shoulders. They gathered in groups, obviously dealing or just hanging out on the railings of the promenade that ran alongside the river. Marthe saw where her train of thought was running whenever Ellen glanced across the water in their direction.

"It's terrible what they are doing to themselves," she said.

Her observation served only to darken the shadows of fear that lurked in Ellen's curiosity, and she staunchly refused to be drawn into any discussion that touched even remotely on Frank. She knew that Dr Zellweger was already waiting in the wings for this opportunity.

It was the first time Ellen had returned to the clinic since the day she arrived so full of expectation from London. It seemed far sadder that afternoon than she remembered it – perhaps because the grounds now lay completely washed out with the winter and the building had been dampened to a dark grey by the rain. Marthe accompanied Ellen and led her down the long dingy corridor to her husband's office.

"Ah, Mrs Goss," he said, getting up from his desk as they entered. He gave Ellen his hand with a ritual posture as if in some kind of pretence that they did not see each other almost every day in the privacy of his own home.

"I see my wife has brought you. Very good."

From the way he moved, the way he touched his bow tie and adjusted the waistcoat under his white clinician's coat, before self-consciously buttoning it up, gave Ellen the feeling he was nervous.

"*Schatz,*" he said, turning to Marthe, "I was talking with Lorenz this morning – he is an old colleague in Zurich," he added for Ellen's benefit, "and he has offered us to use his chalet in St Moritz at the end of the month. He says it will be free for a few weeks. Unfortunately, I will be much too busy preparing for a symposium, but it would be a nice opportunity for Mrs Goss to see another side of Switzerland than psychiatric clinics. Do you ski, Mrs Goss?"

"I'm afraid not," Ellen replied. She could not help wondering as he spoke these words whether he knew that Marthe and she had slept together. Was this the explanation for the appointment in his office, an attempt to formalise his wife's relationship with her in some way and give it the air of respectability? She recalled what Marthe had said about how ridiculous she found her own husband's body, and tried to picture him with no clothes on, without even his bow tie. Would this be the last layer to fall? Ellen wondered. It was hard for her to imagine this pillar of correctness making love to Marthe with any passion, let alone satisfying her. Ellen's wayward thoughts were broken by a knock at the door.

"Ah, Professor Abegg. Please come. You remember Mrs Goss."

Ellen too recalled him, the tall but frail-looking figure from her first visit to the clinic, not so old, but prematurely aged by all the cares of his profession. He had grown a wispy beard since they last met. Perhaps for strength, Ellen told herself. He gave her his hand, while Dr Zellweger drew the earlier conversation with his wife to a close.

"I suggest you phone Lorenz when you get back home and arrange a little holiday in the mountains for you and Mrs Goss."

This was Marthe's cue to leave. Did he really not know what Marthe and I had been getting up to? Ellen asked herself. Or was he actively encouraging it with this invitation? The speculation was tantalising. But futile. And it died a sudden death as she watched Marthe close the door behind her, leaving Ellen to face the inquisition alone. Only Marthe's promise to wait for Ellen outside kept her from falling into a panic when Dr Zellweger returned to his desk, fixed her with his eyes and addressed her so solemnly that she was convinced he had some terrible news to impart.

"Although I now have responsibility for your husband's case, Professor Abegg is with us today in his function as the head of department," he explained.

Dr Zellweger smiled nervously at the professor with this introduction. Ellen had the impression that he was not enjoying the experience, that he had been thoroughly ticked off for letting the patient discharge himself and just walk out of the clinic. Dr Zellweger rested his elbows on the desk and leaned on them awkwardly as he shifted his gaze from Ellen to the books in front of him.

"I must confess," he continued, "that we are making worries for ourselves."

It was not the first time Ellen had noticed how his English suffered when he felt uncomfortable. Now in the oblique backlight of the window behind his desk she saw a dense white – almost silver – in the hair around his temples; it had never struck her before. She wondered if it had appeared overnight with the worries he shared with the professor. Or was it just a trick of the light?

Professor Abegg sat beside the desk nodding in agreement with a discreet smile on his lips. The weakness of the smile was somehow accentuated by the half-hearted growth on his chin. Ellen speculated on how these two ever managed to cope with a patient – were they suddenly invested with self-confidence when they found themselves in a position of advantage, she asked herself. Then he spoke:

"You see, Mrs Goss, we are knowing your husband since too short a time, but we are becoming a picture which confuses us."

Dr Zellweger was sharp enough to see the blank expression written on Ellen's face and came to his colleague's rescue. "What

Professor Abegg tries to say is that your husband has not been with us under observation since long enough to make a diagnosis."

"He's not here now, is he?" she asked. Perhaps it was the panic in her eyes that made Dr Zellweger flinch slightly when she interrupted his train of thought. Or was it a self-consciousness as he struggled to get his English back into shape, Ellen wondered.

"I'm sorry to say he's not. No. But I am confident we will find him very soon, especially now where we are having the police on our side."

"I'm afraid I don't follow. Whose side are you talking about?" Ellen asked. His choice of words quietly enraged her. "I certainly don't feel they're on my side."

"You must understand, Mrs Goss, that your husband is very labile and could be a danger."

"What do you mean a danger? You admit yourself that you don't even know what's wrong with him."

The look which Dr Zellweger exchanged with his professor had a conspiratorial quality. It suggested to Ellen that they knew more than they were letting on.

"That is precisely the point," he said, finally getting to grips with his English. "We cannot be sure about anything, and for this reason we are having to be very cautious."

Ellen watched him get up from his seat and walk over to the window, his hands deep in the pockets of his white coat. He seemed anxiously pensive, as if looking for inspiration or help, which he knew he could not expect from Professor Abegg. Ellen was unable to let go of the feeling that he knew of her relationship with Marthe. The impression was reinforced when he turned round and resumed the conversation with a faster and more frenetic turn of speech that suggested to Ellen he was trying to cover something up. Or suppress an unpleasant truth.

"It's really a fascinating case," he continued. "We cannot be sure, but something which Professor Abegg and I agree, we are both thinking that your husband is showing features of a schizoaffective psychosis."

"Psychosis?" Ellen sensed her mouth hang open in disbelief.

"Thought disorder. Delusions. Auditory hallucinations. And his behaviour generally would appear to suggest this," he insisted. "It is possible that this condition has been induced by drug abuse."

"Oh no, not that again. Please Dr Zellweger, there's no way Frank would have anything to do with drugs. I've been through all this with the police. Is this what you mean when you say they're on our side?"

All of a sudden, Ellen was beginning to appreciate why Marthe was having difficulty with her husband. And she could see in turn that he was becoming impatient with her – as far as his sense of correctness would allow it.

"It is possible that he is acting through what he sees as failures in his life." It was Professor Abegg who took the reins now, but Ellen had the feeling he just wanted to have something to say, and she sensed an irritation in Dr Zellweger's eyes at the interruption. "People who take drugs are often having a very poor self-esteem," the professor insisted.

Perhaps Dr Zellweger agreed with the sentiment. But Ellen could see he was not impressed by the way it was put across.

"Mrs Goss, we are not concerned about the moral or the legal aspects of the case. We are concerned about the health issues – both for your husband and for you," he added ominously as he fiddled with his bow tie again and searched for his next line. "After what he said in the clinic, he appears to feel great resentment for his mother."

"I'm not surprised," Ellen chipped in, and earned a withering schoolmasterly gaze for the interruption. He knew that story. They had spoken of relations with her mother-in-law at length.

"And he is almost certainly rejecting outside help. He probably sees this as interference or pressure. It is interesting that he never mentioned your name. But we have discussed this once before. You see, we cannot be sure whether he also rejects you in his psychosis. It is very unpredictable. And there is no way to know how he will behave when he sees you."

"Dr Zellweger, I don't think you can possibly imagine how tired I am. My husband has been missing for goodness knows how long now. I've been told by the police that he's a drug-dealing criminal. Now you're telling me he's a dangerous psychotic. And slowly I'm beginning to wonder whether I've even got a husband. So even if I believed a word of what you're trying to tell me, I don't actually care anymore. It doesn't mean anything to me any longer. I'm just tired. So I hope you won't think me rude and callous when I say that all I'd like right now is to go home."

Ellen's outburst left an awkward silence in its wake that seemed to last forever. The pensive concern on Dr Zellweger's face eventually prompted him to get up and walk with slow deliberation around his desk to where she was sitting. She felt the firm reassuring pressure of his hand on her shoulder.

"I understand. We will talk another day," he said, and went over to the door. "Marthe, Mrs Goss would like to go home already." His voice was muffled by the door that he held between them as he talked to his wife. The Swiss German was incomprehensible to Ellen, but she did pick up the mention of St Moritz.

In the car back to her house, Marthe confirmed what she suspected their conversation had been about.

"Urs thinks you need a break. I will telephone to his colleague in Zurich, and we will have a nice time together in St Moritz. Just the two of us. It's very beautiful there."

The comfort of her hand on Ellen's knee as she spoke these words put her instantly at ease.

"I've never been to the mountains," she said.

"You will love it," Marthe reassured her.

"But we'll need to find something more suitable for your feet," she added, glancing down at the thick platform soles on Ellen's high-heel boots.

"St Moritz," Ellen repeated. It was a name she had often heard, but it had always been another world for her, a stamping ground for rich playboys. She never imagined for one moment that she would ever spend a holiday there.

"Isn't that where the Cresta Run is?"

Marthe nodded, and Ellen could see from the smile on her face that she found her ingenuousness faintly amusing.

"That always used to fascinate Frank. He was always saying he'd like to try it again someday." Her words became lost in the sound of an aeroplane taking off from the nearby airport. It was still very low in the sky, and Ellen could see quite clearly that it was a BEA flight. Presumably on its way to Heathrow, she told herself. At that moment, Ellen felt further from home than ever.

Chapter 21

Frank sensed that Patricia would not go through with their trip to the mountains and would stand him up. But putting these defeatist thoughts to one side, he had dropped into a bookshop on the way to the station to buy a copy of *Les fleurs du mal.* And to feel the book now resting in his pocket imbued him with a new sense of optimism as he made his way to meet her. Not even the clouds that gathered overhead as he strode to the station could dampen this excitement.

They had agreed to meet at the top of the steps down to the underpass that ran under the station. As he was approaching, he caught sight of a tall figure wearing a light grey fedora. The man emerged from a grand building with a woman unknown to him, but the man himself was uncomfortably familiar. It was Silverstone. He glanced in the direction of Frank, but was too focused on his female companion to notice him. While curious to know who the American's companion might be, Frank felt a keen sense of relief when they turned and walked in the opposite direction towards the Schlotterbeck garage.

The central square itself resembled a global playground that lunchtime. Children romped and tumbled in a Babel of languages and dialects that were mostly beyond Frank's powers of recognition. Some he identified as approximately Slavonic. Others betrayed something of the Hungarian cadence he had come to know from his frequent visits to the Csarda restaurant all those lifetimes ago in Berlin. And a number of the children laughed and played with a clearly Yiddish lilt in their voices.

The scene was one of uncommon happiness that defied the dark clouds above. It surprised him, until he recalled that space had been made in one of the station buildings to accommodate the growing stream of refugees in transit. These were plainly some of the refugee children, who had been allowed a lunch-time opportunity to escape from the tedium of their new freedom. But their happiness saddened him. They put him in mind of Achim's baby boys.

"Refreshing, their innocence, isn't it?" Patricia's voice instantly lightened the load on his heart. He turned around to her smoky, captivating smile. He was instantly comforted to see that his doubts had been unfounded and, in that moment of relief, planted a kiss on her lips that almost knocked her off balance. Yet, in his excitement, he had failed to hear the flatness of tone in her words.

"Come on," he said. "Let's go and get the tickets."

But taking her by the arm, he was still unable to shake off the sighting of his American bugbear.

"I saw Silverstone just outside the station," he said. "Did you see him?"

Patricia shook her head.

"Do you think he's following us?" he asked.

"I think you said he works at the Bank for International Settlements," she remarked. "So it's more likely he's just going back to work after lunch. The bank is just over the road, where the Savoy Hotel was requisitioned for their work."

While the sighting of Silverstone still troubled Frank, and he could not bring himself to point out that Silverstone was leaving the hornet's nest and plainly not going back to work, her matter-of-fact tone at least put his mind to rest.

Approaching the counter, he took out his wallet and opened it. He failed to notice the lock of strawberry-blonde hair that dropped out and fell to the floor. It caught in the draught of a passer-by and landed behind Patricia's feet.

"What was that?" she asked, looking behind her.

"What?"

"Something fell out of your wallet."

He looked down at the floor around him. But the lock of hair had already been swept up by the feet of another passer-by and disappeared from view.

"It looked like a lock of blonde hair," she said. Her eyes flashed a look of quiet confrontation.

He looked askance at Patricia. Her lips, always a gloriously sensual source of fascination for Frank, betrayed a new kind of vulnerability that disturbed him. But he was as perplexed as she was. There was nothing he could say.

"Well, it doesn't matter now," she continued mysteriously, when the silence between them led nowhere. "But you can at least tell me where we're going."

"Let it be a secret," he said. And after a pause for reflection, then added: "I'll give you a clue. We change in Landquart."

But she was not playing. Her gaze had returned to the innocent games of the children in the square outside. She did not appear to hear his words, and seemed oddly distracted. Her thoughts elsewhere. He had the impression she was not really interested in where they were going, and he began to wonder again whether she even wanted to make the journey.

On board the train, her mood showed no sign of lifting. Frank watched the rain stream over the window and leave trails of water that obscured the rolling countryside, as if to compete with it as it passed: the trees, the rivers and the tired brownish-yellow pastures waiting for the end of winter. But the countryside won through. And brought a huge sense of relief to Frank as he felt the landscape banish the menacing streets they had left behind. Yet Patricia seemed to see none of these things. Her eyes did not move, or even flicker at the images as they passed. It was as if she was staring at a blank wall. In the reflection of light on the glass, her beautiful dark eyes were suffused with a deep sadness. It plainly stemmed from a private pain that she preferred not to share with him. Her distance troubled him. She might as well have been a stranger, a bewitching apparition caught for an instant in his field of vision as she sped past on the other line. Yet she was here in this compartment, an intimate companion travelling with him to the mountains – and silently weeping into her own mute reflection in the window.

"What's wrong, Pat?" Frank asked, leaning forward to touch her hand. She accepted the gesture without response, and sat like this in perpetual silence. It was not until the train was chuntering out of Zurich, and the steely blue of the lake began to drape its deceptively inviting canvas out beside the track, that she ventured out of her privacy.

"I had some bad news this morning after you left," she said. Frank waited, his hand still on hers, while another prolonged silence passed.

"Léandre's been killed."

Frank recalled the pasty, undernourished individual she had introduced to him in her flat. An unhealthy-looking specimen, but with an air about him that more than made up for his dubious constitution. Frank's suspicions of a liaison between them had seemed unlikely at the time, but he could never completely lay the idea to rest. And now he saw the thrust of these suspicions brutally confirmed in her sorrow. He wanted to express his sympathy. But he found it impossible to let the words cross his lips because – in a way that intensely disturbed him and offended his sense of decency – he was not in the least sorry. Indeed, he even entertained the cynical observation that Léandre looked so close to death when he met him that it could not have taken very much to finish him off.

"How did it happen?" was all he was able to manage.

"How?" Her eyes glistened with inexpressible sadness as she spoke. But she would not give in, and stubbornly refused to let the tears come, as if this might be taken as defeat. "What does it matter how? A man is killed fighting for what he believes in – who cares how it happened? Who damn cares?"

"Where did it happen then?"

"Please, Frank. Don't torment me with your stupid questions. Somewhere in that awful mess they call Spain. Guadalajara, I think. Does it really matter?"

"I'm sorry," he said. Finally an expression of commiseration slipped out, beyond any control on his part. Her words had stung. But more than this, it hurt to see her in such turmoil. He moved across the compartment to sit beside her and put an arm around the circumflex of her shoulder. But the gesture plainly irritated her as much as his questions.

"Please. Just give me a little space," she said, releasing herself from his clumsy efforts at compassion to slide open the door of their compartment and disappear along the corridor of the train. He wanted desperately to go after her. But the rejection had cast a leaden net of hesitation over every iota of sympathy and desire for her.

It was the terror in her cry – faint but still audible over the clatter of the train – that had him on his feet and into the corridor in a single move. He was just in time to see the brutish hand come sweeping down, vanish in the dim corner at the far end of the corridor and provoke a scream of pain in her voice. He knew the hand at once. It belonged to Wolfgang, the henchman of Breitner who had taken such sadistic pleasure in inflicting his depraved obsessions on Frank. He reached into the compartment for the gun in his coat pocket and moved quickly down the corridor as the train lurched to one side. This threw Wolfgang briefly out of view. Then, the moment he stepped back into sight, Frank swung a vicious backhand with the iron butt of his weapon down onto the nape of the gorilla's neck. Horst, his partner in sadistic violence, had Patricia firmly in the ugliness of his fat contemptuous arms. But even before Wolfgang had hit the floor, Frank had the barrel of the gun at Horst's head and eased Patricia from his grip.

"Open the door," Frank growled. He hardly knew his own voice, so distorted was his speech by the tremor of his fury and agitation. But equally new to him was the exquisite pleasure he had in the fear that swam in the eyes of this repellent sadist the moment Horst saw Frank's intention.

"The choice is yours," Frank shouted over the rush of air, as Horst released the catch on the door and let the side wind tear it from his hand. But he hesitated too long on the threshold for his own good. With a sharp boot in the kidneys, Frank helped him on his way. Wolfgang was in no position to offer any more resistance than the dead weight of his body, and with only a little coaxing, he followed his partner without knowing what he had let himself in for.

Closing the door on the pleasures of vengeance proved a tougher proposition than exacting the revenge itself. But when eventually he swung the door to, his elation was complete. And he was unable to suppress a laugh, which bordered on hysteria. Patricia still stood where he had left her, looking beaten, confused and frightened. She had good grounds for sharing in his mirth, but fear had paralysed her every move.

"Come on," he said, putting an arm around her without thinking. "Let's get you back to our compartment and have a look at you."

She accepted his gesture without a word. But he sensed that it was not so much a positive acceptance as the resignation of defeat.

Once in the light of their compartment, he could see that she had been badly beaten about the face. Her left eye was already blue and swollen, as was the embattled line of her bloody upper lip. The trauma lent her face a cruelly misshapen quality that underlined the obtuseness of her beauty. Not certain and not altogether caring whether his attention was appreciated, he touched the bruises lightly with his lips.

"This is a hell of way to start a holiday," he whispered.

The trace of a smile appeared to flicker in the intact parts of her face. But any impression of affection was abruptly censored by her pain. Or perhaps the hint of a smile was simply the flash of light shooting through the trees as they sped past the window. She said nothing.

"What were they doing here anyway? Were they looking for us?" he asked.

"I don't know." Her words came out ravaged and warped by the injury, and made her wince as she spoke.

"Okay, don't say another word."

Frank sat down beside her again, one hand on hers and a comforting arm around her shoulder – more cautiously this time, with the circumspection of a refugee seeking asylum. But she seemed glad to accept the gesture now, and nested herself tenderly in his arms, letting her hair cascade away beneath his coarse unshaven chin. They remained like this, in silence, until they had to change onto a narrow-gauge line up into the mountains.

Patricia sensed the nervous tension when she took Frank's arm as they alighted onto the platform in Landquart to catch the connecting train. Like her, he found it hard to believe the incident with Wolfgang and Horst could have passed unnoticed. Even if he had managed to keep his revenge discreet when he bundled them both off the train – which seemed especially unlikely in the case of Wolfgang, who looked as if he had never known what it meant to be inconspicuous from the moment he was born – it struck him as highly improbable that the two of them would be travelling without Breitner. And if that were the case, then he would be wondering where they were right now.

Since the colourful bruises on Patricia's face would only add to her glaring presence on the station platform, she covered herself as best she could with her scarf and installed herself in a quiet corner of the waiting room. Frank meanwhile made sure their path was clear and went to locate their connecting train to Davos. Although he could see no sign of Breitner, he felt uneasy. He had convinced himself by now that even a first-class train journey would be below the dignity of a man like Breitner; that he would almost certainly get Lutz to drive him wherever he wanted to go in his Maybach Zeppelin. But he could not shake off a sense of being watched. And he could not escape the feeling that, even if Breitner was not on the train, he was travelling. And that they had a common destination.

It was already dark by the time their little red Rhaetian Railways train rolled through the sleepy village of Klosters and on into Davos. Even in the railway station, the air was clean and fresh. And when they walked outside, the bracing Alpine chill invigorated the lungs so agreeably that he could appreciate why doctors all over Europe sent their wealthy tuberculosis patients here. As if to reinforce this liberating sense of vigour that came with the mountain air, he felt a sense of relief to find that Breitner was not among the holiday-makers who poured from the train. This made him feel a little easier about suggesting to Patricia that they walk from the station.

"It's not far," he said, taking her suitcase, "and the cold night air will do the swelling good."

For the first time on their long journey, she managed something that unmistakably passed for a smile.

"It already feels much better," she assured him. "But you still haven't said where you're taking me."

"It's a little place that belongs to a friend of the family. My father's lawyer, actually. After my father died, he said I could have the use of the place whenever I felt in need of a holiday."

It was good to feel the crunch of snow underfoot and the cold air in the lungs. It took him away from the oppressive greyness of the last few weeks around the basin of the Rhine. Put him in mind of the times he used to come on holiday to the Alps with his father, who always maintained it was for Frank's education. But Frank felt his father saw it more as a good opportunity to get away from home whenever he was back on leave. His mother never joined them. The altitude was not good for her circulation, she said. But his father always insisted that the Alps were nothing by comparison with the mountains in Kashmir. So tame, like the difference between a wild tiger and a spoilt hearthside cat, he said. He promised to take Frank with him one day when he was old enough to see for himself. He never did. But the crunching of the snow beneath their feet now as Frank and Patricia walked up the narrow streets at the foot of the Weissfluh mountain recalled these memories of his father, his tales of savage exotic beauty, and filled him with a sense of having been there so real that he began to wonder whether he had. He was transported to another world, just like the dreams Patricia lived so vividly with Bartok.

The chalet stood modestly alone in darkness on the edge of the forest that draped away up the mountainside. The path that had been cleared through the snow to the front door testified to how thoroughly the place was looked after in the absence of its owner.

"Just wait here a minute and look after the suitcases," Frank said, "while I go and fetch the key."

He left her standing beneath a solitary lamp that seemed pathetically inadequate for illuminating the length of the road it had been given to serve. What little light it managed to let out appeared to catch only on the initials of Patricia's name that were emblazoned in brass on her suitcase – and glinted at him through the gloom and darkness.

The man who played janitor to the property, a certain Gaudenz Cavegn, lived in the next house about fifty metres along the road. Although it lay around the corner, just out of view behind a bank of snow, the still mountain air – crystal clear and cushioned against the sounds of habitation by the freshly laid carpet of white – ensured that it remained within comfortable calling distance.

When Frank knocked on the solid wooden door of the house, the noise echoed through the valley with a loneliness that seemed out of place, almost sinister, after the bustle of activity they had just left behind at the station. Only the muffled resonance of an occasional vehicle on the main street below competed for the night air. The resounding effect of his fist on the door made Frank slightly self-conscious when he knocked a second time. But still nothing stirred in the house. It seemed darker and more lifeless even than the forest that ran uncomfortably close to the building. Resigned to the prospect of having to search for a hotel room for the night, which would not be easy on a Friday that was enjoying the influx of next week's holidaymakers, he made his way back to Patricia.

But she was nowhere to be seen. The emptiness of the road where he had left her tore an instant chasm of terror through his heart. The suitcases too had gone. Their absence lent her disappearance an air of finality. The gleaming initials of her name shone now through his memory with a cruel vengeance.

The narrow street lay still and deserted. Like a face with no features. A dumb witness to secrecies it could never betray. Frank stood helplessly in the road not knowing what to do. Or where to look.

'Why had she not called me if she needed help?' he asked himself. 'She knew that I was only round the corner.'

Her absence overwhelmed every fibre in Frank's body. It was not simply the sudden loss of substance to his life, its meaning cruelly erased. Above all, it was knowing what a shaky frame of mind she was in and the kind of turmoil she had suffered these last few hours. He was seized by a panic that told him the only course left open was to run back down to the main street as fast as the snowcovered road would permit, in the vain hope that he might find some evidence, the slightest trace, of her.

As futile as it was stupid. He knew she would not even have been able to carry both suitcases down that steep slippery slope without help. He thought of Breitner.

When he reached the town centre the quiet self-contained activity that he found there mocked his foolishness with its indifference. But the image of her that was embedded now in his memory – her dark fragile form against the snow as she stood waiting for him in the lamplight, bracketed by the suitcases one each side of her – stalked his reluctance to believe that she was gone.

He picked his way slowly back up the road to the chalet that was to have been their heaven for the next two or three weeks. Hoping with the superstition only a madman could entertain that he would find her there just as he had left her, that it had all been a bad dream, he was struck instantly by a new difference that set his pulse racing. The chalet, which had been in darkness before, was now lit up in every window. Frank stopped in his tracks. Dumbstruck by the lights, and by the sinister implications that beamed out over the snow towards him.

A growling male voice rumbled through the darkness as he approached. A voice that was instantly familiar to Frank. It was the voice of Gaudenz Cavegn. He had the strong, compact walk of a man experienced at dealing with the rigours of mountain life. While his voice was unmistakable, the features of his face were lost to the shadows of the night, until he was close enough for the condensation of his breath to take the chill off Frank's face. It was a breath that came with more than a hint of his home-distilled brandy. And the fabric of his clothes infiltrated the air with the essence of pipe smoke. Cavegn blocked his way and scowled. But showed no inclination to acknowledge Frank's presence by either speaking or moving aside.

"Good evening Mr Cavegn. Have you seen a young lady?" Frank asked, as breathless from the tension as from the climb up the hill. "Small and slim, black hair, wearing a navy coat." Then he remembered she had a scarf over her head, but his description held no interest for the man anyway.

"Eigenmann?" he grunted. Then mumbled: "You don't deserve a pretty little girl like that."

The man called Cavegn then stood aside and walked off into the night. It was at that moment that Patricia's voice fetched Frank back from his nightmare.

"Where on earth have you been? Come on up and have a look. It's beautiful."

She was standing on the balcony. The light silhouetted the modest line of her body and invested it with a mature serenity that contradicted her girlish excitement. Her explanations as to how they had managed to miss each other were lost on him, as befitted their unimportance. What tugged most sweetly at his heart was not simply that he had found her, but that she seemed to have found herself again, that thoughts of Léandre appeared to have been banished – bruised and battered, but smiling. She exuded a charm that moved from smoky enigma to girlish effervescence and back again with disturbing ease.

He took her in his arms with the zeal of a missionary holding on to his dream for fear it may evaporate. She winced.

"My ribs took a bit of a beating this afternoon," she explained.

"I'm sorry."

"Don't be silly. I'm the one to say sorry. And thank you," she added. "Yet I've said neither. I've been very selfish, and there's no excuse. Except that I was so upset by the news of Léandre's death. He was such a dear friend. It's hard to believe that I shall never see him again." She paused for a respectful silence that Frank was unable to share. "Have you ever lost anyone very dear to you?"

"I thought I'd lost you just now," he replied. But his words irritated her and did not even elicit the pretence of a smile.

"Don't be flippant, Frank. Please."

"I'm quite serious. I honestly thought something terrible had happened to you."

His words this time must have convinced her, because she ran a hand through his hair in reply with a look so exquisitely tender it radiated to every pulsatile cell of his body. "Why do you think that janitor said I don't deserve such a pretty thing as you?"

"Perhaps it was the charm of my French accent. Or maybe you just intimidated him with that awful German of yours. I expect he thought it was you who beat me."

She laughed at this afterthought. A giggle that played sweetly on his vanity. He held her slenderness just firmly enough to kindle the passion in him and just loosely enough for her to slip away still laughing from him the moment his lips went to caress the bruises on her face.

"So this is what your father's lawyer looks like," she said as she span elusively towards the open wooden staircase.

"What do you mean?"

'Well, he's left enough clues to his inner self. I'll ignore the furnishings, they're the mark of a good Hausfrau; he'd leave decisions like that to her. But the books are definitely his domain, property of the thinking man – Stefan Zweig, current legal issues like corruption in public life by Rudolf Wassermann – awful man, I attended one of his lectures – or *Le cas Gustloff* (he reads French it seems). Gustloff lived here in Davos, you know, when he was assassinated."

Her words called to mind the fraught conversation with Achim in the restaurant where they had met for their reunion.

"Strange, isn't it?" Patricia added. "The Gauleiter for Switzerland living almost shoulder to shoulder with Kirchner, one of your country's most 'degenerate' artists in such neighbourly exile. I wonder if they ever met."

She savoured this thought for a moment before returning to the examination of his father's lawyer.

"A man who obviously takes his job seriously. But then…" she said, taking one of the books from the shelf, "just to show that not all is lost, that he's still a boy at heart, a single volume of Karl May and a copy of *King Solomon's Mines*. It must be that romantic boyish streak that compelled him to buy this place in the mountains, because the rest doesn't fit at all. Just imagine, this whole secret side of him that no one else back home knows about has been carried up to this mountain lodge as a kind of undeclared investment. Come to think of it, as your father's lawyer he's made you an indirect investment partner too, hasn't he?"

At last she paused for breath, became slightly pensive, then asked:

"You've never told me anything about your father. What sort of a man was he?"

"You talk the most wonderful nonsense, Patricia. Do you know Rudolf Wassermann?" Frank asked back, ignoring her question. Once again, he was put in mind of his own boyhood, and he wondered whether this man was any relation to the Wassermann he had known, the bane of Volker's life.

"I just attended a lecture of his once, that's all," she said. "But don't be so evasive. I asked you a question."

"I'm not," he replied, thinking of all the evasions that she lived by, but said nothing. "It's just a name that puts me in mind of someone I was reminded of recently when I returned to the memories of my childhood." And he described the abortive visit to his mother – but above all, the discovery he had made about his father and the mysterious photo from the young woman calling herself Neeti.

"Goodness knows why, but I brought it all back with me for some reason. It intrigued me I suppose. Unfortunately, the book and I have since parted company, but I still have the photo."

He fished it out of his wallet, where they had been left to mature, untouched since leaving Cologne. Patricia seized on it with a ravenous curiosity.

"Everyone seems to have a secret side," Frank said. "Burow, my father – what about your father?"

It was so slight as to be almost imperceptible in her preoccupation with the trophy of his father's past. She showed such composure. So marginal it was almost intuition that alerted him to the agitation sparked by his innocent question. She concealed her disquiet almost effortlessly.

"Burow?" she asked.

"My father's lawyer," he explained. But for once his own curiosity was aroused, and he pressed home the point. "Now who's being evasive?"

For an instant her eyes betrayed a darkness that had nothing to do with the bruising in her face. It unsettled him. Even the seduction she attempted to initiate was unable to dispel his disquiet. It was the only time he had seen her commit such a clumsy subterfuge. Reluctantly, he bowed to her need for this privacy. But although his desire for her swelled with each button of his shirt that she prised open so deliciously with her delicate white fingers, he could not escape his disappointment that she felt unable to confide in him.

Perhaps it was the desire for her that allowed his sense of discretion to overcome this disappointment and defeat his burning curiosity. At all events, he made no further mention of her father, and actively avoided the issue. This was made all the easier for him by the sweet distraction that she offered.

Yet, wherever his mind turned, he was confronted with a scrapbook of the evil that hounded her every move: the contusions on her face, the sorrow in her eyes and – when she slipped off her blouse – the large black bruise just below her left breast. It spread down her body like an outsized shadow, an unkind caricature of her womanhood screaming at him from her delicate marble-white skin. Gently she eased the gracile form of her body back to rest on the bed like a bone china figurine she was putting on display. And his lips touched the blemish on her rib cage as if hoping by this to remove it.

"Ouch."

"I'm sorry." Instantly he retreated, embarrassed by his clumsiness.

"No. It's not your fault," she said, playing a hand through his hair to reassure him. "It just hurt a bit when I moved."

Little more was said that night. They lay in each other's arms, enjoying the intimacy of the moment and contriving at the same time to keep their bodies at a discreet distance from each other for fear of further inflaming the anger of the bruises. Perhaps it was the intensely erotic nature of this precarious balancing act that focused their minds and kept them from wandering into the darker realms of their separate anxieties as they both drifted into a deep sleep. Or perhaps it was apprehension of what they might uncover if they wandered too far.

As the ensuing days unfolded, the latter explanation began to seem ever more likely to Frank. They spent their time together laughing, playing and savouring the closeness of each other's presence. Stubbornly skirting even the most vaguely uncomfortable issue just as carefully as they had avoided touching the bruises. But Patricia's spirit was plainly even more embattled than her body. Her trauma stubbornly refractory to any balm that he could offer. So they lavished their hours on those important trifles that held them together.

The days were spent mostly riding up the Weissfluh and back or crunching their way along snowy paths around Davos. The weather was far from ideal for winter walks. Cloud obscured the heavenly blue skies from view on most days. The air had become a little too warm for comfort. And the greyish light threw a flatness over the snowy landscape that troubled Frank.

This mood of disquiet was underlined by the glaring unseemliness of his own homeland every time they walked through the village and back up to their chalet. He had not realised when he spent holidays in Davos as a young boy just how much it had been colonised by his compatriots in search of healthy mountain air. Wandering now past the sanatoriums and the Fridericianum, the elite school for Germany's wealthy children and now no doubt the offspring of high-ranking party members, he wondered what Thomas Mann might make of it all today. But it seemed unlikely to Frank that he would be inclined to pay a visit to this German colony anyway. Not only were the elders of Davos less than amused by his depiction of sanatorium life in The Magic Mountain. But it was barely a year since he was stripped of his citizenship, and the palpable influence that his native country clearly had on almost every corner of the town would be more than enough reason to avoid the place: even some of the buildings were decorated with the hateful flags and symbols so ubiquitous north of the border. Frank could have kicked himself for bringing Patricia to this expat hotbed of Nazism.

His efforts to distract her by taking to the slopes and introducing her to the delights of skiing proved to no avail. The bruising of her ribs was still too fresh to cope with the unaccustomed twists and turns. So they committed themselves to gentle Alpine strolls by day. And by night they sat reading to each other beside the open log fire.

"Have you read Rilke's *Duino Elegies*?" he asked. "I have a copy with me."

"Oh, please don't. I'd much rather try Karl May. I've heard so much about him. But girls don't get to read that kind of literature."

The surprised excitement on Frank's face quickly gave way to a questioning smile.

"There's no need to give me such a condescending look," Patricia said, flashing an angry smile at him in return.

"I'm just surprised. That's all," Frank insisted.

And so he led her into the world of boys' adventure with one of Karl May's Wild West tales of Old Shatterhand. Then followed this with Henry Rider Haggard's yarns from Africa. All courtesy of Burow. But he found little enthusiasm for this escapism.

"You know, this kind of stuff puts me in mind of the human zoos they used to stage," he said when he reached the end of the Rider Haggard yarn. "Bringing people from Africa and putting them on show for people's entertainment. They still do it in some places. There was one at Basel zoo a year or two ago."

"I've heard about them," Patricia replied. "They sound quite disgusting."

"Believe me, they are. My mother took me to one in Freiburg when I was a kid. She was fascinated."

The distaste voiced in the delivery of Frank's words matched the revulsion in his eyes.

How much sweeter he found it listening to Patricia as she recited from Baudelaire with her enchanting lilt, which transported him at once to the smoke-filled cafes of Montmartre. He looked out for every sign of emotion in her eyes as she recited from *Les fleurs du mal.* Watched every beguiling movement of her sweet lips as she spoke, listening all the while for them to whisper the cryptic words about her great swan, with his crazy gestures. But the words of that poem never came. And their absence made them all the more enigmatic to Frank.

For the best part of two weeks, they remained encapsulated in this cocoon. Every so often, she would lapse into her own dark, impenetrable reflections, bringing to the surface the prurience she had encouraged in him for the affairs and secrets of others. And he would contemplate the possible reasons she might have for avoiding that particular poem. Was it too painful for her, he wondered. Did it have something to do with the mysterious Léandre, who had died in Spain?

But the honeymoon was too sweet and too precious to be sacrificed to any unkind histories that may have been lurking in the shadows they had left behind. And far too brittle. So, with the dedication that might be expected of a restorer attempting to preserve the beauty of an Old Master from the

Early Renaissance, they handled every moment with devotional care, working silently to keep the bonds intact.

Between days, tucked into the narrow warmth of their bedclothes, a special kind of circumspection was called for. They were encouraged in this by the cold, verecund board down the middle of the bed that was so typical of bedsteads in the German-speaking world – built to keep its occupants apart. But the makers had not reckoned on the slenderness of Patricia. And defiantly they slotted together in their snug rapture, flesh upon flesh, her breasts exquisitely modest against his clumsily worn body, and her eyes more beautiful each night as the bruising became friendlier and lent a new sensuality to their expression.

It must have been about two weeks after arriving in Davos when this idyllic veneer finally cracked, when even his most tenacious efforts to avoid the arrogant backslapping SS types that filled the pavements and restaurants fell miserably short. Frank and Patricia were strolling through the village towards the Parsenn station after lunch, having avoided the rush of skiers on their way to the mountain top. The streets appeared to be enjoying the peace. It was still a little overcast and slightly chillier than usual for the time of day. Patricia walked closer to him that afternoon, one arm wrapped snugly around his – whether she was feeling more affectionate or simply colder, he was unsure.

He enjoyed the closeness, but at the same time it troubled him the way the tightening of her grip on his arm coincided with the sound of a brass band striking up somewhere out of sight. The significance of the music was not immediately obvious. It was only when Patricia's grip on his arm grew tighter still that its familiarity became plain to him. But no sooner had he registered the swagger of his country's national anthem than this celebration of arrogance gave way to the even more sinister theme of the hymn to Horst Wessel.

The overbearing presumption of this insult on the tranquil hospitality that had been theirs for the last two weeks filled him with a sense of nausea. And Patricia plainly more so. But his feelings at once came into conflict with a morbid curiosity. And when she steered him away from the noise, he resisted.

"Come on," she pleaded. "We don't want to have anything to do with that."

"It was you who encouraged me to be inquisitive," he observed. So, against Patricia's better judgement, they moved in the direction of the arrogance that masqueraded as music. If only he had respected her wishes.

The scene that greeted them when they turned the corner into the square was already enough to sicken the heart: banners flying their emblems of evil were held erect like ugly pylons in the snow by mostly young, earnest-faced men, some in the shameless colours of party uniform and others in civvies so normal they chafed at the credulous innocence that still clung stubbornly to the more comfortable corners of Frank's spirit. Grouped around them stood a group of men in long black coats conveying the impression of sinister intent – like carrion crows gathered around in the hope there might be some pickings on offer. The scene put Frank in mind of his mother's nurse and her vivid description of the thugs who killed her dog.

But the band, the flag-bearers and the crows were not alone. They were simply the more conspicuous extras among a gathering he found disturbingly respectable in appearance: a few women, who were dressed up in their expensive furs, but mostly men fumigating the area with their thick cigar smoke. They were all absorbing a message from the mean pinched mouth of a man so strikingly ordinary that Frank wondered what it could be that made this man so presumptuous as to believe he had anything worth saying to so many people. His words were nothing less than a diatribe of hatred. A ranting paranoid indictment of some international conspiracy against men like Wilhelm Gustloff, who died in the service of his people. A heroic champion of the Third Reich cut down by the vicious craven rat of a decadent community. The word 'Jewish' did not cross his lips. It did not need to. Everyone knew what he meant. And nodded wisely in agreement.

"Please, Frank. Let's go. I can't stand this any longer."

Patricia's appeal betrayed a pitch of anxiety he had never heard in her voice before. And he could not listen to it any more than she could stand the hate-filled ravings of his fellow countrymen.

It was just as they turned to go that Frank saw an all too familiar figure standing in the crowd. The features were partly hidden under a large felt hat. But the supercilious expression of his thin lips was unmistakable. And for an instant, just sufficient for the animosity to register, their eyes met. Hoping that Patricia had not seen him, Frank guided her into the nearest side street.

"I'm sorry," he said, surprising himself by his composure. "The assassination of Gustloff is not an event that figures in my calendar. If I'd known it was just a year ago, so close to where we're standing now, I wouldn't have brought you here this week."

As he looked back, he saw Breitner detach himself from the crowd of onlookers, move around behind them with his characteristic swagger, cigar in mouth, and follow them into the side street. At the next junction, Frank manoeuvred Patricia to the right and, finding a tea-room round the corner, persuaded her that some refreshment would do them both good.

As a refuge, it proved a curious place. It sorely needed a coat of paint. And the aroma of cheap cigars hung in the air. But this was thankfully overpowered by the sweeter fragrance of pastries and chocolates displayed at the counter. They sat down and ordered two cups of coffee.

"Please forgive me," Frank said. "I hadn't realised how deeply colonised this part of Switzerland has become by my fellow countrymen. And it certainly never occurred to me that we'd face Nazi marches and demonstrations in Davos. Such a far cry from the sanatorium atmosphere of *The Magic Mountain*."

"Don't be too sure about that. Their death cult is just the kind of self-destructive urge explored by Thomas Mann. Especially in the tedious *Tristan* theme he obsesses about in so many of his novels."

Patricia's melancholy words brought to mind the story she had told him of her school days, when she played Isolde to the Tristan she had been so madly in love with. They hinted at the never-ending sense of bereavement that appeared to pursue her. And he desperately searched for the right words of comfort. A hopeless venture.

As the elderly, sour-faced waitress placed the coffee on the table, Patricia's gasp startled Frank even more than the voice that snaked its way around the waitress and almost caused her to spill the coffee.

"Good morning, Patricia. Mr Eigenmann. What a pleasant surprise. May I?"

Without waiting for an answer, Breitner planted himself between them at the side of the table. Despite his arrogance and self-assured swagger, he struck Frank as more vulnerable than he remembered the man from their first encounter. Perhaps it was the way he kept his hat on in the tea-room, as if he had something to hide. Or perhaps it was the pastiness of winter that he needed to shake off. Or maybe it was simply an impression engendered in Frank by the feel of the gun that still sat faithfully in his pocket.

"I've been looking for you," he said, directing his attention at Patricia. Then, turning his cold lupine eyes towards Frank, he added: "I've been looking for both of you."

"I'm sure you didn't come all this way in search of us," Frank replied.

"Just one of life's happy coincidences that you should also be here paying tribute to our fallen hero," he said with a sarcastic smile. And savoured the idea with a supercilious smirk on his lips as the elderly waitress, who looked as though she had not set foot outside her tea-room for the last twenty years, remained standing silently between Breitner and Patricia. Waiting. Patricia spent the whole time looking down at the table like a schoolgirl who had been caught in a compromising situation and did not seem to notice her. But Breitner was plainly irritated by the woman.

"All right, bring me some Black Forest gateau," he grunted, when he realised at last that she would be satisfied with nothing less than an order.

"We only have carrot cake," she replied, wrapping her words in a slow, deliberate enunciation of every syllable that did nothing to conceal her impatience.

"Good. Bring me some carrot cake, then," Breitner said with a nauseous look on his lips. "And make it sharp."

The old lady endeared herself to Frank by defiantly refusing to show any respect for his arrogant posturing, and she shuffled back to the counter more slowly than ever.

"I can't stand the cretinous way they address you in this country. They don't talk to each other like that. Why do they talk to me like it?"

He chose to ignore the smile on Frank's face and turned a cold dismissive stare on him to underline his complete indifference to any opinion Frank might have of him.

"One way or another, Eigenmann, you cause me a lot of trouble. And you've still not found Lola for me," he added, piercing Frank with his cold steely stare.

"If you're not collaborating with the communists, you're interfering in my private affairs." He looked at Patricia. Her eyes remained firmly on the cup in front of her. But Breitner was determined to demonstrate his dominance. He reached out a hand and lifted up her face to examine the trace of bruising that still showed around her left eye.

"Then look what happens," he said, letting her head drop and looking back at Frank. "And if you're not pestering Mademoiselle Roche, you're molesting my people."

"You mean Wolfgang and Horst? I trust they made it home safely?" Frank said.

"Horst unluckily struck a telegraph pole as he fell. I'm told that death was instantaneous. Wolfgang was more fortunate, probably because he was unconscious when he left the train. He's still recovering in hospital, but I shall be seeing him on my way back. I'll give him your regards."

"And you can tell him that the bruises he inflicted on Miss Roche are also healing nicely."

Breitner's expression turned stone-cold with contempt as he watched the old lady put the carrot cake on the table in front of him. He studied it in silence, as if wondering what he should do with it. But his thoughts were plainly on more sinister plans.

"It would be amusing to have you put away, Eigenmann." His mouth twisted with malice. "Manslaughter is the very least we could get you on. And we might even stretch to murder."

"You would get nowhere without witnesses," Frank observed with a naivety that embarrassed even him as the words came out.

"I have Wolfgang," he said. "And I have Mademoiselle Roche – a witness of impeccable character."

Patricia looked up for the first time since Breitner walked in. Panic filled her eyes. It was a look that told Frank she had an understanding of the man so intimate it gouged a deep furrow through his heart and deposited its heavy waste in the pit of his stomach. A look that told him her tormentor was no longer playing. He was deadly serious.

"You said yourself that Wolfgang was unconscious, so he can testify to nothing. As for Miss Roche," he added hopefully, "I cannot imagine she would have any interest in becoming your witness for the prosecution."

"Don't be so sure, Eigenmann." His confidence unnerved Frank, much to Breitner's enjoyment. "Patricia," he added, "I think it's time for us to go."

She said nothing. Her eyes were still frozen with panic. But Frank could see from the stirring motion of her body that she was ready to go with her tormentor. Disbelief and feverish confusion seized hold of him.

'What's she playing at?' he asked himself. He had to stop her. Decisions forced themselves on him with a crazed logic that had him act more quickly than his disabled brain was able to follow. With one hand securely on the gun in his pocket, he took the key to Burow's chalet from the other pocket and laid it firmly on the table in front of Patricia.

"Go home, Patricia, and wait for me there. You don't have to go anywhere with this rat."

To Frank's dismay, she did not instantly reach for the key, but looked at him with a desperate appeal in her eyes. And hesitated.

"I think you'll find, Eigenmann, that she would prefer to go with me."

And she reinforced Breitner's smug assumption: "Please, Frank. Don't make a scene. I know what I'm doing."

The blood in Frank's veins ran hot with an acrid bitterness that set his head spinning. His thoughts raced around in fragmented confusion. But the largest fragment stuck, an embolism of hatred that knew only one remedy. He took the gun from his pocket and laid it on the table concealed under his arm to all but Breitner.

"Take the key Patricia, and go back to the chalet," he insisted, his gaze fixed on Breitner.

"Look before you leap, Eigenmann. I have a lot of friends here."

Patricia too lent her support to his arrogance: "Let me go with him, Frank. Please. You don't know what you're doing."

But they had long since passed the point where Frank could listen to her appeals. His mind was locked on Breitner.

"Then your friends will enjoy the opportunity of paying tribute to another hero," Frank said, picking up the key and thrusting it across the table into Patricia's hand.

"Could I have the bill, please?" Frank called over to the counter and saw Breitner making ready to leave. Frank put a restraining hand on his arm.

"We wait. She goes first."

Frank returned the gun to his pocket and, as the old lady shuffled over with the bill, Patricia got up to leave. A peculiar petulance on her lips, but fear still in her eyes.

"You didn't like the carrot cake." The old lady's half-questioning observation lay somewhere between rebuke and disbelief. And it brought a sick expression to Breitner's face that was not lost even on her failing eyes. Only its significance escaped her.

"Well, the world would be a sorry place if we always had what we wanted," she mumbled, and took the ten franc note Frank offered her.

"Keep the change," he said in cheery tone.

She was an unlikely ally, this crotchety old woman with her folk wisdom. And Frank appreciated her commitment, however unsuspecting it was. He gave her a conspiratorial smile as she turned to shuffle her way back to the counter, her duty reluctantly done. But she wanted no part of an alliance with any foreigner, and she scowled at his smile with contempt.

"Go back to the chalet and just wait there," Frank insisted as Patricia sidled uncertainly towards the door.

"You're making a big mistake, Eigenmann," Breitner growled. But the more he tried to throw his weight around, the firmer the ground became for Frank's blind obsession, which matured with every second that he kept his gaze on Breitner's visible discomfort.

He enjoyed watching the layer of smug self-assurance peeling off. The lupine eyes that earlier had flashed a cold detached indifference now shifting. Nervous and vulnerable.

"Let's take a walk," Frank said, and reinforced the image of vulnerability by lifting Breitner from his seat with a supporting arm and leading him out of the tea room.

"*Auf Wiederluege*," said the old lady. Frank's unwitting ally was plainly not sorry to see them go. And he was no less sorry to leave the air of chocolate and cheap cigars.

"*Auf Wiedersehen*," he replied without conviction. In his relief to breathe the fresh mountain air again as he stepped out behind Breitner, he overlooked the atmosphere of sneering arrogance that he and Patricia had left behind them when they entered the tea-room. But it was still there in the street, in the speeches that continued to presume their self-celebration on to an Alpine village that was too comfortable with the ways of nature to put up any kind of resistance beyond the crotchetiness of the old lady in the tea room.

Frank nudged his hostage in the direction of the Parsenn station. When they turned the corner, Frank saw two young men approaching. Breitner quickened his pace slightly, opening up some space from Frank, as they drew closer. The men wore the uniform of what he knew at once to be Germany's so-called youth sports group. They swaggered down the street looking for all the world as if they thought the emblems of hatred they were dressed up in invested them with authority over every inch of the world. Frank's watchful eye could not escape the movement of Breitner's shoulders expanding with a new confidence as they came closer. He quickly closed the gap and pushed the barrel of the gun into the small of Breitner's back. Frank sensed him stiffen.

"Not a word," Frank grunted.

The two men appeared to recognise his captive. They invoked their leader's name as they passed – "Heil Hitler" – and their arms shot out like serpents' tongues – threatening, sinister and at the same time rather ludicrous in their forage caps. He saw that one of the men bore a scar on the side of his face that had a cold deliberate look about it, suggesting it had been self-inflicted, as if deliberately to underline his menace.

Breitner made no response. It took another prod in the back to prompt any kind of reply. But his half-hearted effort brought questioning looks in their direction. Frank was a stranger to them, so his evident influence over Breitner aroused their curiosity. And when Frank glanced back, he saw the two men had stopped to watch their conspicuous walk to the Parsenn station. His looking round was plainly the signal they had been waiting for. As soon as his head turned, they exchanged a few words, then moved suspiciously in Frank's direction. They stayed on Frank's tracks all the way to the station and stood in the doorway watching as he bought two return tickets up the mountain.

"Going to the top, Mr Breitner?" the one with the scar called out. "It looks a bit too cloudy up there for my taste. And it'll be getting dark soon."

Breitner said nothing. His submissiveness irritated Frank. It seemed to him a consciously exaggerated effort to arouse their suspicions. The two men watched expectantly, waiting for a reply. His silence would be a signal to intervene, and this was plainly what he was counting on. He had to say something.

"We just need the fresh air," Frank called back. "We're not going for the view. Come on, Willi. We'll miss the train," he added, ushering Breitner out of the foyer and onto the platform of the funicular railway with a hasty "*Auf Wiedersehen*" to the two watchdogs as they vanished from view. The pretence of intimacy suggested by his use of Breitner's first name went so hard against the grain that it almost wedged against Frank's tongue before he got it out. But it gave him the short gap in their mistrust that he was looking for. And the train was heading out of the station before the two youth sports thugs could do much about it.

"I told you I have a lot of friends here," Breitner said smugly, preening himself on his sense of position and authority, as the train pulled them up from the station and out onto the mountainside. It was Frank's turn to say nothing. The train was otherwise empty. They were alone. Whatever Breitner might think about his position, Frank was the one with the instrument of authority in his pocket. He could relax, and let his nerves do the talking.

"I don't know what you have in mind, Eigenmann, but I have an appointment this evening in the Davoserhof. If I'm not there, my friends will get worried. And they'll come looking for you." He fixed Frank with his cold stare, and added with dark emphasis: "Davos is a very small place."

He maintained a cool exterior, but Frank could not escape the jittery, agitated edge to his words. He was used to cracking the whip. And to watch him now without the whip in his hand was like witnessing the desperate fidgets of an alcoholic in search of his next gin. Frank enjoyed every minute of the spectacle. Nonetheless, those words had managed to chip away at the self-confidence that had been sired by his blind rage. And now that this rage had given way to a certain clarity of mind, doubts began to grow in the cracks.

The chill that pricked at his face as they left the station and walked out onto the mountain did nothing to dispel the doubts. But he had taken on a mission, and he had to see it through. The last train down left just after four according to the sign at the exit. That gave him three quarters of an hour. He nudged Breitner out onto the snow, and they took the path towards the Strelapass.

Despite what the scarfaced watchdog had said, the cloud cover was quite thin, and the limpid light over the sheer expanse of snow made the air almost sparkle with clearness. The few remaining skiers of the day were beginning to make their way down. Frank was put in mind of the long walks he had taken here with Patricia these last few days. How different his circumstances were now.

Frank watched him trying to negotiate the slippery path in his smart city shoes. He was not dressed for mountain walking. Frank had the advantage over him in every respect. And he meant to keep it that way. This was emphatically not the time to expose his weaknesses. Breitner had to know that he was in the mood for vengeance.

"Breitner," he called after him, his hand as firm as ever on the gun, "There's something I've been meaning to ask you."

Breitner stopped, and turned uneasily on the icy surface, but said nothing. Just waited.

"Whatever happened to Achim Zimmermann?"

"Your friend?" A thin contemptuous smile twisted its way across Breitner's lips. "He was a fool."

"What do you mean 'was'?" Frank repeated.

Breitner's smile thickened.

"I really should be grateful to you, Eigenmann."

The puzzled expression on Frank's face was not necessary. Breitner was going to elaborate anyway.

"For putting me onto Zimmermann. We might never have known about his little games if you had not made such a spectacle of yourself with your clumsy advances towards Mademoiselle Roche."

Frank recalled that stupid evening in the wine tavern waiting in vain for Patricia. His first encounter with Lutz.

"Weak, so weak," he heard Breitner say, and the man's expression widened with a look almost of sympathy. "What a man will sacrifice for a woman. One might almost think you had gypsy blood in you." He peered narrowly at Frank as if to test the truth of this hypothesis. It was plainly intended to be a defiant show of contempt. Frank ignored it.

"And his family?" The horrific scene flashed for an instant through his mind as he spoke these words. "What did they ever do to you?"

Breitner's eyes snaked their way through the light reflected off the snow. Colder than ever. "I've never met his family." He spoke with a slow deliberation which seemed to be saying that, for once in his life, he was telling the truth and he wanted Frank to know it. Then he turned his back on him to continue his slippery progress down the mountainside. For a good few minutes, Frank watched him from behind as he followed in his tracks, the images of Gertrude and her two baby boys flashing a collage of carnage across the landscape of white light.

They were completely alone now, and there was something pathetic about the sight of that arrogant bully sliding awkwardly over the vast expanse of snow. A solitary figure with the bearing of an injured animal. Now was the time to put the beast out of its misery. There was no going back.

"Breitner," Frank called.

Again Breitner stopped, and turned on the side of the path in time to see the gun emerge from Frank's pocket. The smile never left his lips. Frank moved closer to enjoy the fear in his lupine eyes. But there was none. They remained colder than the ice that chiselled away the rocks around them. And they glared at Frank with stony disdain.

"Put that thing away, Eigenmann. You're not going to shoot anyone. You haven't got the stomach for it. People like you have too much respect for human life." His voice lingered on these last two words, and turned about on them like a thick boot stubbing out a cigarette butt in the gutter.

He was right, of course. But for all the wrong reasons.

"Trouble is, Breitner, you're not human. You're not even alive."

As if to test the truth of these words, Frank dug the barrel of the gun into his ribs. Deep. Breitner winced. And instantly lost his balance in the snow. His smooth city shoes carried his feet from under him with exquisite treachery. A hand grabbed at Frank's sleeve as he fell. But he was already out of reach, so fast was his ungainly body gathering speed as it dropped and slithered down the slope. A helpless bundle plunging into insignificance. With growing satisfaction, Frank watched him dwindle away into the distance until the dark heap came to rest a good hundred metres or so below him.

The chill of the breeze off the mountainside nipped at Frank's face and reminded him that daylight was beginning to fade. But he felt comfortable in his sudden solitude – which was probably more than Breitner could claim as he staggered shaken and uncertain to his feet. Frank left him to his predicament and made his way back to the station before he too missed the last train down.

Yet, as he sat alone in the top compartment of the funicular, the comfort quickly began to show cracks where Breitner's words still echoed through his mind. What did he mean about the spectacle of his advances towards Patricia? And what was the connection with Achim? He recalled that clumsy evening, the image of Lutz raising his glass to him as he left the bar, the clinging sense of menace that pursued him through the streets, the rustling leaves, the suspect shadows. He was convinced at the time that someone had been following him. So was it really he who had been so stupid and unwitting to lead Breitner to his old friend?

The severe rock face slipped away from him with a scowl on its icy black countenance, as if reminding him that he did not deserve even the tiniest comfort which its heartless austerity could offer.

'And I have the gall to ride in luxury,' he told himself.

Quietly, the train sank down the mountainside and dragged him with it into the pit of his own dull conscience. Into the terrors of his memory. Gertrude, her boys, and the squealing rats that crawled over their decomposing bodies.

'Oh Achim, my dear old friend. How could you ever forgive me?' he asked himself. 'It was not you who betrayed our friendship. I was the traitor from the outset. And your family the defiled victim, sacrificed by my dumb stupidity.'

When the train eventually jolted to a halt, Frank stumbled out like a scatterbrained imbecile waking from a troubled sleep. What he had not anticipated was the devoted vigil of the two watchdogs. They had plainly been waiting for him to return with Breitner. And these attack dogs now barred Frank's way when he emerged from the station alone.

Chapter 22

The two sports youth louts filled the width of the pavement with their overweening presence. They said nothing. But Frank was in no mood to play their boy-scout games. He was tired. And desperate to see Patricia.

"Your friend took it into his head to come down on foot. He just wouldn't listen to reason."

Frank showed them the cold iron barrel of the gun, inched closer to the one on the outside of the pavement and thrust it into his nose.

"Don't get the wrong idea. Just take a sniff of this. Not been used, has it?" He paused, savouring the young man's discomfort. "Not yet."

He left them standing there, looking impotent and just a little self-conscious, and hurried back to the chalet. They made no attempt to follow him.

Although evening had already set in by the time he got back, the chalet was in darkness. It gave the impression of being empty. The dense black cover of the trees seemed to have edged much closer to the building than he remembered it from their first night there. It had the effect of drawing in the night even earlier, even colder, around their refuge. To his surprise, the door was open. He called Patricia's name, but the house remained quiet and unresponsive. His mind clouded over, seized by a sensation that lay somewhere between panic and profound sadness. The pounding of his heart was almost audible. Not until he went into the bedroom did he find her, face down on top of the bed, fully clothed, motionless. Only the shadows cast by the light from the landing gave any clue to the subtle rhythm of her body as it followed the mechanics of her shallow breathing.

With a sense of relief, he lowered himself gingerly onto the bed beside her. She stirred at this movement and curled up like a snail retracting into its shell. He watched her as she slept. Her hair draped in the shadows on the bed like a curtain, blacker than the night, over her dreams. The dismay and dread that appeared to haunt every corner of her waking hours was in such stark contrast to this shell of peaceful innocence. This helix of unspoken beauty. The quiet concentration with which he watched over her made the shock all the greater when, without warning, his presence startled Patricia from her sleep.

"Frank! You're back!"

He said nothing, just ran his fingers through her hair.

"Frank!" There was panic in her voice, as she reached out for the light switch. In the sudden glow of the bedside light, he could see that she had cried herself to sleep. Her eyes had the look of raw meat that had been washed clean. "What have you done, Frank? Where's the gun?"

He took it from his pocket and laid it on the bed between them. A dark destiny still untested. A look of horror filled the washed-out spaces in her expression.

"You haven't?" She stared in disbelief.

"No. He literally slipped away before I had a chance."

Frank smiled to himself at the memory as he reassured her, taking her hands in his, and explained how Breitner had unwittingly escaped his clutches.

"When it came to it, I suppose I lost my nerve. However monstrous he is, I couldn't just gun him down in cold blood." He felt her hands tense in his. "I imagine he's still picking his way down the mountainside in his smart leather-soled shoes at this very moment."

"You're a fool, Frank." She flung his hands back at him in disappointment. Or maybe contempt. And she began to pace the floor. Her fragile vulnerability had turned to outright fear.

"Once you've got someone like Breitner on the hook, you don't just throw him back in the water. Oh, Frank, you're such a fool."

"You were the one who warned me off. What was I supposed to do?"

"Finish it. You should have finished it. Once and for all. Finished it."

There was a venom in her voice that shocked him as she hurled the words at him like balls at a coconut shy and continued to pace the room. Her eyes sparked again with life. But Frank felt the obsessive quality of her words open up a disturbing distance between them. He had never seen her like this before. It was at odds with everything he knew about her. And it kindled a new fascination.

"I'll make some coffee," he said with a naive desire to please. But she caught his arm as he tried to leave the room.

"There's no time for coffee. We need to pack and get out of here before he finds his way back."

"What's the hurry? He doesn't even know where to start looking for us."

"Davos is a very small place." Her words were not only identical to those Breitner had used on him earlier. Even the way she spoke them was the same. They carried an edge that threatened to widen the distance between them further. "And you saw yourself that he has a lot of friends here," she added.

The new side to her that she revealed that evening made him slightly uneasy in her company, like a new acquaintance with so much ground for him to make up. And so little time to do it. It created a self-conscious urgency. A sense of gaps to be closed. But he recalled the two faithful watchdogs at the Parsenn station. And had to admit she was almost certainly right.

The next train out of Davos was heading for Filisur. Once they were on it and heading out of the station, they both relaxed and settled back into a kind of harmony that, while still a little edgy, had sufficient substance to let them laugh together at the day's events: Breitner throwing his weight around over a slice of carrot cake in a shabby tea-room; the thought of him sliding his way down the mountainside in the dark; or the ludicrously earnest gathering to honour one of the most forgettable figures in a chaotic nation's history.

"I'm sorry, Patricia. If I'd known, I wouldn't have brought you to Davos."

"You should have told me what your plans were," she said and rested a forgiving hand on his arm. "But it's my fault too. I remember him mentioning that he would attend the event. He wanted me to come with him." She stopped herself, but too late. She had already said too much and withdrew momentarily into a dark, impenetrable silence reflected in the blackness of the night, which sped past them unannounced behind the carriage window.

Frank was desperate to pursue her thoughts. But although she had taught him the art of curiosity, he still shied away from indiscretion. And she was more than eager to gloss over her own lapse and led them quickly onto a safer track. She rested a seductive hand on his and caressed his hapless desire for her with the obtusely captivating smile of her embattled lips and bewitching ebony eyes.

"Frank, I can't go home now. Let's stop off somewhere else. Just for a few days at least. Please," she implored. She knew instinctively how to fill him with boundless warmth whenever she wanted to.

"How about St Moritz?" he suggested, handing her the newspaper he had bought at the station. "It says here that Winston Churchill is due to arrive there shortly for his winter break. After the nest of vipers in Davos, perhaps you'd feel safer in the proximity of a man of his stature."

"You don't have to make fun."

"Actually, Pat, I'm quite serious. If you really want to go somewhere else for a few days, I can't think of a better place. But I shall have to go to the bank tomorrow."

"I wish you wouldn't call me Pat."

"I'm sorry. When I was in England, many people used it as a term of endearment. They call their cats and dogs 'pets', just like you call me squirrel in your dafter moments," he teased her, before adding a sting in the tail: "What do your other lovers usually call you?"

"Only a German could fail to notice any distinction in pronunciation between 'pat' and 'pet'," she said with a look of dismissive scorn. Then added:

"Do you think they allow pets in the hotels of St Moritz?"

She had chosen to ignore his last question. And he was glad of this. Even if it did come with a crushing put-down, it at least indicated that she had approved his suggestion.

They were fortunate that the last connection for St Moritz had not yet left by the time they reached Filisur, so it was still a respectable nine o'clock when their little red train pulled them into their last resort in the upper reaches of Engadin. Frank had already telephoned the Suvretta House from Filisur and managed to book a room.

"We shall have to take a taxi," he explained. "It's a little way out of town. But at least we shall be safely isolated from the Breitners of this world."

She rested her head on his shoulder as the taxi swept them over the snow up the hill to their hotel. Although she was exhausted, the look in her eyes remained stubbornly alert. Frank could sense the trouble turning in her mind as he caressed her lips and the deep seductive furrow of her philtrum with his thumb.

"I've been told the more pronounced it is, the bigger the heart," he whispered, "and those who have not been touched at all by your angel Lailah are completely heartless. Do you think that's why Mr Hitler wears that ridiculous moustache? To conceal the absence of any soul?"

Patricia sat silently enjoying the caress of his fingers on her lips. But her mind was elsewhere.

"Can you imagine anyone wanting to bring children into the world?" she asked.

Frank was startled by the digression. For some reason, he had never imagined she would entertain such ideas, even from the remotest of theoretical viewpoints. She had always seemed to him to be above the untidy biological dimensions of life. It was one of the many qualities he liked about her. So he was glad the taxi was already pulling into the driveway of the hotel before the commitment of an answer could be expected of him. But her question stayed with him like a thorn, pricking him every time he touched it. Yet teasing, and inviting his vanity to play with its implications.

Patricia had taught him sufficient curiosity to want to return to the subject once their luggage had been delivered to their room and they were left alone for the night. But perhaps he was too fearful of where the conversation might lead. After the day's untoward surprises and unplanned travel, he was too tired for any kind of serious conversation anyway. So they both sank into their private worlds, side by side in bed, without exchanging more than a few words. Only touching.

When it was he woke, he could not say, but it was still dark. Nor was he certain what it was that woke him – whether it was the unseen hand of his conscience or the communication between their tangent bodies. But even in his stupor, he was instantly aware that Patricia too was awake. He sensed her staring into space. Trying to lose herself in the darkness that surrounded them.

"Patricia," he whispered. "Are you awake?"

But night remained possessive of her thoughts. Not a peep filtered through the grasping darkness, until he felt driven to switch on the bedside light.

"Uhh! What are you doing?" She blinked violently and hid her face under the sheets. "Please!"

She said nothing more. Frank switched off the light again. And waited. It was the faint tremor of her weeping body that eventually shook the night into some kind of action. He took her in his arms. Her head on his shoulder. The soft flesh of her breasts caressing his belly as she breathed. And her tears trickling onto his chest. Not a sound passed her lips. He could only offer her closeness and warmth. He felt powerless to help. And sensed that she felt the same.

How much of the night passed over them in this impotent embrace it was hard for him to tell, as sleep kept trying to drag him off in other directions – until her words finally pulled him out onto the cold ledge of consciousness.

"It's hopeless, Frank," was all she said. But it was enough.

"What?"

"Everything," she replied. And the waiting game continued, until she added: "We'll never shake off Breitner. As soon as we get back, he'll be there."

But Frank had the impression this was not all she wanted to say, that something else was eating away at her heart.

"We don't have to go back," he suggested.

"I do."

The ominous reflex of her response urged him to try the light again. He had to see her expression, the story in her eyes. But he held back. He feared the exposure would prompt her to pull the blanket of silence over her again.

"I have to return, Frank." Her voice betrayed a flutter of agitation.

The night seemed ready to snap with the tension, as she lapsed into a hesitant pause – and prepared for the leap.

"I told you about my father, that he's Jewish. And Breitner's threats if I didn't toe the line."

"Is that what you call it nowadays?"

His flippant question gagged her for a moment. He could sense her struggling, attempting to maintain her balance on the sheer, unlit face of her confession. And he instantly regretted the callous archness of his words.

But her burden was already too heavy to carry, and she ignored the mean stupidity he threw at her.

"I love my father dearly. He's so kind and understanding, always has a smile on his face, nothing's ever too much trouble. He can be a bit stern sometimes when he feels he has to be, but he wouldn't be a good father if he didn't, would he?"

Frank sensed her head turn lightly on his shoulder, as if looking up for confirmation.

"And I'm so grateful that he sent me here to study. I might never have discovered such treasure..." – Frank interrupted her with a gentle kiss to her brow in vain anticipation of her next words and was instantly deflated by the folly of his conceit when she ignored his gesture – "I knew little about the jewels of Swiss art before I came here. People like Anker and Böcklin. Or Segantini. Although he's not strictly Swiss; he was actually stateless. A little like me in a way."

Patricia paused for a moment at this last thought and let the darkness speak for her. Then added:

"But my father can be ridiculously sentimental – like that business with the Chateau Haut-Brion. And of course I adore him. I'd do anything for him."

Despair filled the space left by these last words as she paused again. Frank could almost hear her fighting to keep it at bay while she gathered her thoughts.

"You remember I said that Breitner promised me protection for my father in exchange for..."

"... certain favours," Frank added with sarcastic emphasis on the last word to complete her sentence for her. He was still unable to let his foolish jealousy rest. But she skirted around the clumsy bait.

"I was with my father in Stuttgart recently," she continued. "The first time I'd seen him for more than a year. You can't imagine how a person can change in such a short space of time. The smile was gone, the kindness a thing of the past. He was irritable and impatient the whole time I was there. Suddenly I didn't know him any longer. He was not the man I knew as my father. In fact, he made it plain I wasn't welcome.

"And I soon realised why: it must have been embarrassing for him to have his daughter in the house when he was entertaining all those local dignitaries and officials with their impeccable party credentials. Especially the SS men. Hardly a day went by without someone knocking on the door, at all hours, often late at night, dinner parties that stretched into the early morning, fat guffawing boorish pigs with opinions of themselves even bigger than their bellies, behaving as though they owned the place. And my father with it. They've probably long since drunk his cellar of 1913 Chateau Haut-Brion dry. You know what he's done? He's made his pact with the devil, sold out to keep his head above water.

"Not that I blame him for that. I think it was probably around three years ago, after the pogrom of Bloody Palm Sunday, when he realised that some kind of insurance was called for. It's all about survival these days, after all. But what really hurt was to find he didn't need all that protection I've been buying for him. He never did. And Breitner knew it all along. He was just playing with me from the very beginning."

"What makes you say that?" Frank asked.

"He virtually admitted it to me." Her voice took on a guttural edge that told him she was fighting off the tears, as she added in a tone of disbelief: "He was there. In my father's house. Being wined and dined. I knew that one of the local SS leaders in Stuttgart was supposed to be a close friend of his, but I never imagined I would have to sit and watch my father fawning over him like that. He was so amused when I walked in and he saw the expression on my face. It was sickening, utterly nauseating to watch him feasting on my father's grovelling hospitality. To see the smugness fill his face when my father poured him a glass of wine. It made me feel so cheap and dirty. In my father's house. The house I grew up in. Can you imagine? He so enjoyed my pain. It was not simply the disappointment at finding that my father had climbed into bed with them. It was the sure knowledge that the day would come when he would have served his purpose. And he would be cast aside like all the others. That's what really hurt.

"Breitner came to me later that evening, not only to gloat in that disgusting way of his, but just to make it clear that of course nothing had changed. Said that, although my father was obviously a resourceful man and understood well enough how to safeguard his own interests (said he had the survival instincts of a rat, but that this was only to be expected of a Jew), he needed the support of his loving daughter more than ever now that he was making so many enemies. And what a tragedy it would be if for any reason my father should make enemies of his – Breitner's – friends. If they should ever turn against him. But it can so easily happen if you expose yourself the way my father had chosen to, he said. Oh, he was so revolting, it turns my stomach every time I think of it."

Her words trailed off into the darkness and left a vast hole of desolation. Only their bodies touched, gently, and hers seemed cold and drained of life. He felt powerless beside her. Uncertain what to say. But he knew that any words from him would have been completely out of place: she was gathering the strength to continue this guided tour of her own private hell.

"You can't imagine what it was like," she said. "All this happening in my father's house, under his roof, where I had so many happy memories. I think that's probably what Breitner found so titillating. But just to ram the message home and make sure that I appreciated the power he had over me, he said he would be taking me to Berlin with him. He had some business there and expected me to go along and…"

"Keep his bed warm?"

"Just like in that tea-room in Davos. You remember?" Still she was trying to avoid his juvenile interjections, but this time Frank sensed that he had pushed her off course. It was not the response he wanted to hear. But he had only himself to blame.

"Damn it, Frank, you don't make it any easier. Do you really want to go into every detail? Are you so thick-skinned?"

He had no reply to her rebuke. Patricia – at last relieved of her burden – finally gave in to exhaustion and sank into a deep sleep. But his skin was a lot thinner than she gave him credit for. Her story was too uncomfortable for him to sleep on. As the dawn light slowly insisted itself through the single window of their room, his head began to clear and his thoughts crystallise – like the freezing light of the valley that stretched away beneath them: the snow-draped fir trees; the hotel's ice-rink laid out with last night's fall of snow; and further down the valley the frozen lake recognisable only as a flat expanse of virgin white. Everywhere he looked, the untouched beauty of an Alpine morning. Clear, innocent, undemanding. Just waiting to be violated.

He turned his gaze from the window to Patricia. Only her hair visible. Like a cascade of jet-black water frozen to the landscape of her bed linen, and the gentle clasp of an arm half-open on the pillow. So vulnerable. Captive to a history that was not of her making. And of course, she was right. She had to go back. But it had to be on new terms. He would not allow her to endure another day enthralled to Breitner. All he needed was to buy a little time, to steel his nerves and let his dark ambition take shape.

It was already late in the morning when Patricia woke. The sun was streaming through the window, as if to celebrate the rare event of an uncompromising decision from Frank Eigenmann. It was the first time for some weeks that they had seen the sun shine with such vigour. It lit up Patricia's sleepy face with a warmth that lent new depths to her beauty. Despite the traces of sleep that still lingered in her eyes, the way she sat up in bed and stretched – the curvature of her body flexed into the morning light – betrayed a freshness which suggested a sense of liberation. But Frank knew this lightness of being was only a surface reflection, that it concealed an immense hole of despair which threatened to swallow her up if he failed to act soon.

It was over a late breakfast that he began making preparations for his last curtain call. The large breakfast room seemed to him a fitting place for drawing up these plans. He and Patricia were alone except for a few staff who still lingered, clearing away the last remnants of the day's first meal and making ready for lunch. Although they tried hard to be as servile and ingratiating as the staff in these luxury hotels are always trained to be, they were reluctant to bring their guests anything at all. But they did grant them a pot of coffee and some bread and jam.

"Coffee is all I need," Patricia insisted when Frank put a sad-looking bread roll on her plate.

"I still haven't apologised for my stupid remarks last night," he said. "They were completely juvenile and absurd."

"Please, squirrel, let's forget about it. I'd rather think of other things while we're here. And enjoy the sun and snow."

"Agreed. But we're not going to be here for long, are we?" He spread his bread roll with jam while he considered his next words.

"Patricia, you must contact Breitner and invent some story about me. Above all, he has to know that you're alone, that you need some time to yourself and that you will contact him as soon as you get back in the next few days."

The searching expression in Patricia's eyes was tainted with a host of emotions. Under any other circumstances, they might have intimidated him, but now was not the time for faint hearts. He had made up his mind.

"It's likely he will be returning home today," Frank continued, "so I suggest you phone this evening. If he's not there, leave a message that you will call again tomorrow – and keep calling until you speak to him. He needs to know that you're still 'toeing the line'."

"What are you playing at, Frank?" she asked, staring at him over her cup.

"Trust me, Patricia," was all he said, and it seemed to be all she needed to hear. From that moment, her expression lightened, as if he had just removed the last burden from her shoulder and she could now walk upright. She became as carefree as every other tourist in St Moritz. Even the phone call she made to Breitner later that evening failed to chip away at the screen she had thrown over the giant hole of despair. Quite the contrary, she found the conversation hugely amusing.

"You should have heard him," she giggled. And Frank was reminded of her girlish enthusiasm during the concert that became such a horrendous experience for him at the hands of Bartok.

"The way he was blustering and choking. It'll be a long time before he gets over his walk down the mountainside."

Frank smiled.

"When did he get back down?"

"I didn't dare ask. His pride was far too injured to tell me that." She laughed, so free at last that Frank felt his task was already half done. "But he did say you would live to rue the day you met him."

"That day has long since passed."

She reached a hand across the table and held his arm as he was about to put the last piece of buttered roll in his mouth.

"Frank," she said, "promise me you'll take care."

Her concern excited the conceit within him. But it expressed itself as irritation: "Why is it that my sacrifice is any less worthy than yours?"

"What do you mean, Frank?"

She was hurt. His words had plainly taken her aback. And he had to admit that he was unable to explain them. But this brief preoccupation with the darkness that was lurking in the wings would not be allowed to unhinge their extended honeymoon.

"Come on. It's time we enjoyed some of this Engadin sunshine."

He guided her out through the expansive lobby and past the other hotel guests milling around the aspidistras in opulent fur coats that looked far too large even for the most overweight of them. Patricia clung to his arm like a wicked young koala and whispered: "What on earth made you bring me to this place? It must cost a fortune."

"Childhood memories, maybe," he replied, conceding quietly to himself that it was more likely he just wanted to impress her. And of course, she was right: he could not afford it. But issues of this kind were unimportant as they walked out into the sun, into a week that would come the closest to heaven he would ever be. And a week also that saw his decision harden and carry him relentlessly towards the final act.

Much of their time was spent either watching the bobsleigh teams practising for the world championships or following the horse-racing down on the flat. It had always fascinated him as a boy when he came here with his father to watch the horses. The snow and ice of the frozen lake under the beating hooves added a new dimension to the excitement of the race. Perhaps it was the resonance of their pounding hooves in the cold thin air. Or maybe it was the crowd. The atmosphere was so unlike anything he had met anywhere else in his narrow world at the time.

Patricia was even more spellbound by the activity than he had been as a boy. The heavy breath of the beasts on the cold air and the steaming of their sleek bodies. It pleased him that he had been able, however unwittingly, to provide her with some nutriment for her dreams. In fact, so taken was she by the festive, gaming mood of the spectators all around them, as they buzzed with expectation at the final Grand Prix race, that he could not restrain her from trying to throw nearly all their money away on one of the horses.

"But you don't know the first thing about horses," he insisted.

"You don't have to. All you need is intuition and a sense of fun," came the bubbling reply. She was in thrall to the race even before it had started and her chosen beast had taken the lead.

"Come on, Broiefort!" she screamed with a power in her voice that was new to him – and did not altogether meet with the agreement of the spectators around them. A tall distinguished-looking man in his early sixties with a white moustache and a fresh-faced appearance that told Frank he was not unaccustomed to a winter climate in the mountains even went so far as to offer his sympathy for the loss he was about to incur.

"I regret to say that your young lady has made a most unwise choice," he said, instantly identifying himself as an Englishman.

"I knew his father, Blandford. Derby winner. Beautiful creature. But this horse is not a patch on him," the man explained, before adding: "Something of a failure as a two-year-old, you know. Tends to fade when the chips are down. You know the type. Not to be trusted."

But Patricia was too enthralled by the race to hear his words. "Broiefort! Broiefort!" she continued to scream.

And perhaps this support was the fillip which the horse had been waiting for. If so, Frank knew precisely how the creature felt and fully understood how, much against his English neighbour's judgement, the horse managed not only to win, but to lead from start to finish.

"Well I'm blowed," was all the man could say. His eyes widened in amazement, as Patricia wrapped every inch of her excitement around Frank. But he could not resist overcoming his English reserve to interrupt their embrace.

"Beg your pardon, madam," he said, raising his hat with an emphasis that seemed to say he was not accustomed to such forward behaviour and would she please forgive him the indelicacy, "but may I be so blunt as to ask whatever possessed you to put your money on Broiefort?"

"If it's a choice between a horse called Reichsherold and a horse called Broiefort, what else could a French lady do?" she laughed.

Frank had never heard Patricia speak anything but German, except when she read Baudelaire to him beside the log fire in their Davos chalet. And to hear the sweet cadence of her French accent now turn to the language of Shakespeare and Noel Coward was strangely arousing, as if she had just put on a new dress that highlighted her figure in a way he had never seen before.

"As a colonel in the British Army, I share your antipathy, madam. But don't be misled by the label. Broiefort does not have an ounce of French blood in him. He's English to the core."

"But of course." Patricia was in effervescent mood. She sparkled more freely in English than Frank had ever seen her do in his own language. And although he found it bewitching to observe, the power of this fascination tugged at his jealous nature. "The English have a monopoly here, don't they? You dominate the bobsleigh racing, so it's only right that your horses should also win. Is that why Mr Churchill comes here?"

"Winston?" The colonel seemed pleasantly surprised, as if she was talking about a member of his family. Patricia looked across at Frank with her pleading expression, and he felt obliged to become involved in the meaningless banter of this absurdly self-satisfied colonel, who looked as though he had long since retired from any kind of service that might warrant leaning on the privilege of rank.

"It is standing in the newspaper that Mr Churchill comes to St Moritz." Frank was aware of his clumsiness with the English language and added "His wife is already here", sensing that this allusion to family and the implicit intimacy with the affairs and gossip of his establishment would meet with the colonel's favour. But he was irritated by his own incomprehensible desire to please a man who plainly had no time for the likes of anyone remotely German.

"I say, do you happen to know where they're staying?" the colonel asked. But Frank had to disappoint him.

"And where are you two charming people staying?"

The question had to come, but Frank was not prepared for quite such a ready reply from Patricia. The colonel beamed like a little boy when he heard the name of the hotel.

"What a stroke of luck. That's my hotel," by which Frank assumed that he was also staying there. Not that he owned it. "We must have dinner together one evening," he added with an air that suggested it was not so much an invitation as a command. And again Frank was taken aback by Patricia's readiness to obey the bugle call.

"That would be nice," she said in all sincerity. Frank could see that the table was already mentally reserved. Her excuses when the colonel had taken his leave and Frank had a chance to express his annoyance – "He seems so lonely. And he's harmless enough" – failed to impress him. Their time together was too short. He felt the brittle texture of every second perish between their fingers whenever they touched, and he was not prepared to forfeit a fraction of her attention for anyone so pompous. On the other hand, nor did he want to sacrifice a single moment of their rapture to bickering or argument. So he did not pursue the matter and hoped that nothing would come of it.

"You're right, Patricia. I knew there was something different here. It's the English." He was trying to move their thoughts in a new direction, but his irritation was still kicking and bent on him having the last word. "They're very present, aren't they? It makes an odd contrast to last week in Davos. I'm not sure which strain of arrogance I dislike the most."

"Do you always have to be so negative?"

The rebuke in her voice was unmistakable. And became even sharper when she fetched her winnings. "Well, you needn't worry about having to waste your precious money on the poor old man – or on me either."

The rapture had been sacrificed long before Frank was even aware of what was happening. But her anger with him did not compromise her beauty one inch. On the contrary, it enhanced it all the more. And made his pain all the greater.

They left the jostle of the racecourse and walked over to the Cresta Run without exchanging another word. She locked her arm in his. But it was more as support to help her keep her balance on the ice than an expression of intimacy. The crowds grew steadily thinner as they approached, and the afternoon sun was warm on their backs. But it was unable to thaw the frost that had settled between them. The toboggan run was already closed when they got there, the ice too soft, so they wandered aimlessly along the snowy paths overlooking St Moritz, their uneasy silence broken only once by Patricia's words:

"He reminds me of my father in a strange sort of way."

She was speaking of the colonel and thinking of her father, but at the back of her mind he detected Breitner. And he knew the moment could not be put off much longer – an awareness that gnawed at him for the rest of the day. It was not until sometime later – as the mountain light was beginning to fade and they were walking into the driveway of their hotel – that he responded to her remark.

"All right. I'll leave a message for him at the desk inviting him to have dinner with us tonight."

But the gesture proved superfluous. As he approached the desk, he caught sight of the colonel waving a stick in the air that would have brought the chandelier down had the ceiling been much lower. Frank's heart sank.

"What a stroke of luck," the colonel shouted, hurrying over to them, excitement in his step and pathos in his eyes. "I was just about to take a pot of tea. Would you charming people care to join me?"

Frank had the distinct impression that he had been waiting all afternoon for them.

"We'd be delighted to join you for a coffee," he replied, surprising himself with the ring of sincerity. But tea was anathema to him, so the colonel would have to meet them halfway if he wanted their company. It was for Patricia's sake that he had made the gesture, and her smile did not escape him as the colonel led them to a far corner of the lobby with the pleased pride of a little boy taking his parents off to show them his secret den.

"Don't like to be too close to the bar at this time of day. Too much of a temptation."

The colonel pulled out a chair for Patricia and, in so doing, drew attention to Frank's own lack of manners, which he suspected was the colonel's intention. Over the throng of people gathering after their return from a day on the slopes, the sound of a piano carried across the lobby to their table. It drew with it a melody as languorous and melancholy as it was familiar. But he could not quite place it. All he knew was that it seemed grossly incongruous in the setting, even though the pianist was plainly doing his best to match it to the warm homecoming mood of the guests.

"'The Man I Love'," Patricia said. She glanced across at Frank as she spoke, the words carried by a silky warmth that came unexpectedly after the frosty afternoon together. "It's a beautiful song when Billie Holiday sings it. Why can't people leave well alone?"

"It doesn't fit, does it?" Frank agreed. "But then neither would Bartok."

"What's Bartok got to do with it?" she asked.

"Nothing at all," he replied. "It was simply an observation."

"Then it was a silly observation. You know I love them both – passionately." She teased him with an almost imperceptible pause that was just long enough to let the full enchantment of her last word sink into the willing flesh of his heart, before she added: "But then, you're not French. You wouldn't feel it with the same passion."

With those words, Patricia lowered her voice, leaned over to the colonel and whispered in his ear. The ex-army wallah rose from his chair muttering "Of course my dear. My pleasure," and strode off like a man with a mission. With burning curiosity, Frank watched him approach the pianist and engage in a brief exchange of words.

"Don't have time for music myself, especially this modern stuff," the colonel said when he returned and sat back in his chair. "Except maybe Elgar once in a while. 'Pomp and Circumstance' – that sort of thing, you know."

How fitting, Frank thought. But the colonel was not finished. He wanted to lead the conversation down a path he felt more comfortable on. He turned ominously to Frank.

"Have you done the Cresta Run yet, old boy?"

At that moment, Frank noticed the music change.

"'These Foolish Things'," he exclaimed, fully aware of the ludicrous smile that instantly lit up his face as he ignored the colonel's question. He recalled the Billie Holiday record he had bought for Patricia and looked across at her, a delicious teasing sparkle in her eyes.

"We were there this afternoon," she said, replying to the colonel for him when it became plain that Frank's mind was somewhere else altogether at that moment.

"This afternoon?" the colonel said with a sceptical expression, evidently puzzled by Frank's words. "It would have been closed then."

"It was," Frank affirmed.

"Just plucking up the courage, eh? When are you going down?"

"Well, I hadn't really…"

"What? You can't come to St Moritz without doing the Cresta Run. The ladies expect it, you know." He sent a conspiratorial wink in the direction of Patricia, who surprised Frank by her amusement. What was it about this man that appealed to her? Frank asked himself. He was certainly not as he imagined her father to be.

"Did it regularly myself when I came here with the chaps, you know. Wager I could still manage it today. Not in the sixty-odd seconds it took me in those days of course. Maybe foolish, as you say. Takes nerves of steel, you know, but I wager I could still do it today."

'Nerves of steel', Frank repeated silently to himself, while in the background the piano continued its refrain. Was it that little gesture of Patricia's – just one of those foolish things – which was beginning to concentrate his mind?

"Tell me, colonel, with your experience as a military man, what takes more nerve? To ride the Cresta Run or to kill a man?" Frank asked.

He saw the teasing amusement in Patricia's face flicker like a light in the first gust of a storm. She knew the implication. But the colonel was undeterred by the question.

"Couldn't tell you, old chap. Never looked upon the enemy as men. More like rats in the cellar. Excuse the bluntness, my dear," he added, putting an apologetic hand on Patricia's arm. To Frank's disappointment, she accepted the gesture with a smile that he would have seen as darkly seductive had it been directed at him. But the colonel appeared not to notice. He still had the army in mind. "The discipline of military training, you know. As long as you don't think of them as men, it's not a problem. Now, the Cresta Run is a different cup of tea altogether. Tame that, and you can do anything."

"Colonel," Patricia interjected at last, "I'm afraid you must excuse us. We have to go and dress for dinner." She was plainly unsettled by the direction the conversation had taken. Frank sensed she was angry with him for allowing it to happen.

A feeling he felt was vindicated by the afterthought she added as they got up to leave: "Frank was wondering whether you would care to join us for dinner?"

"What a splendid idea. I'd be delighted." The colonel's face lit up with a boyish enthusiasm that almost endeared him to Frank – and at least made it easier for him to lend the semblance of truth to Patricia's mischief-making:

"Is seven-thirty all right for you?" he asked.

"Splendid," the colonel said again, and they left him with a smile on his face as he settled back into his chair to finish his pot of tea.

Dinner ran a similar course. The colonel was punctual, as to be expected, and positively bounced with excitement at the occasion. Frank had the impression they were the only people he had talked to the whole time he had been in St Moritz – apart from the hotel receptionist, the waiters and, almost certainly, the chambermaids. Patricia for her part played the attentive daughter substitute with conviction, flattering him with her smile and complimenting him on his choice of wine. For although Frank was ostensibly the host, he suggested that the responsibility for such an important decision as choosing the wine should not be left to the inexperience of youth. And all the while he was unable to imagine what it was about the colonel's company that amused Patricia.

"Excellent, this dried beef," the colonel said, as he devoured the last wafer-thin slice of his entrée and smacked his lips under cover of his moustache in a manner that Frank found faintly disgusting. The colonel appeared relaxed. But the slow deliberation with which he put down his wine glass and fixed his host across the table with his ageing, slightly washed-out eyes unnerved Frank, who once again suspected this was his intention.

"Well, old chap. Have you made up your mind yet?" the colonel asked.

Frank feigned incomprehension. But the colonel knew he was faking, even if he did not let on. And he knew the question had been occupying Frank's mind ever since they had left him in the lobby. It was written all over the smug expression he used to wrap up his words. Frank suspected he also knew the answer.

"The Cresta Run, old chap. When are you going to do it?"

Frank's reply was impulsive, but inevitable.

"I thought I'd give it a try tomorrow."

"Knew you wouldn't be able to resist it for long."

'Of course you knew,' Frank said to himself. The self-satisfied smile on the colonel's face irritated him intensely. But in a curious way he was beginning to look upon the man as an accomplice, if not an ally.

"Colonel, would you do me the honour of coming along?" he asked.

"Show you the ropes, you mean? Be only too pleased." For a moment the colonel hesitated, as his smugness gave way briefly to a look of uncertainty. "Not sure I'm fit enough to do it myself, though. Not as young as I used to be, you know."

It was as if he wanted to attempt an honourable retreat from his earlier posturing before Frank forced him onto the defensive by calling the bluff of his absurd bragging. And Frank wondered whether the colonel sensed the ambivalence of his invitation and the deep resentment he felt towards the man.

But it was settled. At nine o'clock in the morning, they would meet in the lobby. He had expected Patricia to be pleased that he was offering her lonely old colonel his company. But for the remainder of the evening a dark anxiety filled the expression in her eyes and told him that all was not well. Even later, when they were alone together in their room, her mood did not change. She made it plain that she wanted nothing to do with his plans.

"You're not worried, are you?" he asked. "I'll be in safe hands with your colonel."

A stony stare told him that she did not appreciate his flippancy.

"I don't know what you're playing at, Frank. But I don't like the sound of it. And I want no part in it."

Although he was unsettled and slightly perplexed by this reaction, her intuitive knowledge thrilled him for the way it underlined the intimacy between them. But it was not this that kept him awake for much of the night, caressed by her breathing body as she slept. It was his apprehension at the gulf that he could sense opening up between dream and reality. A fear of failure. Tomorrow, his ambition would get the chance for a practice run, but would it match up to the task? Would it be strong enough? Would it show him that he was capable of leaping that gulf? He could not afford another failure. It was this that occupied him while the silky touch of Patricia's body teased the man in him.

He had hoped that at the last minute she would change her mind. But it was not to be. So, when he met up with the colonel in the lobby the following morning, he made the necessary excuses for her. The colonel seemed surprisingly relieved.

"Just as well," he said. "Not really the place for women."

And he spent the next thirty minutes or so on their way over to the toboggan run explaining the ropes to Frank, as he put it. Coaching him. Preparing him for what he was about to embark on.

"Battledore is important," he kept saying. "You'll see a marker at Battledore. Get your steering line right here and you'll sail round the horseshoe at Shuttlecock easy as anything. Get it wrong and you're in trouble. And remember, don't drag your rakes too heavily. If you must use them at all, then use them properly. If you don't, you'll be thrown all over the place." And he proceeded to explain the technique with the detail of a military strategist that went right over Frank's head as he began to wonder why it was he had considered this such a necessary plank in his preparation. But the colonel was in his element.

"Makes me feel thirty years younger," he said. "Perhaps I should give it another try after all. Tomorrow maybe," he added. And escorted Frank over to the office to put his name down and have him kitted out.

It surprised Frank to find that he was far from alone in embarking on this hare-brained enterprise. The whole area at the top of the run was teeming with wholesome chisel-jawed types who looked very much as if they knew what they were about. Frank wondered whether they shared anything even approaching a common motive. It seemed unlikely. They looked very much at peace with themselves and the world around them. But they had plainly tamed the Cresta Run already. They had steeled their nerves on the wall of ice. They had every reason to be at peace.

"They'll call your name on the loudspeaker when you're on," the colonel explained. "Let's go and enjoy the sun while we wait, old chap."

He led Frank over to the run. The snow crunched affably beneath their feet, and the warmth of the sun's rays came pleasantly packed in a crisp air that carried every sound with precious individual care. An atmosphere in stark contrast to the growing tension that had Frank's heart already racing.

"As a novice, of course, you start down there at Junction."

He pointed to a box some thirty metres down the run. Frank listened with growing trepidation for his name to be called. His pounding heart competed with the insistence of the loudspeaker so effectively he wondered whether he would even hear his name when it was called. He thought of Breitner. Pictured the rats in the cellar crawling over the decomposed bodies of Gertrude and her two little boys. Imagined the gun in his hand. But his heart almost lurched to a complete standstill when he heard an unexpected name over the loudspeaker. Crystal clear in the mountain air. It was unmistakable.

"Silverstone," called the disembodied voice. "Silverstone." The name seemed to boom down from every mountain peak around them. Frank craned his neck as the next toboggan appeared on the run.

"Is this really Silverstone?"

"What's that, old chap? Do you know him?"

"No. Nothing. I was just thinking aloud."

The colonel paid no further attention. Frank's eyes meanwhile focused on the man on the toboggan as he slid past down the mountainside. It was impossible to identify him, just another figure lying prostrate on a slab of steel and looking a shade ridiculous.

But he had the build of the Silverstone he knew. And he started from the top – Silverstone could never be seen to start from a novice's junction, no matter how uninitiated he was. He heard scattered cheers of "Hopp-Hopp!" as the tobogganist disappeared from view.

Was this really the Silverstone he now recalled trying vainly to hold on to the last remnants of his dignity in a public convenience?'

"You'd better get over to the box at Junction, old chap. Your name will be coming up before too long." The colonel took the momentum out of his thoughts. "I'll make my way down to the Kulm and have the drinks ready for you on the terrace. Good luck," he added with a military wave as he turned to poke his way gingerly down the slope with his stick.

For once, the colonel was wrong. It was a good forty minutes before his name was called. Someone had apparently fallen badly at Shuttlecock, which was not the kind of news he needed to send him on his way. He tried consoling himself with the thought that maybe the victim was Silverstone. But any consolation he could find was short-lived – his time had come.

Flat on the tray, his face barely inches from the ice that moved away from under his chest, he began the descent – sedately to begin with – and for the first few seconds wondered what the colonel had been making all the fuss about. Then, as if from nowhere, it opened up before him like the mouth of a monster whale. And swallowed him whole. Down he plunged into the vortex. The weight of his frame opened up an ever-widening gap between the callous cruelty of the ice that blew its mocking breath against his face as it passed and his battered thoughts that lingered some thirty metres behind him. He wanted speed at all costs and kept his rakes contemptuously off the ice to let the steel underneath his belly throw him high around the banking. But where was Battledore? His line marker? All he could see was Breitner, his crimson carcass split open on the ice before him, laughing as a ghoulish raw head of a creature – tentacles rising from its blood-engorged skull – crawled out of his body to a roll of drums and dragged behind it Frank's mother, white and drained of any life. She and Breitner buffeted their way endlessly past the steel bullet that shot Frank high around a bend so tight he was not sure whether he was clinging to his toboggan or the ice. It was only as he came out of the bend and the visions of sweet death were swept away that he realised Battledore was already well behind him and he had just come through Shuttlecock. A smile tried to break through his shaking jowls as he came onto what looked like the home straight.

But his smugness was premature. Lulled into the comfort of the straight and a self-satisfied disinterest in his gathering speed, he was already looking forward to the celebration of his survival on the terrace of the Kulm when the toboggan lost contact with the ground and he shot into the air. Visions of Patricia flashed through his mind, heavy chains around her slender ankles. He thought of Breitner. And as he crashed back onto the ice with a belly flop that punched the wind right out of him, he saw the bloodied carcass of Patricia's tormentor once again buffeted along the track beside him, felt it dragging at his feet, slowly putting the brake on his steel bullet. The course lay crimson red like a carpet of blood rolled out before him.

Frank lay on his slab of steel, savouring the stillness of the ice, letting the sun warm his back and filter out these images from his mind. Only the precious clarity of the air washed over him. He felt strangely purified.

"Come on, old man. You can't stay here all day. The next chap will be on his way down before long." It was the colonel. He put a hand under Frank's arm to help him up. "Come on, let's go and have that drink. You've earned it. Did jolly well. Beat my best time by a good two seconds."

The colonel clapped him on the back as he imagined he would pat his pet dog. And Frank felt an urge to growl and gnarl at his master.

"What'll it be?" he asked, as he led Frank onto the sunny terrace of the Kulm. The place thronged with steely Titans of the Cresta Run toasting their prowess and others who were there just to bask in the sun and the excitement. Aromas of coffee and cigar smoke mingled with the oily fragrance of sun creams. Hardly a free seat was to be had. But the colonel had the hawk eye of a military strategist and a bearing that commanded respect. He led Frank straight to a couple of seats at the end of a table that was otherwise exclusively French. Frank thought of Patricia, and wished she was here.

"This is my invitation, colonel," he said. "And since I have something to celebrate, let's have a bottle of champagne."

"Well, that's jolly decent, old chap. Don't mind if I do." And as the waitress departed with the order, he added: "Must confess, old boy. That was a splendid run. The Germans could do with you in their bob team this week."

At that very moment, Frank's eyes fell on the vain expression of a face he knew so well at the far end of the terrace. He was with a group of jovial back-slapping people, none of whom he recognised, and was himself in mid-slap as their eyes met. What promised to be a swaggering all-American thwack on some poor unsuspecting shoulder was suddenly sapped of all energy. The joviality hollowed out to a shell of disbelief, as his grin took on the appearance of a crevasse in one of the Bernina glaciers. The shoulder was reprieved.

"Colonel, you see that man over there, coming towards us?"

Frank nodded discreetly in the direction of Silverstone, who was already battling his way through a large crowd of expectant newcomers just arrived on the terrace in search of a table. The woman Frank had seen with him at the station in Basel was trailing along behind.

"Tall, about fifty, wearing a green pullover."

"Got him, old boy," he said, as if he had just spotted one of the enemy. The colonel's curiosity was aroused, and Frank sensed he had him on his side.

"He's an American, called Silverstone. He won't leave me alone, follows me wherever I go. You know the type. Could you do me a favour and distract him while I go to the toilet? We'll meet back at the hotel and have our champagne there," he added. "With Patricia."

"American, you say? My pleasure, old boy."

Suddenly the colonel was fired with the prospect of adventure. A mission to be accomplished, however small. His fingers fidgeted and his eyes flashed with the excitement, allowing Frank to slip away from the terrace, confident that the colonel would fulfil this mission with dedication.

With grudging reluctance, he was beginning to feel deeply indebted to the colonel, a man who irritated him intensely and stood for everything he disliked about the English.

'What's the American doing here?' Frank asked himself. Whatever it was, he would plainly be seeking revenge for their last encounter. Frank knew he would need to tread carefully for the rest of his brief time in St Moritz.

But he had only one goal in mind. And it was this that occupied his thoughts as he walked back up to the hotel. Nothing would divert him from his goal now he knew that he had the substance and the passion to achieve it.

It was a discovery that filled him with impatience – as if his life had been one huge tangled ball of thread that he had only now taken into his hands to consider the practicalities of unravelling it. And he was consumed with an urgency to get the job done. He needed to find Patricia and share the galvanism of this discovery.

So much greater was his disappointment when she refused to come and celebrate his triumph over the Cresta Run with the colonel. Her eyes seemed darker and more beautiful than ever. But he failed to appreciate either the depth or the quality of her sadness.

"I told you, Frank. I want nothing to do with your plans," was all she had to say. It both irritated and mystified him, since it was she who gave him the motive and encouragement. And it was she who stood to gain from all the fretwork. Now he saw the delicate inlay cracked and broken by a ferment he had not anticipated. It was a damage he failed to understand. He had no idea how deep it ran, nor how it should be measured. He knew only that he had to repair the damage before he left. And that would take time. Champagne celebrations would certainly not help. So he made his excuses to the colonel later that day.

The rest of their time in St Moritz he devoted to Patricia, to the restoration of the precious sparkle in her eyes and the defiant sensuality of her lips. They spent many hours walking the most deserted circuitous paths they could find in the snow, circumventing all the issues that teased at the forefront of his mind. And he let her lead him back into her dream world of Baudelaire. Or to her childhood in Normandy, catching crabs in the rock pools and picking wild primroses in the woods. Anything but the sinister demimonde that gnawed greedily at their being. It was a strange and telling irony that they found themselves compelled to avoid even the smallest detail of their shared experiences – of all those things that tie lovers up in knots and keep them forever entwined.

All the while Frank was unable to shake off the image of Silverstone on the terrace of the Kulm, ploughing a way through the crowd towards him. Or the certain knowledge that he would be seeking revenge and doubtless now trawling through all the hotels in St Moritz in search of him. But as time passed, and there was no further sighting of Silverstone, he began to wonder whether he had simply imagined hearing his name over the loudspeaker, whether the man on the terrace at the Kulm was just an innocent American tourist. Nonetheless, he remained alert to the danger and kept his eyes open for that brash figure. But he never saw him again. And his suspicions of an overactive imagination saw their hunch slowly harden with every day that the American remained absent from Frank's remaining days in St Moritz, especially when they went to watch the final races of the bobsleigh championships.

He was reluctant to go, not only for fear of running into Silverstone, who would certainly be there, but also because the toboggan seemed to have acquired a symbolic value of unpredictable force in his relationship with Patricia. But it was she who insisted with that effervescence he had come to adore in her that they go.

For Frank, this was the first tangible sign of the damage beginning to mend. So, even at the risk of being confronted by his American persecutor, he agreed. Her enjoyment was infinitely more important than this threat, which dwindled to insignificance as he watched her becoming steadily absorbed in the excitement on the ice. To see the joy in her eyes was bewitching. And his own heart reached a new pitch of exhilaration whenever she clasped her hands around his arm. He could sense the mend becoming stronger and firmer by the minute, and he savoured every unexpected moment of her delight. But what surprised him was her unabashed support for the English teams over all the others – even the French. And it was not that the English confirmed their position as favourites and ran away with one trophy after another. That was more likely to irritate Patricia, who was always better disposed towards the underdog.

"I just wanted them to win for the colonel," she explained. "Because I know it would please him."

Her continued liking for the colonel baffled Frank all the more since the man's active encouragement of his exploits on the Cresta Run, which she had so disapproved of. But it gave him an idea.

"I'm surprised he's not here," he said, "but I've been thinking about the colonel." Which was not entirely true. "I've been wanting to take you on a sleigh ride in the Val Roseg ever since we arrived here. And it occurred to me that it might be a nice idea if we invited him to come along with us."

"That's very sweet." She held his right arm tighter in her grip as she stretched up to plant a kiss on his cheek. "When did you have in mind?"

"I thought Sunday would be a good day."

Sunday would be a perfect day, he told himself. But he would need somebody to look after Patricia, to take her mind off things. And the colonel was the ideal choice.

So it was settled. The colonel proved every bit as keen on the idea as Patricia, especially since he was returning to England on the Monday and it would make a fitting finale to his holiday, he suggested. In a curious way, this pleased Frank, because he felt he owed the colonel something after letting him down on the champagne celebration.

The night that carried him into those last decisive hours was long and wakeful. And the darkness swelled with emotion, while Patricia slept into the innocence of her dreams, her peace with Frank restored. Or so it seemed.

He ran his hands over the silky slenderness of her body. Every touch brought a new dimension to his rapture, whispered to him in a new voice, felt different, as if she was somehow a complete stranger to him. This freshness invested his arousal with a charge that was hard to resist. But these moments are too precious to be felled by a deciduous passion, he told himself. They needed preserving. And yet he knew they would evaporate eventually. Before dawn at the very latest.

There was only one path to any lasting kind of conservation. And he was impatient to get on with it. To get moving. To see it through. It was this impatience that kept him awake. Kept him prowling the darkness with his eyes as he acted through every sequence of events in his mind and prepared for every twist and turn.

When the light of day began gradually to penetrate the curtains on their window high up above their little frozen corner of the Engadin, the sweeping wastes of snow that stretched away below them still slumbered quietly. Their tidy repose scorned him in his dishevelled unslept state. Only the overcast sky came close to matching the grey fuzziness that filled his skull. With his oedematous eyelids barely capable of opening, his head thick with unrest and the exhaustion of his fidgeting mind, he felt as if he had spent all night on the tiles. But this woeful condition could not have fitted more neatly into his designs, and helped lend credence to his excuses when Patricia eventually woke.

"I'm sorry, I just don't think I can face that sleigh ride today," he said. "You're going to have to make my excuses to the colonel." It took little theatrical talent to present a convincing picture of his debility. All the outward signs were there. He needed only to paint in some covert detail, such as a sore throat and aching limbs. "Would you mind just the two of you going on your own? I'm sure he'll look after you."

The way she pampered Frank and tucked him comfortably up in his bed made him feel shoddy and mean in his deceit. But this failed to prevent the ludicrous pangs of jealousy that tugged at him when she accepted his suggestion with an enthusiasm that went far beyond the gestures of self-sacrifice he had anticipated. It seemed an absurd idea, but he wondered whether there might be more to the attraction than his appeal as a father substitute. But these wild thoughts were too thin and tenuous to get the better of his vanity. And they faded into oblivion under the sweet commitment of the kiss she left with him when she departed. An indelible keepsake of his deepest wishes sealed into place.

But he could not afford to linger too long in the delicious realms of this sentiment, since there was a risk it might carry him off into the sleep that he had sorely missed. There was time enough for him to recuperate on the train, he told himself.

However, he was not prepared to leave sentiment entirely on the side lines. So he contacted room service and arranged for dinner to be served in their room at nine o'clock that evening – fillet of beef in Madeira sauce with a bottle of Chateau Haut-Brion, which he had noticed on their wine list. The vintage was tantalisingly wrong – a 1931, not a '13 – and his superstitious nature talked him into regarding this as a good omen. Of course, he would have some explaining to do when he got back, and a candlelight dinner in their room seemed a better framework for confessions than most. As long as the railway service did not let him down. He had checked the departure times, and a nine o'clock return appeared just about feasible.

Chapter 23

The early afternoon sun was making a half-hearted effort to break through the clouds when Frank walked out onto the central square outside the railway station, scene of his rendezvous with Patricia on their flight to the mountains. He found it hard to believe it was already three weeks ago that they had met here. So much water had passed under the bridge since then. Yet it seemed like only yesterday. Time seemed indefinably confused. A sensation that was reinforced by the babel of tongues which filled the air outside the station – the same sounds he had heard the day they left. Seemingly so carefree and open to the world. Were they the same young migrant children at play? Frank wondered. The same unsuspecting fugitives in permanent transit? Their faces all looked vaguely familiar. Yet he could not be certain that he had seen any one of them before. What struck him above all was their joyful laughter, the sparkle of their play, the ease of their every move competing defiantly with the sadness in their eyes, the truth of their exile. In this, they reminded him of Patricia.

The paradox of their captive freedom stayed with him and fed his thoughts of Patricia in the tram that carried him close to the border with Germany. To the smart suburban streets where Breitner's villa violated the quiet reserve of the streets with an aggressiveness that matched the style of its owner. The sight of the place prompted a painful re-enactment in his mind of the only other visit he had ever made here. The familiar Maybach stood in the driveway. But the house itself appeared deathly still. Frank's hand rested on the gun in his pocket, as it had done during most of the journey from St Moritz.

He was surprised by the calmness of his step as he walked up the driveway. Only a vague thrill undulating through the wall of his chest betrayed a hint of anything that might approach anxiety or tension. Nerves of steel tempered on an anvil of ice. His thoughts turned to the colonel, and he sensed them bring a faint trace of amusement to his expression as he lifted the heavy black knocker on the front door. It had the same feel, the same shape and the same dull thud of the knocker on the door to his mother's house in Cologne. He half-expected to be greeted by the sour-faced vulture, or even his mother herself.

His hand gripped tightly round the gun in readiness, as he heard the busy shuffling and fidgeting of an elaborate unfastening ritual. Slowly the door opened, just far enough for a face to peer through the crack. He had not anticipated that Breitner himself would answer his knock. On the other hand, nor had it occurred to him that he might find Lutz here. So he was uncomfortably taken aback when he met the gaze of the man's unpleasant, bulbous eyes gaping at him through the narrow doorway.

"Mr Eigenmann," he said. "Really, this is most unwise."

There was a consternation in his expression. Lutz hovered, plainly at a loss to know what he should do. "Does Mademoiselle Roche know you are here?"

"Are you going to announce me to Breitner? Or shall I do it myself?" Frank asked with gruff impatience. Perhaps too much impatience. But he wanted to get it over with. Lutz hesitated. His eyes scanned the street outside. Was he looking out for danger? Or searching for support?

"Come in."

With these uncertain words, Lutz stepped back. And Frank entered the lair. A gloom hung over the hallway that deepened even further when Lutz closed the door behind him. A hallway that had stamped itself so vividly on his memory. The staircase steep and vicious. The deep red carpet that concealed his blood stains. And that image of Breitner's brightly polished shoes laughing in his face before he was turfed out into the street.

"Where is he?"

"Mr Breitner is at a meeting today," Lutz said. "He won't be back until later this evening."

"On a Sunday? Is there anybody else here?"

Lutz shook his head.

"I'll wait."

But Frank had no wish to have Lutz keep him company while he prepared himself for Breitner's arrival. However protective of Patricia the man had become, Frank did not trust him an inch. He would feel more comfortable sitting in a snake pit.

Frank pulled the gun from his pocket as if about to offer Lutz a cigarette.

"Is there a cellar here?"

Lutz eyed the firearm and nodded. Like a docile dog, he led Frank past the staircase to a door in the darkest, farthest corner of the long hallway. He knew Frank meant business, that Breitner's time was up, and without any further bidding led him down into the cellar. Lutz moved with a lightness that suggested a sense of deliverance, as if this was the moment he had been waiting for all his life.

"Just tell me one thing," Frank said before shutting the door on Lutz. "What happened to Achim?"

"Mr Zimmermann?" The expression in Lutz's eyes displayed a look of cold resignation. "I only know that he was shipped back across the border."

"Shipped back?" Frank repeated. "Like rejected goods?"

"That's all any of us are when it comes to it," Lutz said with a shrug of the shoulders.

"And his family?" Frank asked. He caught the trace of a flinch in Lutz's eyes. And a hint of tearfulness in the reply.

"His wife became very excitable when they took her husband. Almost uncontrollable. Until Horst…"

"Horst?"

A sense of revulsion filled Frank instantly with nausea as he repeated the name. He knew painfully well what kind of animals Horst and his sidekick were.

"And her little boys?"

Lutz said nothing. But he could no longer mask the tears.

"The baby boys?" Frank repeated. The anger in his voice was seized with a sense of alarm. He tightened his grip on the gun.

"They were there," Lutz whispered, the words almost inaudible.

"And you? Were you there?"

"I only know what I was told," Lutz mumbled with a timorous shake of the head.

With a look of disbelief and disgust on his face, Frank relaxed his grip on the gun. There were bigger fish to fry. He turned and shut the door, leaving Lutz with a single naked light to keep him company and a strange look of relief, almost gratitude, on his face as Frank locked the door on his captive.

He pondered Lutz's words as he returned back up the stairs to the room where Breitner had received him all those weeks ago. At least they gave him the satisfaction of knowing that he had meted out justice of a sort on Horst.

The waiting dragged deep into the night. It left too much space for reflection, a pondering so deep it let the bottle of Bordeaux waiting in St Moritz slip completely from his mind. For in that one room, he was cloistered within the whole limited compass of Breitner's personality. From Biedermeier to kitsch. There was a temptation to scratch beneath this surface and look for the man. But it was not a search to be encouraged, as the colonel had made plain to him. Better to focus on the rat.

Yet it was more than this that stopped him. Much more. For although it was Patricia who had taught him to be inquisitive, she also guided him in other ways. And it was she who now gave him the motive to suppress his curiosity, because he knew only too well that – if he scratched too deep – he would run the risk of finding her here as well between these walls of degradation.

So Frank let this room become his own cellar. And he plumbed the darkness with a brooding sense of vengeance. Listening out for the sound of rats.

He could already sense the night beginning to recede when at last he heard the sound of the door. He must have just been nodding off to judge by the way the noise drove a painful wedge into his semi-conscious state. He fancied that he heard talking. But Breitner was alone. He seemed unsteady on his feet as he passed the door and made his way upstairs, the arrogance washed away in the drunken privacy of his home. As rats go, he cut a pathetic, tired figure. Frank's grip tightened on the gun that still lay faithfully in his hand. His palm felt sweaty on the metal. He was about to follow his target when Breitner's erratic progress up the stairs came to a halt. Frank heard him turn and clumsily retrace his steps, almost falling back into the hallway. He recalled his own fall into that hallway and smiled at the trivial show of justice, watching with satisfaction as Breitner stumbled into the room where Frank sat. He groped for the light switch, but missed it, and cursed his way uneasily towards the desk on the far side of the room, where he fumbled for some minutes in the dimness of what little light reached into that corner from the hall. It was not until he returned, with a file in his hand, that he saw Frank.

Frank's finger by now was on the trigger. His aim on the narrow space between Breitner's vermin eyes. He saw the rats gnawing at the flesh of Gertrude and her boys. Fighting over Achim.

"What…?" Breitner's eyes were still not focusing. He squinted through the two metres of drunkenness that separated him from Frank. "Eigenmann!" he blustered.

Frank allowed him just this split second of recognition. There could be no hesitation beyond that. The first bullet blew a hole in his chest and contorted his face with pain. The second was a chance hit that smashed into his skull as he crashed behind the sofa. So easy. So still.

Frank edged cautiously around the sofa to examine his handiwork and found him where he had fallen. Crumpled and motionless. The blast still rang in his ears. And the blood still flowed from the gaping wounds. But it was over. And as the colour drained from Breitner's face, the quiet countenance of death reminded him of his mother the last time he had seen her.

Frank licked the sweat from his upper lip. The saltiness mingled with the sweet satisfaction of seeing this evil expunged forever not only from his own life, but from the lives of countless others. It was hard to imagine this man had enjoyed such influence. He looked so ordinary and forgettable in death. His eyes even emptier now. And his body more vulnerable than it must have been since his first few minutes as a new-born infant. Now he lay at Frank's feet like a meaningless overgrown afterthought, parenthesised by the blood that trickled from the gaping wound in the promontory of his skull and onto the file caught half-open under his head when he fell.

Like a nightmare, it screamed from the slowly filling claret lake. Patricia's photo staring up at him. The unmistakable beauty of her eyes mocking his revenge and crying through the sickly, congealing pool of Breitner's blood. This was her file that he had fetched from his desk. But before Frank could do anything with the discovery, his mind took another jolt when a heavy pounding on the door seemed about to bring the walls down around him.

"Mr Breitner! Mr Breitner!"

The voices rang in his ears and came with the desperate sound of breaking glass. Instinctively, he pulled the blood-wet file out from under Breitner's body and ran. By the time he reached the hallway, the first intruder was already through the door. Frank recognised him instantly as one of the two German sports youth louts who had been so suspicious of him in Davos. The other one was close behind. Elated by the power of the weapon in his hand, Frank fired another indiscriminate blast in their direction. He saw the first of his pursuers go down and turned tail through the kitchen door. Once again, his presence of mind took him by surprise when he scooped up a briefcase that lay on a chair in the hall and slipped the file inside it as he went. A freshly blood-soaked document was not the kind of thing to be seen carrying through the streets in the early hours of the morning.

He did not sense any attempt to pursue him out into the darkness. But he would not feel safe until he was on the train back to St Moritz and Patricia. He was late. He had long since missed their dinner together. It was a knowledge that left him with the uncomfortable image of her sharing their Chateau Haut-Brion with the colonel. The earliest he could be there now would be early afternoon. At least this had the advantage that the colonel should have left to return home by then, Frank told himself. And above all, he had accomplished his mission. He was beginning to feel that time was on his side again.

The feeling was confirmed when he saw the early tram into town coming down the line just as he approached the tram stop. It was not until the doors were closing behind him, and he looked back, that his growing sense of security suddenly cracked. He watched in despair as both his pursuers slipped into the last carriage just before the tram moved off.

'So I missed,' Frank muttered to himself, recalling how the first of the sports youth louts slumped to the floor when he turned the gun on them as they burst into the house.

He knew this tram would not take him directly to the station. At some point, he would have to get off and either change trams or walk. He fancied that taking the side streets to the station from the centre of town would offer the best chance of giving his predators the slip. So, when the tram was about to leave the market square, he leapt out through the closing doors and into the side street that led up to the wine tavern where he had arranged in vain to meet Patricia all those weeks ago, and encountered Lutz instead.

Frank glanced back to see the tram carrying off his pursuers. They had not even noticed that he had jumped off. He could relax. Could now make his way to the station without the need for furtive backward glances. But to be on the safe side, he kept to the side streets anyway.

When he reached the station, the next train was due to leave in ten minutes. He found an empty compartment at the front of the train, put the briefcase he had snatched up on the seat beside him and took a deep breath. He smelled the cordite still clinging to his memory of that moment. His heart still pounding from the execution of Breitner, from the sight of his prostrate, bloated body.

The solitude of the empty compartment was the first opportunity he had had to catch his breath since the crushing tension of that moment. He closed his eyes and contemplated the clear, crisp mountain air that lay ahead. The gentle crunch of snow underfoot. And above all the snug warmth of Patricia in his arms and the fragrance of her unique perfume enveloping his senses.

He was not prepared for the scene that greeted him when he felt the train begin to move and opened his eyes. Leaping onto the train several carriages back were the new bane of his life: the two youth sports louts in their forage caps.

'They clearly have an idea where I'm heading,' he told himself. The palm of his hand rested on the gun in his pocket for reassurance. There was no way he would lead them to Patricia. He knew he would have to find some way of shaking them off.

When the train pulled into Zurich about an hour later, Frank jumped out, made for the ticket office and bought a single to Como. A quick glance back told him his stalkers were following his every move. But with the ticket to Italy in his wallet, he was confident that he could shake them off around Lake Como at the very latest. If necessary, he would draw them into the forests along the lakeside and finish them off there. He would then take a ferry to the northern end of the lake and hope to hitch a ride up over the Maloja Pass. If all went well, he could be back with Patricia the next day.

Settling into his new compartment with these thoughts as the train pulled out of Zurich, his attention was drawn to the briefcase beside him. He had not dared open it until now for fear of what he might find inside. But he knew it contained a record of Patricia's life.

When he slipped his hand inside the briefcase and removed the file, he saw at once that it was still smeared with dried traces of Breitner's blood. He glanced nervously at the corridor outside the compartment. He was alone. It was a thin file and, when he opened it, he found only two pages inside. Frank took some comfort from this; he saw it as a sign that she had not played such a big part in Breitner's life as he had feared.

The first page was a potted family history that contained little Frank did not already know – aside from the names of her parents, which were recorded here as: "Father: Roche, Léon (J)" and "Mother: Sommer, Ingeborg", together with details of the schools she had attended in France, Stuttgart and now at the University of Basel. Alongside her father's name was an inscrutable reference in parentheses: (See File D7LY.MK3-RL). Other than this, the only surprise was a short paragraph devoted to a year spent in London as an au pair with a family that suggested some kind of association with the corridors of power. She had never once mentioned this to Frank. He wondered why.

The other page was simply a long list of names, many of which were suffixed with the same designation that followed her father's name: (J). Frank assumed this was to identify them as Jewish. The names meant nothing to him until he reached the bottom of the page, where he found Zimmermann, Joachim (J) and Eigenmann, Götz. A line had been ominously drawn through Achim's name. Against his own name there was a bold question mark.

Attached to the back of this page with paperclips Frank found two photographs. One was of Patricia. Her hair was longer, which lent an added layer to her intriguing beauty. He gently eased the photo out from under the paperclip and sensed a warm thrill as he slipped it into his right inside pocket. The other photo was a group picture of half a dozen men in SS uniform, all except for one; this man wore a black homburg hat and a black coat that seemed almost too long for him; he looked decidedly uncomfortable in the company of all those uniforms. Frank assumed this to be Patricia's father.

He folded these two pages with the remaining photograph and tucked them into the left inside pocket of his coat, intrigued to see what Patricia would make of these two pages when he showed them to her. Then he slid the now empty file back into the briefcase and placed it on the rack above the seat opposite in an effort to disown it.

These thoughts of Patricia and the image of her father preyed on his mind like clusters of doctor fish nibbling at every corner of his brain. But eventually the movement of the train carried him off into a deep sleep that kept his overactive imagination quiet. Even the stops between Zurich and the Italian border, with their whistles and the bustling activity of people getting on and off the train, were not enough to rouse him.

It was not until the train lurched to a stop at the border station of Chiasso that Frank finally woke. Before he was even able to get a grip on his surroundings, still dazed and disorientated as to his whereabouts, he was rudely stirred into action by a Swiss border guard demanding to see his passport. Fumbling around in his coat pocket for the document, Frank was aware of the border guard's growing impatience. And when he finally produced his German passport, he sensed this impatience turn instantly to suspicion.

The border guard looked Frank up and down and carefully scrutinised every entry in the passport. Frank felt his heart begin to race. Was it possible, he wondered, that news of Breitner's demise had already reached the southern border of the country? Was he already the subject of a manhunt? His fears appeared to be substantiated when the border guard disappeared down the corridor with his passport.

Frank sensed panic threatening to take hold as he considered his rapidly vanishing options. But he knew it was pointless trying to get off the train. He would have to bluff his way through somehow. A full ten minutes passed as he attempted to rehearse a credible story against the backdrop of a pulse rate so high that he could almost feel his heart pounding against the wall of his chest. All to no avail. The rehearsal proved unnecessary when the border guard returned. He handed the document back to Frank without another word and moved on to the next compartment. Frank slipped the passport under the cold metal of the firearm that still lay ready in his coat pocket.

After a further ten minutes or so, the train slowly pulled out of the station, across the Italian border and Frank started to relax. Until the train lurched to a stop again. It was the turn of the Italian border guards to demand his travel documents.

When the official in his navy uniform and jackboots appeared outside his compartment, Frank instantly reached into his coat pocket. But he was a little too ready to please. A touch too eager for his own good. In the meantime, the passport he had slipped into his pocket now cradled the barrel of the firearm between its covers. Unaware of the shifting landscape submerged inside his pocket, he pulled out the document to show it to the border guard, dragging the firearm with it. The weapon crashed to the floor.

In a flash, the right boot of the border guard trapped the firearm underfoot. Suddenly Frank found himself staring into the barrel of another gun. Its owner was yelling back over his shoulder in an incomprehensible rapid-fire barrage of Italian. It took just a few seconds before two more dark navy uniforms appeared behind him. They instantly trained their own firearms on Frank, as the first border guard kicked Frank's gun out into the corridor, pushed him head first down onto the seat and slapped on a pair of handcuffs. Frank was dragged to his feet, wincing as the metal cuffs cut into his wrists.

By now, the commotion in his compartment had attracted an audience around his carriage. His captors had to manhandle him off the train and force a way through the throng that had gathered on the platform. Beyond the crowd, further up the platform, Frank caught sight of the sports youth louts who had tracked him all the way from Breitner's house. They stood watching the spectacle from a distance. The expression on their faces betrayed a look of disappointment that they had been deprived of their opportunity for vengeance.

They watched in silence as Frank vanished from view behind the crowd.

Chapter 24

As the wintry brown meadows and lowland streams slipped past them on the train, Ellen could not escape the feeling that Frank too was fast receding from her life. It was a sentiment that stayed with her for the entire journey, as the meadows gave way to a looming horizon of white mountain peaks, and she and Marthe changed to the narrow-gauge railway up through the twisting snow-covered landscape to St Moritz.

When eventually they stepped off the train into the crisp, cold air, Ellen took a deep breath, enjoying the freshness of the Alpine atmosphere. She was struck by the way the fading sunlight sparkled gently in Marthe's dark hair, revealing shades of auburn she had not noticed before. It lent a new dimension to the beauty of her companion.

"The chalet is a little way out of town," Marthe said. "So we'll need a taxi."

"Your hair glistens so beautifully in the sunlight," she added, running a hand through Ellen's strawberry-blonde locks as they climbed into the car. Ellen smiled. The coincidence of their thoughts both teased and unnerved her.

As the taxi carried them up through the town, past the luxury hotels and out to the more sparsely developed, snow-covered slopes, Ellen pondered Marthe's remark with a growing sense of excitement intermingled with wariness. She could not help seeing in her words a confirmation of the intimacy between them that Marthe seemed keen to keep alive. The thought sent a tingle of anticipation coursing through Ellen's body.

The drive up to the chalet took little more than five minutes. But already the sun was dipping behind the mountains when

Ellen stepped out of the car and felt the crunch of snow underfoot. She was struck by the intense quiet. The deep snow around them seemed to absorb every sound – from the noise of the car as it disappeared back down the mountainside to the crack of a twig that succumbed to a squirrel darting up into the trees.

The chalet itself lay in splendid isolation close to the forest. It was a cosy little lodge. More modest than Ellen had been expecting. The perfect place to put the events of the past few weeks behind her, she told herself, when Marthe took her on a short tour of the house and showed her where she would be sleeping. It all seemed so perfect to her. The walls and floors and ceiling all of wood. The red and white gingham curtains over tiny windows that looked out onto the snowy slopes and enhanced her sense of cosy comfort all the more. And in the lounge a stone fireplace just waiting for them to sit by the log fire together in the evening to chat and contemplate the flames.

Ellen knew of course that any conversation would go deeper than mere chat. But she had come prepared. Throughout the train journey to the mountains, she had mulled over the point of her being here at all. And now, as she unpacked her suitcase and then lay on the bed to relax after the journey, her thoughts began to settle on a decision.

Marthe had taken the precaution of bringing two packets of soup and some coffee with her.

"Tomorrow, we can get in some food from the Konsum," she said, when Ellen emerged from her bedroom and found Marthe in the kitchen opening one of the soup packets. "Or we could go out to eat if you prefer."

"I'm happy to eat here," Ellen replied. "It's so nice and cosy."

While the soup was heating up, Marthe disappeared through a side door in the kitchen, before re-emerging a few minutes later with an armful of logs, lighting the fire and opening a bottle of red wine she had brought with her.

"I'm sorry it's only Maggi soup," Marthe said some thirty minutes later as they settled down to eat beside what by now was a roaring log fire.

"It tastes fine," Ellen assured her.

"It's not so much the flavour that bothers me," Marthe explained. "It's more the image. The idea of consuming products from a company with such a dubious reputation."

Ellen looked quizzically over her soup at Marthe.

"Urs insists they were pioneers. Not only in nutrition. As employers also. They provided their workers with benefits that everyone else could only dream of back in the Thirties. But all I know them for is the pact they made with the devil just before the war. Perhaps it was necessary to survive, but it left a nasty taste – until they were de-germanised by Nestlé. Even then a lot of people found their soups hard to stomach for a long time to come."

"Well, let's drink to Nestlé then," Ellen said, raising her glass. "Cheers."

"Santé," Marthe replied with a smile.

"I'd really like to thank you, Marthe."

Marthe reached out and placed a hand on Ellen's arm.

"Whatever for?"

"For inviting me. For being there for me all the time. For being such a comfort."

"It's been my pleasure. Really," Marthe insisted, moving closer and taking both of Ellen's hands in hers. "I enjoy your company. Urs does not always have as much time for me as I would like. He's often at the clinic or away at conferences. Or with his protégé Stefan."

"Even so, I'm sure you would be relieved to have me out of your hair for a while," said Ellen.

"What do you mean?"

"I was thinking about Frank in the train up here. The way he's slipping away from me. I've been in limbo for the last few weeks. Not knowing where he is. Or what's happened to him. Always fearing the worst. Going round in circles chasing someone who is supposed to be him, but who keeps evading our searches."

Marthe clasped Ellen's hands tighter as she spoke.

"For all your wonderful kindness and hospitality, Marthe, this is really not a life anymore. It's purgatory. And all the while, I have an employer back home, patiently waiting for me to get back to work." She paused. Marthe relaxed her grip before Ellen continued: "So, I've been thinking that maybe it's time I returned home. For a time at least. We'll stay in touch of course. And as soon as you have any news for me, then I will fly over right away. But at the moment, I believe it's the right thing to do."

"I understand how you feel," Marthe said. "But you don't have to make any hasty decisions. While we're here in the mountains, you will have plenty of time to consider it in depth."

"I already have," Ellen insisted. "I don't need any more time. I've really made up my mind."

"Well, at least you can enjoy the mountain air for a few days," Marthe said, withdrawing her hands and sitting back in her chair. "Tomorrow, we'll have a late start and stroll down to Suvretta House for lunch. They have a fabulous restaurant there, where we can talk more about your plans, and then go shopping in town."

Ellen was adamant in her own mind that any further talk would be pointless. But she told herself that lunch and shopping would provide a pleasant distraction. So she and Marthe spent the remainder of the evening contemplating the flames of the log fire and punctuating each other's thoughts now and then with idle chatter.

When Ellen eventually closed the outside shutters in her bedroom, drew the quaint little gingham curtains over the windows and climbed into bed, she fully anticipated that Marthe would come knocking on the door and sneak into bed beside her. Ever since she felt her hands play appreciatively with the strawberry-blonde tresses of her hair when they arrived in St Moritz, Ellen had the feeling that she was keen to renew the intimacy they had shared a few days earlier. The prospect excited her in a curious way that she would not have imagined possible until a short time ago. As she lay in the snug warmth of her duvet, she longed for the door to open. Yet the frisson that came with this anticipation was also fraught with unease and self-doubt. And it was these misgivings that she eventually carried with her into a deep sleep. Not until the morning did her self-doubt give way to a sense of disappointment when it dawned on her that Marthe had kept her distance after all. She wondered whether it had anything to do with her decision to return home.

Marthe was already up and about by the time Ellen woke to the sound of activity in the kitchen. And music. It was 'Lola'. The track that Ellen was surprised to find what seemed like weeks ago to be a source of such excitement for Marthe. And she was no less surprised to hear the music now playing in the kitchen below.

By the time Ellen emerged, it was already on 'This Time Tomorrow'. Where will we be? What will we know? It all seemed so apposite. Why is it, she asked herself as she entered the kitchen, that every song ever written seems to have been penned for that given moment when its words carry such meaning?

"Good morning Ellen," said Marthe breezily, switching off the music when she turned and saw Ellen in the doorway. "I'm sorry. I hope the music didn't wake you."

"It's already well past nine. Normally I'd be awake much earlier than this. So, no. The music didn't wake me," Ellen said, catching sight of a cassette player on the table as she spoke.

"Did you bring it with you?" she asked.

"The cassette?" Marthe replied, flicking a switch to boil the kettle. "I thought it would be nice to have a little music in our retreat."

"I would never have taken you for a fan of the Kinks. Or of anything but classical music really."

"Well, Ellen. You should never be taken in by appearances," Marthe said, throwing two spoonfuls of tea into the teapot next to the kettle and glancing at Ellen as she did so. The glance came with a smile so engaging that it struck Ellen as almost flirtatious. She felt the colour begin to rise in her cheeks.

"I like all kinds of music," Marthe added, instantly delivering Ellen from her embarrassment. "But my favourite song on this album is 'Lola'."

"It's one of mine too."

The wistful expression in Ellen's eyes and the musing tone of voice as she spoke these words were not lost on Marthe. Ellen could see from the way she was hanging on her every word that she was expecting more.

"It so reminds me of Frank," she said, not wanting to disappoint. "I was constantly dropping hints and trying to persuade him to get it for me. We were always teasing each other about it, because he wasn't so keen."

"Did you need his permission? Could you not buy it yourself?"

"We have an agreement that we never buy things for ourselves, but only for each other," Ellen explained.

"But from what you tell me about those impulse buys, he doesn't always keep to that agreement, does he?"

"In his own mind, I think he does."

"But he never bought 'Lola' for you?" Marthe asked, as she poured the boiling water into the teapot.

"No. He never did."

These words cast Ellen's thoughts adrift. She sank back into a deep pause for reflection. Caught in a tangle of memories.

"I suggest we take a walk in the snow this morning," Marthe said at last, placing a cup of tea on the table for Ellen. "And work up an appetite for lunch. I've already phoned and booked a table."

For all her attention to detail, Marthe was not the most efficient of women. The morning was already half over by the time they had dressed for the snow and found themselves on a trail that skirted alongside the forest with only the occasional squirrel to distract them. Perhaps it was the raw chill of the morning air that reduced their conversation to pleasantries and idle chat. But Ellen was not so sure.

Her doubts were vindicated when they eventually arrived at the hotel restaurant for lunch at noon. Their entrance was accompanied by the sound of a piano playing in some unseen corner of the lobby. There was a luxury to the place that Ellen had never experienced before – elegantly upholstered furniture, plush carpets and strategically placed aspidistras. It gave her a sense of disquiet, a feeling she was out of place here, until Marthe led her into the restaurant, where they were guided to a table with a stunning view over the snow-covered valley. It took Ellen's breath away. And in the cosiness of the restaurant with Marthe, she instantly felt at peace.

"I'm going to miss you," Marthe said once the waitress had taken their orders and disappeared with the menus. She stretched both hands around the vase of flowers on the table between them and rested them on Ellen's hands as she spoke.

"I will be back, you know." Ellen gave Marthe's hand a reassuring squeeze. "I really appreciate your friendship. At the moment, though, I need to get back to work and return to some semblance of a normal life while the search for Frank continues. Being here, so close to the whole story, is just beginning to make me question everything. My own sanity. Who Frank is. Or even who I am."

"Believe me, there's nothing wrong with your sanity or who you are."

"So you agree that there's still a huge question mark over who Frank is?"

"We'll find an answer to that question eventually," Marthe insisted. "Urs is also not convinced by the idea that he is involved in drugs. He believes Frank is suffering a schizoaffective psychosis."

"Is he a good psychiatrist?" Ellen asked, bringing a smile to Marthe's lips.

"Oh yes. Perhaps not very imaginative and too quick to accept conventional thinking. But he's very caring. The thought and care he showed when he supported me in the referendum are very typical."

She paused and contemplated the vase of flowers for a moment, before adding: "Which makes it strange that he's not so good at personal relationships."

"How do you mean?"

"He has a problem showing his emotions. It's probably something to do with his background. He's from the most eastern part of the country. Very conservative. And I'm originally from the French-speaking part in the west. That's a big difference. They call it the Rösti Curtain where I come from. It's not quite the Iron Curtain, but it defines the cultural divide between the German and French speakers. That's why I like it in Basel: although it's a German-speaking city, the Rösti Curtain is so frayed at the edges that it's more like the French-speaking part. They show their emotions more. Even vote the same way very often. In the referendum to give women the vote, more than eighty percent of men voted yes. Just like in Lausanne or Geneva. Thank goodness! Because there were some German-speaking areas where most men voted no!"

"I didn't realise there was a problem between you and Urs," Ellen said, unwilling to dwell on the referendum as it reminded her too much of Frank's mission here. "You always seem to get on so well."

"Oh, it's not a problem. We do get on well. And I'm proud to say he was one of the eighty percent," Marthe reassured her with a smile. "But we have our differences. And I think I've become more aware of them since you've been here."

Ellen felt the colour rising in her cheeks.

"Oh gosh, don't look now," Marthe said, and unwittingly helped to spare Ellen's blushes. "The man who has just walked in and taken the table behind you is the most perfect example of that difference I was talking about."

Ellen discreetly turned her head to witness the fuss being made of the man who took the table behind her. He glanced up as she looked. He had a rather doughy and slightly chinless, but inconspicuous face, wore horn-rimmed glasses and boasted a supremely confident parting in his brilliantined hair.

"He's a member of parliament," Marthe explained in a whisper that succeeded in expressing extreme revulsion despite the hushed tone of her words. "From Zurich."

"He looks harmless enough," Ellen said.

"That type often does. I've been told he's distantly related to Bismarck. But he's a completely heartless beast. A throwback to darker times, when he belonged to the National Front in the Thirties. He was especially good at organising violent demonstrations to intimidate political cabarets that were critical of Nazi Germany and forcing them out of business. I can imagine what his position was on the Jews and other refugees fleeing to Switzerland at that time. Now he sits in parliament as a member of another party under a different name. But it's basically no better than the old fascist party.

"Last year he made a name for himself with a referendum to kick out immigrants. Especially the *Tschingge*, as he calls Italian guest workers. No one thought he had a chance of winning. And fortunately he didn't. But it was very close. Much closer than anyone thought was possible. About 51 to 49, I think. Some of the German-speaking cantons even voted yes. Of course, only the men were allowed to vote then. If we had the referendum today, maybe we women would have made a difference. But now everyone is talking about foreigners. He's made the divide in the country wider than ever."

"We have something similar in England. A politician who talks about rivers of blood if the tide of immigration isn't stopped," said Ellen. "But no one really takes him seriously."

"They should," Marthe replied. "The last time anyone in this part of the world talked about a river of blood was in the 1930s. And we all know what happened then. Countries thrive on migration. Switzerland has. Almost twenty percent of the population are immigrants. In fact, many of our big companies were founded by immigrants. Most were started by Huguenots from France. Just like Frank's Triumph motorcycles you talked about recently, built by German engineers."

By now, Marthe's eyes were alight with the irrepressible fire that Professor Abegg had spoken of.

"People like him see immigrants as a threat to their precious identity," she continued, and nodded in the direction of the man behind Ellen. "Which is nonsense of course. Identity is not static. It evolves. Countries, like people, also evolve the more they're exposed to what lurks beyond the boundaries that hold their identity back. And that's what makes them prosper. I just thank God women have a vote now. Maybe we can help to change the way men think."

"So, is Urs anti-immigrant?" Ellen asked.

"Good heavens no! That's not what I wanted to say. Urs is a very decent man. I was trying to explain the difference between the language regions here. Then I got carried away when that awful man came to sit on the table behind you. I forgot that St Moritz is his favourite haunt. You know, only a couple of years ago an Italian guest worker was beaten to death in this town just after he started his campaign. He's a disgusting man.

"Perhaps it's time to order coffee and then settle up," Marthe added with an abruptness that was completely at odds with the cosy prospect of roasted coffee beans.

"No coffee for me thanks," Ellen said, feeling moved to decline the offer by the sight of a Marthe who was visibly seething and could plainly not to wait to get out of the restaurant. This was another side of her that Ellen had not seen before. It surprised her almost as much as the more appealing, intimate side.

Once they were out of the hotel and strolling in the crisp mountain air again, Marthe had calmed down. She linked arms with Ellen.

"Come on. Let's go shopping."

They strolled down into St Moritz and spent the rest of the afternoon browsing the upmarket shops. Ellen had already eaten into much of her savings in the last few weeks, and there was no way she could consider splashing out on any of the luxury clothes or accessories on the shelves. But Marthe was intent on spending her way out of the anger she had allowed to upset her mood and also, to put Ellen's mind at rest, on buying her a silk scarf from Chanel.

"Please, I insist," Marthe said, when Ellen attempted to turn down her offer. "I'd really like you to have it. As a souvenir. Something to remember me by when you get back home."

Framed in this way, it was impossible for Ellen to refuse. So she politely tucked it away in her handbag and allowed Marthe to spoil her for the rest of their stay in St Moritz.

They spent the next few days shopping, walking in the snow and strolling over the frozen lake. Although there were plenty of other people wandering there, Ellen sensed a flutter of nerves the first time she stepped out onto the expanse of ice.

"You really don't need to worry, Ellen," Marthe reassured her with a smile. "They hold horseraces on the lake. So I'm sure it will take your weight."

The thought of thoroughbreds pounding their way over the snow and ice seemed improbably bizarre to Ellen. But she glanced around at the other people promenading on the ice, and she had to admit they all looked perfectly at ease.

"Sadly, we missed the racing by a week or two," Marthe added. "You would have enjoyed it. When you stand on the corner and watch the horses come round the bend, it's so exciting. The drumming of their hoofbeats on the ice and the tourbillon of snow behind them. There's nothing quite like it."

The passion in Marthe's words as they stood there on the lake brought the scene so vividly to life that Ellen could just imagine the excitement all around her. Could almost hear their hoofbeats on the ice, almost see the horses bunching up and jockeying for position before they raced away down the straight, kicking up the snow behind them.

She looked about at the women in their expensive furs and the men keeping themselves warm with their fat, pungent cigars as they strolled over the lake. She could just imagine them cheering on their favourites. And for just the fraction of a second, she caught a familiar movement among them. A mop of thick brown hair bobbed into view. Then vanished again. For the briefest of moments, Ellen's heart appeared to stop. She clutched Marthe by the arm.

"Are you all right?" Marthe asked.

"Yes, of course. I'm fine," Ellen lied.

At that moment, specks of snow landed on her face as if from nowhere and bathed her in a singular sensation. As she looked up through the flurry of snow at the mountain peaks above, she wrapped an arm around Marthe.

"This is another world," Ellen said.

The audible thrill in her words concealed a nervous tension. It really was another world. So remote from life as she had known it until a few weeks ago – and from Frank himself, who with every twist and turn in the search for him had become increasingly unfamiliar, her memory of him vanishingly faint. It was almost as if he had ceased to exist, while she was discovering a new part of herself each day. If it had not been for that mop of dark brown hair.

But Marthe only heard the thrill in Ellen's words and smiled with her sparkling, sapphire-blue eyes.

"Tonight is our last night before we head back home," she said, "and I think we should dine in style this evening. So I've booked a table at Badrutt's Palace." There was an air of defiance in her voice that struck Ellen as odd. Was this a rebellion against her husband, she wondered, or against the ordered life Marthe's sister led with her watchful accountant and neatly kept cash book.

"But for now," she added, let's walk back up to the chalet before the sun goes down completely."

They were less than halfway back and the sun had already tucked itself firmly behind the mountains. The light was fading fast. They quickened their pace past the shops and luxury hotels and on up the hill to the lodge.

"What's that?" Ellen asked, pointing at a building on the other side of the road. They had walked this way every day since arriving here, but this was the first time the modest domed construction tucked away in the wooded slope above them had caught her attention.

"It's the Segantini Museum," Marthe explained, then added in response to Ellen's blank expression: "Segantini was an Austrian artist. Or Italian, whichever way you want to look at it. Born an Austrian in an Italian region. But the Swiss also like to think of him as one of theirs, because he lived so much of his life here, where he painted all his great work. But he remained stateless his entire life. A true citizen of nowhere, who spent much of his time crossing borders. A *frontalier* all his life. I wonder what the member of parliament behind you at lunch earlier in the week would have thought about Segantini if they had lived at the same time…

"But it's closed now," Marthe added, raising her voice as Ellen wandered over to take a closer look.

At the entrance to the museum stood an imposing marble sculpture. The beautiful naked form of a young woman with long flowing hair rose from a marble crag that was populated in relief by a group of sheep and lambs. Inscribed on the base of the sculpture were the words: *La bellezza liberata dalla materia.*

"Why didn't I notice this place before?" Ellen asked, turning to Marthe, who by now had caught up with her.

"You were too preoccupied perhaps," Marthe suggested.

"It's so beautiful."

"Beauty liberated from the material world," Marthe said.

Ellen gave her a mystified look.

"That's what the inscription means. It was originally made for his tomb. I have no idea why it ended up here. He's actually buried in a village not far away called Maloja, close to the Italian border."

Ellen was transfixed. In that moment, the sentiment carved into the marble appeared to encapsulate exactly the feelings that imbued every sinew of her soul.

"Come on Ellen." Marthe tugged at her arm. "It will be getting dark very soon, and we need to change for dinner."

The jerking motion of Marthe's hand brought Ellen back from her dreamy captivation.

"Not far from here, high up on the mountaintop, is the hut where Segantini lived and painted," Marthe added. "It's still standing after all these years. When you come back in the summer, we'll take a walk up there. As you put it earlier, it's another world."

'When I come back,' Ellen repeated quietly to herself, sensing a tingle of anticipation at the idea. "But it's not my world, is it?" she said.

Her words were tinged with sadness.

"I mean, I'm sure it's beautiful in the summer as well. But will I have found Frank by then? Will my world have returned to the way it was until a few weeks ago?"

Marthe placed a comforting hand on Ellen's left arm. But had no answers for her.

For the rest of the evening, Ellen continued to turn these questions over in her mind. Even the haute cuisine at Badrutt's Palace, which Marthe had hoped would mark the perfect end to their stay, failed to put these questions to rest.

"I recommend the Capuns," Marthe said. "They're a local speciality, and I'm told they do it perfectly here."

Ellen could not say whether it was the troubling uncertainties on her mind or the spaetzli dough wrapped in Swiss chard leaves that wreaked havoc with her digestion. But whatever the cause, she was left feeling uncomfortably bloated.

"Try this," Marthe said, when the waitress placed two small glasses on the table. They contained a concoction that looked as toxic as a solution of Congo red salvaged from some long defunct chemical laboratory. "We call it Röteli. It's good for the digestion."

Ellen looked askance at the glass in front of her. She was unconvinced. Only when Marthe picked up her glass and downed the contents in one was she reassured that at least it was probably not poisonous. Gingerly she followed Marthe's example and downed the potion. The sweet medicinal flavour may have lent credence to the claims of digestive relief. But it brought an expression of disgust to Ellen's face. And in fact did nothing for her indigestion.

Yet she managed a smile through her discomfort as she recalled the digestive woes inflicted on her by Frank's culinary skills.

"You see," said Marthe, "I told you it was good for the digestion."

"It's not that," Ellen explained. "I was just thinking of the meals Frank sometimes cooks for me. He comes from

Lancashire, where he grew up on things like tripe and vinegar, so I suppose it shouldn't have come as any surprise the first time he tried one of his own specialities on me."

The smile morphed into a wince at the memory of the time Frank had spoken of a trip to Hamburg, where he had discovered their local speciality Labskaus. What probably excited him more than anything, she explained, was the similarity in name to the lamb scouse his mother used to cook for him. But what he tasted in Hamburg was quite different, he said. And he insisted on making it for her one evening. Ellen could not understand how he could even contemplate eating it. The mash of corned beef and beetroot with a side of herring not only looked awful and tasted terrible, but smelled even worse.

"… but then he always did have a strange sense of smell," she added, recalling that this was something he always put down to the slightly misshapen bridge of his nose.

"Do you think that's possible?" Ellen asked, as they left the restaurant and wandered back up the hill arm in arm through the snow.

"I'm sure it is," Marthe assured her.

Ellen mulled over these memories and uncertainties all the way back to the chalet. And contemplated the evening which Marthe had intended to be so perfect yet ended in digestive disgruntlement.

But perfection of another kind came eventually once they closed the door on the cold night air. After they had both turned in and Ellen had settled down under the cosy warmth of her duvet, she heard the gentle squeak of her door opening. It was Marthe. Not a word was said. Ellen felt her pulse quicken and sensed a tingle as Marthe slid in under the duvet and put an arm around her. They remained in each other's embrace for the remainder of their last night in the mountains. And Ellen carried the memory of that night with her all the way back on the train the next day.

After their return, Urs Zellweger appeared unsurprised when Marthe told him of Ellen's decision to return home.

He received this news with the kind of clinical psychiatrist's response that Ellen had come to expect from him.

"A wise decision under the circumstances," was the way he framed it. All trace of Frank, he conceded, seemed to have dried up. And it was probably best if she returned to her normal routine at home in London while the search continues. They would of course contact her as soon as they had any news.

Ellen had the impression Dr Zellweger would be quite pleased to see the back of her. It would be understandable, she told herself. But it did make her wonder whether he suspected his wife had struck up a relationship with their house guest that was just too intimate for his comfort. She coloured at the thought. When Marthe promptly jumped in with the suggestion that they go to the station the next day to check on departure times and get a ticket, Ellen sensed that she had noticed her blushes. And this made her colour up all the more.

"That's a good idea, Marthe," Dr Zellweger said, glancing at Ellen with a smile. "And you can be sure we will contact you as soon as we have any news," he repeated, setting Ellen's mind at rest that he had given no thought to the colour in her cheeks.

It was not that he was actively encouraging her to return. Nor did Ellen have any doubt that, as a psychiatrist, he would have understood what a wrench it was for her to leave behind the last known links with Frank, however tenuous. But she was very much aware of how wedded he was to his psychiatric hospital. Yet some weeks had now passed since the man who was said to be Frank absconded from the clinic. And in the meantime, this stranger appeared to have become more a person of interest to the police than a patient of Dr Zellweger's.

Ellen sensed the blushes fade with these thoughts, and she became outwardly more composed. But inwardly she was beginning to wonder how the return to her normal routine would shape up. Whether it would even be possible to revisit life back in London as it had been until a few weeks ago. Simply to carry on as normal. Constantly awaiting a call from Marthe or Dr Zellweger. Or from the police.

Chapter 25

Countless months in Italian custody had left their mark on Frank. After his arrest in possession of a firearm by the Como police, he was interrogated for weeks by the local Carabinieri, who suspected him of antifascist motives for entering Italy. When they concluded he must be an agitator for the Justice and Liberty movement, he was transferred to Milan for more aggressive questioning. For his entire incarceration he was kept in solitary confinement. The only thing that kept him going was the memory of Patricia and his determination to get back to her as soon as he could. He recalled the very first time he laid eyes on her, when she captivated him with the fullness of her raven hair. The indescribable beauty of the moment when she threw her head back, letting her hair catch in the corner of her mouth. And the way she would discreetly part her lips to sweep away the black strands with her fingers. Or the beguiling motion of her ankles when he followed their effortless progress up the steps and watched the seam of her stockings as they traced every movement. But these sweet memories remained forever in the shadow of the bitter knowledge that she had no idea where he was or what had happened to him. That maybe she even thought his failure to return was his way of dumping her.

He had no idea just how many months passed before he was eventually allowed to pass on a message to the office of his father's old lawyer. Burow himself was now retired, but if he could persuade a lawyer's office in the country of Italy's closest ally to vouch for him, he felt that he might stand a chance of getting out of the hole he was in. Whether it was this that did it, he had no idea. But one day, out of the blue, they began to treat him with a little respect. And as the interrogations became less frequent and less intense, he sensed that his case was being handled more seriously.

So it was that, in due course, he was charged with nothing more than unlawful possession of a firearm. Just a few weeks later, he was deemed to have served a sufficient sentence for this crime and was quietly released.

When he finally got to taste fresh air again, Frank was shocked to find it was mid-winter. He must have been in detention for the best part of a year. And all that time there had been no contact with the outside world. They had refused him permission to contact anyone except immediate family. But he saw little point in contacting his mother, since she would probably not even know him.

And, as Frank had remained entirely cut off from Patricia, the vast gaping hole that now defined whatever there had been between them totally consumed his every waking hour. He was desperate to know how she was and what had become of her after he failed to get back over the Maloja Pass as planned. So, on his release from prison, he wasted no time finding a tram to the station.

His prolonged incarceration had made him acutely aware of how time had left him behind. So much had passed him by. On the tram, he was struck by shop facades now sprayed with the words 'Negozio Giudeo' under the Star of David in evil imitation of his own country. It was something he had never seen in Italy before. On a more cheerful note, some of the newspapers on the newsstands at Milan's sparkling new triumphalist central station were full of pride in the national football team's bid to retain the World Cup in Paris during the summer. But his acute awareness of time past was brought home to him above all when he bought a newspaper to read on his journey north.

The headline that caught his eye was the news that Ribbentrop had just been appointed to head the Ministry of

Foreign Affairs in Germany. How much deeper into its swamp of incompetence can this country stoop, Frank asked himself, when it appoints a dull salesman of cheap, sparkling wine to represent it abroad? But if nothing else, the news made him thankful that his own case was now closed and hence no longer a foreign affair.

Other than this, the newspaper offered little newsworthy content, and after crossing that fateful border at Como, he soon fell into a deep sleep.

It was an early March morning in 1938 when the train pulled into the central station at Basel. The square outside the station bristled with too much activity for so early on a Monday. Frank sensed a buzz of excitement in the air. Even the trams were running. It was as if the whole city had come out to celebrate his arrival home. The return of the hero who had rid the streets of the Third Reich's ambassador for thuggery in Basel. For the first time in this city, he felt the world was on his side, and he leapt onto the first tram that came along with a heart which was lighter and more carefree than he remembered it having been for a very long time – until he tried to find a seat amid the swarm of excited faces that crammed into the carriage more tightly with every stop as it headed into the city. Why so early in the morning? Frank asked himself. Where were they going?

As the heat and noise in the tram rose, memories of his last night in this city impinged on every direction his mind tried to take in an effort to shake off the images of Breitner bleeding onto Patricia's file. A whole year had passed. Yet it seemed like only yesterday when he fled the scene of reckoning, with Breitner's youth sports thugs in hot pursuit. He pictured the whole place on high alert when the killing was discovered. Imagined it could well have led to a local diplomatic crisis while he was incarcerated in Italy – in the same way the killing of Gustloff did in Davos. And today, the moment he stepped off the train, he felt the eyes of the city were on him.

When Frank was released from his Italian prison, he was surprised to have the two pages from Patricia's file returned to him by his jailers, complete with photographs. They kept the gun, of course. But he had expected them to hold on to Breitner's file contents as well. Now, finally back in the place where he had come under her spell, he was tempted to take the pages out and pore over the contents before their reunion. But he felt deterred by the people crowded around him on the tram. The cause of his hesitation lay deeper than mere inhibition. It lay right down in the fragile new roots of his existence – roots that were struggling to establish themselves in the rocky soil of an entangled past which seemed already close to withering. He knew the contents of the file would lend a definition to this past which reason told him would be best left in darkness. It served no one's interest. Certainly not his, nor Patricia's, nor her father's. As he was contemplating where the pages with their photograph of Patricia's father might be safely and permanently disposed of, his thoughts were interrupted by a disembodied voice:

"*Endstation.*"

The tram was already grinding to a halt. It was the end of the line. But he could see that they had not even reached the city centre. Like a lost sheep, he followed the crowds that poured out onto the pavement. And it dawned on him as they streamed onto the street that the city's three days of Fasnacht were just getting under way. He recalled from the last time he was here that the carnival started at four on a Monday morning with drums, pipes and an endless parade of vast painted lanterns. The dense thronging crowds and droves of people on the streets came to him as a godsend. Gave him the cover of anonymity he needed on his journey through the city. And he let them lead him wherever they were headed – a murderer in their midst, however heroic he thought himself to be.

When he came to the bridge over the Rhine, he slipped away down the steps to the river where he had been accosted by Silverstone and the cloth cap. It occurred to him that there could be no better guardian of Patricia's secrets than these swirling waters. He hunted around on the promenade for a stone that would take the pages and anchor them firmly to the river bed. Finding one of suitable size, he then wrapped the pages around the stone and threw it as far out into the river as he could. As it sank from view some thirty metres out, Frank knew that he would never be confronted any longer with the truths in Breitner's file. He felt the last burden slip gently from his shoulders.

The relief proved premature. When he looked up, the crowds were still flocking above him towards their mysterious goal. They reminded him of lemmings, and he wondered whether it was wise to follow them. But what unsettled him in particular was the sight of a solitary figure standing out above them all. It was not only the fedora or the way he was moving more slowly, out of step with the rest, that caught Frank's eye, as the familiar figure stopped now and then searching the crowd around him. Silverstone would catch his attention under any circumstances.

'Is it me he's looking for?' Frank asked himself. 'Has he seen me?'

He even wondered whether Silverstone might have also been at Breitner's door on the night of the killing. Everything had happened too quickly to get a clear picture of how many there had been.

Silverstone's role in the events that had so irrevocably shaped Frank's life before he was thrown into prison remained as impenetrable as ever. But one thing was clear to him: whenever the American crossed his path, he seemed to be waving a flag of huge yet baffling significance in his face. This cold and absurdly early winter morning was no exception. Feeling safer with him in his sights, however, Frank hurried back up the steps and re-joined the flocking crowds on their flight across the bridge.

But in the time it took Frank to reach the throng, he had already lost sight of Silverstone. The American had melted into the mass of heads and shoulders marching on ahead of him. He could have been any one of a hundred or more figures bobbing up and down over the river. And by the time the flow of eager faces had carried him with them away from the swirling waters of the river that now held Patricia's secrets in their grip and into the market square, Silverstone could have been anywhere.

The pavements around the square seemed fit to burst with all the people heaving into it to watch the cortège. The massive lanterns artistically decorated and daubed with obscure satire. The groups of drummers and pipers, like a macabre military parade in their grotesque masks and costumes. And confetti cast by clog-wearing figures in blue smocks and outlandish masks whose huge upturned noses competed for attention with bright yellow straw that passed for hair.

With the appearance and instant disappearance of Silverstone in this babbling current of colour and noise, Frank sensed an unseen menace in the shelter which this crowd had earlier seemed to give him. A menace he felt could strike from any direction at any time. He sought the refuge of a wall and sidled his way around to the far end of the square, where he found the relative safety of a shop doorway opposite the old town hall.

The cortège continued its procession through the square. Turning away from the heaving crowd in front of him, which was completely immersed in the parade, he slipped into the back streets and headed towards the zoological gardens and Patricia's flat. The very thought of the sparkle in her eyes and the sweet charm of her lips as she opened the door had his heart pounding in expectation as never before.

The let-down came step by step. At this hour, he would expect the light in the window of her flat to be on as she prepared coffee and breakfast. The place was in darkness. It occurred to him that she might be out already enjoying the carnival. He tried the outside door, but it was locked. Frank recalled that, when Lutz had found this accommodation for her, he insisted that the nameplate beside her door bell be left blank as a precaution. But as Frank reached out to ring the bell, he saw that it now bore a name: 'M. Hunkeler'. He searched the other nameplates. 'P. Roche' was nowhere to be found. Had he come to the wrong address?

No. Although Frank had only been to her flat once before their retreat to the mountains, this door was etched on his heart. And to see her nameplate now expropriated in this way overwhelmed him with alarm. As he was considering what to do, whether to ring the bell that should be hers anyway, the door opened. A man emerged. Mid-forties, well-dressed.

"Excuse me, does Miss Roche no longer live here?" Frank asked.

The man looked Frank up and down with suspicion.

"I don't know anyone by that name," he said.

"She lived here a year ago," Frank insisted. "In the top flat."

"I only moved in last week. In the top flat," the man said with a passing smile that betrayed the kind of smart-aleck sarcasm Frank might have expected from Silverstone.

"Mr Hunkeler?"

"Yes?" the man said, who had already reached the end of the path by now. He was plainly taken aback at being addressed by name, and he turned to face Frank, as if to challenge him.

"Do you know where she went?" Frank asked.

"No idea."

Impatience had driven M. Hunkeler out onto the pavement by now. And he headed off towards town. He had no further time for interrogation by this intrusive stranger.

Frank was devastated. The last time he had stood on the steps to this house, they had offered him boundless comfort. Today they stood for infinite despair. All at once, he found himself swallowed up in a vast gaping hole of fathomless gloom. Irretrievably lost and adrift. Like tears in the rain. No sense of direction. No ties. No attachment. Ineffably alone. Where could she possibly be?

He was barely aware of what he was doing or where he was going as he followed in the footsteps of M. Hunkeler and made his way back through the back streets to the city centre. Drawn towards the sounds of carnival that filtered through the streets ahead. The drums and pipes. The steady hum of the crowd. Would he find her there, among the milling crowd?

When he came to the steps that ran down to the market square, Frank instantly stopped in his tracks. The stairway below was eerily empty except for one solitary figure. Approaching slowly up the steps came a lone piccolo player, dressed in the costume of a jester. The two horns of the cap swayed to the rhythm of the piccolo. A mask covered the face to the tip of the nose. The piccolo player headed straight towards Frank at the top of the steps, seemingly oblivious to his presence. There was something both sad and sinister about that solitary march. A foreboding sadness that was underlined by the dark inscrutable eyes buried deep behind the mask.

Frank moved aside and let the piccolo player pass. He watched the swaying horns of the cap recede to the incessant tune of the flute. Silhouetted against the far end of the street, the diminishing figure was gradually lost in the shadows. The bleakness of the jester's lone march into the distance perfectly encapsulated Frank's own condition.

As the sound of pipes and drums rippled up the steps from the market square, Frank was brought slowly back to earth. The constant hum of people on the streets below reminded him that Silverstone was still out there somewhere in the crowd.

Reckoning that his best move for now would be to get a room at the Kolping house, he decided to make for the other side of the river. It may not be open yet, he told himself, but at least it was not on the route of the parade, so he could lie low outside until it opens. Since the only way there lay through the carnival celebrations, he knew he would have to be on his guard all the while as he let himself be jostled to his goal amid a masquerade of oddly earnest frivolity: the grotesque figures with their yellow hair and huge noses forcing confetti on him with a menace that seemed ironically out of place; piccolo players dressed as ducks parading in newspaper uniforms; and smart city gents beating a solemn rhythm on their drums and led by a vast bloodsucking creature with enormous tentacles that rose out of its head. Snatches of the weird procession seemed strangely familiar. But the heaving mass of bodies that pushed him in all directions at once levered open a gap in Frank's aching skull. His head began to spin. And his disjointed mind had its work cut out negotiating even the narrowest path through the thicket of people that lined the pavement.

He recalled that Silverstone was given to the use of a flick knife, and it struck Frank that this slow progress, cheek by jowl, through the carnival crowds would be just the kind of situation he would relish. An opportunity to slip the blade quietly into his back and vanish in the throng. The closer they pushed and pummelled against him, the more vulnerable he felt.

The bizarre carnival masks only added to the sense of menace, until suddenly Frank caught sight of him. The burly American figure stood sentry on the step of a corner shop which lifted him head and shoulders above the rest of the crowd. The twilight of the lanterns gave Silverstone's face a ghostly quality, but he was distressingly real. And although Frank now had him more safely within his line of vision and could measure the danger, this gave him little comfort as the American commanded a view over the whole street. Frank knew he would never get past without being spotted.

He stopped in his tracks and began to edge back the way he had come. But there was no path back. Only a few steps away and moving hungrily in his direction was one of the two sports youth louts together with a familiar figure looking horribly recovered from Frank's last encounter with him. It was Wolfgang.

Frank sensed his destiny closing in on him. His mind paralysed by a desperate indecision that had him marking time when time was fast running out. It was a wavering that epitomised every twist and turn of his life. Save maybe one. And no prospect of reprieve – until a group of carnival revellers swallowed him up and bundled him through the doors of a tavern that opened onto the pavement behind him. A typical Basel pub.

As the crowd disgorged Frank from its midst to find a table, he saw Wolfgang's bull neck and head just disappear from view past the window outside. He had evidently not seen Frank. The atmosphere in the restaurant was thick with cigarette smoke and the tenacious aroma of onions and gruel. The place had the unappetising feel of a soup kitchen for the starving homeless. But it was a safe haven for the time being and, although his head still span with the noise of drums and pipes, it gave him a chance to catch his thoughts. In a smoky corner far away from the door, where the air was almost too thick to breathe, he found a spare seat at a table and ordered a bowl of gruel in the hope that it might at least warm him up inside. But his mind was too embattled. Too preoccupied with that gaping hole where Patricia ought to be, with thoughts of their last moments together before they said goodbye. The sweet taste of commitment on her lips.

The sound of knives on the plates, the ostentatious roars of laughter and other desperate signals of enjoyment droned and echoed through his shelter. Scythed their way into his skull, splitting it in two. His head pulsated with the pain. And the vapours of gruel that wafted up from his bowl of soup brought a retching nausea to his throat. He pushed the bowl away from him. And found it instantly shoved back in his direction by an anonymous arm, which pushed a steak knife back in its wake. This disembodied limb was wearing a wristwatch so loud and garish it almost screamed the time at him. But the pain was too intense, the nausea too deep, and his eyes too blurred for it to register. He needed to get out. To find his way to the Kolping house. And then start his search for Patricia once the carnival was over.

Seizing the steak knife for protection, he manoeuvred his way out of the tavern and into the fresh air. On the street outside, the crowds had begun to thin out. Morning had arrived. It proved to be a warm and sunny day for early March. But a dark menace still hung in the air. A chill nipped at his face like hungry crows in search of winter food. And Silverstone still stood sentry across the street some fifty metres from the bridge. But he was not alone. In front of him, staring out over the bridge, stood a woman Frank sensed he knew.

'Are the two of them together?' Frank asked himself. And: 'Who is she? Where have I seen her before?'

This oddly familiar woman had the look of a vulture, as she hovered on the pavement's edge, her beak ready to tear into the carrion. Frank inched closer, his head throbbing so intensely he could barely focus his eyes. His hand was clammy on the handle of the knife in his pocket. He tightened his grip as he drew nearer to Silverstone and to this woman who was so strangely known to him.

Images of his mother forced themselves on him as his hand gripped the handle of the knife ever tighter: images of the way she had lain there before him, her face drained of colour, or of anything that could be associated with the woman he had known as his mother. All bones. Not even sufficient food for a vulture.

'That's it,' he muttered to himself. 'The old crow who called herself his mother's nurse.'

That was the woman he saw before him now, their eyes close enough to meet. But where was Silverstone? He had disappeared. What was his game? In his place now, Frank saw the huge ungainly frame of Wolfgang some distance behind the woman. And could not escape the crazed, burning appetite for retribution in those ugly eyes. He briefly caught the glint of metal. A gun aimed directly at him. Frank pulled the knife from his pocket and lunged past the woman.

Too late. The searing pain that came with the crack of gunfire ripped through Frank's chest and felled him instantly. Struggling for breath from the clear sky above as he lay where he fell, racked with pain, he saw the sky turn dark from the ugly frame of Wolfgang standing over him. Saw the gun aimed straight at his head. Felt the shot.

Frank lay motionless. A small dark crater between the eyes lay exposed to the elements. A hole quite unremarkable, except for the trickle of blood that ran a steady path down the neck and mingled with the colours of confetti on the pavement around him.

Chapter 26

Climbing the stairs to her Fulham flat after so many weeks away, Ellen was struck by just how alien everything appeared in all its familiarity. And the moment she opened the door to all the memories of life with Frank, she felt instantly engulfed by a deep sense of being totally alone. All the time she had been in the company of Marthe, she could convince herself that Frank would eventually be found. Now she was back in this place that had once been the home she shared with him, she was not so sure.

She put the suitcase down, loosened the silk scarf that Marthe had bought her and let it slip out of her hands onto the coffee table, where it curled around the words 'Bank of England 1920–1944'. She ran her fingers over Frank's spidery handwriting. Would he ever get to finish his article? Ellen wondered.

There was a part of her that wanted to look for somewhere else to live at the first opportunity – to put as much distance as possible between her present life and her memories. But there was another part of her that saw this as defeatism, if not betrayal. So, as she settled back into the routine of life in London, the idea that one day she would eventually hear from Frank began to take root again. It was an idea that accompanied her every day on her way to work and back. Across Putney Bridge, where she would stop to watch the wheeling gulls or the passing of an occasional 'boat beneath a sunny sky'. And think of Frank.

Marthe kept in touch and, true to her promise, invited Ellen to join her for a week or two in the mountains and visit the Segantini hut. But Ellen declined. She preferred to get on with her life and wait until Marthe had tangible news of Frank before returning to Switzerland.

It was not until around twelve months later, in 1972, that Ellen eventually accepted an invitation from Marthe. The call did not come with any news of Frank. Nor was Ellen initially inclined to accept, despite Marthe's attempts to sell the local carnival as a unique event in the city's calendar that no one should miss. What clinched it for Ellen was the second call that came some days later. No longer was it framed as an invitation. It now took the form of an urgent dispatch. Frank had been found.

Ellen took the Night Ferry from Victoria that same day, changing in Paris for the early morning train to Basel.

The perfume of Marthe's warm embrace when she stepped onto the platform in the early afternoon reminded Ellen just how much she had missed her companionship over the past year. Her husband on the other hand offered Ellen the kind of cordial handshake and welcoming words she had long since come to expect of him. Courteous and correct to the last. But there was an air of ministration about the way he took Ellen's suitcase and guided her out to the waiting car. It suggested to her he was there more as psychiatric support than anything else.

"Where is he?" Ellen wanted to know. "Where did they find him?"

"Let's get you home first," Dr Zellweger said. "We can explain everything there before we see the Kommissar."

"The Kommissar?" Ellen asked.

"He has news of Frank," Marthe added, placing a reassuring hand on her arm as they climbed into the car.

"News? I thought they'd found him."

"A man answering his description has been seen," Marthe explained. "The Kommissar will tell you more when we see him tomorrow."

The disappointment on Ellen's face was plain even to Dr Zellweger in his rear-view mirror.

"The Kommissar wanted to see you this afternoon, then phoned to say that he had been called away on an important case," Dr Zellweger explained. "But he will be there for you in the morning."

Marthe had initially invited Ellen over to experience the Fasnacht. But this idea was abandoned the instant they heard news of Frank's appearance. Now that Ellen was forced to wait yet again for any kind of explanation, and Marthe pointed out that the carnival celebrations would already start at four in the morning, she suggested they could at least kill time by seeing some of the parade before their appointment at the police presidium. So they were both already wide awake when the phone rang, getting ready to join the carnival crowds.

"Normally, I would take the tram," Marthe explained. "But no trams will be travelling through the centre during Fasnacht. Of course, it will be impossible to park in the Storchen. It would already be full by four in the morning."

"That's where they found Frank sleeping, isn't it?" Ellen asked.

"Yes. There used to be a smart hotel there many years ago. But they pulled it down in the Fifties to build the car park."

"It's strange to think Frank chose to sleep there, isn't it?" Ellen remarked. "Almost as if he knew that it was once a hotel."

Marthe looked across at Ellen with a curious expression in her eyes that slightly unnerved her.

"Of course," Marthe said, as she brought the car to a halt around the corner from the large grey featureless building that Ellen had come to know so well, "one big advantage to be invited to the police presidium, is that we can drive almost to the door without any problem. So it doesn't matter if the Storchen is full."

In this respect at least, Marthe was proved wrong. She needed all her charm to persuade an exceptionally humourless traffic policeman that they had an appointment at the police station which entitled them to leave their vehicle there. He wanted to know who they were going to see, why and for how long. Even took their names and registration number to check on the story. It was an officiousness that was completely in keeping with the dull leaden greyness of their uniforms and the building from which they took their inspiration and their orders. It was something Ellen had grown used to on her first trip here. She had met too many grey officials and had to wait too often and too long only to be rewarded with the anti-climax of no news and no progress. Perhaps for this reason, Ellen was not unduly surprised or upset, but simply frustrated, when they were led into an empty side-office on their arrival and told to wait.

"The Kommissar has been called on an urgent case suddenly. He comes back as soon as possible," the fresh-faced young assistant said as he ushered them inside. No clue as to why they had been called. And no apology for making them wait.

"That's something you're probably used to here already," Marthe said. "They never tell you anything unless you ask the right questions. But you can never know what the right questions are."

"Oh, and they never say sorry. Especially to a woman," she added with her index finger raised as if to punctuate this afterthought with an exclamation mark.

It was plain to Ellen from the sour look the man gave Marthe as he turned to leave that he had understood every word. And to underline their displeasure before he disappeared into the corridor, Ellen gave vent to her own frustration.

"I thought from the phone call it was urgent. I mean, if it was important enough to drag us out at seven in the morning, then the least you could do is give us a clue what it's all about."

The man smiled uneasily over to Marthe, repeatedly muttering a word that sounded to Ellen like 'mort', as if this explained everything. Again and again he repeated it in what Ellen saw as a nervous response. To her, his manner carried the look of a helpless and lost little boy on his first day at school. Suddenly he did not appear to understand a word of English, and she almost began to feel sorry for him. Then Marthe explained:

"Seven is not really that early here, especially during Fasnacht," she said. "I told him we would come back later. In the meantime, we can watch the parade. The Kommissar will probably not be back for a couple of hours. He's been called out on a murder case."

It was not until they were out in the chill of the dark early morning, mingling with the crowds and the noise of the carnival, that the significance of Marthe's last words dawned on Ellen.

"Did you say murder?" Ellen shouted out over the rat-a-tat of the drums and shrill sounds of the piccolos. The last word fell in the brief fraction of a second between beats and seemed to descend on the whole carnival procession in their vicinity. All heads turned in Ellen's direction. But they were not distracted for long. Their imagination was caught by the huge painted lanterns that bobbed and floated through the streets above their heads.

"But the Kommissar is not in the murder squad, is he? Why should he be called out on a murder case?"

Marthe said nothing in reply.

"You don't think it has anything to do with Frank, do you?" Ellen persisted, but Marthe's attention was elsewhere. Her eyes were alight. She was in another world.

Ellen had never seen Marthe so disinhibited in public before. And it was clear that these questions had no place here. But she did not ignore Ellen. She was plainly keen to take her along into the celebrations. Yet it was an occasion for which Ellen felt the word 'celebration' to be a peculiar description.

As the huge painted lanterns passed by, with inscriptions that she was unable to decipher, it all seemed strangely serious to Ellen. When Marthe told her it was a carnival, she had imagined something like Rio or Venice. But no one here was letting their hair down. No one was dancing. It appeared more like a ceremony to Ellen. And yet, from the look on their faces, like little wide-eyed children, everyone appeared to be enjoying all the pageantry, the lanterns in the darkness, and the almost military sound of drums and pipes that filled the air. Marthe was no less enraptured than anyone else. Taking Ellen by the hand she started moving, almost dancing, through the jostling crowds.

"It will start to get light soon," she shouted to Ellen through all the noise. "We shall go and have a soup then to warm us up before we see the Kommissar."

But Ellen found it hard to share Marthe's enthusiasm. There was something ominously sinister about the military rat-a-tat of the drums in the air – and the lanterns floating huge and ghostly in the darkness with their indecipherable messages – which disturbed her to the core.

"What do they all mean?" Ellen asked, pointing at the lanterns as they passed.

"They're all making political and social statements. Making fun of the politicians. Or the city's big companies," Marthe shouted over the noise. "Like that one there," she added pointing at one that Ellen could at least vaguely understand as a comment about Vitamin C and Hoffmann–La Roche.

"But that's the most controversial one this year," Marthe said with an oddly chilled glee, pointing at the image of a man at the mercy of a woman. And alongside this picture the words *Der dressierte Mann*.

"Also the most disturbing," she added. "After everything we won in the referendum last year, this Esther Vilar comes along to undermine us. And the men love it."

"Is that *The Manipulated Man*?" Ellen asked with a hint of recognition in her voice. "I was reading about it recently. It's caused quite a stir at home as well."

Marthe let out a hiss of disdain, which was instantly swallowed up by the piccolos and drums.

Every group of pipers and drummers, each led by a drum major, were all dressed in a variety of costumes with huge grotesque masks on their heads. Ellen found the bizarre militaristic mood to the parade unnerving. And on the corner where Marthe had positioned herself and Ellen, it was a mood that only added to her sense of vulnerability.

'Or am I just paranoid?' she asked herself.

They had been standing on that corner for a good half an hour, when suddenly Ellen became aware of a loud enthusiastic voice of what seemed a particularly artless American behind them. His drawl put her in mind of Bill Plattner – even the way he kept repeating his appreciation with a facile "awesome!" reminded her of the way Frank's sculptor mate would caress his granite artwork with such wonder – when at that very moment she could have sworn she saw him.

"Frank's here!" Ellen shouted, beside herself with disbelief.

She had never known until then what the expression 'a sight for sore eyes' truly meant. The shape of that head, the mop of hair so delightfully, so intimately familiar to Ellen – even in the deceptive light thrown by the lanterns, the street lamps and the slowly dawning sky. She was certain it was him, and she grabbed Marthe's arm.

"Where?"

Marthe craned her neck in all directions, her eyes alight with expectation. She appeared more excited even than Ellen was, as if it was *her* lost property that had just been found.

Ellen pointed over to the other side of the street where she had spotted him. But he had already vanished. Then, from behind a crowd that was drowning in a sea of confetti just tossed into the air by a carnival-goer, he reappeared. A little closer now.

"There!"

Ellen wanted to tug at Marthe's arm, but it was not there. She was gone.

"Marthe!"

Her companion was nowhere to be found. But by now Frank had seen her. And he was moving in her direction. Yet strangely. He moved in a way that she had never seen in him before. His expression was foreign to her. He wore a hunted look. A crazed desperation widened his eyes.

He began lunging towards Ellen. Dr Zellweger's warning words that Frank may be suffering a psychosis flashed into Ellen's mind. And she panicked. Suddenly she was terrified of her own husband. But this was not her Frank. This was not the man she had married.

"Marthe!" she cried again. "Marthe! Frank's here!"

Frantically, she searched the faces around her. Where was she? And in the corner of Ellen's eye a glint of metal from Frank's hand. It was the scream of a woman's voice beside her that made her spin round…

… just in time to see him fall. His face stared up at Ellen from where he lay, a trickle of blood from his head mingling with the colours of confetti on the pavement around him. So far away. So distant.

The scene that took shape around Ellen as her senses slowly returned told her she was back in her own bed in England. But this was only the cruel kind of trick the mind plays halfway to waking. For a moment, which extended far too long for comfort, it was a scene that was completely alien to her. A room she did not know. A bed she had never slept in before. Wearing bedclothes that were not hers. And a clean smell of sterility in the air. But Marthe was beside her, holding Ellen's hand, as if there to lead her back to consciousness.

"Where am I?" Ellen asked, and she realised as she uttered those words that she was with the only person who had brought her comfort in the last twelve months.

"You've had a terrible shock, Ellen," Marthe said. "You're in hospital."

"But Frank. What about Frank?"

"You need to rest, Ellen. I'll let the doctor know you're awake," was all Marthe said in reply, and the softness of the voice instantly lulled Ellen back to sleep.

How long she slept it was impossible for her to tell. But she suspected it was only a few minutes, because the doctor was just entering the room when she woke again. With his shock of dark brown hair, it could almost have been Frank, and her heart momentarily leapt at the sight. But the white coat quickly brought her down to earth.

The doctor shook Ellen's hand as she sat up and introduced himself with a name she was unable to understand. But he spoke impeccable English.

"You have suffered a shock, Mrs Goss," he explained (as if she needed to be told), "but all the vital parameters seem to be in order, so I think we can discharge you into the safe hands of Dr Zellweger's wife."

Marthe's reassuring hand rested on Ellen's arm.

"Come on, let's get you home," she said. But Ellen was far from reassured by either Marthe's hand or the doctor's words.

"What about the police?" she asked. "We were supposed to see the Kommissar."

"The Kommissar will want to speak with you, of course. He will come to the house once we've got you home."

The anxiety that had permeated Ellen's every thought since she received Marthe's call was shot through now with a wholesale fear made inconsolably real by her memory of Frank lying at her feet on the pavement. Or had she just dreamt it in the melee of grotesque masks and incessant drums?

She knew the answer, of course, without having to ask. And the knowledge cowed her into a timid silence on the drive back to the Zellwegers' home.

"Now, you relax in the lounge, while I make you some tea. And I will be with you in a moment," Marthe said as she disappeared into the kitchen. Ellen retreated to the sofa in the lounge and listened to the boiling of the kettle.

Sitting on the sofa that had been so familiar to her the best part of twelve months ago, she was struck by how little had changed in the intervening months. The same newspaper, the *National-Zeitung*, lay on the table. And the same magazines. Only the headlines and pictures had changed. And the erotic watercolour still hung there on the wall. Tantalising. Ellen smiled at the sensual scene as the thought occurred to her at that moment – knowing Marthe in the way she now did – that perhaps Marthe herself was one of the women in that naked embrace.

It was a thought that prompted oddly unconnected memories of a day out with some school friends when she was fifteen or sixteen. They were strolling through a narrow, wooded valley carpeted with primroses and bluebells on the southern fringes of Dartmoor one afternoon, when suddenly the idyllic peace was shattered by a thunderous crash. It shook the earth they walked on. They all instantly froze to the spot in trepidation. Ellen had never felt such paralysing fear in her life. When the group finally plucked up the courage to continue on along the valley, they soon came upon a clearing at the foot of a rock that rose above the trees like a monument to the bucolic nature that surrounded them.

There on the ground lay a man. Quite still. Ellen and her friends stood watching the lifeless body. Was this the cause of the thunderous crash? Had he fallen from the rock? Had he thrown himself off? The girls looked uncertainly at each other, immobilized by their fear.

"Feel his pulse," one screamed. "We need to feel his pulse."

But nobody moved. Until Ellen stepped up. She gripped the man's wrist in her hand and felt for the pulse with her thumb. She felt nothing. Not the slightest movement. Not the vaguest hint of life. The man was plainly dead.

Ellen had never before been confronted with death in any form, let alone in such a stark and direct encounter. What shocked her most was the ordinariness of the scene, the unremarkable picture of the man who now lay before her. A life completely expunged.

Two of her friends instantly ran to find the nearest village where they could phone for an ambulance. While the rest of the group waited at a safe distance from the corpse, Ellen casually wandered off into the woods and picked bluebells to help her through the long wait, as if the trivial pursuit of woodland flowers would blot out this confrontation with death.

And today, in the slightly disturbing comfort of the Zellwegers' lounge, her bluebells were these two naked women in their erotic embrace.

Ellen did not cry. Did not even gently weep to herself when Marthe sat down beside her, poured the tea and explained what happened when she fainted. Ellen was imbued with an intensely uncomfortable feeling of guilt that she was unable to shed any tears. In her heart, she had long since come to terms with the idea that she would never see Frank again. She had sensed it the moment she decided to return to London. And yet, when she did set eyes on him, face to face, he came to her like a figure in a dream. Lunging in her direction from a crowd of strange faces and masks, before instantly vanishing again. It was hard for her even to comprehend the idea that this could actually have been Frank. After all these months.

"Can I see him?" Ellen asked.

"You will have to identify the body," Marthe said. She placed a comforting hand on Ellen's arm. "And they may want to perform an autopsy."

"An autopsy?"

"Kommissar Staehelin will send someone to pick you up tomorrow morning," Marthe explained.

"I still don't understand," Ellen said.

"Do you remember just before you returned home last year that a man was attacked on a shooting range and his gun was stolen? And the police suspected it might have been Frank?"

Ellen gave Marthe a look both incredulous and disapproving.

"Apparently a gun like that was used in the killing of a gangster around the time you returned to London," Marthe continued. "Last night, a man was shot in the same house. That is the murder case which was occupying our Kommissar yesterday, because they think that Frank may have had something to do with it."

"That's ridiculous!" cried Ellen. "My Frank a killer?"

As she spoke these words, her memory of that fleeting sight of Frank resurfaced, the glint of metal in his hand.

"The Kommissar will speak with you later. You know, the police are watching the house where the dead man lived since many months already. He was in a drugs gang, and now they are thinking that Frank has had something to do with it."

"No, it's ludicrous," Ellen insisted. Then asked: "What happened exactly? After I passed out?"

"Ellen, my love." Ellen had never seen such tenderness in Marthe's expression before. Even when they lay in each other's arms, it was usually lined with a certain severity – hardened maybe by years of disappointment.

"You can tell me, Marthe. I saw him fall. I remember his face staring up at me, deathly white and empty."

Marthe placed a hand on Ellen's arm.

"They are not sure until they have made an autopsy, but it was probably a heart attack."

Just like his mother, Ellen thought. Or was it? There were still so many unanswered questions. Yet all of a sudden none of them interested her any longer. She had spent so long searching and waiting for Frank, only to discover a huge unexplained hole. And she had no wish to spend any more time filling this hole with pointless questions and answers. She was too tired for that. Frank was gone. He was dead. That was all she needed to know.

"It's all over, then."

Marthe nodded.

Chapter 27

The next morning, when Ellen was called to identify Frank's body, she was on edge. Her nerves frayed. She was wondering after all whether she could cope with seeing his lifeless corpse. What bluebells could there possibly be to help her through this ritual?

Marthe suggested they go and have a drink at a café in the market square beforehand to calm her nerves. They found a table on the first floor next to a window overlooking the market square.

"I have been thinking a lot in the months while you were away, Ellen," said Marthe as she sipped on their coffee. Ellen was lost in her thoughts, gazing out over the stalls in the market. The winter vegetables. Cheeses. And cut flowers to add a splash of colour.

"What you said about Frank and how difficult his mother found him when he was a child," Marthe continued. Ellen turned her gaze back at Marthe, who could not escape a hint of curiosity in her eyes. But there was also a resignation, a flatness to Ellen's expression.

"What of it?" she asked.

"When I was in America with Urs, I was reading some fascinating articles by a psychiatrist there about the survival of human personality after death. I think his name was Stevens. Or maybe Stevenson. It was really thought-provoking. Of course, Urs found it complete nonsense. Like most of his colleagues. He just laughed at the whole idea, which really shocked me at the time, because I knew how much he admired C.G. Jung's work. But 'it was Jung's contribution to psychotherapy that was so important,' Urs said. 'Not all that visionary, occultist nonsense.'"

"What does all this have to do with Frank?" Ellen asked.

"This Stevens man wrote about children with memories of a former life. They recalled places, people and also past events, things that happened long before they were even born and which they could not possibly have known. And when he checked their stories, he found those people and places had really existed. The events had really happened. They corresponded exactly with the memory of the child – although the child could not possibly have had knowledge of those places and events. It's even been suggested that injuries in a past life can show up as deformities in the next life."

By now the resignation and flatness of expression in Ellen's eyes had vanished. She was slowly becoming hooked on Marthe's words.

"So, it makes me wonder whether the wild stories Frank would tell his mother – and perhaps his nightmares also – were memories of a past life. And if so," Marthe speculated further, "whether these memories were triggered again when he came to Switzerland. Like a *frontalier* of the consciousness, crossing a very private, unknown frontier."

Ellen now stared at Marthe, open-mouthed. She was lost for words.

"Of course, Urs would dismiss the whole idea as absurd."

"So you haven't spoken to him about it."

"Of course not," Marthe scoffed. "He can only consider tidy explanations."

"Maybe you underestimate him," said Ellen. "His refusal to accept his colleagues' assessment of Stefan suggests his mind is not the straitjacket you imagine it to be."

"As I've said before, Urs is a very decent man. All he could see was a tormented, abused boy who was not receiving good care. But he doesn't have the imagination to consider anything beyond the boundaries defined by his profession."

"And do you really think it possible that Frank might have been reliving memories of a past life?" Ellen asked.

"Why not?"

This improbable idea lodged in Ellen's mind and would not be budged for the rest of the day, as her memory of Frank's odd quirks came flooding back. The books that he would buy. The Bartok LP. And the strange deformity in the bridge of his nose. These images and the notion that they could be the shadows of a past life – the markers of some dark frontier that Frank had crossed – followed Ellen every step of her way to the mortuary.

To see him laid out, as if for some ritual event, was the strangest experience in what had become a whole catalogue of bizarre experiences for Ellen. It was plainly Frank, the man she had shared so much with in their short time together. The man she had known so well. But had she?

His face looked worn. Embattled with troubles completely alien to her. She was struck by the way the strangely buckled bridge of his nose appeared more prominent than ever. She recalled Frank telling of his father's cruel description of this odd deformity: as if shot between the eyes at birth. And that was exactly the way it looked to her now as he lay on the slab. It underlined her sense that Frank seemed to have assumed an entirely new persona in his absence from her. It was unmistakably Frank. But was it really Frank in a past life? Was that deformity the mark of an injury sustained by a different Frank from the one she had known? It seemed an absurd idea. She almost preferred Dr Zellweger's diagnosis of a psychosis.

"Yes," she said, turning back to Kommissar Staehelin, who stood at a discreet distance behind her. "It's my husband."

For all his discretion, however, the Kommissar was a persevering man. And after the identification, he left Ellen no peace. He called her into an interview room.

"Please take a seat, Mrs Goss," he said, beckoning her to one of four seats next to a table. Aside from the table and chairs, the room was bare. The spartan air lent a particularly cold edge to the Kommissar's rasping voice, which made every word sound as if it was being dragged over a cheese grater as he spoke.

He was joined by a colleague from the drugs squad, and together they visited one preposterous theory after another on Ellen. Each one more nonsensical even than the idea that Frank may have been reliving a past life. She was glad that Marthe had insisted on staying with her for moral support. Perhaps it was the way the Kommissar reminded Ellen of her brother-in-law, Malcolm, which caused her to dislike the man so much with his moustache, white socks and black slip-on shoes.

The colleague from the drugs squad was no exception in this respect. And while she was being bombarded with their questions and assumptions, Ellen wondered what they could be so afraid of that they felt the need to make such a pathetic show of their manhood. What are they trying to prove? Ellen wondered. She imagined that Marthe would put it down to women finally winning the right to vote.

In the case of Kommissar Staehelin it was clear. He was burdened with the obligations of protocol. And the proofs he had to bring were all as neatly defined for him as the topiary trimmed so tidily across his upper lip.

Convinced that Frank had been mixed up in some international drug syndicate, the Kommissar was bent on getting every scrap of information she could offer him on Frank's movements. Who his friends and acquaintances were. What his job was. What he did in his spare time. And although the whole scenario he painted appeared ludicrously far-fetched to Ellen, she could not deny the glint of metal in Frank's hand. Or the witnesses: not only had a person matching his description been seen in the house a year ago; that person had even gunned one of them down. Apparently, he had also made off with a briefcase, which they thought probably belonged to the victim.

It was at this point in his account of events that the Kommissar became especially persistent, because they had failed to locate the missing briefcase, and they suspected it might contain crucial evidence that could help break the whole syndicate. So he wanted to know exactly what Frank had been carrying when she saw him. Did he have anything which might have fitted that description and might have fallen into the hands of a bystander, he wanted to know. And had she noticed anyone suspicious lurking nearby at the time ('As if I might have been taking notes in my panic,' she remarked to herself).

She had often wondered whether men with moustaches are so busy trying to cope with their complexes that they have no time to consider anyone else's feelings. It was certainly plain to Ellen that the Kommissar did not even entertain the idea she might have any feelings at all. She began to think he actually suspected her of complicity.

Ellen had the impression that he thought she was lying through her teeth when she presented such a normal picture of Frank and their marriage. That he found it impossible to imagine she had not noticed anything odd about Frank's behaviour before he disappeared – which of course she had, but surely nothing of any relevance that would interest the Kommissar.

It was Marthe who suggested that maybe Bill Plattner was connected with the whole story. And Ellen had to admit that, when she added up all the features of Frank's relationship with him, the theory was not implausible. The man certainly had a strange influence on Frank – she recalled the time she found them together in Bill Plattner's studio – and he always had plenty of money to throw around. His expensively renovated cottage was only the most obvious example. And it was after becoming friendly with him that Frank started acting so strangely. Maybe that's what he meant by "reinventing" himself, she thought. Perhaps it really was the psychosis of drug abuse. Suddenly nothing seemed impossible any longer.

The Kommissar's ears pricked up at this part of Ellen's story. His eyes were alight with the excitement of making what he saw as a significant discovery. It was clear that he found the Bill Plattner connection plausible as well. At last Ellen had given him something he could get his teeth into, and for once her words had left him with a satisfied smile on his face. This gave her hope that it would be the last time she would be subjected to his tedious questioning. In the last months of searching, wondering and waiting, she had become so estranged from Frank and everything about him that the flat insistence of the Kommissar's one-track mind struck her as a huge waste of time for both of them. And it irritated her intensely. She was thankful to Marthe for her inspiration, albeit it slightly worried by the trouble that might now be brewing for Bill Plattner. For deep down, Ellen was quite sure the man had nothing to do with drug dealing or mafia-style killings any more than Frank.

When Marthe and Ellen took their leave of the two policemen, Ellen hoped dearly that she would never have to see them again. All she wanted now was to put everything behind her and get on with her life. As they left the interview room and walked into the corridor, Marthe touched Ellen on the arm, as if to detain her for a moment, and turned back to the Kommissar. It was a short conversation, and Ellen could not understand a word of what was said.

"I expect you would like to take Frank's body back to England with you," Marthe suggested when she turned back to Ellen and they were walking down the corridor.

"I hadn't really thought about that."

"Well, the Kommissar just explained that it will be some time before they can release the body. He will contact us when they've completed the autopsy."

They did not exchange another word as they walked out of the building and back to the car. Heavy clouds loomed over them. But when the first drop of rain caught Ellen in the eye, it barely registered. She remained deep in concentration. And Marthe had no wish to disturb her thoughts.

As they drove to the Zellwegers' house on the Bruderholz hill overlooking the city, Ellen imagined Frank wandering these streets, walking by the Rhine. He was always so fascinated by rivers, she told herself. He would surely have loved it here.

"You know," she said, turning to Marthe at the wheel, "I'm sure Frank never thought for one moment about what should happen to him after his death. We certainly never discussed it, except to agree that we would both prefer to be cremated than buried. But I can imagine he might have liked the idea of his ashes being cast into the Rhine and carried away into the North Sea."

Marthe looked askance at Ellen.

"How much would a funeral cost here?" Ellen asked. The question met with a long pause as they stopped and waited for traffic lights to turn green.

"I have no idea," Martha replied after some hesitation. "But I can find out for you, if you like."

Ellen interpreted her words as an offer rather than a commitment. But as soon as they arrived back at the Zellwegers' house, Marthe fished out the yellow pages and began to make enquiries.

Ellen wondered how she could possibly have managed without the help of Marthe. It was not simply the way she took the onus of helping to cope with all the questions from the police, organising the practicalities of the funeral arrangements and collecting all the necessary documentation. It was also the selfless friendship she offered.

When the police eventually released Frank's body, and they were able to set about making concrete arrangements for the funeral, Marthe even took it upon herself to select the music for the service. She noticed a flicker of discomfort in Ellen's expression at mention of the word 'service' and was reminded of her difficulty with religion and the problem she had when they visited the basilica the year before. Marthe reassured her that it would be a secular event held in a chapel at the cemetery.

But when it came to the music, Ellen could not imagine even a secular service would sit comfortably with Frank's taste, which probably would have been Led Zeppelin, Pink Floyd or, at best, Miles Davis. So she was grateful for the exquisitely ethereal piece from Erik Satie that Marthe selected. And she was certain that Frank would also have approved.

But at the last minute, just the day before the service, Marthe included another piece.

"It's just been released," she explained. "And when I heard it on the radio, it seemed the perfect choice to close the service."

It was Vicky Leandros singing *Après toi*. Luxembourg's entry for the Eurovision Song Contest, which sounded to Ellen like a fairly crass choice. But when Marthe played the song, she had to admit that it did seem perfect. It could have been especially written for the occasion.

Even the clouds in what seemed to be an otherwise perpetually overcast sky parted briefly on the walk up the monumental steps to the chapel. This unpretentious rectangular edifice at the end of a long arcade lit up briefly in the sun as they entered, as if to welcome them. The service itself was a modest affair. Only Marthe and Dr Zellweger were there with Ellen. And she knew that this quiet departure would have been exactly the way Frank wanted it.

It was not until Ellen saw the coffin disappear behind the curtains to the melody of *Après toi* that she was overcome with emotion. She had said goodbye a year ago, had seen him fall before her feet without a word only recently, and now she was watching the final moment of his obliteration. After all that she had been through since Frank left their flat over twelve months ago and her slow acceptance of the likelihood that she would never see him again, this moment did not come with the eviscerating sense of loss she would have originally expected. But still it was the most bitter moment of her life. The tears were unrelenting. Marthe held her hand, squeezing it until the music eventually faded.

As they were leaving the chapel, and Ellen slowly regained her composure, Marthe and her husband tried to persuade Ellen that one of the cemetery vaults would be the ideal place for the urn. But Ellen had got it into her head that Frank's ashes should be dispersed into the Rhine and left to journey their way north. It was a proposal that drew a look of disapproval from Dr Zellweger.

"It's not the kind of thing that is encouraged here," Marthe explained in a whisper. "But I think it's a very romantic idea. We will go together when Urs is in work."

Dr Zellweger remained silent as they walked back down the steps from the cemetery to the car. And the quietus cast over that day was punctuated by the sound of the car doors closing with a thud.

Apart from that brief moment of sunshine in the cemetery, the sky remained overcast for the rest of the week. But it remained dry. And when Ellen was driven into town a few days later to cast Frank's ashes into the Rhine, she detected a sense of spring in the air.

As they were approaching the bridge, Marthe's attention was caught by a voice behind her.

"*Salü* Marthe!"

Marthe span round. And Ellen's gaze followed. They came face to face with a man Ellen estimated to be about forty. She found him strikingly handsome, with dark eyes that had an intensely magnetic attraction and an engaging smile that would have made her heart leap, had she not had Frank's ashes in her arms.

"*Salü* Jack," Marthe said, and gave the man her hand. "This is Mrs Goss from England," she added, switching to English for Ellen's benefit. "Ellen, this is Jack Hruby.

"I'm pleased to meet you," the man said in perfect English and gave Ellen his hand. He was carrying an object wrapped in a blanket. It looked to her like a picture.

"How is Anna?" Martha asked

"She's well. We just got back from Locarno. We had a wonderful time, together with Esther. I think it did Anna a lot of good. She even persuaded me finally to get rid of this painting," he said, lifting the blanket-covered object.

"Where are you taking it?" Martha asked.

"A gallery has offered to take it off my hands."

"Can I see it?"

Jack rolled back the blanket to reveal a painting of a woman with long tresses of red hair that fell down over an emerald green dress.

"Lola," he said. "It's an old painting my mother bought in an auction here many years ago."

"She's beautiful," Ellen chipped in, and was mesmerised by the smile in his eyes when he looked up at her.

"You should offer it to Urs. He would love it," Martha said, then added with a knowing smile: "and we could then move your own painting to a more suitable location."

"That's a good idea," Jack replied, returning the smile.

This brief exchange intrigued Ellen. It gave further nourishment to her suspicion that Marthe was one of the women in the painting on the wall of her lounge.

"Look, why don't you take it with you now," he continued, and handed it to Marthe, "and see what Urs thinks. If he likes it, he should make me an offer. It's an unknown artist from the Twenties, so it's probably not worth much. The gallery offered me 400 francs."

"It was a pleasure meeting you," he added, turning to Ellen to give her his hand, and then headed off in the direction he had come from.

"Come on," Marthe said to Ellen, the painting now tucked under her right arm. She then locked her left arm around Ellen's right and they continued on their way.

When they reached the middle of the bridge, Ellen stopped and contemplated the river. Again, by what seemed to her to be the strangest of coincidences, the clouds briefly parted, allowing the sun to cast its sparkling light onto the water. All at once, a barge silently appeared from under the bridge, heading north. Ellen instantly thought of Frank's mysterious words on Putney Bridge – 'a boat, beneath a sunny sky' – and smiled. Stooping down to take the urn from the bag she had been carrying, she felt Marthe's cautionary hand on her arm.

Ellen looked up. The other side of Marthe, a few metres further along the bridge, stood an older woman, probably in her sixties, with a large scarf draped over her shoulders and a bag on her arm. She was staring over at Ellen with what Marthe took to be a disapproving curiosity.

"Not here," Marthe said. "I think it best if we throw the ashes in from the side of the river, where it's more discreet."

She led Ellen back over the bridge and down some steps to a mooring point for boats. Here Marthe watched Ellen deep in contemplation before she slowly cast the ashes into the river, where they followed in the wake of the now distant barge until they disappeared from view.

It was on their way back up the steps that Marthe suggested Ellen take a few days' break in Ticino before returning home.

"I've been thinking, Ellen. When Jack said he had just come back from Locarno, it occurred to me that this would be a perfect place for you to relax by the lake and take your mind off everything for a few days before you return to England."

Ellen was not sure she needed any further reprieve from the reality of life without Frank. But when Marthe insisted that she would join her in a few days' time, Ellen was persuaded.

"I have some things to do for Urs first," Marthe explained, "but I can be with you in Locarno at the weekend."

Chapter 28

Ellen recalled from her A-level studies that Wordsworth saw Locarno spreading out like Heaven before him. To her it seemed more like a dark underworld. And on reflection, she was quite glad that Marthe had been unable to join her after all. It left her free to focus her thoughts without any distraction. But they had proved uncomfortable thoughts, made all the more disagreeable by the strange behaviour of Signor Sciarone. So, the moment she found her seat on the train out of Locarno, she felt an instant sense of release.

And when she arrived back at Marthe's place before making the onward journey back to England, Ellen was imbued with a sense of awakening. The start of something new – albeit tinged with sorrow. She was keen to get back home at last.

Nevertheless, even the intimacy of Marthe's embrace that she was leaving behind only partly explained the heaviness of heart that Ellen felt when the moment finally came for her to say goodbye. A good four weeks or more had passed since Frank's death, and she was filled now with a strangely subdued kind of eagerness as Marthe drove her to the station and the start of a new life. Already there was a hint of spring in the air, but the warmth of the sun through the windscreen was deceptive. The streets still had a colourless, dejected look about them. It was a look that seemed to reflect Ellen's own traces of disquiet, which were still held uneasily in place by an ill-defined cocktail of guilt and a sense of regret at not having had a chance to say her farewells to Dr Zellweger. He had been called out on an emergency.

"Don't worry about it, Ellen," Marthe reassured her. "If it was not an emergency, he would have been too busy organising his next symposium. He does not have enough time even for me at the moment. But I will say goodbye to him for you."

Once again Ellen put herself in her debt, but Marthe was already on another track.

"Are you going to your bank when you get home?" Marthe asked.

Ellen was thrown by the non sequitur of her question, and it took some time for its significance to sink in.

"Once I get home, of course. I hadn't really given it much thought."

"Do you think the bank would accept me as a customer also? Urs and I have been discussing whether to buy a small apartment in London."

Her concentration was on the traffic, which obscured the expression in her eyes, but her lips in profile quivered slightly with what might have been a smile. Or was it nervousness? Ellen did not know what to say, but Marthe's line of questioning intrigued her, and she could sense it teasing both of them as they continued the remainder of the journey to the station in silence.

They had to say goodbye just inside the entrance, because Marthe had forgotten to bring any identification that would allow her through customs to the platform on the French side of the border. It was the most self-effacing frontier crossing Ellen had ever seen, as if it was trying desperately to be something else. An oddly nondescript corner of the station for one of the country's main gateways to France. It looked more like a left-luggage office that had not been given a coat of paint for fifty years. Not the kind of place for fond farewells.

Only a solitary traveller ventured down the narrow corridor ahead of them which led into France. A lady with a familiar-looking air, who evidently had no one to say goodbye to, except for the porter who wheeled her baggage along beside her.

Ellen and Marthe both watched as they vanished from sight. Neither wanted to say goodbye. And neither of them spoke. Ellen felt Marthe's arm around her waist.

"Promise you'll come and visit soon," said Ellen. "Come and stay. You could look for a flat while you're there."

Marthe said nothing in reply, but her arm tightened around Ellen's waist.

"Easter would be a good time," Ellen added, and Marthe kissed her gently on the cheek. Their lips touched fleetingly as she pulled away from Ellen. It was quick and painless in the end. And silent. Not until Ellen was halfway down the corridor into France did she hear her voice.

"I promise. Have a safe journey," she said, and Ellen turned to see her blowing a kiss.

The train to Paris was almost empty, for which she was thankful. She wanted time to herself. To relax and not have to puzzle over the mysteries of the past year or so. It was all the more inexplicable, then, that she chose to sit in precisely one of the few compartments in the train that was occupied by another passenger. Her travelling companion was the elegant lady that Ellen and Marthe had observed earlier making her way down the customs corridor. For some peculiar reason, she was instantly drawn to this woman.

Ellen put her luggage on the overhead rack, took her collection of Daphne du Maurier stories from her handbag, placed it on the seat beside her and settled down for the journey. She was looking forward at last to completing the story she had been unable to finish in Locarno. It was not until she was settled into her seat that she looked across at her travelling companion and greeted her with a smile.

"Hello my dear," the elegant lady said, smiling back at Ellen. "It's so nice to meet you again."

It was then that Ellen noticed the cream-coloured silk foulard draped stylishly around the lady's neck and the Louis Vuitton bag beside her on the seat. All at once, it dawned on Ellen why the air about the woman as she walked along beside the porter had appeared so familiar. This was the woman who had insisted her company on Ellen as she tried to enjoy her cappuccino in Locarno and to whom she had confided so much of her history.

There was no sign of surprise in the woman's voice, but above all a deep sense of pleasure. For all her unruffled composure, however, she appeared inwardly agitated. After fussing around in her Louis Vuitton bag, which put Ellen in mind of their first encounter in Locarno, she stood up and eased another bag off the rack above her. There was a fierce independence about the busy way she dragged it down and rifled through it on the seat beside her. But the limits of her independence were rudely exposed when this search proved to no avail, and she gazed up in despair at the heavy suitcase that lay tantalisingly on the rack above her. She turned towards Ellen with a pathetically beseeching look in her eyes, but said nothing. She needed no words. Her expression was compelling enough.

"Can I give you a hand?" Ellen asked, springing to her feet without waiting for an answer.

"That's very kind of you, my dear. Thank you so much," she said, and continued the hunt after Ellen placed one of the suitcases on the seat beside her and put the other bags on the rack.

"Ah, there it is," she announced at long last with triumph. "It's very fortunate for me that you decided to travel in this compartment. Otherwise I would not have found it until I reached my destination. And that would have been such a shame."

She pulled out the table flap by the window as she spoke and placed on it with careful pride the bottle of red wine that she now took from her suitcase. With slight embarrassment in her expression, she looked across at Ellen.

"I'm sorry to bother you again." She looked across the compartment and then cast her mournful eyes back up to the rack above her, where Ellen had put her other bags. Without any further bidding, Ellen leapt to her feet again.

"The Louis Vuitton bag," she said, half-guiding Ellen with her arm.

"Thank you so much, my dear."

And from this same bag that Ellen had seen in Locarno, studded with the initials P.R. in large gold letters, the woman took a corkscrew and proceeded to turn it into the cork of the bottle. Her wrists looked so frail that Ellen fully expected to be recruited to this part of the ritual as well, but this proved unnecessary as she removed the cork with little effort. It was only when she wanted to put the bottle back on the table top that the attentions of advancing age had their fun of her, making her misjudge the height of the flap and let the bottle go as she knocked the bottom of it on the table rim. It was fortunate that Ellen found the pantomime so riveting. For she was following every movement so avidly that she was alerted to the danger long before her travelling companion realised what was happening. And she managed to catch the bottle without losing too much of the precious liquid.

"Thank you so much. I'm really getting very clumsy in my old age."

Ellen pulled a tissue from her handbag to mop up the spillage for her, bringing with it from the bottom of the bag a scrap of paper that she had almost forgotten existed. Once the table had been cleared of the few small pools of wine, she picked up the scrap of paper from the floor and was about to throw it into the bin with the tissue, when she realised it was the strange verse that Frank was said to have written. She studied it again, but its meaning was no clearer to her now than it had been when she first read the scribbled text twelve months ago. And it belonged to a chapter of her life she preferred not to dwell on. She was not prepared to let her new future be haunted by some indecipherable sentiment. Without giving it any further thought, she scrunched up the paper in her hand, put it on the table in front of her, then watched as her travelling companion on the other side of the table reached forward, picked up the cork and laid it in the nest formed by this crumpled piece of paper.

The purplish-red butt of the cork lay like a dismembered torso in Frank's first words. And in this new setting, Ellen became aware of a significance she had not seen before. The creases in the paper conspired with the sunlight shining through the carriage window in such a way that the first letter of each line stood out almost in relief. Together they spelled the name Patricia.

Ellen's heart missed a beat. Suddenly, as if from nowhere, she recalled Frank's words on Putney Bridge:

'Still she haunts me,' Ellen muttered to herself, 'an acrostic… such a lovely device, he said it was.'

"Excuse me?" said her travelling companion.

"Sorry, I was just talking to myself."

Ellen was excited by this discovery. It sang to her like a ploughed field that had released up some archaeological treasure. She wondered what other secrets might be buried in these words. Although she had no stomach to dig deeper, she wanted desperately to take the paper in her hand again and examine its strange message. But the elegant lady beat her to it.

It was probably the sense of tidiness that comes with age that prompted her to seize on the piece of paper, scrunch it as tightly round the cork as her slim wrists would allow, and throw both into the bin under the table.

Deep down, Ellen was grateful to the woman for sparing her the pain of any further curiosity. And, almost as if she knew what was going through Ellen's mind, she smiled sweetly across the table at her.

For the next half an hour or so, as the train rumbled north along the foot of the Vosges Mountains and their neat tawny fringe of sleepy vineyards, they sat smiling at each other over the bottle of wine, only occasionally exchanging pleasantries.

"Are you going all the way?" Ellen asked.

"Pardon me?"

"To Paris?"

"Oh no. Only as far as Strasbourg today. I shall be travelling on to Normandy next week."

"How on earth will you manage with all your luggage?"

"You're quite right, my dear. Porters are not so easy to find nowadays. But I shall manage somehow."

The words gave Ellen the distinct feeling that she was the one who would be recruited to the task. But she could not begrudge her this, especially when her travelling companion later offered to share her wine with Ellen.

"I think it's been breathing long enough, don't you?" she said. "Would you care to have lunch with me?" And from her Louis Vuitton bag she took two glasses, together with a small parcel. This she unwrapped and passed over to Ellen. It was a makeshift plate of sandwiches.

"Please take one. They have cheddar cheese inside. Not easy to find in Switzerland, unless you know where to look."

She then poured the wine and handed Ellen one of the glasses. "A rather special Bordeaux. Couldn't resist opening it now."

Ellen lifted the bottle and examined the label. Château Haut-Brion 1913. She knew nothing about wine, but it seemed a trifle old to her. And the scepticism in her face did not escape her companion.

"You'll find it's survived the passage of time rather well," she assured Ellen. "I picked up a job lot of six bottles at an auction. Quite a stroke of luck." Then she raised her glass to Ellen and took a sip. "It goes rather well with the cheddar, don't you think?"

"I'm afraid I don't know very much about wine," Ellen confessed, but at once the lady put her at her ease.

"Between you and me, even if it had not been jolted around over the last few days, it could not be said in all honesty to have aged awfully well. But it's a very special vintage for me, and sentiment plays funny tricks on an old woman."

"Would it be very indiscreet of me," Ellen said, "if I asked where you learned to speak English so well? I remember you said you had a very good teacher, but I can't imagine you learned it in school."

Frank had always admonished her for being too inquisitorial. She knew that, had he been with her now, she would certainly never have been so bold. But her travelling companion did not seem at all put out by Ellen's clumsy question. On the contrary, she beamed a sweet smile across the compartment and broke into a litany of nostalgic reminiscence so private that Ellen almost felt something of an intruder.

"I did warn you that I can be rather sentimental," she said, as if to apologise for causing Ellen any discomfort. "England was home for me during the war," she continued, "thanks to a dear old friend who took me in when the rest of Europe was under threat. He was a colonel in the British army. Retired. A very dear friend."

"Judging from the slight trace of an accent, I assume your home before the war was France."

"I suppose it was, yes." It seemed an oddly uncertain answer to Ellen.

"That is to say, if you mean my country of birth. But I spent much of my childhood in Germany and also studied in Switzerland, so I have always been a little rootless. That's why those years in England were so important to me. They gave me somewhere I could put down roots when the rest of Europe was being devastated. They even gave me a surrogate father. They were probably the happiest years of my life."

"Did you not have a father?" Ellen asked, and instantly sensed that her tactlessness had gone too far. It seemed to have touched a central nerve. "I'm sorry. Please forgive me. You must think me terribly nosy."

"Oh, it's all such a long time ago now, my dear." She paused, as if in need of time to find the right words. "A lot of ghastly things were happening in Europe at the time. That's why my father sent me to Switzerland to study. Unfortunately, I was unable to keep an eye on him while I was there." She paused again, only for longer this time, before adding: "I did what I could."

Ellen sensed a tearfulness in her eyes and had the impression she wanted to say more, then thought better of it. She rearranged the scarf around her neck instead and turned her gaze to the grey industrial estates that slid past the window as the train rolled quietly through the outskirts of Colmar.

"Why didn't you stay in Switzerland?" (Oh Frank, you would be so ashamed, Ellen said to herself.)

"I couldn't."

The reply was abrupt when it came, and Ellen sensed the sweet sentiment of her companion turn sour with unspoken memories. She was reluctant to interrupt the long pause that followed. And stared out through the silence now at the vineyards speeding past north of Colmar.

"My English colonel kept in touch, you see," Ellen's travelling companion added at last, as if this explained everything. "We corresponded quite frequently for some months. And then, almost a year to the day after we first met, I received a very concerned letter. I remember the day well. It was a Saturday in February 1938. Schuschnigg had just come to an agreement with Germany, and the colonel worried that it was only a matter of time before Hitler marched into Austria. From there it was just a short step to Switzerland, he wrote, and urged me to move to England as soon as possible."

"So you just upped and left?"

"There was no one to keep me there any longer," she replied. Ellen could not escape the audible sadness that crept into her voice with those words.

"I'd lost interest in my studies by then as well. And the colonel was right. It felt very unsafe living right on the border in those days. So I left my apartment at the end of the month. And a few days later I got on this same train to Paris and made for England.

"It was a good time to leave, just before the carnival, which can be very tiresome for a foreigner. But more importantly, it was barely a week before Germany marched into Austria, as the colonel had predicted."

"Did you ever marry your English colonel?" Ellen asked, wanting to bring her back onto the gentler slopes of her past. And her colonel proved to be the right cue. Her eyes twinkled with a private merriment, as she adjusted her scarf again.

"No. He was very much older than I. Just a wonderful friend to me."

"Age doesn't have to be an obstacle. A lot of women like to marry a father figure."

"No, I never married, my dear." And the twinkle in her eye suddenly faded again as quickly as it had appeared, like the embers of a fire that had long since ceased to burn. Only deep down, beneath the ash, was the trace of an occasional spark exposed by a passing breeze that spoke of the flames which must have danced in her heart at one time. So sad, yet somehow warm and content in her resignation.

"Only once might I have come close to marrying," she added in a deep reflection that seemed to shut Ellen out entirely. "But I lost him. Poor little squirrel. That's what I used to call him. But he was more of a swan really. An injured swan adrift in strange waters. Such a fool he was. In the end it was probably his foolishness that betrayed him. Then he just disappeared. As so many people did in those days."

She paused and took another sip of wine.

"He had a lot in common with my father in some ways. I don't think he ever realised just how fond of him I was. But it would never have been a great success – we would only have tried to make different people of each other, and heaven knows I had no wish to do that to him." She carefully mulled over these last words as she put the glass to her lips and took a final sip of the wine. "So, I drink a glass of Chateau Haut-Brion to him now and then, and hope that he can still hear me."

A smile swept across her face like sunlight racing cheekily over the winter landscape, hunted by clouds. Poor old thing, Ellen said to herself. She carried her past so heavily, and looked far too frail for the burden. But there was something about her, so robust, she would never let the weight drag down the sweetness of her temper. Frank had always had a soft spot for sweet old ladies, and Ellen could imagine he would have been especially taken by this intriguing woman.

She played with her scarf, constantly rearranging it, and stared out onto the passing fields. They looked tired, yellow and drained by the winter. Private reminiscence occupied her eyes where the twinkle had been.

Ellen left her to her thoughts. She could picture her as a young woman in the chequered history that she was going over at this moment. Not conventionally beautiful perhaps, but she had a strength of character in her face that must have been very striking in her youth. And Ellen could imagine she had an allure that must have made quite an impression on the men. But what did she have from it, apart from a fading memory?

She must have sat fidgeting with her thoughts for a good fifteen minutes before eventually jogging herself into action. Horrified, Ellen watched her take another bottle of wine from her suitcase.

"You've been such a charming travelling companion," she said. "Would you do me the honour of accepting this?"

Ellen could hear her English tutor, the colonel, in her choice of words, and smiled at the thought of this quaint liaison.

"That's very kind of you, but I couldn't. Really."

"Don't be so English. Here," she insisted, and thrust the bottle into Ellen's hands. Then, taking a paper handkerchief from her bag, she wiped the wine glasses clean, put them away, and looked at Ellen with an expression that spoke of so much unhappiness which only she would know. Just as only Ellen would ever know her own.

"I have to get out at the next stop. Could I impose upon you one last time?" Her eyes wandered over the luggage. "The porter wanted to put it in the guard's van, but I preferred to have it all with me. You never know what might happen, do you?"

There was really no way Ellen could refuse even if she had wanted to. So, for the third time on that short journey, she sprang to her feet for the elderly lady, leaving her to continue the stroll through her reminiscences, while Ellen hauled her luggage down from the rack.

"I shall be glad when I get home to Normandy. I think I'm getting too old for all this travelling. You know, it was the colonel who took me back to Normandy in a manner of speaking, though he never knew it. It was his most lasting legacy to me. Such a beautiful part of the world, do you know it?"

Ellen confessed that she knew very little about France at all.

"I was born there, you know. But that's only partly why I returned. You see, it reminds me so much of southwest England, where the colonel lived. He had a beautiful cottage on the edge of Dartmoor."

Ellen almost dropped a suitcase on the woman's head as her heart stopped for an instant. She knew what was coming. Yet she could not quite believe it.

"I'm sorry, my dear. That one is rather heavy, I'm afraid – I should have warned you – it has the other bottles of wine in it." She smiled with a slight embarrassment in her eyes, which Ellen noticed were starting to twinkle again at the memories of her colonel.

"It caused quite a stir in the village, you know, when I moved in." The smile broke into a mischievous chuckle. "He never really lived it down. But he enjoyed that. It appealed to his sense of fun, the idea of the scandal. And I was very happy there, especially when spring came round – the wild primroses, the daffodils and the honeysuckle crawling over the hedgerows. It was like a dream. Reminded me so much of my early childhood. He left the cottage to me, but I could never live in the place on my own. I tried, but it was never the same after he died. So eventually I sold it and came home to find a place in Normandy. That must have been about twenty years ago. Of course, Normandy is not quite the same. But the colonel would often take me to Penzance for weekends just so that I could enjoy the view of St Michael's Mount, because it reminded me so much of my childhood in Avranches, where I grew up. He was very sweet like that.

"But there are no moors in Normandy with their beautiful granite outcrops. I found it a hauntingly beautiful landscape. So my sentimental streak often took me back to see the old place again. But the last time, I found it had changed so much that it no longer meant anything to me. So I don't go anymore. The cottage was bought by an artist, an American, who converted it into a studio. Lost all its character. I feel so guilty when I think of it, for letting that happen. The poor colonel would turn in his grave if he knew."

Struck dumb by the sheer scale of the coincidence, Ellen let the reminiscences wash over her. If she could have spoken, she would have told her that she knew the artist in question, would have offered her sympathy, since he had taken something very precious to her as well. But there was no time for such complications. They were already rolling into the station at Strasbourg as Ellen fetched the last of her baggage out and deposited it in the corridor.

Ellen was a willing recruit to the last task she set her: it seemed the most obvious and natural gesture to help her down from the carriage and unload her luggage onto the platform.

"Thank you so much, my dear." She knew she had left Ellen no choice but to lend her this hand. And Ellen could not begrudge her the small manipulation, especially now she knew what they had in common. When she insisted that Ellen get back on the train before it went without her, that she would soon find a friendly porter to help, Ellen hesitated. She felt that she was letting her down in some strange way. That she should stay with her. But there was still sufficient independence there. She did not need Ellen.

Slowly, the train pulled out of the station, and Ellen's travelling companion was left on the platform, bracketed by all the baggage that seemed to hold the last remaining bouquet of her past, the sum total of a sad unwritten life. She waved sweetly as she receded into the distance, and Ellen returned to her compartment. The bottle of wine she had left Ellen still lay on the seat, and the sight of it filled her with an oddly uncomfortable feeling. It was a part of the woman's life that held a special significance for her. Twenty percent of all she had left from a job lot. And she had given it away.

Ellen wondered whether she would be as profligate with what Frank had left her, such as it was. It was this thought that prompted her to rummage through the waste bin and retrieve the scrap of paper with the strange words that he had written. She had pondered over Marthe's theory about past lives, what she called *frontaliers* of the consciousness. And wondered whether Frank's cryptic verse might hold any clues to his own dark frontier.

She read the words once more and found them no less baffling than the first time she had read the verse. But she hoped that, if Marthe could translate the German parts for her, they might enlighten her a little more. So she tucked the paper safely back in her handbag and spent the rest of her journey to Paris and on to Calais writing a long letter to Marthe. She was so looking forward to her coming to stay.

CPSIA information can be obtained
at www.ICGtesting.com
Printed in the USA
BVHW081759290321
603655BV00001B/25

9 781913 962180